From This
Moment

Books by Elizabeth Camden

The Lady of Bolton Hill

The Rose of Winslow Street

Against the Tide

Into the Whirlwind

With Every Breath

Beyond All Dreams

Toward the Sunrise: An Until the Dawn *Novella*

Until the Dawn

Summer of Dreams: A From This Moment *Novella*

From This Moment

From This Moment

Elizabeth Camden

BETHANYHOUSE
a division of Baker Publishing Group
Minneapolis, Minnesota

Published by Bethany House Publishers
11400 Hampshire Avenue South
Bloomington, Minnesota 55438
www.bethanyhouse.com

Bethany House Publishers is a division of
Baker Publishing Group, Grand Rapids, Michigan

Printed in the United States of America

Library of Congress Control Number: 2016930779

ISBN 978-0-7642-1721-0

Scripture quotations are from the King James Version of the Bible.

This is a work of historical reconstruction; the appearances of certain historical figures are therefore inevitable. All other characters, however, are products of the author's imagination, and any resemblance to actual persons, living or dead, is coincidental.

Cover design by Jennifer Parker
Cover photography by Mike Habermann Photography, LLC

16 17 18 19 20 21 22   7 6 5 4 3 2 1

Romulus White stood motionless in the crowded ballroom, staring at a woman he'd once longed for more than his next breath of air.

It was not a pleasant experience, especially since Laura stood alongside her doting husband. Even from a distance, her copper-red hair gleamed in the candlelight and made her stand out from the crowd.

It had been several years since Romulus had last seen her. He braced himself for the blinding wall of anguish that was sure to clobber him, but surprisingly, it didn't come. He waited, holding his breath, but the only emotion Laura's presence summoned was a cloudy swirl of bittersweet memories, an almost-pleasing sort of ache. Wasn't that strange? But perhaps that was the nature of a first great love. If such a profound experience didn't leave the trace of a scar, it would be disappointing.

"Are you going to say hello to her?" His cousin Evelyn drew up alongside him, pressing a glass of mulled cider into his hand.

He took a sip before responding. "Who?" he asked casually, but Evelyn sent him a shrewd look. Evelyn was three years younger than his thirty-two years, but she'd already perfected a disapproving stare that could terrify lesser mortals. They'd grown up together, and she knew all about his epic fit of despair when Laura broke their engagement ten years ago. It was not his proudest moment. He'd rather think of anything—a plague of locusts, perhaps enduring a public execution—anything other than those ignominious few weeks following Laura's rejection.

"You know who I'm talking about," Evelyn said pointedly. "It might be nice to exchange a few words to let her know there are no hard feelings."

"I'm here on business, not to make pleasant chitchat with Laura Rittenhouse."

Tonight's gala was in celebration of the next round of funding that had just come through for the greatest engineering project in Boston's history. Hosted in the lavish country club overlooking one hundred acres of rolling woodland, this was an unprecedented gathering of the city's leading politicians, engineers, bankers, and businessmen, all of whom had joined forces to create the nation's first subway, which would soon be running beneath the streets of Boston.

Romulus intended to shake as many hands as possible to-night. His career as the editor and publisher of *Scientific World* depended on his ability to capitalize on friendships with the engineers and scientists who were forging the new era of invention. He'd spent more than a decade cultivating these alliances, and he was good at it.

"You haven't stopped staring at her since she entered the ballroom," Evelyn observed.

"Laura no longer means anything to me," he said, relieved there was no stirring of those turbulent emotions that had once knocked him flat. In hindsight, Laura had been right to cut him loose. He would have been a terrible husband, and she was surely better off with Dr. Rittenhouse.

Besides, it was quite possible that no man in Boston enjoyed bachelorhood more than Romulus M. White. He adored women and had cut a wide swath through their ranks over the past decade. Someday he would marry, but not anytime soon. The woman he married would be a good mother and suitable companion. His future wife would make him smile, but never roar with laughter. She would be capable of holding an intelligent conversation, but she would not hold him spellbound and entranced. Nor would she have the ability to make him weep in despair or plunge him into melancholy merely because she withdrew her favor. He had already dipped his toe into that particular pond and had no desire to sample it again. Ever.

He didn't want to think about Laura tonight. A far more fascinating woman had just arrived in Boston and captured his professional interest. He had never even met Stella West, but his letter to her was burning a hole in his pocket.

He leaned down to whisper in Evelyn's ear. "After the speeches are concluded, I need a few minutes of your time to discuss business."

Evelyn was not only his cousin, she was his business partner and the managing editor of *Scientific World*. They shared ownership of the magazine on a fifty-fifty basis, so he was legally obligated to gain her consent before major decisions. Although they usually worked smashingly well together, there had been tensions over the years, and the envelope in his pocket was *not* going to make Evelyn happy.

"Dare I hope you are about to tell me you've approved the list of technical articles for the April issue?"

"Completed just before I left and already on your desk. You

can get everything on the production schedule first thing Monday morning. There is something else we need to discuss."

And it was going to have to be handled delicately. Evelyn ran a tight ship at the magazine, and she was likely to fight him tooth and nail over his suggestion. *Scientific World* would have crashed into insolvency years ago if Evelyn had not been there to reel him in from his more extravagant indulgences, but on this issue he intended to remain firm.

"Are you wearing a *pink* vest?" The voice belonged to Michael Townsend, the attorney general of Massachusetts and Romulus's weekly sparring partner in the boxing ring. With patrician features and prematurely gray hair, Michael was a handsome man despite his bland taste in fashion.

"It's coral," Romulus corrected. "I'm wearing it in honor of the marine life exhibit currently at the Smithsonian. We are featuring it in next month's issue."

Michael looked skeptically at the vest, but his tone carried a glint of humor. "It looks pink to me."

Like most men in the ballroom, Michael wore a black swallowtail coat and vest, but Romulus had had an appreciation for style from the day he was old enough to understand the concept of complementary color schemes. Standing over six feet tall, with black hair and a face that turned heads, he never shied away from a dash of color or a sparkly gemstone to liven up his wardrobe.

"Brace yourself, the speeches are coming," Michael said, and a balding man with a walrus mustache stepped up to the podium in front of the orchestra.

The music came to an end, and the clinking of forks on champagne glasses caused a hush to settle over the crowd. Henry Whitney was the improbable hero of the evening. A businessman with a lifelong interest in railroads, Henry was intrigued by the possibility of creating a railway that ran beneath the streets. Two years ago, he had finally cobbled together the necessary financing, technical plans, and political clout to begin building America's first subway.

Traffic congestion had always been bad in Boston, with its narrow, twisting streets first laid out in the seventeenth century. More than half a million people now lived in a city whose streets were choked by lumbering streetcars, wagons, and pedestrians darting among the potholes and horse-drawn carriages. It had been even worse for the past year as streets had been torn up for the digging of the subway tunnels, but the first leg of the subway was due to open soon.

As the applause settled down, Henry began speaking. "My friends, it is surely no coincidence that the first attempt at a project as technically challenging and politically risky as a subway should happen in Boston. Our city has been blazing trails into the unknown since the first settlers arrived in America. We carved a great society out of the raw wilderness, and now our factories, publishing houses, and universities are the envy of the world. Our colleges support the research that is fueling the innovation that will lead us into the twentieth century. Our ships sail to ports all over the world, and our buildings are rising high into the sky. Soon we shall expand into an entirely new realm, deep beneath the city itself, to launch the first underground subway in America."

A hearty round of applause greeted the words.

"London may have been the first city in the world to build a subway," Henry continued, "but the London subway runs on steam, and ours shall be powered by the miracle of electricity. It shall be a clean, well-lit, and well-ventilated subway, a model for all future projects."

Mr. Whitney proceeded to introduce the mayor, the chief

engineers, and the bankers who had pulled off the latest round of funding that would permit breaking ground on the Tremont link. If all went well, digging on the Tremont leg would happen within the month, and the subway would be ready for business by the end of the year. Henry continued introducing key players in the Boston subway while Romulus fought the temptation to let his gaze wander back to Laura Rittenhouse on the far side of the ballroom. Then Henry's voice interrupted the struggle.

"And I would be remiss if I did not recognize Mr. Romulus White, whose magazine, *Scientific World*, has done so much to educate the public about the subway project."

Romulus felt pole-axed. This kind of recognition was unexpected and stunning, but not to be taken lightly.

"Romulus? Where are you?" Mr. Whitney asked from the podium.

"Here, sir!" he called out in a hearty voice. The crowd around him parted enough for the renowned financier to spot him.

"Egad," Mr. Whiney burst out. "A pink vest!"

Romulus raised his glass. "Only the best for a night like tonight!"

Applause mingled with laughter as every face in the room swiveled in his direction.

When the laughter settled, Mr. Whitney continued in a sober voice. "We could not have commenced this project without the support of the public. *Scientific World* has done more to ease fears about safety and stoke excitement for the coming subway than an army of politicians could have done. We are grateful, sir."

This time the applause was mingled with foot-stamping and some good-natured cheers. Michael clapped him on the back, and Evelyn beamed.

He swallowed hard. Oh, this felt good. Was Laura still in

the ballroom to hear? Ah yes, there she was, standing by the ice sculpture and politely clapping.

He bowed his head in acceptance, when what he really wanted to do was shout from a mountaintop. For a man who had barely graduated college, floundered with finding a career, and whose glittering wardrobe disguised a lifelong sense of insecurity, this was nice. For a few seconds, he had the esteem of every person in this room.

But they didn't really know him. Not like Laura did.

He pushed away the thought. These misgivings rarely plagued him anymore, for he had launched a magazine with scientific influence that reached all four corners of the globe. By the time he managed to draw a breath, Mr. Whitney had moved on to congratulate the team of geologists whose work charting the terrain beneath the Charles River was a vital step for the next leg of the subway.

He turned to Evelyn and kissed her on the cheek. Evelyn was an attractive woman, with glossy black hair and a willowy figure that belied the backbone of pure steel that had propelled her into a field normally closed to women.

"None of this would have happened without you," he murmured, and Evelyn sent him a grateful smile. It wasn't fair that he received all the acclaim for their magazine's success, but he'd always been the public face of *Scientific World*, while Evelyn quietly labored behind the scenes to keep the operations humming like clockwork. The two of them had been inseparable since childhood, and what a miracle that they'd found a way to turn their unique talents into a profitable career for both of them. He only hoped the letter in his pocket would not throw a bomb into their sometimes contentious relationship.

"Enough with the boring speeches," Mr. Whitney intoned with a nod to the orchestra. "Let the dancing begin!"

Romulus had no interest in dancing. He needed to win Evelyn's consent regarding the letter in his pocket. It took some maneuvering, but he managed to lead her out to the enclosed patio overlooking the wide expanse of lawn. The March evening was chilly, and there were fewer people out here, but some had gathered amid the potted palms and flickering lanterns that cast circles of warm light into the evening. Soft laughter mingled with a violin sonata, and the air was perfumed by night-blooming jasmine. He guided Evelyn into a secluded corner, for he didn't particularly care to be overheard.

"Stella West is in Boston," he said. "She is the final missing piece we need to make *Scientific World* soar."

It was hard to mask the excitement leaking into his voice, for Stella was an artist of extraordinary skill. He'd been trying to hire her for years. They had never met, but he could tell merely by looking at her illustrations that they were kindred spirits.

Scientific World was the most prestigious science magazine in the country, but they'd never been able to produce full-color illustrations on the amazing topics they covered. Developments in lithography now made high-speed reproductions of color artwork possible, but it required an artist of both technical and artistic mastery. Stella could do it. Her illustrations could capture the translucent quality of a butterfly wing or the breathtaking colors of the Grand Canyon. No grainy photograph could capture the wonders they covered, and Stella's artwork hinted at an exuberant love of the natural world that had captivated Romulus from the moment he'd seen her fantastic lithographs.

"I thought she lived in England," Evelyn said. "And that she told us it would take a barbarian horde armed with pitchforks and a battering ram to pry her out of London."

He held up a letter. "This was my latest offer begging her to work for us. I sent it to her London apartment, but her landlord wrote a forwarding address to Stella here in Boston."

Evelyn's brow wrinkled in confusion. "So how did *you* get it?"

Romulus grinned. "The post office made a mistake and returned it to me rather than Stella's forwarding address. So now I know where she lives. I'll need you to set aside eight thousand dollars to make her a tempting salary offer."

Evelyn nearly choked. "No, no, no," she sputtered. "*Noooo.*" Her voice was a swirling mass of disapproval, but Romulus had anticipated resistance and kept his face a pleasant mask.

"I've always admired how you can pack an entire kaleidoscope of disapproval into a single word. Now that we've got that out of the way, let's proceed with a salary offer for Miss West."

"No. Absolutely not. We've got a perfectly adequate illustration team."

"We need better than *adequate*; we need the best."

Two spots of color appeared on her ivory skin. Ever since they'd been children, Evelyn's porcelain complexion had betrayed her when she was upset, and there they were, the visible signs of agitation sneaking out from beneath Evelyn's iron control.

"We can't afford her, and she's already rejected every offer you've ever made to her. Quite colorfully and persistently."

It was true, but he wasn't ready to give up yet. After he'd seen Stella's work on display at a gallery, he'd instantly known she must be recruited to work at his magazine. He sought out everything he could learn about her. She was an American, the daughter of a New York physician, and she had studied at Cornell University. She left before completing her degree when the London art world beckoned, and her reputation had been on the rise ever since.

13

He and Stella West had enjoyed a lively correspondence over the years. She was blunt and funny and wisecracking, but one thing was always the same—she refused to leave London.

Which made him exceedingly curious about what had lured her back to the United States. It didn't matter, for the thrill of the hunt had seized him. Stella West had wandered into his city, and he'd go after her with the speed of a comet hurtling through space.

"All I need to do is figure out what she wants, then offer it to her," he said. "Pearls from the bottom of the ocean, rubies from the Far East, whatever it takes. I want her onboard at the magazine."

"How long have you been trying to lure her to *Scientific World*?" Evelyn asked.

"Three years. That means we have published thirty-six issues without the best illustrator gracing our pages. Don't ask me to tolerate a thirty-seventh." He snatched the envelope back from Evelyn.

"Stella West is a luxury we can't afford." She was about to launch into a classic Evelyn tirade but stopped when a group of ladies wandered onto the patio to admire the jasmine. Evelyn nodded politely to the ladies, then turned her attention back to him and spoke in a calmer voice. "We can't afford it," she said. "I'd rather finish paying for the office renovation first. We overspent shamelessly on the main office."

Evelyn was still prickly over the parquet floors he'd installed in the editorial wing of the building. He'd designed the oak parquet floor himself, modeled on the geometric pattern found in quartz crystal structures. Hardly anyone noticed the similarity, but their magazine was founded on the principles of scientific wonder, and if he wanted to spend a fortune on a parquet floor that mimicked the six-sided prism of a quartz crystal, he would do so. The same went for the artwork in the magazine.

"Art can move people in a way no written words can do," he said. "I want to inform and inspire anyone who has ever dreamed outside the limits of their own daily life. Don't you see it, Evelyn? Our magazine is reaching people in sod houses in Kansas, in frozen villages along the Yukon River. We just got our first subscriber in Mongolia. Those people will never see the Grand Canyon or the inside of a museum, but they see our magazine and it opens the entire world to them."

He couldn't afford to pay for a new artist unless Evelyn loosened the purse string, so he chose his words carefully. "Stella West is one of us," he said, barely able to control the undercurrent of passion in his voice. "I can tell merely by looking at her artwork. She captures the radiance and the immensity of God's creation. She can immortalize it in brilliant color. If we can get her on our team, our subscription rates will soar."

Evelyn still looked skeptical. She rarely made a decision without triple-checking every conceivable angle, but on this move he knew he was right.

"I'll see what I can do," she said grudgingly, and he breathed a sigh of relief. The magazine was the most important thing in the world to him. On his deathbed he suspected he would still be strategizing ways to polish its content, recruit better writers, improve their circulation rates—

"Hello, Romulus," a soft voice murmured.

He stiffened. Laura must be standing directly behind him, for he'd recognize that honeyed voice anywhere. In front of him, Evelyn winced in understanding and sent him a sympathetic smile. This wasn't going to be too horrible, was it? In any event, it seemed there was no escaping it. He plastered an agreeable expression on his face and turned to greet Laura.

"Mrs. Rittenhouse," he said with a slight bow. "You look as lovely as ever."

She made a polite reply and introduced her husband. He'd met Dr. Rittenhouse many times before, of course. Romulus made it his business to attend the conferences of scientific organizations throughout New England to keep abreast of developments in the field. Dr. Rittenhouse owned a pharmaceutical company that produced a drug for immunity against tetanus. It was real work. Not like what Romulus did . . .

Laura proceeded to chat with Evelyn about her new house in Beacon Hill. Apparently people paid handsomely for the doctor's tetanus drug, for no house in Beacon Hill could be purchased cheaply. She probably wouldn't think much of the hotel room where he lived, but why did he need a house when all he did at home was sleep? The hotel suited him perfectly fine.

Evelyn elbowed him, and he realized Laura had asked him a direct question. "My apologies. Could you repeat that, please?"

"There is a gaggle of young ladies near the punch bowl who wondered where you disappeared to," Laura said. "I gather they were hoping for a dance. Greta Fitch was particularly interested in securing a waltz with you."

Was Laura trying to play matchmaker? It was totally unnecessary, as he tended to enjoy women's company far too much as it was. And Greta Fitch was becoming a problem. They'd enjoyed a brief flirtation last summer, but she was reading far too much in to it, and he'd been trying to avoid her. She was a nice lady, probably too good for him, but her pursuit was becoming a little awkward.

"I'd prefer to remain out here and enjoy the night air," he said.

"Why?" Evelyn asked. "Greta is remarkably intelligent and has a genuine interest in natural science. I think the two of you might make a go of it."

"And you consider yourself an expert on matrimonial bliss?"

Evelyn raised her chin and shot him an icy glare. "Don't be small," she warned.

But on this particular issue he *was* small. And annoyed and disappointed in Evelyn.

Evelyn was his best friend in the world. They were only first cousins but had always been as close as any brother and sister. They'd been through difficult times together, they'd built a world-class magazine together, and their friendship was the bedrock that grounded his entire world.

With one notable exception. Ten years ago, Evelyn had married Clyde Brixton, the best friend Romulus had ever had, but the marriage had collapsed after only a few years. Evelyn had even reverted to using her maiden name on the masthead of the magazine, which Romulus thought was both petty and inaccurate, but he could hardly dictate to Evelyn on this point. Evelyn and Clyde had been separated for the past six years, and he doubted they'd ever mend the chasm between them.

Which was a problem, since rumor had it that Clyde was back in Boston. Whatever happened, Romulus intended to stay out of the line of fire should Clyde be preparing for another go at winning Evelyn back. There had been a time when Romulus had tried to be a coolheaded mediator between the two of them, but he had finally given up in despair. The collapse of Clyde and Evelyn's marriage only confirmed every one of Romulus's misgivings about romantic love. He wanted nothing to do with it.

"I enjoy women's company far too much to settle down with just one," he said. "Greta is perfectly charming and intelligent, but if I married her, she'd soon be a millstone around my neck. I'm simply not cut out for marriage—"

"Thank you, Romulus. You certainly have a way with words."

Greta Fitch stood at the far end of the patio, hands on hips, fire in her eyes.

He froze, horrified at what she'd just overheard. "My apologies, Greta. I truly didn't mean—"

"You certainly *did* mean it!" Greta called out, her voice full of artillery fire. She advanced toward them with measured steps. Laura and her husband both politely stepped a few feet away, but everyone on the patio had noticed. Everyone was listening. More than a dozen pairs of eyes watched as Greta marched toward him, and she did not bother to lower her voice as she flung the barbs at him. "I think you are so terrified of genuine emotion that you flee any woman who gets too close," she said. "You'd rather set yourself up as king of your precious magazine because it lets you hide behind your subscription lists and sycophants begging to be profiled. That magazine is nothing but a stack of papers! And you sacrifice your entire life to it."

He tried again. "Greta, I said I was—"

"Sorry? Yes, you are! Don't worry, Romulus, I won't impinge on your time or the sanctity of your precious magazine. I know how much those pages stoke your over-inflated vanity. I hope that someday a woman trounces your heart so hard you'll have a little taste of what you've been dishing out all these years. I hope she rips away every artifice and illusion you hide behind, because underneath it all, I don't think she'll find very much."

Greta whirled away before he could speak another word. The door to the ballroom slammed so hard it made everyone on the patio startle. Excruciating silence hung in the night air. Well, he supposed he deserved that kick in the teeth. He'd been honest with Greta from the outset, but she'd simply ignored all his warnings.

After a few moments, the clusters of people who'd stopped

to stare in drop-jawed amazement turned back to resume stilted conversations, but he sensed their surreptitious attention.

He looked at Evelyn, who did not have much sympathy in her eyes. Which was ironic. She'd survived a miserable marriage, so why should she nudge him toward the same matrimonial inferno?

Romulus asked, "So when can I expect you to come up with an appropriate salary offer for Stella West?"

"Romulus! Aren't we going to discuss what just happened?"

"I think Greta was quite thorough in her assessment." Not too far off base, either. He moved closer and lowered his voice so no one could overhear. "I'm not going to rush to the altar just because Greta Fitch has a nesting urge. The only woman I'm interested in courting right now is Stella West. Frankly, I hope she has the face of a barnyard door and the personality of a python, because I don't need any more trouble with overly emotional females."

It really didn't matter what Stella looked like. He'd been dazzled by her from the instant he'd seen her artwork, and he would move mountains to get her onboard at *Scientific World*.

Until four months ago, Stella West had enjoyed a charmed life.

As an infant she had been delivered by her own father, a physician who adored his wife and showered his two daughters with an endless supply of love and opportunities. Stella was also blessed with beauty, artistic talent, and a quick mind. Her parents provided her with a childhood anchored in sunshine, butterfly hunts, piano lessons, a world of good books, and most importantly, the blessing of a happy family she loved with all her heart.

Stella's parents were forward-thinking people who had sent both their daughters to college. She and her sister, Gwendolyn, had shared the same dormitory room at Cornell University, flirted with the same set of young men, and laughed in the same sun-dappled meadows. Stella had inherited her father's love of science, just as she'd inherited his Scandinavian blond hair, blue eyes, and soaring Viking confidence to go forth and conquer the world.

It was at Cornell that Stella had mastered the art of lithography, a complicated process that required artistic talent, an eye for detail, and an aptitude for technology. The full-color lithographic prints she made had been sent to competitions all over the world. Her real last name, Westergaard, was hard to spell, so she'd signed her lithographs simply *West*. The name Stella West had flare and was easy to remember, so she'd adopted it for all her professional work. Soon she had an international reputation and contracts with famous publishing houses.

Those things made her life interesting, but not truly charmed. What made her life extraordinary was the string of events that capitalized on her love of art and science, sending her to London and the pinnacle of artistic success. How many American-born girls could claim to have been toasted by the Prince of Wales? Had seen their artwork on display at the Louvre? Been courted by the world's most prestigious publishers to license her illustrations in the pages of their books and magazines?

Until four months ago, Stella had all that and more.

Perhaps it was only fitting that those who flew so close to the sun were most in danger of getting scorched, but she'd never realized how badly it would hurt until it happened.

Her world had collapsed on a cold December morning when a telegram arrived at her London apartment. The only thing Stella could now be certain of was that life would never be quite as golden as it had been before that telegram arrived.

Stella pushed away the memories as she trudged down the steps of Boston's City Hall. Her neck ached from leaning over a stenotype machine all day, her eyes were bleary from transcribing text, and she felt frumpy in this plain dress. It was important to blend in with all the other clerks at City Hall, so immediately after arriving in Boston, she'd bought simple dresses in shades of brown, beige, and bland.

She strode the half mile to her rooming house, sighing in relief as circulation returned to her cramped limbs. Her appearance and the tedium of her new job were irrelevant. She'd come to Boston for a single purpose, and the only way she could accomplish it was to blend in. She wore dowdy clothes and averted her gaze from anyone who tried to make conversation with her. She had become quite good at pretending introverted modesty.

But through it all, she never stopped listening, watching, and observing. The entire scope of her world had narrowed to a single task, and she fixated on it with all pistons firing. Each morning, she awoke with a sense of urgency propelling her as she silently gathered information on a steadfast quest to discover who had killed her sister.

There was no longer room in her world for art, flirtation, or fashion. The tree-lined streets of Boston were lovely, and the city was vibrant and engaging, but she allowed none of it to penetrate the hard shell she'd built around herself.

Stella trudged up the steps to her boardinghouse on tired legs. She'd been fortunate to find a respectable room so close to City Hall, even though it meant climbing to the fourth floor each day. The rooms were leased mostly by single men, but Mr. Zhekova had allowed her to board because she was willing to pay three months of rent in advance.

She walked to the row of brass mail compartments at the end of the dimly lit hall on the first floor. She checked her mailbox daily, always eager for news from home. Her mother's fragile mental stability was deteriorating again, and if it got any worse, Stella would feel compelled to return home despite her father's pleas to stay away. Both her parents were floundering, and she couldn't be certain letting them handle this on their own was the right thing to do.

She inserted the tiny key into the lock and opened her box to see a single letter propped inside. She reached for it.

"Ouch!" she shrieked, jerking her hand back and dropping the letter on the tile floor. A low buzz came from the mailbox, and to her horror, a bee careened out of the opening. A second dart of pain pierced her thumb. Bees crawled all over her hand! More poured from the mailbox before she could fling the door shut. She shook her hand, running down the hall in panic.

A cluster of bees still followed her, and another sting pierced her wrist. She snatched a newspaper from the dining table and tried to swat them away.

A slew of foreign words sounded from behind her, and Mr. Zhekova came stomping into the room, surprise on his round, bearded face. She twisted and shrieked as a pair of bees buzzed about her. Mr. Zhekova grabbed another section of newspaper and batted at the bees, as well.

She doubled over in relief as her landlord beat another bee into immobility, then crushed it beneath his boot.

"Thank you," she gasped out. Four stings made her entire hand ache and throb. "They were in my mailbox," she said as soon as she could catch her breath.

"Why did you put bees in your mailbox?" Mr. Zhekova demanded.

If she wasn't so upset, she would have laughed. "I didn't put them there. I don't know where they came from, but we'd better check the other boxes. Where there's one, there's usually more."

She followed her landlord down the hallway. Mr. Zhekova was a mountain of a man, at least six feet tall, and he ate very well, so he waddled from side to side as he headed to the row of brass mail compartments. Her letter lay on the floor where she'd dropped it, and a single bee still circled the room. Mr. Zhekova used the newspaper to swat the single remaining bee to the ground, then stomped on it. He headed around to the narrow room behind the mailboxes to examine them from the other side.

"Ha!" he shouted. "There is a bee's nest in your box. Not in the others."

She ought to be relieved that none of the other people living here would be confronted with such a rude shock, but Mr. Zhekova was angry as he returned to the front room.

"What did you put in your box to attract bees?" he demanded in his thickly accented Bulgarian voice. "Have you been storing food in there?"

"Of course not!" Who stored food in a mailbox? But her landlord was not finished.

"You are a woman," he grumbled. "You wear perfume?"

"Sometimes." Actually, she wore perfume every day. Before leaving London, she'd stocked up on three bottles of her favorite orange blossom perfume, imported from Paris and sold for shocking prices. Indulging in the appallingly overpriced fragrance was one of the few luxuries she still allowed herself.

"Well then, your perfume caused the bees," Mr. Zhekova concluded.

It was the most ridiculous statement she'd ever heard. She visited the mailbox once per day, with her hand inside it for no more than a second or two. It was hardly enough time to infect the mailbox with a flowery scent destined to attract bees from outside the building, down the hallway, and directly into her mailbox.

But this wasn't the first time something odd had happened to her. Two nights ago, a baseball had been hurled through her window. It was ten o'clock at night, and surely no children were still playing in the street. She lived on the fourth floor, so it would have taken a strong arm to get to her window, and thus it was hard to believe the baseball was a random accident.

She'd told Mr. Zhekova about the baseball the next morning, and by the time she'd returned from work that day, the glass had been replaced. He'd been quite decent about fixing her window, but now he looked at her with clear disapproval.

"Well, stop wearing perfume and maybe we'll stop having bees in the building."

"Fine," she mumbled. Her hand hurt too much to argue, and her legs were unsteady as she reached down to pick up her letter. She had done nothing to cause the bees—or the baseball, either. Perhaps someone in this boardinghouse did not like a woman rooming amid all the men? She hoped so, for the only other explanation was too frightening to contemplate. She was walking a dangerous tightrope in Boston, and the longer she could go about her business without attracting attention, the safer she would be.

A glance at the letter showed that it was not from her parents, so it wasn't urgent. She tucked it inside her bag and trudged up the stairs to her room.

It was a plain room, with only a bed and a wardrobe in which to store her dresses. The single window overlooked an alley and had a depressing view of a brick building directly across the street.

But she hadn't come to Boston for a view. She'd come to salvage what was left of her family, but with each passing day, those golden, halcyon memories seemed farther away.

The mattress creaked as she sat down. It was hard to open the letter with only one hand, but the blistering stings on her right hand hurt too badly to flex. Anchoring the envelope to her lap with her elbow, she tore the flap with her clumsy left hand and extracted the note inside, her brow lowering as she recognized the signature.

How had Romulus White learned she was in Boston? This wasn't good. She'd never even met the man, but he'd been pursuing her for years, and he was relentless.

Once again he was offering to hire her at *Scientific World*. There had been a time when she'd been amused by his impassioned letters to her, so full of enthusiasm it had been hard to turn him down. She admired people who had a passion for their work, and his letters sparkled with intelligence and the sheer love of sharing the wonders of science and technology with the wider world.

His letters were untethered by reason or restraint, and she always found them amusing. Their correspondence brimmed with delightful barbs and a professional rivalry that sizzled despite the three thousand miles separating them. She enjoyed his letters but was never tempted to move, for the great publishing houses of London beckoned. She dared not tempt fate by leaving her idyllic life in England to work for a man whose unbridled passion rivaled her own. They would either get along smashingly well or be tempted to kill each other on sight.

All that was over now. She no longer had a career in art; she was merely a clerk at City Hall. Even doodling in the margins of her papers made Stella feel guilty. It would be best to not even respond to this latest missive from Romulus, for it would only confirm that she had relocated to Boston, and the fewer people who knew she was here, the better.

Her heart sank a little deeper as she folded his note and returned it to the envelope. Romulus White and his dazzling offers belonged to her past, and there was no room for him in her new, darker world.

She dropped his note into the trashcan. She would not think of him again.

―∽✧∽―

By the next morning, Stella's hand hurt even worse. It was awkward to type with her right hand swollen from the stings, and she hoped no one in the office watched as she painfully pecked out keys on the typewriter. Stella shared the office with six other stenographers, and their desks were only a few feet apart, meaning she had no privacy.

"How did you hurt your hand?" Nellie Carlyle asked from the neighboring desk.

"Bee sting," Stella replied but did not look up from her work or offer more information. She had no desire to make friends with her fellow stenographers. She didn't trust anyone in City Hall, and the more anonymous she was, the easier it would be to gather information as she sneaked around the building. All the stenographers here had known her sister, and Stella could not afford to let anything slip that might reveal her connection to Gwendolyn Westergaard.

Poor tragically murdered Gwendolyn. Of course, no one in Boston believed Gwendolyn had been murdered. Everyone from the police department to the medical examiner's office insisted it was a simple accident, but Stella suspected otherwise.

And she was here to find proof.

When she applied for this job, she used her professional name, Stella West. She was grateful for the name, for it meant no one would suspect an association between Stella West and the tragic Gwendolyn Westergaard.

"That must have been a lot of bees," Nellie said. "I imagine you'll be even slower than normal in typing up your notes."

"I can handle it," Stella said, although it was no secret that she was the worst stenographer here, barely able to keep up with the rapid-fire discussions at the meetings. While in college, she and Gwendolyn both had studied stenography, the art of typing shorthand notes during important meetings, but that was eight years ago, and her skills were rusty. As soon as she'd arrived in Boston, she'd bought her own stenotype machine and practiced for two solid weeks in the privacy of her room. Summoning up her old training from college, Stella worked hard to resurrect her dormant stenotype and typewriting skills. She bought training books, exercise manuals, and studied by lamplight into the early hours of the morning. She used a blindfold to force herself to learn the keys without looking. By the time she applied for the vacant position at City Hall, she was adequate to the task.

She sat at the same desk where Gwendolyn had once worked. She was meeting the same people Gwendolyn had once known. And in the course of this tedious, mind-numbing work, she expected to learn who had killed her sister.

She had been on the job for six weeks, but even on her best days she struggled to keep pace with the deluge of notes she needed to type, and now the bee stings slowed her even more. She couldn't afford to lose this job, for it provided a front-row seat to everything and everyone Gwendolyn had known during those final months before she'd died under such mysterious circumstances.

"Well, if you don't hurry up, I think you should be reported to management," Nellie said. "We have a professional reputation to maintain."

The clattering from the typewriters trickled off as other stenographers sitting nearby eavesdropped. In an office where women were measured by the speed at which they could type, Stella wasn't surprised she was the object of derision.

"Don't be catty," Janet Davis said. Janet was the youngest and the only friendly stenographer here. "I'm sure Stella is trying her best."

"She should try harder," Nellie said. "I could type faster than Stella after only a week on the job."

"You're right," Stella said agreeably. "I wish I could be as good as you, Nellie. I could practice for years, decades . . . oh

28

heck, I could practice for an entire geologic epoch, but I doubt I'd be close to how famously good you are." She flashed Nellie a wink no one else in the office could see, and Nellie's mouth twisted in fury.

She turned her attention back to her typewriter. She didn't care what her coworkers thought of her. They had no power over her job—but the men at her next meeting did. The officers of the Boston Transit Commission held their meetings in a large auditorium so members of the public could attend, for the subway project attracted a lot of spectators. Hundreds of people usually attended the meetings to argue over funding, traffic disruptions, and subway routes.

She didn't spare Nellie another glance as she headed out the door to her next meeting. Members of the Transit Commission sat at a conference table at the foot of City Hall's raked auditorium. Stella took her seat at a small table off to the side, where she would dutifully use the stenotype keys to make a shorthand transcript of every word spoken. The auditorium's seats were already packed, and it seemed to be a rowdy bunch today.

Boston was the first city in America to attempt the construction of an underground subway, and it had profound implications for property owners throughout the city. As streets were excavated for the subway, the city's water, sewer, and gas lines all needed to be pulled up and re-plumbed. Streets would be excavated, traffic diverted, and businesses would struggle to survive during the months their customers could not reach their stores. Despite the political and economic quagmire, construction of the subway was careening ahead at an astonishing pace.

Not long ago, recording these meetings had been Gwendolyn's job. Now it was Stella's.

Gwendolyn had learned something dangerous while working here. Throughout Stella's years in London, she and Gwendolyn had carried on a lively correspondence, and in the months before her death, Gwendolyn wrote that the subway project was drenched in graft and corruption. Gwendolyn wrote that she practically had to hold her nose to sit in the same room with certain corrupt officials during their meetings. Stella suspected it was one of those crooked government officials who'd ordered Gwendolyn's death.

At each meeting, she scrutinized every person who attended. Was it possible to spot corruption on a man's face? The great artists had always been able to endow the villains of history with signs of wickedness. Perhaps it was a dissipated expression or a beady gaze. She only wished life were as easy to interpret as great art, for the businessmen and engineers who attended these meetings seemed competent and professional, with no glaring signs of corruption.

The meeting commenced, and her fingers moved across the keys of the stenograph machine, tapping out the phonetic code to produce a transcript of every word spoken. The bee stings made each keystroke hurt, but she couldn't stumble, couldn't slow down. These meetings were always loud, boisterous, and fast, but they were her best chance of spotting the corruption Gwendolyn had discovered.

The transit commissioner stood to deliver his report of growing discontent about the "sandhogs" hired to excavate the tunnels. Many of the sandhogs were Italians, and members of the Irish unions were snapping mad. When the commissioner insisted the Italians would continue to be employed, a tomato came hurtling through the air from somewhere deep in the auditorium. The commissioner ducked in time, and the tomato splatted on the blackboard behind him, leaving a wet, seedy stain.

The tomato sparked a chorus of hoots and jeers as various

Italian and Irish observers rose to their feet. These meetings were always contentious, but this was the first time Stella had seen flying vegetables.

"Officers, clear the room of protesters," the chairman ordered.

More than a dozen policemen swarmed the room. It took a while to clear the rowdy spectators, as some refused to leave and needed to be hauled away.

Stella took advantage of the time to rest her aching hand. It throbbed from the past half hour of vigorous typing, and she savored the lull. About a dozen spectators remained after the rabble-rousers had been cleared, but only one man caught her attention.

He stared straight at her. Tall, dark-haired, with a firm jaw and a beautifully sculpted face, he was an outrageously handsome man. And the way he lounged in his seat, with one arm casually draped across the back of the neighboring chair, suggested the easy confidence of a man born to power. Beneath his fine black suit he wore a vest of lavender silk shot with threads of gold. Only a man of immense confidence could wear such a color and still appear to be the most masculine man in the room. The half smile on his mouth as he stared at her was disconcerting.

Stella was accustomed to male appreciation, but this sort of scrutiny was uncomfortable. The way he watched her . . . was it possible he knew her from London? She'd always accepted that these public meetings were putting her at risk of exposure, but the artistic set she'd mixed with in London were unlikely to appear at a municipal government meeting in Boston. And the frumpy dress she wore looked nothing like the spectacular ensembles she'd flaunted in London.

She risked a second glance at the man. He still stared at her.

They had never met, she was sure of it. She would remember a man with such a flair for style.

A gavel banged, and the meeting was recalled to order. The transit commissioner resumed his position at the podium, looking a little haggard after the hectoring. "If there are no more concerns about employing Italians on the project . . ." The commissioner let the sentence dangle, hope in his eyes. A single hand rose, and the commissioner reluctantly acknowledged him. It was the man in the lavender vest.

"Your name, sir?"

"Romulus White of *Scientific World*."

Stella gasped, and it echoed in the half-empty auditorium. A handful of men swiveled to stare at her, but she disguised the blunder with a cough, covering her mouth and turning away to hide her face.

Was his presence here merely a coincidence, or had he come to continue his pursuit? It seemed impossible to believe, but if he had managed to track her down to her boardinghouse, he could probably find her at City Hall, too.

And that would be a disaster. Her mouth went dry and she held her breath, waiting for his question. If he dared mention anything about her skills as a lithographer, it would be impossible for her to explain what she was doing here.

Romulus stood. "Berlin is about to break ground on a subway system," he said. "Their plan is designed to cover the city on radial lines, which seems far more efficient than our design of mirroring existing street patterns. Have you interviewed the Berlin engineers?"

Stella breathed a sigh of relief. Apparently his attendance at this meeting was entirely coincidental, for innovative engineering projects were regularly featured in the pages of *Scientific World*. The conversation droned on for almost an hour, and

Stella did her best to record every word, the clacking of the stenograph keys keeping pace with the discussion.

At the close of the meeting, some of the remaining spectators mingled with Transit Commission members. Stella put the stenotype machine back into its leather box, still aware of Romulus White, who chatted amiably with the director of public engineering, but she sensed him repeatedly glancing her way. Surely it was because she was the only woman in the room, for he couldn't possibly know who she was.

Or perhaps that was wishful thinking. As she left the room, Romulus was close behind and gaining on her. The hallway was crowded, with voices and footsteps echoing off the vaulted marble ceilings. If she reached the elevator ahead of him, she could escape to her third-floor office where the public was not allowed to follow. She was almost at the elevator when a voice called out from across the hall.

"Miss West!"

Her heart plummeted, for now it was a certainty that he knew who she was. She couldn't let him catch her. If what she suspected was true, any one of the men milling about in this lobby could have been involved in Gwendolyn's murder. At all costs, she must avoid anything that drew attention to her.

"Miss West . . . Stella, wait."

She slipped inside the crowded elevator, its brass doors closing before he could catch her.

She sighed in relief. She had escaped.

─◦◦◦◦◦─

Stella worked hard the rest of the afternoon, transcribing her shorthand notes into a transcript that would be filed in the official record in the archives. At precisely fifteen minutes before the end of the workday, she looked up and scanned the room. "I'm heading down to file my work in the archives. Would anyone like me to take their notes, as well?"

As anticipated, every woman in the office eagerly accepted, reaching for their paperwork and hastily assembling it into files and noting a date on the tab. Stella waited patiently for all six women to hand over their day's work.

"I don't know how you can stand that man," Janet said. "Mr. Palmer is just so odd. No matter how hard I try, I can't warm up to him, so thank you." She turned over her notes from the School Board meeting to Stella.

Stella nodded but said nothing as she carried the stack of files down to the archives, where she would turn them over to Ernest Palmer, the city's archivist.

Ernest Palmer was the butt of jokes throughout City Hall, but she liked him anyway. Stella suspected that his overly large eyes, magnified by the thick spectacles he wore, might be part of the reason people teased him. Ernest worked in the basement archives all day, and who wouldn't be odd if they never saw the sunlight? He smelled of camphor, continually pushed his thick eyeglasses up his nose, and talked incessantly to anyone who visited the archives, usually about his passion for the history of typography. He could rattle on for hours about the beauty of Garamond type or the challenges of italic font. Mr. Palmer was especially eager to talk to the stenographers, for he assumed they must share his passion for the printed word.

Stella always enjoyed chatting with Ernest. She had no interest in long-winded discussions about typography, but she liked people who had a passion for something, even if it was as pedantic as the beauty of a typeface. The eccentric Mr. Palmer would have fit in quite well with the crowd she'd run with back in London, as artists had a high tolerance for unconventional people.

She dashed as quickly as possible down to the basement, her heels clicking on the marble steps. At the stroke of five o'clock, people would come pouring out of their offices, leaving her precious little time for her most important task of the entire day: skimming the notes typed up by her coworkers.

She stood in the vacant corridor outside the archives, flipped open Nellie's file, and scanned the neatly typed transcript from the Board of Taxation meeting. Names of the attendees were always typed near the top of the page, and Stella read them quickly, but there was nothing of interest here. She closed the folder and moved on to the next.

Her offer to carry their notes downstairs was not motivated by kindness. Rather, it let Stella quickly learn the names of every government official who had been at City Hall that day and in what capacity. She skimmed the notes of her coworkers every day, on the lookout for the name of the man who might help her unlock the clues to Gwendolyn's murder.

In Gwendolyn's many letters to her, the one person she'd mentioned as wholly trustworthy was a mysterious man she'd referred to only by his initials, A.G. He was the man in whom Gwendolyn confided when she first discovered evidence of graft at City Hall.

I thank the Lord I had an ally I could trust with the evidence of corruption I had found, Gwendolyn had written. *He is wonderful, possibly the most valiant man I've ever known. He knew exactly how to handle the evidence I turned over to him.*

Gwendolyn went on to report that he was in a sensitive position in the government and she hesitated to name him, referring to him only by his initials. She said he was an idealistic man who had long been frustrated by the rampant corruption in the government and was quietly mounting a campaign to root it out.

Stella was almost certain A.G. worked at City Hall, for

Gwendolyn knew him well and trusted him implicitly. So lavish was her praise that Stella suspected her sister was half in love with the enigmatic man.

It bothered her that Gwendolyn would not confide A.G.'s full name. It seemed peculiar, especially since everything she said of him nearly glowed with admiration, portraying him like a crusading archangel from the legends of old.

I love feeling useful, Gwendolyn had written her. *A.G. and I are a team, and I've already seen some of the men I've named brought up on criminal charges. We are making a real difference in Boston.*

Toward the end, Gwendolyn began to suspect her work was putting her in danger. In her final letter, Gwendolyn wrote that she feared for her life. She sounded almost embarrassed as she wrote it. *I hope I don't sound too melodramatic, but should something strange happen to me, please consider it foul play.*

A woman of Gwendolyn's swimming abilities drowning in five feet of water qualified as *strange.* So did the stonewalling Stella had received from the medical examiner's office and the Boston Police Department.

Stella's chief objective in working at City Hall was to discover the identity of A.G. As soon as she found Gwendolyn's mysterious ally, he would be able to tell her everything Gwendolyn had learned and provide his perspective on exactly what had happened to her sister that cold December night.

It was why Stella skimmed the notes of every meeting taking place at City Hall. She flipped open the next file in the stack, and her eyes widened in pleasure. Andrew Gaines, director of the Parks Department, had been in the building today.

He was a possibility. Director of the Parks Department was a powerful position in the city. He controlled huge swaths of public land and was instrumental in designating routes for the subway. He was someone Gwendolyn would have encountered in the course of her work. And being associated with such an idealistic job was the kind of thing that would have appealed to Gwendolyn.

So far, Stella had found fourteen men connected with City Hall whose initials matched A.G. She kept the names of all fourteen men on a scrap of paper taped to the underside of her desk drawer. Soon she would begin seeking them out to determine if they could be Gwendolyn's man.

After skimming the other files, she found no additional men with the proper initials, so she opened the door to the archives to turn over the files. "Good afternoon, Mr. Palmer."

The archivist was hunched over a newspaper at the front counter, and he barely glanced up as she entered. Which was unusual. Normally he pounced on her the moment she walked through the door to chat about whatever oddities he was obsessed with that day. She set the files on the front counter, but he still didn't look up. Whatever was in the newspaper he examined so studiously had caused furrows on his brow, and she was worried about him.

"Is everything all right?" she asked.

He grimaced and stood upright. "There is going to be an auction of old printing presses and typefaces in Philadelphia. The announcement says it is the largest collection of antique printing equipment to surface in the past decade."

"Well, that's wonderful . . . isn't it?"

He shook his head. "The auction is next month. I don't know if I should go. I can't afford a set of antique type, and seeing it go to someone else would be unbearable."

Her colleagues upstairs would have laughed at the despair in Mr. Palmer's voice, but Stella understood. "You still ought to attend," she said. "It will be like visiting the Louvre. You can't buy any of the artwork, but just having the chance to admire it is worthwhile, don't you think?"

A few of the tension lines eased on Mr. Palmer's forehead. "There is going to be a complete collection of Caslon type on display. Including the Hebrew and Greek fonts. Can you imagine what a labor of love it must have been for William Caslon to create fonts in three different alphabets? I've never seen a complete set of Caslon fonts before, they are *that* rare."

He continued to ramble about the eighteenth-century gunsmith who had given up his profession to design a new form of typeface. Stella did her best to pay attention, but she needed to get back upstairs and record Andrew Gaines's name onto her slip of paper. Still, she sensed Mr. Palmer had no one to share his obsessive interests with, and he seemed so lonely down here in the archives all by himself. She listened to him gush about the brave gunsmith who had ventured into the risky world of typeface design, driven by nothing more than a craving to create beautiful text. Against her will, Stella began developing a reluctant admiration for the long-dead typographer.

Ernest abruptly stopped. "Hey, it's Tuesday," he said. "Aren't you going to call your parents?"

Stella glanced at the telephone in the corner. Ernest had generously allowed her to use the telephone in the archives to call her parents each Tuesday afternoon. It was far better than trying to place the call from a crowded pharmacy or hotel lobby, where it was always so noisy it was hard to hear. Whenever Stella called, she needed to listen hard for clues about her mother's condition. A hitch in her voice, a change of cadence . . . these were the signs her mother's stability was wavering again.

"Not today," she said. "I've got an appointment this evening I can't miss. Might I call them tomorrow?"

"Sure thing," Ernest agreed before turning back to his newspaper.

As she walked back up to her office, she hoped Mr. Palmer would go to the auction. Life was too short to hold back from the pure elation that could be found from the pursuit of a dream.

Of course, the irony was that Stella's entire life was now completely devoid of passion, art, or anything else she had once cherished. That was okay, though. Until she found out who'd caused Gwendolyn's death, the rest of her life would be held in suspension. Only after she exposed a murderer would she be free to try to gather the frayed threads of her world and weave them once again into a thing of beauty and meaning.

She trudged back up to her empty office and recorded the new name on the list taped beneath her desk drawer.

Now came the hardest part of the day. After weeks of trying to make contact, she had an appointment with Freddie McNeill. The prospect sent a chill straight down to the marrow of her bones, for Freddie was the waterman who had found Gwendolyn's body floating in the river.

And he had information she needed to know.

S tella drew a fortifying breath as she descended the staircase at City Hall. Was there anything more distressing
than learning the details of your sister's final moments
on earth? Or seeing the place where her body had been pulled
from the frigid river?

But it had to be done. The police had lost patience with her
and no longer took her appointments. They insisted Gwendolyn's death was an accidental drowning, but that didn't make
sense. When they were children, Gwendolyn had laughingly
challenged the neighborhood boys to see who could swim
across Windmill Pond the fastest. It was half a mile to swim
the length of the pond, and Gwendolyn always won. She was
a strong swimmer who would not have drowned in five feet
of water.

For Gwendolyn to die by drowning was morbidly ironic.
While Gwendolyn loved frolicking in the water like a dolphin,
Stella had always been terrified of water, too afraid to even learn
how to swim. And yet it was Gwendolyn who had drowned.

Freddie McNeill was the city waterman who rowed the

Charles River each day, scooping out muck that built up in the city's inflow and drainage pipes. Without regular raking out, the pipes got clogged with sludge that could cause pressure difficulties at the pumping station. It was a messy job and best done at low tide, which meant Freddie was often the first person out on the river each morning.

And on a cold, drizzly morning in early December, Freddie McNeill had been the first one to spot the beautiful dead girl floating facedown in the freezing river.

Stella pulled her shawl tighter as she headed outside. Boston in early spring was chilly, and getting to the wharf where Freddie had asked her to meet him was going to be a challenge. Huge sections of the city's streets were ripped up for subway construction, causing the streetcars to be rerouted and more crowded than normal. She needed to get all the way to south Boston within the next hour. As she scurried down the impressive steps in front of City Hall, she almost missed the tall man leaning negligently against a lamppost.

The instant she spotted Romulus she averted her face.

"Miss West," he drawled casually.

She ignored him and headed north on Court Street, but he pushed away from the lamppost to follow alongside her. She should have known he wouldn't be discouraged so easily, but she still had no intention of confirming his suspicions that she was the artist he was looking for. There were probably dozens of women named Stella West in the country.

"I like your shawl."

She kept marching straight ahead without breaking stride. Perhaps if she ignored him he would leave her alone.

"William Morris?"

She glanced at him in surprise, for the ornate tapestry of her shawl was indeed from the great designer William Morris.

The extravagant shawl was out of place with her bland clothes, but it had been chilly this morning and she'd succumbed to the temptation to wear it. Wasn't it just her luck that Romulus White seemed to have a keen appreciation for textile design and felt compelled to comment on it. She didn't even know if William Morris's fabrics were available in the United States, for this shawl had been a gift from the artist himself shortly before he died.

She walked faster, but Mr. White kept pace with her. "It's a spectacular shawl," he said. "It gives you a wonderful medieval flare, like Eleanor of Aquitaine striding down the streets of Boston."

She fought to keep the smile from breaking onto her face. It would only encourage him.

The crowds were terrible at the next intersection due to an overturned wagon that had dumped hundreds of turnips across the cobblestone street. A policeman directed traffic, but Stella was trapped beside Romulus until the officer let them pass.

"I should properly introduce myself," he said. "I'm Romulus White. I've admired your work ever since I first saw it on display at—"

She cut him off, desperate to avoid anything that hinted she was anything but an ordinary stenographer. "Romulus. What an unusual name."

"My mother goes through periodic phases with historical eras," he admitted. "For a while, she was enchanted with Roman mythology and couldn't resist foisting the name of Rome's founder on me. I'm grateful I wasn't born during her medieval phase or I'd have been named Beowulf."

He paused to squint at the overturned cart. "I wonder why that cart was carrying turnips?" he asked in an abrupt change of topic. "No one likes turnips. They aren't fit for anything but cattle feed, and even that seems like cruelty to animals. I know a physician named Dr. Lentz who swears that root vegetables are the most nutritious things to eat, but I'm convinced the joy from a single ounce of chocolate does the body and spirit more good than a whole cartload of turnips."

He continued to ramble, but she stopped listening the moment she heard the name Dr. Lentz.

"Dr. Lentz?" she asked. "Dr. Rupert Lentz, the medical examiner?"

"Yes, do you know him?"

Stella had never been able to get past the ring of clerks, security officers, and red tape surrounding the medical examiner. All she knew of Dr. Lentz was that he performed Gwendolyn's autopsy and was chiefly responsible for insisting that it was an accidental drowning. She'd been trying for weeks to pierce through the blockades and speak directly to Dr. Lentz, but she'd been routinely brushed aside. The last time she'd tried to force her way into his office, the police had been summoned. She fled before they arrived, but she was still determined to confront him in person.

"No, I don't personally know Dr. Lentz," she said. But this was an interesting development. If Romulus White had a connection to the medical examiner's office, he could be useful to her.

The cart had been set upright, the driver scrambled to toss the turnips back into the wagon's bed, and pedestrians were finally allowed to cross the street.

"You never did tell me your name," Romulus said as he set out across the street alongside her.

"Stella," she admitted. "Just Stella."

"Well, just Stella," he said with an amused tone, "did you know that I've been corresponding for years with a young lady named Stella West and that her landlord just informed me she works at City Hall? Imagine my surprise when I learned that one of the city's stenographers shares an identical name with a talented lithographer who, until recently, has lived in London. I can't help wondering if the lithographer and the modest stenographer walking alongside me might be one and the same. What do you say, just Stella?"

The more she denied who she was, the more curious he would become, and that could be problematic. The best she could do was appeal for his silence. When she reached the other side of the street, she turned to face him. "If I am this woman you are referring to—" she began, scrambling for the best way to frame this delicate conversation.

"Stella West," he supplied. "A lithographer of some note."

"A lithographer of *spectacular* note."

"Let's not get carried away, just Stella," Romulus said, but the gleam in his eyes brightened.

"If I am this woman, and if I have been bombarded by slavishly admiring letters for the past three years, might that be enough for me to get a bit carried away?"

He pretended a wounded tone. "Did my letters come off as slavish?"

"I'm afraid they did," she said in a conspiratorial whisper. His letters had been delightful, glittering with wit and lighting up her day, but she had the perfect life in London and never seriously considered his offer. Now more than ever, she needed to focus on her mission without any distractions. She had an appointment to keep and had no business indulging in a flirtation on a public street.

"So if I am this lithographer who walked away from a celebrated career in London to work as an ordinary stenographer in a city office, don't you think I would have a very good reason for that decision?"

"Certainly," Romulus said. "And I wait with bated breath to hear about it."

As much as she was tempted to stand here and flirt with him, a wave of exhaustion settled on her. She missed her parents. She missed the life she used to have, but none of that mattered. She dropped all the playfulness from her tone and looked Romulus directly in the eyes. "I came to Boston because I believe that my sister was murdered," she said bluntly. All humor vanished from Romulus's face, but aside from a single raised brow, he made no move to comment, so she continued. "Everyone from the police department, the medical examiner, and the court system insists it was an accident, but I don't believe them. I've tracked down the man who found my sister's body, and I am due to meet him within the hour. He's going to show me the spot where she was found."

He looked appalled. "To what end?"

"To figure out what really happened."

"Isn't that best left to the police?"

She fought the temptation to roll her eyes. She and the police department were not on the best of terms. They'd been respectful the first few meetings, but as her refusal to accept their conclusion solidified, they dug in their heels and stopped answering her questions.

"I have lost confidence in the police. Also, they quit speaking to me after I threatened to sue the entire department for incompetence. Besides, if you want something done right, it's best not to trust outsiders."

"Some would say it is best to trust the experts. This doesn't seem like the kind of thing a woman should do."

How little he knew her. Some people collapsed when they were hurt. They floundered while waiting for someone to rush to their rescue and solve their problems—but that wasn't her.

She raised her chin and stared at him. "Let me be clear," she said. "When I wake up in the morning, I live, breathe, and function only in the interest of solving Gwendolyn's death. I intend to hunt down exactly who is responsible and drag him, her, or them before a court of law. So, please, I don't have time to talk about art or pretty pictures or working at your magazine. I'm pleading with you not to pester me at City Hall. I need that job, and I don't want to worry about you showing up to try to lure me to your magazine. That sort of thing raises questions. Right now all I need is to find the streetcar so I can meet the waterman on time."

"Where do you need to go?" Romulus asked.

"South Boston, down by Cooperman's Bridge. I've never been there before."

His brows lowered in concern. "That's a rough part of town. I'll take you."

"Would you?" She didn't mean to sound so stunned, but this was the first time someone in this city had offered to do something nice for her. Perhaps she'd gotten so used to hostile officials and slammed doors that this bit of kindness seemed extraordinarily chivalrous.

"Let's go," he said confidently.

—◦◦◦—

Stella's nose wrinkled at the marshy, decaying scent as she and Romulus stepped off the streetcar near Cooperman's Bridge. Tenements and warehouses were built close to the cracked and rutted street, with no trees or greenery anywhere to be seen. They headed toward the river, where the ground sloped downward. The wet, peaty smell grew stronger, and she covered her nose with the corner of her shawl. Sometimes even the scent of water was enough to set her teeth on edge.

A break in the warehouses revealed the river, wide and still. She kept her gaze averted from the shoreline as they headed toward the boardinghouse where Freddie McNeill lived.

Romulus sent her a worried glance. "Are you sure you wouldn't rather have me handle this? I can ask him whatever questions you want and will report back fully."

"No, I'll be fine," she said smoothly. She'd rather have a tooth pulled than confess her fear of water. She needed to shove those inconvenient feelings aside and get the task done.

A man smoking a pipe on the covered porch of a boarding-house noticed her. He dropped the chair back onto all four legs and rose. "Are you Stella Westergaard?" he called out.

"I am." She used her real name every time she interacted with anyone related to Gwendolyn's case, for it tended to buy her a degree of cooperation. She glanced up at Romulus, who looked at her curiously. "West is merely my professional name," she said. "It's easier to spell."

Romulus nodded, and she turned her attention back to Freddie. He plunged his thumb into the bowl of his pipe, snuffing it out and then tucking it into his shirt pocket. He loped down the wooden steps and crossed the graveled yard, his hand extended.

"I'm Freddie McNeill," he said.

Stella didn't mind a few tobacco stains and returned his hearty handshake. This man worked a long and grueling day on the river and was taking his personal time to meet with her. His skin was creased and dark like old leather, his grubby pants were held up by suspenders, and he had the strong build of a man who made his living from the strength of his back.

"I appreciate your willingness to meet with us." She made introductions, but Mr. McNeill's heavily lined face peered at her curiously.

"You look like her," he said simply.

She swallowed hard. "So you can tell that?"

"Oh yes. The sun was barely up, but I saw her face. I doubt she was dead more than an hour or two when I found her, so she was in good shape. Not like some of the ones I've seen who float ashore after a few days. Those bodies are so swollen up and bloated they're hard to recognize."

Stella nodded. This wasn't a pleasant conversation, but it was exactly the sort of thing she needed to know. "Can you describe where in the river she was? One of the early reports said she was directly under the bridge, but another said she was closer to shore."

"I found her bumped up against the pilings in the middle of the bridge," Freddie said. "Come on, I'll take you."

He pointed to an old skiff tied up to the pier. Her heart squeezed, and a fine sheen of perspiration broke out across her skin. It looked like he wanted to take her there in the boat. There wasn't much that frightened Stella, but anything to do with getting close to water did the trick.

"Can we see it from the shore?" she asked.

"Nope, it's around the bend. And it would make more sense in the boat."

This was what she'd come out here to see, and she'd only have to do it once. She nodded. "Let's go."

She refused to let her gaze stray from the skiff. It would be nice if the flat-bottomed boat didn't seem so ramshackle. Freddie sprang into the boat and began moving rakes, buckets, and oars to make room for her. She drew a steadying breath and gathered up her skirts. In a little bit, this would all be over. Any ten-year-old child could get into a boat and be rowed about. She would do it, too.

Romulus held her elbow as she lowered a foot into the boat. It listed wildly as Freddie helped her board. Soon she and Romulus sat on the front bench, with Mr. McNeill on the seat behind them. The oars thudded as he positioned them in the rowlocks, but after a few sloshing drags, the skiff pulled away from the pier. Every list and bob was unsettling. Water surrounded her on all sides. She couldn't even close her eyes to escape it, for she could smell the water and feel it jostling her from side to side.

"Tell me about your job," Stella prompted, scrambling for anything to get her mind off what was happening. "It must be so interesting seeing different parts of the city."

"Oh yah," he said in his broad Boston accent. "I row a different part of the river each day to muck out the drainage pipes. All kinds of stuff gets up in them if you don't watch it. Mostly plants and river sludge, but I've pulled up lots of stuff in my day. Old shoes, broken tools, stuff like that. Mostly fishing tackle, though, which is a shame. People don't realize that when they throw that gear overboard it goes right on catching stuff. Fish are swimming around down there, minding their own business, then they get caught up in an old net or crab trap and they're stuck down there forever until they die. Did you know a salamander can drown? Frogs, too. Can't keep 'em under forever or they suffocate."

It was getting harder for Stella to breathe. She clung so tightly to the dry wood that a few splinters started working lose.

"What can you tell us about the body you found?" Romulus said.

Freddie let go of the oars to point over her shoulder. "That's Cooperman's Bridge. There's an outflow pipe that runs out from the shore. I first saw her as I was pulling up to clean out that pipe."

Stella twisted her body to look. Compared with some of the other stretches of this river, it looked rather pretty. It shouldn't matter what sort of spot Gwendolyn died at, but a tiny piece of her was glad the bridge was lovely, made of old stone and lifting in a gentle arch over the river. The shoreline was lush, with wild grass and cattails swaying gently in the breeze.

Freddie jerked the oars back into place. "I'll get you closer," he said, and she was grateful he'd quit rambling about the drowned salamanders.

"You said she was floating," Stella said. "Don't people who drown sink?"

"They sink at first, but eventually they float back up," Freddie said. "They get all bloated, and after a few days they bob back up to the surface and . . ." His voice tapered off, and he looked at the spot where Gwendolyn's body had been found. "But she wasn't swollen. Looked like she'd only been in the water a few hours. So yah . . . that's weird. She should have sank if her lungs were full of water. It takes a few days for them to gas up enough to float again."

"Did she have any injuries?" Romulus asked. "Something that might have knocked her out so she fell over the bridge?"

Freddie shook his head. "Not that I could see. I rowed alongside her and turned her over to be sure she was dead, but I didn't do more than a quick look-see. Her skin was ice-cold and not a drop of color on her face. I rowed ashore and summoned the coppers."

Stella pulled the shawl tight against the chill as she scrutinized the area. The bridge was made of rock, which held heat and took longer to ice over than a wooden bridge would. There were no boulders or other obstructions in the river that Gwendolyn would have hit her head on. Stella analyzed every detail and committed it to memory before saying a silent prayer for Gwendolyn.

"Okay, let's go back," she said softly.

~ ᴄᴠᴯᴖ ~

She and Romulus were both cold and hungry by the time they reached the shore. They had to hurry to catch the last streetcar heading back into town, but as soon as they arrived in Stella's neighborhood, Romulus guided them to an Irish pub he swore had the best corned beef and cabbage this side of the Atlantic. She didn't care for cabbage, but she'd gladly eat weeds if it made Romulus happy, for she was about to ask him for another big favor.

She needed his help getting into the medical examiner's office. Based on what she'd learned from Freddie, she was even more convinced that Gwendolyn did not drown. She needed to see the autopsy report, but the medical examiner's office refused to release it to anyone but the police, citing departmental protocol. All she'd been able to see of the postmortem documentation was a terse summary in the official police report, but she wouldn't be satisfied until she saw and read the original document itself. She also wanted to question Dr. Lentz, and Romulus could help her cut the Gordian knot and get straight through to him.

Inside the pub, the air was thick with the scent of pipe tobacco and yeasty beer. A fiddler played a rousing tune near the back of the pub, prompting Stella to take a seat as close to the front as possible. She didn't want to shout to be heard.

It wasn't the type of place she normally dined, but the sheer normalcy of the pub was comforting. People laughing, the clinking of glasses, the thump of footsteps banging in time to the music. Perhaps there was truth to the adage that one couldn't appreciate the wonder of the ordinary until it had been snatched away.

And this pub was wonderful. Not because the décor was exceptional or the music anything beyond commonplace—it was wonderful because *life* was wonderful, and she had full view of it here from this scarred and pitted bench. It was in these ordinary hours she could appreciate the hearty laughter of men relaxing after a day's labor, the blessing of familiar food, company, and music. It was in ordinary places that the human spirit was unshackled and free to enjoy the gift of life, transcendent in a way that was almost holy.

Romulus had gone to the counter to order food for them and returned with two tall steins of cider.

"Thank you," she said. She didn't realize how thirsty she was until downing half the mug.

"Perhaps you can thank me by making a few lithographs for the next issue of *Scientific World*," Romulus said. "You can have your choice of topics, and I have a new rotary lithographic press that will tempt the birds from the sky."

She smiled in reluctant admiration, for Romulus was nothing if not persistent. "I'm sorry. I can't concentrate on anything until I find out what happened to my sister." She felt churlish refusing his request, but there was no point in quibbling. On this topic, Romulus had always been relentless, and she knew he would pounce on any opening unless she slammed it firmly closed.

"I would appreciate it if you continued calling me by the name of West," she said. "If anyone at City Hall knew my name was Westergaard, it would raise all kinds of questions I don't want to answer. I need to remain as inconspicuous as possible."

He glanced at her plain wool frock. "I confess that you seemed quite different from what I predicted for an artist. Are the plain clothes part of your attempt to blend in with the staff at City Hall?"

If he could see the clothes she usually wore, it would be quite obvious why she could not wear them to a clerical position. Even among London's avant-garde set, she was always a little forward when it came to dress.

"Yes. When I went shopping for clothes, I gravitated toward

anything that looked like my grandmother might have worn while digging up potatoes."

She took another sip of cider, trying to think of a delicate way to wrangle a meeting with the medical examiner, but then Romulus fired a question she hadn't seen coming.

"How long have you been afraid of water?" he asked.

She set down her mug. "Was it that obvious?" She'd thought she'd been flawless, masking her anxiety with a string of questions to Freddie about his work.

"To anyone with eyes in his head." The way Romulus lounged in the hard-backed chair was outlandishly attractive. With his long legs stretched forth and a hand casually twirling his mug on the table, he gave the illusion of a man at leisure, but Stella knew it was only an illusion. His languid pose masked a fierce curiosity on his face, and it was oddly appealing. She liked a man whose eye for detail was as sharp as her own.

Which was a problem. She couldn't afford to let this man's magnetic attraction lure her away from her goal.

"I've always been afraid of water," she confessed. "One of my earliest memories is standing beside the lake near our house. I was six years old, and Gwendolyn was only four. My mother put us in little sleeveless tunics so we could learn how to swim. My father stood in the lake and tried to coax us in. He told us what fun it would be, how he'd teach us to float like ducks." She smiled, remembering the squawking duck noises he'd made to encourage her.

"Gwendolyn couldn't wait, diving in and splashing around like an otter, but I held back. I remember crying so much that my mother gave up and walked me back home. I never did learn how to swim. I've avoided water all my life."

Romulus had been wolfing down his corned beef and cabbage while she spoke. How could men clean their plates so quickly?

She'd barely taken three bites, and even though she'd been hungry ten minutes ago, she had entirely lost her appetite now.

"Here. You finish this," she said, and he gladly pulled the plate toward him.

"What I find curious," he said as he cut into a juicy slice of corned beef, "is that the first set of lithographs I ever saw of yours was about sea life, with manta rays and conger eels. I specifically remember the delicacy of the way you illustrated the tentacles of the sea anemones. I could almost sense them wafting in the ocean currents. So I am astonished you have such insight into those creatures without firsthand experience."

"Oh, I had firsthand experience," she said grimly. Literally. She had held the sea anemone in her hand and seen dozens of marine specimens preserved in formaldehyde at a marine research institute in Portsmouth. The specimens had been floating in tanks, and she had walked among them to scrutinize everything at eye level. Walking down the aisle of tanks caused a suffocating, strangling sense of panic as she studied the long-dead sea creatures trapped in a tank with no oxygen, submerged in water. The logical piece of her brain told her the massive tanks of liquid were no danger to her, but some raw, primitive fear was stoked to life and impossible to ignore.

But not impossible to overcome. Under the guidance of the marine biologist on duty, she had reached into a tank to lift out a starfish and feel the musculature just beneath its grainy skin. She studied all the other specimens she'd be drawing with equal care, as she had accepted a lucrative commission from the marine society and wouldn't let irrational fears drive her away. She'd learned long ago that courage was not the absence of fear, but the willingness to confront it.

"I took the commission as a way to face my fear," she told Romulus. "By signing the contract, I obligated myself to the task, and there was no going back on my word. I hated every second of it, but I got the job done."

"I wish I could have been there to see it."

"Then you're insane. The specimen room stank, it was a literal icebox, and it was full of dead creatures suspended in their perpetual graves."

"I don't care about the specimens. I wish I could have seen *you*. Even now, the expression on your face is like Boudicca facing down the Romans. I would have loved to have been there."

She managed a smile, but the challenge of the marine aquarium was paltry compared with other things she had endured. She had buried her sister. She had held her father while he sobbed so hard she feared he couldn't keep breathing. Reviewing her sister's postmortem report was merely another task that had to be done. It was time to ask for the favor she needed.

"Thank you for going with me tonight," she began. "Rowing out to the spot where Gwendolyn died was terrible for me, but I could have done it on my own. What I really need from you is access to Dr. Lentz."

Romulus stiffened. She supposed she could have been more diplomatic, but they'd gotten along so well she'd assumed she could be frank.

"And what do you hope to gain by such a meeting?" His tone was ten degrees cooler than it had been a moment ago.

"I intend to rip away the veil of secrecy and expose the incompetence that has been clouding the investigation into my sister's death."

"Ah," he said delicately as he set down his fork and pushed the plate away a few inches. "Sadly, I value my association with Dr. Lentz, a man whose professional credentials, character, and friendship I hold in high regard." He dried his fingers on a napkin, wiped his mouth, and stood. "Good evening, Miss West."

"Wait!" Her only link to the medical examiner's office was slipping from her grasp, and she needed to salvage it. "You can't leave. I need—"

"But I don't." He tossed a few coins on the table. "Your boardinghouse is two blocks south, I trust you can find your way."

His smile was pleasant, but it didn't reach his eyes. She stood in mute bewilderment as he turned his back and walked out the door.

Well! If there was one thing Stella was inexperienced with, it was men turning their backs on her. Perhaps it was arrogant, but she was well aware of the effect she had on the opposite sex. She alarmed timid men, but dazzled the confident ones.

It seemed Romulus White was defying her expectations.

One of the reasons Romulus liked living at the Jamison Hotel was the fine restaurant on the first floor. He had no time for or interest in maintaining a proper household of his own. The hotel had everything he needed. It was two blocks from his work, plus it had a restaurant, laundry, and a clothes-pressing service. What more did a man need?

This morning, all he needed was Otto Stallworth's signature on a one-year contract for full-page advertisements in *Scientific World*, but Stallworth was reluctant to commit.

"I've already bought advertisements in your rag for the next three months," Otto growled as he cut into his omelet in the Jamison Hotel's restaurant. "That will carry us through planting season. No need to advertise fertilizer once the fields are planted."

Romulus didn't particularly enjoy hearing the proudest accomplishment of his life called a *rag*, but he couldn't afford to alienate a major advertiser. "Planting season will be over in America, but not in Brazil or Australia," Romulus said. "Our magazine is distributed all over the world. Do you know how many farms are in Russia alone?"

Romulus could tell by his furrowed brow that Otto was considering his options. Finally, he set down his fork. "I'll sign a contract for a year of advertisements, but I want a discount."

"How much of a discount?"

"Seventy-five percent."

Romulus took a sip of coffee to hide his appalled look. He wanted a long-term contract with Stallworth's company, but he wasn't going to undermine his entire pricing structure to lock in a single contract.

"A thirty-percent discount is the best I can do," he said. "It is a steal, actually. I can hear my managing editor howling in agony as we speak." Which was true. Evelyn controlled the budget because he was a shameless spendthrift and her frugal mind was needed to keep the magazine afloat. It was his job to attract advertisers and negotiate contracts, and Evelyn's job to decide how the revenue was spent.

He continued to idly twirl his cup of coffee—anything to avoid looking at Otto Stallworth's flushed face. Talking business inevitably got Otto's temper up, and engaging in a staring contest would only make matters worse. Besides, he had Otto over a barrel. There was no other magazine to rival *Scientific World* in terms of prestige, circulation, and influence.

Otto's voice was gruff when he finally spoke. "Thirty-percent discount, paid in installments, and I want one of your designers to come up with the advertisements. I want a fancy ad, like that series I saw for Bell Telephones."

"Deal." Romulus rose and shook hands on the agreement. He actually preferred control over the advertising designs, for he wanted no cheap artwork littering his magazine.

And he knew an artist who would be perfect for the job. Most artists of Stella West's caliber would have nothing but scorn for designing a lowly advertisement, but she might pounce on the opportunity if he dangled the possibility of an introduction to Dr. Lentz in exchange for the job.

Stella had been interfering with his concentration repeatedly during the past two days since he'd abandoned her in that pub, and now she haunted his thoughts as he walked to his office. She had an ego the size of Manhattan, but he liked that about her.

She had to be handled with care or she could take a wrecking ball to his reputation. It had taken years to cultivate a network of friends and professional allies who helped make *Scientific World* soar, and Stella's assumption that he'd risk that on her behalf was annoying. Introducing Stella to Dr. Lentz would be like tossing the young doctor a grenade. Dr. Lentz was a nice man, and Stella was a force of nature. She seemed uniquely skilled at annoying people during her short stint in Boston, which wasn't his style of business. He used honey to attract friends, while Stella seemed to fling vinegar wherever she went.

But he still wanted her working for *Scientific World*, no matter how challenging her personality. Offering her the advertising commission in exchange for an introduction to Dr. Lentz could be the first step toward getting her permanently added to his staff at the magazine.

Despite his attraction to Stella, Romulus knew she would be off-limits if she worked at *Scientific World*. Dallying with someone who reported to him would be asking for trouble. He sensed that she had the ability to disrupt his hard-won equilibrium, and he'd invested too much into creating the perfect life to let any woman interfere with that.

The four-story building that housed *Scientific World* occupied a prime lot on Tremont Street. Like most of the buildings on the street, it was fronted with ornamental columns and deeply carved cornices. It contained a modern passenger elevator, but Romulus rarely used it. By walking up the staircase, he could indulge in listening to all the wonderful sounds of production as he climbed to the managerial offices on the top floor.

A café, a stationer's shop, and a pharmacy occupied the ground floor of the building, but the other three floors were the dominion of *Scientific World*. As he climbed past the second floor, he could hear the steady thump and whirl of the electro-type-processing machine pumping out thousands of pages soon to be bound into individual issues of the magazine. The third floor was the domain of the artists who illustrated each article that appeared in the magazine. The clacking of typewriter keys from the writers on the top floor gave evidence to the world of science that was being committed to text and soon to be sent out to all corners of the world.

Romulus strode through the front door to the main office, an oversized room filled with desks for the writers and managerial staff. As usual, he'd arrived before Evelyn. Her desk was placed squarely in the front of the bustling office so she could keep an eye on everything, but Romulus needed to work in silence. He was the only person in the managerial wing with a private office, but having a door he could close was a necessity. It was too easy to get distracted by the conversations around him, and he'd never get anything done if he was out on the floor with the others.

Each morning as he unlocked the door to his private office, he marveled at how he'd managed to arrive at this pinnacle of success. As a child, he'd made terrible grades in school, always too distracted by what was going on outside the window to pay attention to a teacher droning on about nouns and verbs and ancient history. All he cared about was the end of the school day, when he could escape into the natural wonders of his own backyard. On the weekends, he and Evelyn hunted through bookstores for every volume that shed insight into the wonders of the world around them. While other children daydreamed about King Arthur or the Count of Monte Cristo, Romulus was spellbound by the feats of Louis Pasteur and Thomas Edison. He and Evelyn lived in the greatest age of innovation the world had ever seen, and they awaited each new shipment of books with the anticipation of Christmas morning.

When he was thirteen, he spent his allowance on a subscription to a newsletter that printed summaries of recently filed patents. At that time, *Scientific World* had been a flimsy publication, a mere sixteen pages in each issue. The editor was a clerk in the Patent Office in Washington, D.C., and he wrote brief comments beneath each featured patent, speculating on the invention's commercial viability. Romulus's favorite parts of the newsletter were the letters submitted by fellow readers, who shared their thoughts about the featured patents. He and Evelyn devoured each issue cover to cover, often writing their own letters to the editor.

Romulus had soared with elation when, at fifteen years old, he opened the newsletter and saw his letter to the editor printed for all the world to see. Evelyn had squealed with glee, carrying it to every bookstore and newsstand in town to brag about her cousin's accomplishment. He ought to have been embarrassed by her hero worship, but no, it was wonderful. He clipped that letter from the newsletter and hung it on the wall of his bedroom, staring at it before he went to sleep each night, dreaming about what his life would be like someday. He didn't know what he wanted to be, but staring at that letter gave him hope.

It meant that maybe, just maybe, he wouldn't be the profound failure his father thought he would become. Having grown up in West Point with a colonel as a father, Romulus had been expected to outgrow his foolish interest in nature and become a man by joining the army. His mother didn't care what he did, but she was mortified by the terrible grades he made throughout primary school. Who could concentrate on mathematics and grammar when monarch butterflies fluttered just outside the window? He was an embarrassment to her in the closely knit town where the children of officers were held up and compared like melons at the local market.

He was relieved to leave home at eighteen for Harvard. His father had to pull a lot of strings to get him in, giving him a stiff lecture to buckle down and quit embarrassing the family with his foolish inattention and lack of discipline.

Romulus went to college with an abundance of natural curiosity but a complete inability to focus on any one field. He began studying chemistry until botany snagged his interest instead. That lasted a little more than a year, and then a new program in animal science was introduced to the college, and he enrolled in every class he could. His nomadic interest across all fields of science was a wonderful adventure, but not a practical one. How could he translate his unwieldy interests into gainful employment?

As graduation loomed, his anxiety grew. He had no practical skills, no hope of useful employment. Laura was the daughter of a Harvard professor and began fretting that they couldn't get married if Romulus was incapable of supporting a family. He masked his unease with a cocky grin and an endless stream of jokes, but right before graduation there was no more room for humor. Laura threw him over. He was unemployed, and his father's patience was growing thin. He couldn't sleep at night, suffering from the withering fear that he was about to be un-masked as the hopeless failure his father had always claimed.

Then came the notice that the *Scientific World* newsletter was about to go out of business, and a spark of inspiration struck. Evelyn had just gotten married to his best friend Clyde Brixton, a man who shared their obsessive fascination with science and technology. Romulus was perpetually low on funds, but Clyde had a job. As an enlisted soldier in the army, Clyde's salary was a pittance, but he had managed to save a few dollars. Between the three of them, they pooled their money, pawned some furniture, and gathered the hundred dollars necessary to buy the failing newsletter.

Romulus hopped on a train that very day and arrived in Washington by nightfall. By the end of the next day, his wallet was drained, but he possessed the subscription list to *Scientific World*, complete with the rights of ownership and distribution. He intended to grow it beyond the reports of patents into a magazine that would feature articles he and Clyde wrote about science and nature. Romulus persuaded some professors from Yale and Harvard to contribute articles, too. Their page count doubled, then quadrupled. As the magazine's prestige grew, advertisers came knocking. Nine years later, they had grown the subscription list from a paltry 300 names to 160,000.

And although he and Evelyn were usually brilliant collabo-rators, their partnership could be shaky. The weekly meetings to discuss the magazine were almost always torture, and one was scheduled to begin in a few minutes. Romulus shifted in his office chair, fiddling with the miniature gyroscope on his desk. His office was a reflection of his interests, and his desk was littered with various oddities he'd collected over the years. A chunk of petrified wood from Siberia. The jaw of an iguana from Mexico. The upper half of his office wall was a glass window overlooking the interior of the fourth floor, so he had a perfect view as Evelyn gathered her reading glasses and the production schedule and started heading his way. She rapped on his office door and entered.

"Hello, dearest," he said with a wide smile.

She froze and looked at him over the top of her spectacles. Despite the schoolmarm outfit and narrow, rectangular spectacles, Evelyn was the picture of elegance as she swanned about the office. Always graceful, always in control.

"You're up to something," she said as she closed his office door. "You never call me *dearest* unless there's something you need."

He pretended to be hurt. "Dearest . . ." he drawled in his most soothing voice. Yes, he was up to something. He needed to inform her that the advertising revenue from Stallworth's Fertilizer would now be paid in installments and reduced by thirty percent, and it wasn't going to be a pleasant conversation.

Evelyn set the weekly calendar on his desk and pulled up a chair opposite him. "A team of Italian chemists are visiting Harvard," she said. "They've got some interesting theories on helium, and I've arranged for you to meet them on Tuesday. On Wednesday, you've got an interview with the physician who is trying to develop a new vaccine for diphtheria. You might want to watch out for him. I have a sense he is using us for publicity, rather than dissemination of information. And the new electroplating press is due to arrive next week. They'll need another payment before they deliver it. It's a steep bill, but I can juggle our other payments until we have the revenue from next month's subscriptions."

This probably wasn't the ideal time to inform Evelyn that he'd offered Stallworth's Fertilizer a lower price in exchange for a long-term contract, but she needed to know. He used his most placating voice as he told her the news. It still didn't go over well.

"When were you planning on telling me?" she demanded, rising a few inches out of her seat. "I've scheduled payments for the electroplating press through the end of the fiscal year. You can't adjust our advertising revenue without telling me."

He smiled tightly. "Evelyn? The contract was signed only this morning. I made the decision to offer a lower rate because we will collect more money in the long run. I am not so innumerate that I would have sold us into the poorhouse."

The fire eased, and her head drooped a little. "I'm sorry, Rom. I don't know why I'm so tightly wound. It just seems that as the magazine grows bigger, so do the problems. I'm terrified of making a mistake."

The anxiety in her voice tugged at him. Ever since she'd been a little girl, he had tried to protect her, and some things never changed. "Do you remember our first month in business when we had only three hundred subscribers and not a single advertiser? We would have *killed* for these problems."

Her smile was soft as she met his eyes across the desk. It had been a glorious time, running the magazine out of the two-room apartment Evelyn shared with her husband. The publication was a mere sixteen pages back then, hand-typed and copied at a rotary copperplate press they rented by the hour. They addressed each issue by hand, snacking late into the night on German pretzels because that was all they could afford until the next batch of payments arrived.

"You're right, you're right," Evelyn conceded. "But please, *please* . . . we need to lock down the finances. It seems like each month our expenses keep soaring."

"So does our subscription base."

"Nevertheless. We're still paying for the silly parquet floor you were so adamant on getting. Who even notices that it mimics crystalline structures?"

"The floor has been budgeted and accounted for."

"It was still a stunning waste. I'm sick of paying that monthly bill."

He wasn't going to argue with her about the floor again. Evelyn's extraordinary mind for detail had a downside, for she remembered every offense and could drag it out to wave it like a red cape before a bull. The floor had been installed two years ago. They'd waged a battle over it, but he'd trimmed expenses in their mailing account in order to make her happy. It should have been settled two years ago, but she brought up his gorgeous, handmade parquet floor every time she fretted about money.

"If the floor is making you that miserable, I'll pay off the bill with my own money," he said. "It's ridiculous to keep arguing about it."

A movement through the office window caught his attention. Visitors were rare on the fourth floor, and whenever he met with Evelyn, he kept an eye out in case anyone entered the managerial office. His eyes widened as he recognized the familiar figure walking through the door to loiter in front of Evelyn's vacant desk.

This was going to be a problem.

"Would you excuse me for a moment?" He stood, fastening his vest and praying Evelyn wouldn't turn around and notice who had just stepped into their office, for it was probably the last person on the planet she expected or wanted to see.

Evelyn's glare was stony. "Don't think I'm going to forget about this."

"I never for a moment thought you would," he said tightly as he stepped around his desk, relieved she didn't turn around to see who was standing a few yards away.

A smile spread across his face the instant he stepped out of his private office and closed the door. "Hello, Clyde," he said to Evelyn's estranged husband. "Let's step out into the hall, shall we?"

It was the first time Clyde had seen their new building, and he seemed amazed as he scanned the spacious office, noting the high coffered ceilings and shaded wall sconces. His head swiveled to take it all in. "Nice office," he murmured. Clyde's blue eyes looked pale against his deeply tanned face, but his blond hair had darkened a bit since they'd seen each other last.

When the three of them had been running the magazine, they had done so from the tiny apartment Clyde and Evelyn shared. There had been barely enough room for the three of them, and they'd knocked elbows as they wrote out addresses by hand. They didn't even have a proper desk, and Evelyn set the typewriter on a sofa table, sitting on the floor as she typed up the articles written by him and Clyde.

"Is Evelyn here?"

Romulus grabbed Clyde's elbow, turning him toward the door leading back into the hallway. This needed to be handled delicately. "She's here, but now isn't a good time. She's in a bit of a mood."

They stepped into the relative privacy of the hallway. "Still?" Clyde said. "It seems she's been in a mood for the past six years."

Romulus stiffened. He was allowed to tease Evelyn, but no one else could. "Watch it," he murmured.

Was there anything more awkward than being smack in the middle of a marital dispute? He and Clyde had become enduring friends within five minutes of meeting each other ten years ago. And when Clyde and Evelyn had announced their engagement, he had been overjoyed that his two best friends had found happiness together. Just because Evelyn had kicked

Clyde back out onto the streets didn't mean Romulus intended to follow her example.

Clyde held up his hands in surrender. "Sorry. It's a stressful time . . ."

"What are you doing here? The last I heard you were living in New York." That had been the deal when Clyde and Evelyn had split apart six years ago. Evelyn would live in Boston, and Clyde could live anywhere else in the entire world so long as he stayed entirely out of Boston.

Clyde shifted nervously. "New York has just scuttled their plans for a subway. Again."

The wind left Romulus's lungs in a mighty gust. Clyde was one of the lead engineers on the subway that was due to break ground in New York. He'd spent years working on an ambitious plan to tunnel through the bedrock beneath Manhattan, boring beneath historic city streets in a project even more complicated than the subway under construction in Boston.

"I've spent the past two years paying draftsmen and surveyors out of my own pocket," Clyde said. "I was sure to win the contract, but the date to break ground has been set back yet again. The financing has fallen through. I'm flat broke and can't wait any longer."

"So what are you doing in Boston?" Romulus asked, although he was pretty sure he already knew the answer.

Humor lit Clyde's suntanned face. "I don't know if you noticed how ripped up the streets are outside. Rumor has it Boston is building a subway, and I need a job."

Romulus folded his arms across his chest. "About that little agreement you have with my cousin? About living anywhere in the world so long as you leave her in peace in Boston?"

"I've spent the past two years and every dollar to my name designing an electrical grid that can power a subway," Clyde said. "I'm one of the few engineers in the country who knows how to do it, so I'm coming to Boston. Meet the lead electrical engineer for the Tremont link."

Romulus sighed. Unlike most major engineering projects, which were under the leadership of a single contractor, Boston had elected to award the contracts to twelve different engineers, each of whom would have responsibility for a unique segment of the subway.

"Did you have to win the *Tremont* line?" Romulus grumbled. "It's right outside our window."

"I'll be underground most of the time, so Evelyn won't even have to look at me if she doesn't want."

Try as he might, Clyde couldn't disguise the pain in his voice. For most of their marriage, Clyde and Evelyn had done little but hurt each other. There had been a couple years of bliss when the two of them had been so deliriously happy that they could light up any room they entered, but those times were eventually overshadowed by the bad. There was plenty of blame to go around, and Romulus was tired of being a go-between. It had been four years since he and Evelyn had last seen Clyde, but Romulus still remembered what an ugly scene it was.

Clyde had been working at the Menlo Park Laboratory with Thomas Edison, but Edison was famously difficult to work with, as was Clyde. The two of them had locked horns, and Clyde had ended up on the street. He sold a few of his successful patents, but when the money ran dry, Clyde came to Boston, looking to sell his share of *Scientific World*. Clyde and Evelyn were still married, which meant Clyde shared Evelyn's fifty-percent stake in the magazine. He thought an easy solution for his money problems would be to have Evelyn and Romulus buy him out.

Clyde's request wasn't unreasonable. In all the years he had been separated from Evelyn, he hadn't collected a dime from the magazine, letting Evelyn live off the earnings while he traveled the country, a brilliant engineer with a habit of clashing with his employers. Four years ago when Clyde had come to them, he had been broke, desperate for money, and wanted to sell his share of the magazine.

Evelyn had panicked, as had Romulus. The paltry newsletter they'd bought had grown into a world-class operation, but most of the money had been reinvested into the magazine. They bought expensive equipment, paid a monthly lease on a spectacular office building, and spent almost everything else on the salaries of forty employees. He and Evelyn each pocketed a generous salary, but they didn't have a spare thirty thousand dollars to buy Clyde out.

For weeks, Romulus had been unable to sleep. He'd been forced to hire a lawyer to fight his best friend, whose ugly marital difficulties were now reaching out to taint his only professional accomplishment. Evelyn had been so sick at heart she couldn't eat. She lost weight and arrived at the office looking like a stiff wind could blow her over. A court date loomed, and they both knew Clyde would win, which would force them to sell the magazine.

In the end, Romulus asked Evelyn and the lawyers to leave the room so he and Clyde could try to salvage something of the friendship that had never died. Romulus agreed to pull out every stop to get Clyde hired to teach at the newly established engineering program at Dartmouth. Over the years, Romulus had been collecting favors from scientists and academics, and he cashed them in to get Clyde that lucrative job. In exchange, Clyde had signed his rights to the magazine over to Evelyn, and he'd agreed to leave her in peace in Boston.

It seemed most brilliant engineers shared the same Achilles' heel. No matter how kind or easygoing they were in their personal life, when it came to scientific invention, they were fierce and inflexible. Clyde's tenure at Dartmouth hadn't lasted long, and he moved on to the challenge of the subway in New York. This time Clyde's unemployment wasn't his fault. Projects this monumental often took decades before they finally got underway, and Clyde had been caught in the turbulence of the launch.

"Aren't there any other subways in need of a good engineer?" Romulus asked.

"Berlin is the only other city in the world currently building a subway. I don't speak German, and I need this job."

Romulus nodded. "I'll deal with Evelyn. She won't like it, but I'll talk her around."

Clyde looked away, the echo of remembered pain on his face. "How is she?"

"She's fine. I sometimes wonder if—"

The elevator doors opened, and a group of typesetters poured into the hallway, heading toward the front office to collect their weekly paychecks. Clyde's brows snapped together, his lips tensed in frustration. By the time the gaggle of typesetters had funneled into the office, an old memory had surfaced in Romulus's mind.

"In one of the first issues of the magazine, you translated a passage from Otto Lilienthal on his design for a glider."

"So?"

"So you *do* speak German. At least enough to communicate with a construction team."

Clyde's shoulders sagged. The spark of energy drained from his eyes, and he looked beaten and sad. "I can't give up on her. I've tried, Rom. I know she can't stand the sight of me, and when she asked me to stay away, I tried to do as she asked." He swallowed hard, his Adam's apple bobbing as his eyes filled with reluctant humor. "They say that when a zebra is born, the mother won't let her calf look at any other zebra until her pattern of stripes is indelibly imprinted on the baby, never to be forgotten. That's what Evelyn is for me. She was the first and only woman I've ever loved. When I think of the meaning of that word, hers is the face I see. No matter how many years pass, no matter how far I travel, Evelyn White is the only woman I'll ever love."

The door opened, and a pair of typesetters left with their paychecks in hand. Clyde watched them with solemn eyes. The typesetters were young and pretty, but they could have been a troop of army rangers for all the attention Clyde showed them.

He pushed away from the wall. "I wanted to let you and Evelyn know I was in town. I'll try to stay out of her way."

Clyde was halfway down the hall toward the elevator when Romulus called out, "Clyde? Her name is still Evelyn Brixton. Don't let her forget it."

And for the first time, a bit of hope lightened Clyde's face as he nodded and turned away.

5

Chilly rain pelted Stella as she left City Hall, a perfectly awful end to a miserable Monday. Her shoulders ached from stooping over the stenotype machine, a headache throbbed from the clatter of typing in the office, and she'd gone nearly blind transcribing notes from a dreary meeting about the subway contracts. And she'd found no additional men who might be Gwendolyn's enigmatic A.G.

The folded newspaper over her head was a poor substitute for a proper umbrella, and she was soaked by the time she boarded a packed streetcar filled with other damp, irritated travelers.

It had been six days since her meeting with Romulus at the pub, which began with such promise but ended so badly. Given what she'd learned from the waterman, she was more convinced than ever that Gwendolyn's death had not been an accidental drowning. All her attempts to contact the medical examiner had failed, and she was about to embark on her last resort.

An exhumation of Gwendolyn's body for a second autopsy.

She had the funds to pay for a private examination, but it had to be done in such a way that her parents never learned of it. Her mother's mental stability was already tenuous, and her father flat out insisted that Gwendolyn's death was an accident.

She clenched the handstrap as the streetcar bumped and jostled, the stink of wet woolen clothing making her feel ill. She didn't want a second autopsy. She didn't want her sister's body exhumed and prodded and cut open once again, but how else could she be certain Dr. Lentz had been wrong?

She'd lost her best shot at winning an appointment with him when she'd bungled her meeting with Romulus. It seemed everywhere she went in Boston she was making enemies rather than friends. Even her landlord resented her following that incident with the bees' nest in her mailbox. She still had no explanation for the bizarre event, but at least the agony in her hand was finally beginning to ease.

The rain had trickled to a drizzle by the time she arrived at her boardinghouse, but she was still cold, damp, and itchy. She held her breath each time she opened the mailbox, bending over to peer inside before reaching in. There was another letter today. Her breath caught when she recognized the bold scrawl on the outside of the envelope. What did Romulus want?

She ripped open the letter, and a smile curved her mouth as she read the formal proposal.

Miss West,

I am searching for an artist to design a challenging series of advertisements for my magazine. In exchange for your cooperation in such a project, I am willing to use my influence to smooth your way at the medical examiner's office, provided you agree to the standard rules of etiquette. To date you have displayed the manners of a common wood tick, but I live in hope.

> *Sincerely,*
> *Romulus White*
> *Publisher,* Scientific World

A wood tick? She grinned as a surge of anticipation shot through her. Romulus could insult her all he wanted so long as he delivered on his promise. How was she to contact him to accept his offer? His note made no mention of a meeting, but the return address on the envelope was to the office of *Scientific World* on Tremont Street.

She set off to see him the first thing the following morning. She was not required to be at City Hall until ten o'clock, so she ought to have plenty of time to meet with Romulus before her workday began.

If she had any reason to doubt *Scientific World's* prominence, the sight of its office building banished it. The managerial office took up most of the top floor, where a dozen employees busily toiled at various desks as the clattering of typewriter keys filled the air. It was a splendid space, with tall ceilings, a wall of Palladian windows, and the most spectacular parquet floor she had ever seen. She couldn't resist kneeling down to admire it, her fingers tracing the inlaid wood.

"Can I help you?" the woman at a commanding desk in the front of the office asked. She was a willowy woman with ivory skin and dark hair artfully styled atop her head. The nameplate at the front of the desk read, *Evelyn White, Managing Editor.* Romulus's wife? She hadn't realized he was married, and it caused a strange catch in her throat.

She swallowed hard. She had no business indulging an

attraction to any man, not until Gwendolyn's death was solved. "I'm looking for Romulus White. Is he available?"

Was it her imagination or did the elegant woman roll her eyes? If she did, it was quickly masked, and Mrs. White was the embodiment of refined elegance as she replied.

"It's Tuesday morning, so that means he is boxing."

"Boxing?" Stella asked in confusion. *Boxing* must be a publishing term she did not know. Blocking, binding, bumping . . . all these terms she knew from working in the London printing industry, but boxing?

"And . . . where does the boxing happen?" she asked.

A hint of amusement lit Mrs. White's face. "At the Boston Athletic Club, just across the street. I only hope his face won't be pummeled into an unrecognizable pulp, as he is scheduled to meet with the chairman of the Union Pacific Railroad this afternoon, and black eyes always raise questions."

So *boxing* really did refer to the sport. Her heart sank, for it made Romulus even more attractive to her. She adored strong, bold men and had wondered if his fine figure might merely be an illusion created by a perfectly tailored suit. But no, only a fool would step into a boxing ring unless he was physically fit, and Romulus was no fool.

Well. She'd simply have to ignore this niggling attraction, for Romulus's wife was still eyeing her in amusement. Stella excused herself quickly and headed back to the street. From the building's front steps, she had a perfect view of the Boston Athletic Club directly across the street, so she'd be able to spot Romulus the moment he stepped outside. Tremont was chaotic, with hundreds of people going about their business on the tightly packed street. People moved so quickly here. Just watching them made her admire the energy that kept this city thriving, producing, and inspiring.

A few minutes later, she spotted Romulus emerging from the Athletic Club, engrossed in a conversation with a refined, silver-haired gentleman who looked like he might be the president of a bank or a university. Or perhaps France. Some men simply exuded authority, and the silver-haired man was one of them.

Romulus and the man were heading toward *Scientific World's* building, navigating around carriages and wagons as they crossed the street. Maybe this was a mistake. It was going to be awkward to explain her unannounced presence with that distinguished man looking on.

At least the silver-haired man was dressed properly, wearing a somber charcoal-gray suit with a plain black tie. Romulus wore a silk vest of alternating cranberry and ivory stripes, accented with a sage-green tie. In her old life, she would have pestered him for where he'd found it, for it was hard not to admire his unabashed sense of style.

His brows rose in surprise as he spotted her. "Miss West," he said. "Dare I hope you are here to discuss the possibility of designing a series of advertisements for fertilizer?"

She blanched. "You want me to advertise manure?"

"Fertilizer isn't always manure. Sometimes it is bonemeal, blood meal, or night litter."

"Night litter is another word for sewage," she said, still not sure if she should be insulted or amused that the advertisements he wanted her to design were for manure.

"Yes, but *night litter* sounds nicer. Michael, may I introduce you to Stella West? Miss West is a stenographer at the Boston Transit Commission. Miss West, this is Michael Townsend, the top attorney in the entire state and my sparring companion. I quiver in fear each time we enter the ring."

Appalled, she let her mouth drop open. "You've been punching an old man?"

77

The statement was out of her mouth before she could call it back. A hint of displeasure darkened Romulus's face, and Mr. Townsend simply looked embarrassed. He shifted on his feet and straightened his tie.

"I can assure you, ma'am, this old man is up to the challenge," Mr. Townsend said with remarkable recovery. "I was captain of my college boxing team in 1879."

On closer look, Mr. Townsend must be one of those men who went prematurely gray, for his face was free of lines, and if he'd graduated from college in 1879, that meant he was in his late forties. His silver hair lent him an air of dignity and age, but he was still a handsome man with a slender, athletic build.

"I'm sorry," she babbled. "I meant no disrespect. I was simply surprised . . ." She wished she'd inherited one-tenth of her mother's tact. She scrambled for something else to say and turned to Romulus. "Your wife told me you were boxing, but I couldn't quite believe it."

Mr. Townsend looked stunned. "Did you run off and get married while no one was looking?"

"Perish the thought," Romulus said with a mild shudder. "If I ever get married, the entire city will know it, as my mother shall hire a choir of angels to sing from the mountaintops. You probably saw Evelyn, my cousin. We share a last name, which sometimes causes confusion."

The clock tower on the corner chimed the bottom of the hour, and time was running out if she was going to be at her desk by ten o'clock. "I need to leave for City Hall within the next fifteen minutes if I am to avoid the draconian punishments awaiting any stenographer who dares risk tardiness. Might we discuss the proposal you sent me?"

"Absolutely." He said his farewell to Mr. Townsend, then grasped her elbow to guide her into the building.

"Since we're short on time, I'll take you straight up to the third-floor art department. And never fear, I shall be close at hand in case you faint at the sight of our brand-new lithographic equipment. It is a sight to make the strongest of mortals weak with amazement and envy."

Even the elevator was finely fitted out, with an inlaid floor and elegant brass panels. The attendant latched the door closed, then cranked the lever to lift the compartment up. She grasped the railing, always a little disconcerted when she felt the floor beneath her jostle and lift.

"Was that man really the state attorney for Massachusetts?" If so, perhaps Mr. Townsend was another of Romulus's connections she could use to her advantage.

"He really is. We've been boxing together for six years. I've found it useful to cultivate allies within the government, as they have a bird's-eye view of civil engineering projects. Plus, it's simply good form to be friendly with people."

"I've never thought of pummeling each other into insensibility as *friendly*. Boxing is nothing but ritualized barbarity to indulge primitive masculine egos."

He grinned. "It sounds like you've been listening to too many Cornell professors. Incidentally, Cornell has a terrible boxing team, so it is no wonder your professors were bitter."

The elevator jerked to a halt before she could reply. The attendant unfastened the doors, and she gasped at the wondrous sight of the art studio that opened before her.

Soaring windows flooded the room with natural light that gleamed off the polished chrome of the electroplating machine. Artists worked at spacious tables, the scent of linseed oil and turpentine in the air. A lithography press, looking like a mighty table with its gigantic flywheels, inking beds, and rotating cylinders, graced the center of the room, and the comforting scent of ink on rubber rollers filled the air. Stella was struck mute as she stepped into paradise.

"I warned you that fainting was a distinct possibility," Romulus said as he guided her into the artists' wing.

He should have warned louder. Never had she seen such a collection of shining, new, and sophisticated equipment in one studio. This was simply wonderful, but awful, too. A lump formed at the back of her throat. The last time she was in an artist's studio, her sister had been alive. The comforting thump and roll of the electrotyping machines reminded her of days when the world was full of nothing but joy and the thrill of artistic creation. If she closed her eyes, she could almost imagine she was back in London, before a terrible telegram changed her world forever.

At the end of the room was an alcove where the art supplies were stored. Romulus pulled her inside, and she let her gaze wander over the familiar tubes of paint, boxes of pen nibs, and bottles of ink. The scent of linseed oil and cleaning solution enveloped her, stirring another rush of fond memories.

"Well, Miss West?" he said. "What was it you wished to discuss with me? Dare I hope you are ready to abandon a life of clerical drudgery at City Hall in exchange for all this? I can offer you a permanent position if you'll only sign on the dotted line."

She felt like Eve being offered the apple, but her only goal in the world right now was uncovering what happened to Gwendolyn. She turned her back on the spacious studio and looked directly at Romulus. "I'll design your fertilizer advertisements if you can get me a personal meeting with the medical examiner. That's all I can commit to right now."

He raised a brow in surprise. "Is that the best you can do? I'll offer a competitive salary for a one-year commitment, and I can also open doors for you all over the city. I am a highly sought-after member of society."

"I don't know if I can bring myself to work for such a shy and self-effacing man."

He actually preened at her comment, straightening his shoulders as a hint of a smile curved his lips. "A one-year contract with *Scientific World* and I'll ensure you have access to any official in the city."

She shook her head. "I'm not quitting my work at the Transit Commission. Get me an appointment with the medical examiner as proof of your renowned charm, and I'll design your fertilizer advertisements. That's all I can promise you right now."

"And you'll avoid reckless attempts to threaten or sue any government authority with whom you disagree?"

Those threats wouldn't have been necessary had Dr. Lentz simply met with her in the first place. "I'll be a perfect lady."

"Deal." Excitement illuminated his face, as if a live electrical wire had flared to life inside him. It was impossible not to be flattered. He offered a handshake, and it was a firm, confident grasp. If she were a romantic sort, she would swear she'd just felt a zing of electricity charge straight through her.

"I'll make the appointment and notify you of the details," Romulus said. "Is your boardinghouse the best place to contact you?"

"It is," she said, turning around to survey the magnificent sight before her once again. Being in this room was restoring a piece of her soul that had been dormant for the past four months. "Thank you for showing me your studio," she said. "The stenotype machines won't seem quite so dazzling after seeing all this."

Romulus leaned down to whisper in her ear. "That was my purpose in bringing you up here."

She felt the tingle in her ear the entire way to City Hall.

6

Stella snapped awake in the middle of a dream. Her room was still dark, but her heart thumped, for she'd been dreaming of Gwendolyn. They had been laughing. Stella was in the archives of City Hall, going through filing cabinets to search for clues about the mysterious A.G., but Gwendolyn kept slamming the file cabinets shut, laughing and tugging Stella's arm, trying to draw her out of the archives. Gwendolyn tugged so hard they both fell down, gales of laughter overtaking them both.

Was Gwendolyn telling her she was looking in the wrong place? In the dream, Gwendolyn kept pointing upward and laughing. The archives were in the basement, so was she gesturing to someone who worked upstairs?

The dream felt so real. Stella sat in bed, still breathless from her imaginary tussle with Gwendolyn. It was hard to believe they would never laugh together again.

She rolled out of bed, her feet hopping on the frigid floor as she dashed to the wardrobe. She wrapped up in her beloved William Morris shawl as she scanned her clothes, letting her gaze linger on her London dresses, shimmering in the early-morning light in their shades of turquoise, saffron, and lavender. They represented a distant memory of happier days. She traced her fingertips along the sapphire-blue dress of watered-silk before reaching past it to lift out the brown frock of worsted wool. She shrugged out of her spectacular shawl and dressed in the dreary garment she was coming to despise.

Today she would cast a wider net at City Hall. Gwendolyn had said A.G. ran in the highest political circles, but that didn't necessarily mean he was a government official. He could be a rich financier or a college president. He could even be a publisher like Romulus White, for that matter!

She used her lunch break to start exploring other areas of City Hall. She'd always ignored the public gallery that showcased Boston's impressive history, but perhaps it was worth a look. The gallery featured a Hall of Heroes with life-sized marble busts of notable Bostonians such as Paul Revere, Sam Adams, and Nathaniel Hawthorne. Others were portraits of people who had died in the Civil War or the abolitionist crusade.

To her surprise, Ernest Palmer, the archivist, was in the Hall of Heroes, bent over the nameplate on one of the busts.

"Ernest? What are you doing?" she asked, her voice echoing in the nearly empty marble hallway.

He stood up, a guilty flush staining his face, but he breathed a sigh of relief when he saw it was her. "Hello, Stella. I can't figure out the typeface on this bust. Are you familiar with it?"

She drew closer. Ernest had been using a lump of charcoal to make a rubbing of the nameplate beneath a bust of Crispus Attucks, a black man killed during the Boston Massacre. Stella read the commemorative passage beneath his bust, which indicated that Attucks was regarded as the first casualty of the American Revolution. The typeface on the plaque looked like ordinary text to her, but Ernest was unusually fascinated.

"None of the other commemorative plaques use this particular font. I must do more research into where it came from."

Stella didn't quite know what to say, but it certainly appeared Ernest was flummoxed by his inability to identify the typeface. "Do tell me what you learn," she said, for she had no doubt the archivist would obsess over this until the mystery was solved.

But she had her own mystery to solve. Beyond the Hall of Heroes were dozens of framed photographs of important events from the recent past. The photographs memorialized presidential visits, the swearing-in of governors, and groundbreaking events. Nameplates beneath the photographs listed the dignitaries in the picture. Might A.G. be in one of the photographs? She headed toward the photographs at the far end of the gallery to begin scrutinizing the prominent men of Boston, searching for Gwendolyn's man.

One of the photographs was of the groundbreaking for the Boston subway only two years ago, the men wearing heavy coats and bowler hats and lined up around a small stone, a shovel propped in the mayor's hand. Alongside him were other elected officials, engineers, and some of Boston's financiers. She smiled when she glimpsed Romulus White in the line, looking chilly and serious as he stared at the camera. She skimmed the brass nameplate beneath the photograph, looking for someone with the initials A.G. Twelve men were listed on the nameplate, but none matched A.G.

"Miss West!" a voice barked behind her.

She startled and whirled around to see Mr. Grimes, the man in charge of hiring all clerical positions in City Hall. She wrinkled her brow as three police officers trailed after him.

"What precisely are your credentials for being a government stenographer?"

It was a strange question for him to ask, for it was Mr. Grimes himself who had interviewed her for the position. Why was he asking about her credentials now? And why were those three police officers here?

"I learned stenography in college," she said truthfully.

"Which college?"

It was the question she'd dreaded. When she'd interviewed for the position, she had shed both her last name and the name of Cornell from her record. She wanted nothing that might draw a connection between her and Gwendolyn, but she didn't want to be trapped in a lie.

"Why do you ask?" At her interview, she had been required to demonstrate her skills, not produce college transcripts.

"I have reason to believe you may not be adequate to the job for which you have been hired," Mr. Grimes said, and Stella silently groaned as Nellie's smirking face rose in her mind. It seemed her scornful colleague had tattled on her.

She lifted her chin a notch. "This is the first complaint I've heard."

"Not only are you a poor stenographer, it appears you falsified your application when you claimed to learn stenography through personal study rather than classes at Cornell University. That qualifies as a lie on a government application."

This couldn't be happening. It was no crime to omit a piece of information on an application, but it seemed Mr. Grimes had gone through an unusual degree of diligence in researching her background.

He glanced at the officers crowding the hallway behind him. "Naturally I consulted the Boston Police about my concerns, and imagine my surprise when they were already well acquainted with Miss Stella West. Or should I say Stella Westergaard? Surely it is no coincidence that you have schemed your way into your sister's old position. What have you to say for yourself?"

She clamped her mouth shut. Of course she'd been honest

with the police department about her relation to Gwendolyn, for it was her best shot of convincing them she had useful information to share about Gwendolyn's character and ability to swim.

Ernest Palmer watched silently from down the hallway, confusion and concern on his face. It was embarrassing to be badgered like this in front of him, but she had bigger concerns to worry about.

"Search her bag for misappropriated government property," Mr. Grimes said. One of the police officers grabbed her bag.

"You can't do this!" she cried. "That bag is my personal property!"

The officer ignored her as he upended her bag, spilling her coin purse, an engraved silver pen, and some hair pins across the floor. She clenched her teeth as one of the officers squatted down to paw through her belongings.

"Your employment here is terminated. The officers shall escort you from the premises."

She still couldn't believe this was happening, but even as she stepped back from the approaching officer, a terrible thought struck. "I need to get things from my desk upstairs." The note with the names of men who might be A.G. was taped to her desk drawer, and she *needed* that note. She moved to step around Mr. Grimes and head to the elevator.

Mr. Grimes was one step ahead of her, blocking her passage. "You may make a list of any personal property and it will be retrieved for you, but you may not return to your desk."

Her mouth went dry. She couldn't tell him about that list. How could she explain why she had it taped to the underside of her desk drawer? To do so would be shining a spotlight on each of the men on that list, and it might put A.G. in danger. He was the only person who truly knew what Gwendolyn had been up against, and Stella felt an instinctive urge to protect him.

"Well? What shall I have the officer retrieve?"

Every muscle in her body wanted to sprint upstairs and snatch that note from its hiding place, but there were three police officers watching her every move. Her only hope of getting the list back was to remain silent until she had a better strategy.

"There's nothing," she said stiffly, and three minutes later, she had been escorted outside, down the steps of City Hall, and told not to come back.

She stood on the cobblestone walkway, heedless of the pedestrians jostling around her. She'd just lost six weeks' worth of work, all because she had been too nervous to bring that list of names home where her landlord was known to poke through her room.

She didn't know what to do. She had no friends at City Hall and no alternate plan for figuring out what had happened to her sister. Her only hope for finding Gwendolyn's ally was taped to her desk drawer, and for all she knew, that desk was being cleaned out as she stood here on the sidewalk.

She had to put a stop to it. She had to know her rights and, if humanly possible, she had to get that list back.

Romulus White knew everybody and everything about Boston. Before she even had a coherent idea of what to ask him, she'd turned around, lifted her skirts, and begun running toward the offices of *Scientific World*.

—◦◦◦◦◦—

She was breathless by the time she arrived at the top floor of *Scientific World*. Her feet hurt from the blisters rubbing into her heels and she was thirsty, but none of that mattered. She just needed someone to help her, and Romulus was the closest thing to a friend she had in Boston.

It seemed the office was half empty, which wasn't surprising since many people probably had left for lunch. Romulus's cousin Evelyn was at her desk at the front of the office. She was keying a stream of numbers into an adding machine and looked up when Stella barreled in the door.

"Can I help you?" Evelyn asked coolly.

"Romulus," Stella said on a ragged breath. "Is he here?" With every moment, the likelihood of her desk contents being cleared out and tossed in the trash increased.

"May I ask who wishes to see him?"

But Stella had already spotted Romulus through the window of his private office. He was alone, and that was all she needed to know. Stella rounded the front desk and dashed across the floor. She rapped on the glass window and entered his office without waiting for a response.

Romulus had been standing at his window with his back to the door, staring down at the activity in the street below. He whirled around at her entrance. "Miss West! I see you are wearing another of your prison-garb ensembles." He sighed. "Pity, since I know you can do so much better."

She shut the door. It was hard not to feel like a brown wren beside his flawless attire, but she didn't care. "I have to quickly solve a problem, and I desperately need your help."

"Ouch," Romulus said. "What a split infinitive."

Stella couldn't believe her ears. "Are you quibbling over my grammar?"

"No self-respecting publisher can overlook such flawed syntax," he said. "The modifier goes after the verb, not before. I'm surprised they didn't teach you that at Cornell."

While she stood here getting lectured on grammar, the papers in her desk were probably being thrown into the trash and lost to her forever. All her work over the miserable weeks as a stenographer would be useless. She hadn't had a proper night of sleep in months, her feet hurt, and she was further than ever from finding A.G.

It was too much. She plopped down into the guest chair and burst into tears.

"Oh dear," Romulus murmured. He rounded his desk to stand awkwardly at her side, but she couldn't bear to look at him. He was her only hope for finding a way to get into her desk before the horrible Mr. Grimes destroyed her list, and he wanted to argue about grammar. She cried harder.

Romulus tried to offer a handkerchief, but she pushed it away. "Come now," he coaxed. "This is about more than bad grammar. Tell me."

"I don't have bad grammar," she said on a shuddering breath.

"You do so, dearest . . . but please. I'm afraid I've never been able to resist a pretty woman in tears. And you are pretty, despite the potato sack you're wearing."

If she wasn't so terrified of what was happening at her office, she would have laughed. Romulus pulled out his desk chair, folded his hands, and focused his entire attention on her. Blubbering wasn't going to solve her problem, so she forced herself to calm down and wipe away her tears.

"Out with it," he said. "What can I do to help?" All trace of teasing was gone, and his voice was tender and genuinely concerned.

"I got fired from my job at City Hall. It doesn't matter why, but they told me I couldn't go to my desk to retrieve my personal papers. I have an important document in my desk. I need to get it back before they ruin it."

"I don't know how I can help you with that."

"Can they do that?" she asked. "Is it legal? Don't I have any rights to my personal property?" She explained how Mr. Grimes had offered to have an officer fetch specified items for her, but she'd turned it down. "They have no business looking at that document. It's private."

"I'm no lawyer, but it seems you may not be entitled to privacy for things stored in their desk."

"But I need that document," she insisted. "I don't care if I have to hire a lawyer or a private army to get it back, but it needs to be done quickly. If they clean out my desk, it will probably be thrown away."

Romulus shifted in his chair, the corners of his mouth turned down and his eyes darkened in concern. He parsed his words carefully. "Miss West, you seem to be engaged in something entirely underhanded. I can't help you if I don't have a better understanding of what's going on."

His concern was fair. She needed his help, and perhaps if she explained everything, he would be more willing to give it.

"I've already told you my sister died under mysterious circumstances. Gwendolyn uncovered a web of corruption at City Hall and was working with a partner to root it out. All I know about her partner is that his initials are A.G. I need to make contact with this man. I've spent the past six weeks combing through the archives, trying to identify everyone whose initials are a match. That is the list I need. And I can't ask them to retrieve it, because that may put this man in danger, or at least under suspicion."

"Not to question your intelligence, but did you ever consider asking the city for a list of employees? It is a matter of public record."

She rocked back in her seat. "Could you repeat that, please?"

"Ask for a list of payroll employees. It should be a simple enough matter."

It could *not* be that easy. She sat staring at Romulus, her mouth hanging open and a wave of heat flooding her body. She knew nothing about running a business or payroll or what was public record, but he seemed to think it possible.

"Given your circumstances, I can understand why you'd be reluctant to ask for such a list at this point. I can have a clerk run over and put in a request. They ought to be able to produce one within a couple of days."

She unclenched the arms of the chair, and if she hadn't already been sitting, she probably would have collapsed in relief. "You'd do that for me?"

Before she'd even finished speaking, he had pushed away from the desk and stepped outside, summoning a clerk at a nearby desk and issuing the command to send a runner to City Hall with the request. To her horror, another wave of tears welled inside. This level of help was unfamiliar, and she wanted to weep in gratitude. She tamped it down, forcing herself to draw slow, steady breaths as Romulus returned to the office and shut the door.

"How did you learn about this A.G. person?" Romulus asked when he sat back in his desk chair.

She told him how she and Gwendolyn had exchanged long, chatty letters at least twice a week. Gwendolyn's letters initially had been full of sisterly gossip, such as the new almond oil tonic she used to make her hair shiny or the inexplicable way her landlady managed to burn soup. But then Gwendolyn noticed money flowing under the table at City Hall. It was illegal, and she had reported it to the one and only man she could trust.

"And that was when the tone of her letters changed," Stella said, relieved that Romulus had completely dropped his breezy manner and now listened with solemn concern. "Gwendolyn's letters became obsessed with this man. She described him as though he were a hero out of a storybook. He was a courageous man who wanted to expose all the entrenched corruption to the sunlight. He had a utopian vision for America, and Boston would be his test case. He wanted Gwendolyn to help him."

A muscle in Romulus's jaw tightened. "He recruited a lone woman to venture into a den of vice to do his investigating for him?"

"Gwendolyn didn't see it that way. She had always been idealistic, and she wanted to help. I know if I can only find this man, he'll provide insight into what happened to her. Gwendolyn said that she first met him at one of the subway meetings because of his position in the city, but he wasn't a formal member of the commission. Do you know who he might be?"

Romulus frowned. "There must be thousands of men with those initials in Boston."

"If you can get me that list of city employees, I'd be eternally grateful."

"It's happening as we speak. I've also gotten you an appointment with the medical examiner on Thursday morning."

"You did?"

"I did. Meet me here and I'll walk you over."

Relief eased through her like a cool breeze on parched skin. It was strange how quickly she was coming to trust and rely on Romulus, but there was far more to him than it first appeared. His debonair exterior hid a keenly intelligent mind that was highly attractive.

"You're a miracle worker," she breathed as she stood and prepared to leave.

"Aren't you forgetting something?" Romulus asked.

She glanced around the office. Her canvas tote was clutched in her arms, and she'd brought nothing else. She looked at him in confusion.

"An illustration, perhaps?"

Understanding dawned. "Your manure advertisements. Yes, I suppose I owe you that."

"And if you tire of manure, in the coming months our magazine will be running articles about the medicinal properties of orchids and the moons of Jupiter. Both would be more interesting than fertilizer, if you can be persuaded to join our staff."

It was tempting. Now that she had lost her job, what else did she have to do with her days? It would be so easy to slip back into the familiar, exhilarating world of art and leave the grief of the past behind.

Dwelling on the prospect was dangerous. The more she gave of herself to art, the more Gwendolyn's memory would slip away. She would not permit her life to begin again until Gwendolyn's death had been solved, but already Romulus was interfering with that. She'd been attracted to him from the instant she'd seen him lounging so elegantly in the auditorium at the subway meeting, and now . . .

Well, now it was even worse. After teasing and insulting her, he made her laugh, solved her problems, and then dangled the job of a lifetime before her. All while looking devastatingly handsome in a flawless suit with a shantung silk vest.

And he'd taken notice of her, too. The spark of energy humming between them each time they were together was getting harder to ignore. She ought to resist him, but instinct took over.

His eyes flared as she closed the distance between them, placed her hands on his chest, and kissed his cheek. He even smelled divine, like piney soap and the crisp scent of starched linen.

"Thank you, but no," she whispered.

He hadn't moved a muscle, but his gaze flicked over to study her through lowered lids. "Careful, Miss West."

She could feel his heart pounding beneath the silk vest, but still he hadn't moved.

"I'm never careful," she replied as she turned and left the office.

7

From the fourth floor, Romulus had a bird's-eye view of the activity on Tremont as the groundbreaking for the next leg of the subway got underway. Wooden barricades had been erected along the walkways, and stakes with bits of colored fabric marked underground gas lines, water pipes, and sewage drains. Men hefted and swung pickaxes to dislodge the paving stones, while a few yards behind them came another team to pry up the broken stones and hoist them into the wagons to be carted away.

The city had opted for the "cut and cover" method of building a subway, which was faster and safer than tunneling beneath the streets, but it was loud, dusty, and disruptive. Each ten-block portion of street took workers two months to blast, dig the trench, erect the braces, pour the concrete tunnel, and then cover it all over and move farther down the street to repeat the process. Until the subway was complete, they'd be subjected to this awful racket.

The street swarmed with men, mostly the laborers known as sandhogs, whose job it would be to dig up and haul away the soil. Clyde Brixton stood on the corner, talking to a burly Italian man in charge of the sandhogs. Even from here, Romulus could see Clyde's shoulders heave with laughter as he clapped the sandhog foreman on the shoulder. They went to examine a set of blueprints on a sawhorse. It was impossible to see what was on those complicated plans from here, but Romulus was certain Clyde could recite it all from memory.

It was moments like these when his old insecurities came roaring to life. Clyde was brilliant, while Romulus had always been completely unemployable. Except for the fluke of launching the magazine, he would have no way to capitalize on his assortment of arcane knowledge. If this magazine ever went under, he would be broke and jobless, and it would be blatantly obvious he was nothing but an imposter. A man good at faking success, but with no real skills. Clyde had always been a far better man than he.

Evelyn still didn't know Clyde was back in Boston. After the incident four years ago when the squabble over ownership of the magazine had landed them all in court, Romulus had declared himself a neutral party. He would no longer carry messages, negotiate ceasefires, or take sides. He was determined to maintain both friendships, even if Clyde and Evelyn couldn't be in the same room without fireworks.

The office door opened behind him, and Evelyn's voice was bright with excitement. "They've finally broken ground!" she said.

The enthusiasm on Evelyn's face dissolved his gloomy thoughts. While most people loathed the disruption caused by the coming of the subway, Evelyn was dazzled by it. If the world were fair, Evelyn would have gone to college and studied engineering like her father. How ironic that her father, the general in command of the U.S. Army Corps of Engineers, had refused his daughter the opportunity to follow in his own footsteps. Romulus had always wondered if Evelyn's immediate attraction to Clyde had been based on Clyde's respect for her frustrated ambitions. While most couples courted through formal dances or moonlit walks, Clyde and Evelyn's courtship took place while wiring a greenhouse for electricity, and they thought it the most romantic thing imaginable.

Romulus nodded as Evelyn joined him at the window. "I hear Park Street is entirely jammed with wagons loaded down with timber for the tunnel braces. It's going to be a mess."

"I don't care," she said. "It's an exciting mess, and I'm going to love watching every stage of it. Someday every large city in America will have a subway, but we are the first to take the leap." Her voice was a little breathless and trembling.

"Are you getting misty-eyed over the groundbreaking?" he teased.

She blushed but didn't deny it. "I think it's splendid, and I can't help being proud that I'm part of a city that is undertaking such a project. It's a huge risk, and yes, sometimes I get a little emotional over such things."

They weren't the only ones intrigued by the groundbreaking. Across the street, almost every window had curious spectators watching the action get underway. Evelyn still hadn't recognized Clyde, whose wide-brimmed canvas hat was pulled low to protect his eyes from the sun as he hunkered down over a set of plans unrolled on the ground.

Romulus could tell the moment she spotted Clyde. Her entire body stiffened, and she flinched.

"Is that . . . ?" Her voice trailed off, for just then Clyde stood and began sauntering to the other side of the street in his distinctive, rolling gait. It was impossible to mistake that long-legged, loose stride, and Evelyn's entire body recoiled. "What is *he* doing here?"

Romulus turned away from the window to sit at his desk. He dragged the calendar showing his day's appointments before him. "It looks as if he is gainfully employed at a job he is highly qualified for."

"He promised he would stay away from Boston," Evelyn bit out. "He *promised*."

"Yes, he did. And so did you, ten years ago while standing before an altar. I was in the front row and saw it in person."

She turned to glare at him, her normally ivory skin blotchy with patches of red. "You have no idea," she said in a voice vibrating with tension.

"You're right, and I don't *want* to know. I've spent the past six years trying to keep myself out of the line of fire. Clyde is here, and he is likely to be in Boston until the first leg of the subway opens in the fall."

Evelyn stormed out of his office before he could finish the sentence, slamming the door loudly enough to rattle the window glass.

―◌◌◌◌◌―

Evelyn took the stairs down rather than letting herself be trapped in the confined space of the elevator. She wanted to run and scream and hit things. As it was, she locked the emotions down and limited herself to calmly descending three flights of stairs, the click of her boots echoing in the stairwell.

She'd always been so weak where Clyde Brixton was concerned. After the series of cold, unfriendly homes of Evelyn's childhood, the immediate friendship that had formed between herself and Clyde had been a blessing. She was only eighteen and Clyde was a senior at West Point when he came to her house to help her design a hydraulic pump. She'd been entirely self-taught from studying old engineering texts in the library, but she had been desperate to prove to her father that she had what it took to go to college. She and Clyde had fallen in love while fixing a hydraulic pump for her greenhouse, and then they went on to tinker with designing a dry-cell battery and an electric generator as well.

She pushed through the heavy front doors and stepped out onto Tremont Street, coughing at the lungful of dust she inhaled. She clasped a handkerchief over her nose, scanning the crowds to see if it was really Clyde or if her imagination had run away with her.

The clank of pickaxes mingled with thuds of broken pavement tossed into wagon beds. She angled through the crowds on the sidewalk and headed to the hotel next door. Clyde's makeshift table was set up between two sawhorses, and from her position behind a column, she had a perfect view of his back as he leaned over a blueprint.

How naïve she had been to think he would honor his promise not to return to Boston. When she'd heard that the contract for building New York's subway had fallen through, she should have suspected he would turn up here within the week.

Was it possible to feel the weight of a gaze? Clyde had his back to her, but she saw the muscles in his back stiffen, and his pencil froze. He stood and turned around, spotting her beside the column.

A flash of regret darkened his face, but after a moment, he gave her a reluctant, lopsided smile. She'd always been such a fool over that smile.

He set down his pencil and headed her way. It would be childish to run, even though they had nothing to say to each other. The document they'd signed four years ago had finalized their legal and financial situation for all time.

"Hello, Evelyn," he said softly. He swept off his battered hat and ran a hand through his dark blond hair. His face was dusty, streaked with sweat, and his eyes looked impossibly blue against his tanned skin. She'd always loved the sight of a man who was strong and capable of building things. She looked away.

"Clyde," she said with an infinitesimal nod.

"Did Romulus tell you I was here?"

Her eyes widened. "He knew?" Wasn't that just perfect? The only man she trusted in the whole world knew about this and hadn't bothered to tell her.

"Don't hold it against him. He swore four years ago he was finished being an emissary between us."

She was surrounded by a hundred workmen and dozens of pedestrians, but they faded into the distance, making it feel as if she and Clyde were the only two people in the world, pinned together in this awful silence stretching between them.

"How are you?" he finally asked.

"Fine. The damage was confined to my uterus."

He flinched, as she'd known he would. A better woman would feel guilty about flinging this in his face, but she didn't. He hadn't been here six years ago to hold their baby as he died, and she felt no obligation to spare him the details of what she'd been through.

"But you're fine now?" he asked.

It was surprising that she could even think about that awful year without dissolving into tears, but time had built a layer of scar tissue over the wound that had once seared her world. The magazine was the only thing that had saved her. Getting up each morning and scheduling the assignments, reviewing the articles, managing the budget . . . these were the things that gave order and structure to her world. And at the end of each month, she had a beautiful magazine to show for it, filled with page after page of scientific wonders.

Four years ago, Clyde had the gall to try to force her into selling her share of *Scientific World*, robbing her of the only thing she had left. Thank heavens Romulus had kept a cool head and steered them through to a compromise that managed to let her retain her share of the magazine.

"I'm fine, but I wish you hadn't come to Boston."

"It's the only city in America building a subway."

"So you've lost interest in blasting railroad tunnels through the West?" She tried not to let bitterness leak into her voice, but it was hard. After they married, Clyde had promised he would take jobs close to her, or in places she could live. A construction tent in the Bighorn Mountains of Wyoming was no place for a pregnant woman, so she'd stayed in Boston while her husband had gone in search of his next engineering adventure.

Clyde's smile was tight. "I have an interest in earning a living, especially since I signed over all ownership of the magazine I helped finance and establish. And that means I need to work in Boston. And if you can't—" He stopped abruptly, looking away and breathing heavily. "I'm sorry," he said. "I don't want to fight with you. If anything, I had hoped that . . ."

"Hoped what?"

He closed his eyes and swallowed hard. If she didn't know him so well, she'd suspect he was nervous.

"It's going to take at least a decade before the entire subway is completed. That's a long time. Depending on how things go in Boston, I had hoped that maybe . . . well, maybe I could settle down here and we could make another go of it."

"There would be no point in it. The doctor said I can't ever have more children."

The breath left him in a rush. It looked as though an unseen fist had just punched him in the stomach. "Evelyn . . . I didn't know. I'm so sorry. I didn't know."

He reached out toward her, but she stepped back before he could make contact. "So, you see, there really wouldn't be any point in it, would there?" She turned away before he could reply. Clyde had desperately wanted children, and now she was useless for that particular function. All her creative energy was funneled into *Scientific World*.

Her ambition to study engineering had been stifled by her father, and her desire for a happy marriage had been squandered by Clyde. Even her opportunity to be a mother had been destroyed by fate. All she had left was the magazine. How ironic that those sixty-four pages each month had become the most precious thing in her world. They were the distillation of her energy, insight, and intellect. *Scientific World* gave her life a dependable rhythm and a sense of security that Clyde had never been able to provide.

It had taken years after the wreckage of her marriage to regain her equilibrium, but she had accomplished it. She would not let Clyde Brixton waltz back into her life to destroy it once again.

—◦⁊◦◦—

Stella dressed with extra care on Thursday morning as she prepared for her meeting with Dr. Lentz. No longer required to hide beneath a drab exterior, today she was free to let her true colors shine. Her eyes feasted on the clothes she had brought from London, where she'd lived among the literary and artistic avant-garde of society and flamboyant displays of style were common.

But this was Boston, not London. She wouldn't step out in her most outrageous styles, but at least she no longer needed to wear beige. After all, she was going to do battle with the city's medical examiner this morning and needed to look respectable, competent, and a person of consequence.

Her black velvet tailcoat was the perfect mix of severity and style, a dashing and feminine take on a traditionally masculine cutaway coat. The waist of the jacket was tightly cinched before flaring out at her hips with a swallowtail hem in the back. She paired it with a slim-fitting skirt of polished maroon cotton. It was a sharp ensemble—but perhaps needed a bit of softening. Scanning the jewelry in her top drawer, she selected an over-sized starburst brooch of carnelian coral to pin to her lapel. The splash of color was a perfect offset for the midnight-black of her coat. And for her hair? She was thoroughly tired of the sedate buns she had been wearing and opted for a wonderfully soft pile of romantic curls gathered loosely and twisted atop her head. A couple of finger twists and she had blond tendrils framing her face as if she'd just stepped out of a Botticelli portrait.

For the first time since her arrival in Boston, she felt like her true self. She rode the trolley to Court Street, the farthest she could go before subway construction diverted the streetcar route. The air got dustier as she battled the crowds on Tremont. She hadn't expected the chaos to be so bad. Wooden barricades reduced the width of the sidewalk to a fraction of its normal size, and pedestrians bumped shoulders, inching forward on the claustrophobic path at a snail's pace. It took her a full ten minutes to walk the three blocks to Romulus's building.

She rode the elevator to the top floor, where Evelyn's eyes widened in surprise at the sight of her. Before Evelyn could comment, Romulus flung open the door of his private office and headed toward Evelyn with his typical restless energy.

"I'm heading downstairs for a bite to eat," he said. "Miss West is shamefully late. If she arrives while I'm gone, please scold her for me, then offer her a pot of tea until I get back."

He was halfway out the door before she spoke. "Ahem," she said politely.

Romulus froze, then swiveled back around to gawk at her. A flare of appreciation lit his eyes. When she turned to face him directly, he slowly perused her from the top of her jaunty hat all the way down to the polished leather of her high-heeled boots.

"Well, well, well," he said in a measured, warm drawl. "The real Miss West finally appears."

"Indeed," she replied with a bit of humor, but it was quickly replaced with steel. "I'm ready to face the medical examiner and pry a copy of that report out of his tightfisted little hands."

Romulus said nothing, but the way one black brow rose communicated his surprise. He pointed to his office. "Let's have a little chat before we go, hmm?" His voice was polite, but she knew this wasn't a request. She followed him back to his office and lowered herself into the seat he offered. He closed the door, then propped his hip on his desk and folded his hands casually before him. "You look splendid this morning."

"Thank you." Odd, he didn't really seem complimentary; he seemed annoyed.

"Dr. Lentz reviews the articles about health and medicine for my magazine," he said tightly. "He got his medical degree from Yale, which besmirches an otherwise faultless record, as Harvard is clearly a superior school, but I know him to be a decent man. We've served together for years on the board at the Boston Athenaeum, so I consider him a friend, not a tightfisted man with little hands."

Her chin rose a notch. "He has been less than friendly with me. My experience with Dr. Lentz has been one of repeated indifference and stonewalling. Not much better than the police I've dealt with."

"I can't change what's gone on between you and the police, but I am telling you that attacking Dr. Lentz's character is the wrong way to handle him. I know Dr. Lentz to be a highly competent physician. I wouldn't ask him to review our articles for accuracy otherwise. You will catch more flies with honey than vinegar. I did suggest in my letter to you that I'd expect a modicum of etiquette."

"You suggested I had the manners of a common wood tick."

"True, but I suspect you are capable of better. Are you?"

She did love a good challenge, and she straightened her shoulders and lifted her chin as though she were the Queen of England. "Watch me," she said with confidence.

It was enough to convince Romulus, and twenty minutes later they were on North Street, walking toward the office of the medical examiner, which was tucked into a row of elegant Colonial buildings. There was no subway construction here, and life seemed achingly normal.

What a stark contrast to the turmoil gathering momentum in her mind. For months she had been fighting for this appointment, but it hurt to think of Gwendolyn lying cold and lifeless on a mortuary slab. She wanted only to remember Gwendolyn laughing in the sunshine, swimming in the lake near their house, jumping into bed with her on chilly winter mornings. They used to daydream about the men they would someday marry and the number of children they would have. Stella wanted only a single boy and a girl, but Gwendolyn wanted half a dozen children. She would never have any.

"Let me do the talking," Romulus said as they drew closer to the medical examiner's building. "We are likely to gab about Boston baseball for at least twenty minutes, and I know—"

"Twenty minutes! What a ridiculous waste of time."

"Trust me on this," Romulus said. "You've been barging in and telling the police how to do their jobs and have gotten nowhere. Let me soften the ground before we attack Dr. Lentz's professional abilities, hmm?"

She supposed it would be all right. She didn't care a fig about baseball, but if it softened up her opponent, she was all for it.

Romulus walked up a narrow path to a door flanked by Corinthian columns, but her feet were frozen to the ground. He must have noticed her hesitation, for he looked at her with question in his eyes. She drew a fortifying breath. This wasn't going to be easy, but it had to be done.

The stench of carbolic acid greeted her as they walked down the tiled hallway. The clerk at the front counter, the one who had threatened Stella with the police the last time she was here, smiled and nodded to Romulus as they passed into the private wing of the building. Romulus rapped on the door of Dr. Lentz's private office, the thud echoing down the hallway and ratcheting her tension higher.

A young man wearing a white coat over a plain black suit smiled upon opening the door. With tousled brown hair and a skinny build, the man had a boyish look that was charming. *This* was her enemy?

"Romulus," he said, holding out his hand for a quick shake. "Please come in."

His office was remarkably ordinary, with a wide desk facing two chairs. Behind him was a window overlooking a leafy garden.

"You must be Miss Westergaard," the young doctor said with sympathy in his brown eyes. "Please have a seat and I'll be happy to share what I know of your sister's case."

Well, this was a marked difference from the closed doors she'd been treated to earlier in the month.

Romulus nodded to the autographed photograph of Hugh Duffy, the Boston Red Stockings's best hitter. "Are you planning on attending the opening game?"

As Romulus had predicted, the two men chatted amiably

about the coming baseball season. Stella couldn't tear her mind off the plain manila folder placed on the doctor's desk, Gwendolyn's name printed on the tab. Dr. Lentz must have noticed her attention, for after a few minutes, he straightened his spine and abruptly changed the topic.

"Enough baseball, let's get down to business, shall we?" the doctor asked as he opened Gwendolyn's file.

She drew a breath to launch into her spiel, but a quick glare from Romulus froze her. With a barely perceptible motion of his hand, he indicated she should wait for the doctor to speak first. It didn't take the man long to review his notes.

"Your sister's body was pulled from the Fort Point Channel shortly after sunrise on December 10th. Based on the state of rigor mortis, she had been dead for several hours by this time, but her body was not discovered until the sun had cleared the horizon. She arrived at my office an hour later."

"Did you perform the autopsy?" Romulus asked.

"I did. It was a straightforward case of drowning." He spoke the words gently, while looking directly at Stella. She was sure Dr. Lentz was well accustomed to dealing with grieving family members, and he skillfully conveyed the perfect blend of compassion and medical competence as he outlined his findings. He listed the typical signs of drowning and confirmed that Gwendolyn's body showed every one of them.

"Gwendolyn was a strong swimmer," she said. "The bridge wasn't that high over the river, no more than ten or twelve feet. I don't think a fall would have rendered her unconscious."

"It is impossible to know the exact circumstances of your sister's fall," the doctor said. "Her lungs were saturated with water, and there was no sign of foul play. No bruising or other injuries."

"How could she be floating if her lungs were filled with water?" she asked.

Dr. Lentz gave a patient but uncomfortable smile. "I'm not sure you want to know the answer to that. It isn't something for delicate ears."

"My ears aren't delicate. I'd like to hear everything you've got to say."

"Well," the young doctor said, shifting uncomfortably in his chair, "your sister was alive when she hit the water. When she inhaled water into her lungs, it got mixed with air and the mucus secretions in her windpipe. This creates a foam, which is an unmistakable sign of drowning. Her lungs and respiratory passage were entirely filled with this foam. It would have been enough to keep her afloat."

"Were there photographs taken?" Romulus asked.

Stella blanched. Never having pondered the procedures in an autopsy, she hadn't realized there might be photographs. It seemed obscene to take photographs of her sister's lifeless body.

Dr. Lentz cleared his throat. "It was not deemed necessary. In such a clear-cut case, I rarely take photographs."

She released her breath. Under no circumstances would she ever desire to look at such a photograph, and relief washed through her, draining her of strength.

The doctor turned Gwendolyn's file so she and Romulus could see the pages. It was a three-page form, with Gwendolyn's name, age, and a brief description filled in at the top. Various checkboxes indicated good health in all categories except her lungs. A typed paragraph summarized the presence of foam and river water in her lungs. The last page consisted of a pre-printed outline of a female body, with space for the medical examiner to note any unusual marks or injuries. Dr. Lentz had drawn the two-inch scar on Gwendolyn's wrist from a childhood accident with a fishing hook. Stella remembered her father stitching that wound closed, and afterward he had looked more shaken than Gwendolyn.

"That scar was on Gwendolyn's left wrist, not her right," she pointed out.

Dr. Lentz raised a brow and consulted the form. "Ah," he said delicately.

"Your report is wrong."

He cleared his throat. "I remember the scar was quite old. It had no bearing on your sister's death."

It was still a sign of sloppy work. A wall of framed diplomas and accolades testified to Dr. Lentz's credentials, and Romulus had vouched for Dr. Lentz's integrity. Was it possible that Gwendolyn's death at such a young age truly was the result of a tragic accident? Although Gwendolyn had been in the process of documenting corruption at City Hall, that did not prohibit her from falling victim to a normal accident, even though for months Stella had rejected the coincidence.

Stella wanted someone to blame, someone to punish. At the very least, she wanted indisputable *proof* her sister's death was an accident, but perhaps the autopsy report was the closest she could ever come. Dr. Lentz assured her he'd have his secretary prepare a copy of his report and mail it to Romulus the following week.

She hadn't expected this meeting to be so exhausting, but she wasn't even sure if she'd have the strength to stand up and walk to the trolley stop at the end of the street.

Romulus must have noticed as they left the building. He suggested getting something to eat at the Quincy Market, which was only a few blocks away. He needed to buy some buttons, and there were hundreds of vendors there who set out their wares daily. Stella welcomed a chance to free her mind, if only by something as trivial as shopping for buttons.

The marketplace was inside Faneuil Hall, a historic building dating back to the early part of the century. Vendors' stalls flanked each side of the grand corridor that ran the length of the building. The vendors offered everything from cheese and imported coffee and tea to bolts of cloth and leather goods. Stella had a fiendish infatuation with Belgian chocolates, and she bought a small box that she shared with Romulus as they strolled through the marketplace. They found a stall at the end of the market with a double-wide table overflowing with a staggering array of buttons in all sizes and materials: brass, ivory, pewter, polished wood, mother-of-pearl, and even handpainted enamel.

"Have you any stamped brass buttons with a wide shank?" he asked the big-boned woman overseeing the stall. "I have a wool overcoat that is hopelessly drab and could use some spiffing up."

Stella watched in amusement as he perused a tray full of buttons with zealous concentration. It was actually a little fascinating. Romulus was so passionate about everything, whether it was the illustrations for his magazine or the buttons for his jacket. He held dozens of buttons to the light, tossed them to test their weight, and asked her opinion. He finally settled on a brass alloy with the imprint of an acanthus wreath stamped onto the surface.

"Just the right mix of classical formality and a touch of botanical charm," he said as he tucked the sack of newly purchased buttons inside his coat pocket. They started strolling toward the Long Wharf, where flags snapped in the breeze and a salty tang blew in from the harbor. He was hungry and insisted the best clam chowder could be had at a tavern near the wharf. She nodded and followed, even though she'd rather eat anywhere other than a tavern overlooking the water.

But she refused to show weakness in front of Romulus. She followed him to the tavern, which was crowded and dim inside, but there were plenty of places at the tables outside. Romulus ordered two large crockery bowls of chowder and carried them outside to her.

It seemed half the people in the tavern had ordered the same, and she could tell why on her first sip. Rich with cream and seasoned with onions, celery, and a hint of smoky bacon, the clam chowder was both filling and comforting. She and Romulus ate in companionable silence while they watched schooners in the harbor. Romulus seemed unusually pensive. Normally he rambled from topic to topic so fast she could hardly keep pace with him. Finally, he set down his spoon and looked at her.

"So. After speaking with Dr. Lentz, has it changed your mind about what happened to your sister?"

"No. I'm not denying that she drowned, but I can't believe it was a simple accident."

He stared at a distant schooner, his eyes tracking it as it sailed along the horizon. He looked troubled.

"You don't believe me," she said.

"Everything points to an accidental drowning."

"Not Gwendolyn. She was a strong swimmer. She wasn't clumsy, careless, or suicidal. I refuse to believe it was an accident. And Dr. Lentz's report was sloppy. He got the location of Gwendolyn's scar wrong, and it throws his credibility into question."

Romulus stood and adjusted his vest before offering his arm. "Let's head back to the trolley station. I'm not sure I can convince you."

"Perhaps because I'm right?"

He said nothing as he stared straight ahead, but she could tell by the tension around his mouth that he was dying to say something but holding himself back. He was practically champing at the bit.

"Go on," she prompted. "Say whatever it is you are thinking."

"You probably don't want to hear it."

"Say it anyway."

They walked several more paces before he spoke. "It occurs to me that you are not in a position to make a rational judgment about this. You are so loyal to your sister that you may not be able to . . . don't look at me like that . . . you asked my opinion. You aren't displaying sound judgment in this matter, but it's not entirely your fault. Few women in your position would."

"You said few *women*. Are you suggesting that because I am a woman I am not fully capable of rational thought?"

He said nothing for a maddening amount of time. Ever since stepping out into the world as an independent woman, she had dealt with men condescending to her for nothing more than the fault of being female, but she hadn't expected it from Romulus.

"I don't think it's a secret that women can sometimes be irrational," he finally said. "Last year, *Scientific World* published an article on the chemicals released by the female pituitary gland, which seem to regulate moods. It seems some women are biologically prone to irrational mood swings and—"

She whirled to face him, stopping him in his tracks. "Yes, I am irrational about this," she said. "So irrational that if the only way I can learn what happened to Gwendolyn is by crawling over broken glass on my hands and knees, that is what I will do." She pointed her index finger at the hollow of his throat and spoke in a low voice vibrating with intensity. "And if you *ever* insult my intelligence like that again, I will cram those fancy brass buttons down your throat."

Romulus folded a gentle hand over her pointing finger and lowered it. His face and voice were calm. "Try it again," he said.

"Try what?"

"Try putting me in my place without getting surly and aggressive. It's counterproductive, and your attitude is probably the reason you've failed to get Boston's authorities on your side."

Her gaze flew to his. Humor glinted in his eyes, and she realized she'd walked into his trap. Just this morning, he'd advised that her technique for blasting through opposition was causing problems, and already she had been slipping into her old ways.

She closed her eyes, gathered her thoughts, and forced the tension to drain from her muscles. When she looked at him again, she had the poise of a duchess. "While a medical doctor can diagnose the physical cause of death, his knowledge of the behavior and habits of the victim is limited. This is where the insight of a family member will prove beneficial in helping him form a conclusion."

"Well done," Romulus murmured.

"Is it going to get him to reopen the case?" After all, that was the only thing that really mattered.

"I doubt it."

"This won't end here, Romulus. I don't believe Gwendolyn drowned, and I think Dr. Lentz did a sloppy job. As soon as I get a copy of that report, I'm going to look in to this further."

"May I suggest you actually read his report before you sally forth demanding a revision? Being a product of Cornell, I accept you are tragically disadvantaged compared to a Harvard graduate, but I live in hope that you can overcome your educational deficiencies."

"Possibly. But how sad that manners weren't a part of the curriculum at Harvard." She struggled to keep the laughter from her voice. They began walking toward the streetcar stop, her arm tucked companionably in his. "And in case I wasn't clear, I find you to be a perfectly awful human being."

"What a lie," he replied. "You're just having difficulty with a man who doesn't fall to his knees the instant you grace him with your presence. Just because you aren't the sort of woman I typically squire about town—"

"Trust me, you aren't my preferred sort, either," she interjected.

He almost stumbled. "I'm not?"

"I like nice men," she said. "The type who can accept a compliment without demanding another."

"Nonsense," he said dismissively. "I'm exactly your kind of man. Admit it. You need someone like me to keep your ego a manageable size."

Oh, the irony. There was something charming about the way he so freely flaunted his high opinion of himself. He didn't flinch from her, didn't pander to her, and she liked that about him.

"My goodness," she said. "I'm impressed you are able to walk with the weight of that gargantuan ego in your head."

"You'd be surprised at my dauntless strength. Don't let the fine tailoring deceive you. I am a man of awesome abilities."

"Yes indeed. Romulus of Rome, just popped down to say hello to the mere mortals."

She enjoyed walking alongside him. For a moment, she didn't have to dwell on the injustice of Gwendolyn's death and the despair weighing her parents down. She was just a healthy young woman trading insults with the most charming man in Boston, and it was fun.

Even though it had hurt when Romulus said she wasn't his type. She was drawn to him like iron filings to a magnet, and she'd assumed the attraction was mutual. How mortifying to learn otherwise. She must not forget that when she'd kissed him on the cheek the other day, he hadn't moved a muscle to encourage her. Was it possible he really felt nothing for her?

She hid her confusion behind a bright façade of indifference and strolled alongside him, keeping up the flirtation simply because it was so enjoyable.

But it also wasn't getting her closer to her objective. She still needed to find A.G., and Romulus had promised to get her a directory of city employees. "And when can I get that list of personnel working for City Hall you promised me?" she asked him.

"I'm still awaiting a promised fertilizer advertisement," he said. "One extolling the virtues of processed manure in a fashion I'm sure only your creative genius can do justice."

His grin was confident as he tossed off the compliment, and her heart fluttered anew. Even the way he complimented her was thrilling.

"I shall design you the Taj Mahal of manure advertisements," she said, still having no idea how she could blend the necessary threads of artistic beauty and scientific information into a single image, but she'd always liked a challenge.

One of the things Stella liked about Boston was that most of the finest restaurants in town permitted women to dine alone. Other cities looked askance at such women, but since its founding, Boston had been a thriving community of radicalism, revolution, abolition, and suffrage. If a woman strode into one of Boston's fine restaurants and ordered a meal, the only thing that mattered was if she had the ability to pay for it.

And thanks to her healthy bank account, money was the least of Stella's worries. Even after being dismissed from City Hall, she could support herself for years, especially if she continued to live at Mr. Zhekova's modest boardinghouse. Stella didn't need luxury, but she did need a spacious table and suitable light in order to draw. She owed Romulus three proposed sketches for the first fertilizer advertisement, and a table by the window at the restaurant on Washington Street was a perfect place to draw.

By early afternoon, she had three sketches to present to Romulus. It had been a challenge to supply artistic beauty while simultaneously delivering information about the value of the product, but she was optimistic these sketches would work.

She had just entered the managerial office at *Scientific World* when a woman came careening straight toward her. Stella tried to sidestep, but the weeping woman slammed into Stella's shoulder as she barreled out the door, noisy gulps of tears poorly masked by the handkerchief clutched to her face.

Romulus stood in the opening of his office door, his face somber and hands thrust into his pockets. His cousin Evelyn had risen from behind her desk and was staring at the fleeing woman, as well.

"Am I arriving at a bad time?" Stella asked.

Romulus spotted the leather portfolio tucked under her arm and closed the space between them. "Not at all," he said blandly. "Especially if those are fertilizer sketches you are ready to show me. Don't worry about Daisy. She was just indulging in a tantrum for dramatic effect." He turned to Evelyn. "How did she get in here, anyway?"

"She must have gotten in when I stepped outside to use the facilities," Evelyn said. "I suspect she was lying in wait for just such an opportunity. I've asked her to stop pestering you, and she knew she wasn't welcome. What did she want today?"

"An escort to a soiree at the Garden Club next week," he said. "This is my punishment for paying too much attention to her when I took her for a ride on one of the swan boats. Now she is hearing wedding bells, which is ridiculous." He extended both arms and spoke loudly enough for the entire fourth floor to hear. "Have I not sworn repeatedly that I would never marry before the age of forty?" He scanned the room, and the various office workers nodded, some even hiding laughter. "I've got eight more years of bachelorhood," Romulus continued. "I've done nothing to encourage Daisy beyond squiring her about town a few times and compliment-ing her appearance. I've been quite clear that she should never expect more."

Stella shook her head, amused by Romulus's naiveté. "Most women harbor fantasies that they are somehow unique," she said. "They believe they shall be the one to tame the beast, to persuade Casanova to change his ways. Some women have the curious ability to set aside logic and believe the force of her love will bring the knight errant to his knees." She should know; she'd been battling similar fantasies about Romulus ever since she'd met him.

Romulus swiveled a questioning look at Evelyn. "Is that true?"

"I'm afraid so," Evelyn acknowledged with a pained expression.

"I'm not dropping to my knees before I'm forty. And even then, no knee-dropping will be involved. I have more respect for the tailoring of my trousers than that." His eyes brightened. "Come. Have you drawings to show me?"

"I do."

And like magic, a spark of energy brightened his face. His admiration of her work made it hard not to be flattered. They entered his office, and as soon as the door closed, he held out his hand for her drawings.

"Why won't you marry before you are forty?" she asked.

He shrugged. "It's just a number I picked out of the air a long time ago. It keeps women from pestering me too much."

He took the folder from her hand and walked to the other side of his desk. She studied his face as he reviewed her sketches. The smile on his mouth cut deep grooves into the sides of his face. She'd known he would like her drawings, but she was still curious about his fear of marriage.

"Why does the prospect of marriage terrify you so much?"

He didn't move, but his gaze flicked up to meet hers. "Did I say it terrified me?"

"You didn't need to. Any man who makes such ardent declarations of his bachelorhood before his entire office is clearly building a barricade to hide behind. I was just wondering the reason."

He leaned back in his desk chair, one of the newfangled kind that swiveled on its pedestal. A speculative gleam lit his dark eyes as he folded his hands across his waist. "I intend to marry someday. One cannot have children without that preliminary step, so there's no avoiding it. But I will choose my wife carefully, and she will not fall into the *terrifying* category. She shall be intelligent, respectable, and attractive. I don't care for histrionics, so Daisy Callahan is out."

"While you were indulging in your monologue decrying marriage, I couldn't help noticing the redheaded lady at the adding machine," Stella said.

"Millicent O'Grady?"

Stella didn't know the woman's name, but the fetching redhead had seemed spellbound as she hung on every word Romulus spoke, staring at him with a combination of fervor and despair. "She seemed disconsolate over your comments. One of your many admirers?"

He snorted. "I adore women and everything they represent, but I am entirely immune to any woman who works for *Scientific World*, and Millicent knows that. I would no more tamper with a woman in my employ than drink a cup of poison. Both are recipes for disaster."

He turned his attention back to her sketches on the desk, flicking through them quickly and pulling out her sketch showing the Mona Lisa as she smiled enigmatically at the viewer with a bountiful harvest in the background. A large caption read *What*

Is She Smiling About? and smaller text explained the amazing benefits of proper soil preparation with Stallworth's Fertilizer.

"This is brilliant," Romulus said. "I confess I was skeptical you could produce an alluring advertisement featuring manure, but I'd like to present this one to Mr. Stallworth for his approval. It is both attractive and conveys all the necessary information. I suspect he will be pleased."

"I suspect so, as well," she said proudly.

He snorted. "What's it like to be unburdened by an ounce of humility?"

"You tell me," she replied, coaxing a huge smile from him. "Besides, you wouldn't be interested in a woman burdened with humility."

"Not one working for my magazine, I wouldn't. I only hire the best."

She held out her hand for the return of her sketch. "I'll head downstairs to the artist's room and get started immediately."

─◦⟨◦⟩◦─

Evelyn reviewed the ledger of operating expenses on the desk before her, running calculations in her mind. It looked as if Stella was indeed going to begin working for them, at least in the short run. That meant Evelyn needed to find a way to pay another salary.

It would be a challenge, but an enjoyable one. Each month, she choreographed a complicated dance to ensure outgoing expenses came in below their revenue. It required a combination of mathematics, business acumen, and the ability to forecast expenditures. Once upon a time, Evelyn had dreamed of becoming a famous engineer like her father, but that dream had died a long time ago. Never could she have imagined the satisfaction she'd find in managing this magazine and ensuring they had the funds to keep it healthy. Although she'd fretted about the cost when Romulus initially proposed hiring Stella West, as usual, his instincts were probably correct. Evelyn was always far more cautious and resisted anything that might rock the boat, but it was Romulus's insistence on investing in the best writers, artists, and production materials that made their magazine so impressive. It was her job to figure out how to pay for it all, and she loved every moment of it.

It was a far cry from when she'd managed the household budget when she and Clyde had shared a household. Despite his flamboyant ways, Romulus understood the real world, while Clyde had always been reckless and without a care about long-term consequences. The Christmas she and Clyde celebrated their fourth anniversary was a classic example.

They had gone to West Point to spend the holiday with Romulus's parents. She had been furious because their anniversary had been on December 15th, and Clyde had completely forgotten it, as he had every single year of their marriage. She always reminded him before the day was over, but not this time. This year she maintained a steely silence, waiting to see how long it would take him to remember, but he never did. Christmas Day arrived and still he showed no sign of remembering their forgotten anniversary. As they withdrew to their small guest bedroom after Christmas dinner, all Clyde wanted to know was if she could find a few dollars in their budget so he and Romulus could go ice fishing for three days in Maine.

"Ice fishing," she said coldly. "You need me to find money in the budget so you can go *ice fishing*."

Clyde rummaged in the drawer for his nightshirt and had the good grace to look a little sheepish as he tugged it on. "I've put a few dollars aside each week all month, but I'm still a little short. You don't mind, do you?"

And to think, she'd been hoping that perhaps the reason he'd been short of cash all month was because he'd been squirreling it away to buy her a nice anniversary present, or perhaps a nice Christmas gift. But no . . . their anniversary had come and gone, and now so had Christmas. He'd bought her a tea cozy for Christmas but still hadn't realized he'd forgotten their anniversary.

She drew a steadying breath and turned down the blankets. "You're heading to Mexico in two weeks, and now you want to go dashing off into the woods to go ice fishing with Romulus? That's how you're choosing to spend our final few days together?"

She still couldn't say the word *Mexico* without her voice rising in volume. He'd only informed her of the job in Mexico last week. It had come completely out of the blue. He'd come home from work early, announcing he'd quit his safe job at the Boston Power & Light Company to take a job at a smelting plant in Mexico. Clyde assumed she would be delighted because she knew how much he disliked his employer, and the job in Mexico promised to pay well. Electrifying the plant in Mexico would take only three months, so it was a great opportunity, wasn't it?

"Maybe your time would be better spent fixing the leaky window in our apartment before you go running off to go ice fishing with Romulus," she said.

His mouth tightened. "I can fix the window in less than an hour as soon as we get back to town."

"It's been wet and freezing for weeks!"

"Which was why I couldn't fix it before now," Clyde said, his own voice getting louder.

She plumped the pillows with a little more force than necessary. "Wonderful! You'll be warm and toasty in Mexico while I'll be freezing in Boston. Whatever happened to your promise to find work closer to home? If you hated the job at the power company, why didn't you warn me you were about to quit? Why didn't you at least *ask* how I felt about you dashing off to Mexico?"

A soft knock on the door interrupted Clyde's retort. "Yes?" Evelyn asked.

The door cracked open, and Romulus tipped his head inside. "I can hear you from down the hall . . . is something wrong?"

"No!" she and Clyde both said in unison.

Romulus sagged a little, and his voice was heavy with exhaustion. "I hate to ask, but if you could keep it down, it would be best for my mother. She's had a difficult night. My father is out, and it's a sure thing he is with his mistress again. My mother knows, and it's killing her."

Clyde looked astonished. "I thought that ended last summer."

Romulus shook his head. "It did, but he's taken up with someone else. She won't be his last, either. I know it, my mother knows it, and yet she puts herself through these grand histrionics each time he starts up with a new woman."

Evelyn's heart split wide open at the anguish in Romulus's voice. "Oh, Rom! Is there anything we can do?"

"Not really. I've been with her for the past few hours, and she's finally cried herself to sleep. It would be best if we can all keep our voices down so she doesn't wake up."

"We'll be quiet," Clyde rushed to assure him.

"Of course," she added.

A hint of a smile brightened Romulus's tired face. "Thanks. You two are the best." The smile vanished, and he swallowed hard. "You can't imagine what this is like."

She felt hollow inside after Romulus closed the door with a gentle *snick*. The complaints in her marriage were nothing compared with the cataclysmic tantrums that had raged between her aunt and uncle for years. It was petty to keep nurturing the grudge over her forgotten anniversary compared to what her aunt endured.

She found the money so Clyde could spend a few days in the woods with Romulus. Clyde's move to Mexico would be a loss for Romulus, too, and she wanted them to have a good time together.

Two weeks later, Clyde left for Mexico. Everything proceeded smashingly well until the smelting company went bankrupt, and Clyde's final month of wages went unpaid. He took the job in Wyoming later that year . . . and then the baby . . . and then her terrible period of melancholia. She and Clyde bickered incessantly after that.

Well, enough wallowing in the past. She'd made a successful life here at the magazine, and if Romulus wanted her to find money in the budget to hire Stella, she would do so. They had a world-class magazine because she trusted Romulus's instinct for what would appeal to the public. Within ten minutes, she'd made arrangements for her and Romulus to delay their equity dividends for the next quarter, and she reduced their excess printing supplies from three months to two months. It would be enough to meet Stella's salary in the short term.

Evelyn smiled as she made notations in the ledger. Oh yes, she did love the juggling act of keeping this magazine afloat. She liked Stella, too, and she would gladly recalculate the next few months of expenses to make room in the budget for her. Stella was a safer bet than Clyde Brixton had ever been. Stella was an investment, whereas Clyde had always been a gamble.

And if she'd learned nothing else, Evelyn had come to accept she had no tolerance for gambling.

Romulus scrupulously avoided the third floor while Stella began working on the first fertilizer advertisement. He knew she'd already prepared a zinc-lined plate to be used as the template for printing because Evelyn had to put in an order for more zinc powder. Etching the design onto the plate was the longest part of the process and would take her several days to complete.

He'd caught a glimpse of Stella the very first day, wearing a white artist's smock over one of her plain dresses, her hair tied up in a charming scarf. She had her sleeves rolled up and looked like a peasant woman. A radiant, beautiful peasant woman. Stella working at her trade. It was a whole other side to her he found wildly appealing.

But he wouldn't let himself be tempted. For the past two days, he had stayed firmly rooted on the top floor, avoiding any accidental meetings with Stella that would throw his concentration into chaos.

And concentration was especially important this afternoon. He was meeting with a pair of astronomers writing an article on Jupiter and its moons. He'd commissioned them to write a three-page article, and they had submitted eleven pages of single-spaced text far too detailed for his general readership. They had been insulted when he'd asked them to trim the article, but he had finally convinced them to do so by telling them he would work alongside them, so they could approve every paragraph he cut or sentence he translated into intelligible English. It was going to be a long afternoon.

They were two hours into the process when a clerk knocked on his door to hand him Stella's page proof of the fertilizer advertisement. It was in blazing full color, with Mona Lisa in the foreground and a valley of verdant fields behind her. He stood in the open doorway of his office, a stupid grin on his face as he gazed at the advertisement. Both astronomers were dazzled when they saw it.

"Brilliant!" one said.

The other leaned in closer. "Full-color advertisements? My, my . . . quite impressive. Might we have a color illustration for our article, as well?"

This was *exactly* the response he was hoping for. Getting Stella permanently added to his staff would be a complete stroke of brilliance. "I'll see what I can do," he replied. If all went well, maybe he could get Stella to meet with the astronomers and create images of the moons of Jupiter.

The only problem he saw with the ad was some minor bleeding of ink along the bottom edge, but it could be solved by a bit of border work. It was a message best delivered in person. Artists could be notoriously prickly, and he didn't want his message bungled by a clerk.

He glanced at the clerk. "Please tell Miss West I'll be down shortly to discuss the advertisement." He could hardly interrupt his meeting with the astronomers. The three of them had a long way to go editing this article to make it suitable for a lay audience.

By the time the meeting was concluded, it was past five o'clock. Everyone else in the managerial office had gone home for the evening, and he wondered if Stella had left in a pique. He sprang down the staircase as quickly as possible. He'd meant to go down earlier, but he'd completely forgotten she was waiting. It was easy to become distracted when editing a good science article.

He should not have doubted her. As he stepped inside the artists' wing, the air was laden with the scent of wet ink and turpentine solvent. Stella still wore her smock, her sleeves rolled up as she sat curled on the oversized windowsill, a sketchpad on her lap. She turned her head to smile at him. The way the fading sun illuminated her profile made her lovelier than any Vermeer painting.

He mustn't let her get to him. Stella was an employee—or at least he hoped she would become one soon. He was here to examine her work and authorize her to proceed with printing 160,000 copies of a color advertisement. He was supposed to be here on business, yet he couldn't resist taking a peek at her sketchpad.

"May I see?" he asked as he crossed the room like a moth getting dangerously close to a flame.

She tilted the pad for him to see. It was a simple charcoal sketch of three sandhogs working in the street below. One man sat on the edge of the subway trench, and two others leaned against shovels as they took a rest from the backbreaking work. There was a rough dignity to their faces, a strength of character in the musculature of their necks, faces, and strong hands as they held the shovels. It was tough, gritty work that garnered little respect, yet Stella had imbued them with the dignity and heroism rarely afforded such men. They were men working to forge the future, laying a foundation for generations to come. Long after these men were dead and buried, their children and grandchildren would be riding on the subway they had built.

It was an oddly moving sketch, and not something he had expected to see from Stella. It revealed a surprising depth of compassion, stirring feelings deep inside him that were better left untouched.

He cleared his throat and tried to get back to business. "Forgive my delay," he said. "It seems astronomers are fated to speak in a language that flies over the heads of regular people. Your advertisement is brilliant. I noticed a bit of feathering at the—"

"At the bottom," she said. "I'll add a border."

"My thoughts exactly."

"Great minds and all that . . ." She smiled again, and his mind went blank. How could she do this to him so quickly?

He turned away and scooped up a chunk of Caribbean coral sitting on one of the artist's tables. It had been sent by the Smithsonian to illustrate an upcoming article. He scrambled for something to say as he toyed with the coral. "What are you going to do with the picture?" he asked, nodding to her sketch of the sandhogs.

"I've done a whole series on the subway. I'm taking them to my parents the next time I visit them. They will be curious about the subway, and it's easier to describe in pictures."

"You visit them often?"

She sobered, leaning her head against the frame of the window as she gazed outside. "Not as often as I'd like. They mean everything to me. I've always thought they were the best parents any girl could ever ask for. My heroes, for want of a better word."

He couldn't help but be curious. His own family was such a disaster, and it was rare to hear such forthright praise from someone as worldly and sophisticated as Stella. "How so?"

She took a moment before answering. He dragged a chair to sit opposite her.

"They did all the usual things," she said. "They gave my sister and me a foundation in faith and a good education. They taught us to be self-reliant and respectful and curious. Every summer, we used to go upstate to visit my grandparents' farm because my father wanted to teach us about the natural world. We'd tramp through the countryside, and he'd show us how a caterpillar changed into a butterfly, or we'd track the progress of tadpoles in a puddle behind the barn. Nothing extraordinary, but it meant the world to me. Why do you ask?"

Because his own childhood had been so starkly different. He

had no fond memories of his father, only fear and intimidation. "No reason," he said, looking away and pretending fascination with the blob of coral still in his hands.

Speaking of his parents was something he never did, even with Evelyn. She'd been there. She knew of the monumental fights, the thrown crystal, and the broken promises. He'd rather submit to dental surgery than talk about his father. The man had been dead for three years and could still cause a rush of anxiety in his gut. "Let's just say you are lucky to have such parents," he finally said. "Not everyone is so fortunate."

"Given the expression on your face, I gather you did not. It still seems that you survived quite well."

Looks could be deceiving. His fingers pressed hard against the cratered surface of the coral, his fingertips beginning to sting. He wished she wasn't so perceptive, but that was the problem with artists. They noticed everything. Making a conscious effort, he forced his fingers to relax. It was ridiculous to damage a piece of rare coral over a few childhood scars.

After all, it wasn't as if he'd suffered a terrible childhood. The dark hours of heartache had usually been shot through with periods of wonderment and discovery. "My father was a colonel in the army," he told Stella. "He always assumed I would follow in his footsteps, but I wasn't what he hoped for in a son."

She looked confused. "But why?"

He glanced away. It was hard to look at a woman while baring his soul, but he sensed Stella would understand.

"My father commanded a battery at Culp's Hill at Gettysburg," he said. "He took a bullet that broke his arm but kept fighting until the end. He held that hill for two solid days and was a legend before the battle was even over. And I was interested in monarch butterflies. Do I need to explain more?"

Was there any wound more painful than one caused by a

parent? Colonel Samuel White was dissatisfied with his son, neglected his wife, and died in his mistress's bed.

"My father died three years ago, so he lived long enough to see *Scientific World* achieve prominence. I finally earned a grudging respect from him, but I don't think he ever read a single issue."

Stella smiled gently. "Maybe that's why God made us all so different. The world needs warriors like your father, but it also needs men who have the curiosity to look at a butterfly and wonder where it came from. Your magazine does a good job of encouraging that sort of curiosity, but you can't expect everyone to adore it. You should be very proud of what you have accomplished with *Scientific World*."

He shrugged. Of course he was proud of the magazine, even though he lacked the skill to actually be a scientist himself. He couldn't build a subway like Clyde or manipulate a high-speed lithographic press like Stella. If the magazine ever went under, he had no idea what he'd do.

He turned the clump of coral in his hands, studying it from every angle. "You've said I am brash and overconfident, but I'm not. It's all just a disguise. Someday the mask will slip, and I'll be exposed for what I really am."

"And what is that?"

"Someone who can't concentrate on a topic for more than a few minutes without getting distracted. Not really suitable for any job other than the one I have." How had he let himself get drawn into a mortifying conversation like this? It served no purpose, and it was well after closing time.

He set down the lump of coral and reached for her advertisement. "In all the years I have dreamed about our first full-color page in the magazine, I never imagined it would be an advertisement for manure, but I couldn't be happier with the results." He tried to sound lighthearted. He wanted to project confidence and the right degree of artistic appreciation, because his smokescreen was slipping, and he wasn't comfortable letting Stella any farther inside. She was dangerous to him. "Please proceed with a full production run tomorrow." He flashed a nonchalant wink he hoped would communicate the irreverent humor he was most comfortable with. "And fix that sloppy border, will you?"

He could not escape the room fast enough.

—⟨ఌ⟩—

It didn't take Stella long to correct the feathering at the bottom of the fertilizer advertisement. Thickening the bottom border solved the problem, but she intended to get Romulus's approval before moving on to the printing. The cost of producing 160,000 full-color images was not something to take lightly, and it wasn't her money she'd be spending as she loaded up the lithograph's rollers and cylinders with ink and paper.

Before last night, she never would have considered the cost of ink or paper, but now she'd had a glimpse behind the gleaming façade Romulus wore so well. She'd assumed he came from money, but the son of an army officer was unlikely to have a family fortune. She knew enough about the publishing industry to know that no matter how profitable a magazine, costs were high, and only those with additional sources of revenue were truly safe.

She walked up the stairs instead of taking the elevator, in order to have time to gather her thoughts. Which Romulus would greet her today? The pensive, reflective man of last night? Or the *bon vivant* full of irreverence?

"He's been expecting you," Evelyn said as soon as Stella stepped inside the managerial wing.

Sure enough, Romulus sprang out of his chair and opened his

office door the moment he spotted her. "Miss White! Another prison-garb ensemble. Tragic."

So . . . now she knew which Romulus she was meeting. "I've brought you the manure advertisement for your approval."

He grabbed a pair of spectacles and scrutinized the page, inspecting the subtle gradations in tone and pigment as each phase of the lithographic process overlaid a wash of color to create the image.

"Excellent," he confirmed. "Please proceed with the printing. And here, take this as a sign of my gratitude." He tossed a slim pamphlet to her. She reached out to snatch it from the air.

Her breath caught when she read the cover. The pamphlet was an alphabetic listing of all the employees on the city payroll. He'd done it! "You're a miracle worker," she breathed.

"Don't get too excited," he warned. "I've already looked at all the men whose initials match A.G. and don't think you'll find it impressive."

Her fingers trembled as she flipped to the page of last names beginning with G. Luckily, each employee had his or her department and job title included in the directory. Some of the names were familiar. She'd had fifteen names on her list, and there were an additional twelve here.

As she read, her heart sank. It was obvious what Romulus meant. Arnold Green was a janitor; Alvin Griswald worked as an orderly in the city hospital. She already knew about Avery Gottschalk, an accountant who worked on the third floor of City Hall and was so timid he perspired when she tried to make conversation with him. He couldn't be the bold, powerful man Gwendolyn had described. None of the others looked promising.

"Tell me more about what your sister said regarding this man," Romulus prompted.

Stella took a deep breath and closed her eyes. From the moment Gwendolyn had first mentioned A.G., the man had shone like a hero in her sister's letters. "She said he was powerful. Gwendolyn has always been fascinated with King Arthur and his Knights of the Round Table. Gwendolyn thought King Arthur was like an island of valor surrounded by a sea of corruption. When she first told me about A.G., she said he reminded her of King Arthur, a man battling corruption on all sides. She trusted him because of the swiftness with which he accomplished things."

Romulus lifted a brow. "Can you give me an example?"

There were plenty to choose from, but Stella relayed the first incident Gwendolyn had told her. "Gwendolyn approached him when she noticed corruption in the Water Commission. A couple of men in the accounting department were charging an extra tax on all new buildings in the city. It was a bogus tax, and the accountants were pocketing the fees. Less than a week after Gwendolyn turned the evidence over to A.G., the men were arrested and terminated from employment. They were forced to repay the six hundred dollars they'd bilked from innocent people, all of which was returned to the victims. A few days later, an article appeared in the *Boston Globe*, exposing the scandal. A.G. must be a powerful man to act on Gwendolyn's information so swiftly." She glanced back at the pamphlet listing the names of employees. "None of these men are in a position to wield that kind of power."

"Is it possible he works for the *Globe*?" Romulus asked.

"I don't think so. How could a journalist get City Hall to jump like that?" She straightened. "You know powerful people in Boston. Does it sound like anyone you know?"

Romulus removed a slim book from his desk, skimming it with a somber expression. "The only A.G. in my address book is Alfonso Griglio, my shoemaker. I doubt he's Gwendolyn's man." He closed the book and slid it back into his desk drawer. "Why wouldn't your sister tell you his name?"

Stella paused. It did seem strange, but given the clandestine nature of what Gwendolyn had been involved in, perhaps she was protecting him. "I don't know," she confessed. "The way she wrote about him, it sounded like she was in awe of him. Almost as though she was in love."

"Perhaps he is a married man and their clandestine meetings involved more than mere business?"

"Absolutely not!" No one raised in the loving household of Karl and Eloise Westergaard would dare intrude on the sanctity of the marriage vow. Gwendolyn knew better than that.

Romulus held up his hands. "No need to lunge across my desk and tear my throat out. I was only asking. What about your sister's belongings? I assume that, after her death, either you or your parents collected her possessions. Perhaps Gwendolyn had letters or notes from A.G. in her belongings?"

Stella winced at the memory of cleaning out Gwendolyn's modest apartment. It was a week after the funeral, and her mother was still too despondent to leave her bed, so Stella and her father undertook the task on their own. Her father did his best to lighten the mood by rambling about the various types of chowder served at their hotel's restaurant. His voice was artificially bright, and he was trying too hard, but she didn't interrupt. They both needed something to distract themselves from what they were doing.

Gwendolyn's room was pretty, frilly, and feminine. The clothes hanging in the wardrobe still carried a hint of her vanilla and citrus perfume. When Stella opened the wardrobe doors and that lovely scent surrounded her, she almost broke, but she swallowed back the lump in her throat and dutifully folded the clothes into a box to be taken back home. Meanwhile, her father was taking the pictures from the walls, still babbling about spicy chowder versus creamy chowder. Stella clung to his mindless rambling like a talisman, anything to keep from dwelling on the last time Gwendolyn had worn this lace blouse or what she'd been thinking in those final moments when icy water closed over her head.

The chatter from her father stopped, and when Stella turned, he was sitting on the bed, staring out the window, his face bleak as tears rolled silently down. He had lost the battle. Stella rushed to his side, and they clung to each other as they both wept.

It took a while to regain their composure, but after they did, they rushed to finish the task. Even at the time, one thing penetrated Stella's veil of grief and struck her as odd.

Her own letters to Gwendolyn were not in the room. Nor were there letters from her parents, an address book, her calendar, or any other documents of a personal nature. Gwendolyn hoarded things like a magpie, but it seemed the room had been stripped of everything that would shed light on Gwendolyn's private life. Only a few books and her jewelry box remained.

"Did the jewelry box look like it had been plundered?" Romulus asked after Stella had explained.

She shook her head. "Gwendolyn didn't care for jewelry, but what few pieces she owned were there. Mostly it was just a box of stray buttons, a few hatpins, and a tiny little key I could never figure out."

"What kind of key?"

"I don't know. None of the drawers in her apartment had locks on them, and it was too small for any door. I put it back in the box and forgot about it."

"So you've done nothing with that key?" Romulus looked aghast.

"What would I do with it?"

"Take it to every bank within walking distance of your sister's apartment and see if it opens a safe-deposit box."

Stella frowned. She'd heard of safe-deposit boxes but had never owned one, nor did she believe her sister had one . . . but if Gwendolyn had something very valuable or dangerous, it made perfect sense that she would have kept it somewhere safe. Her mind whirled, but Romulus had not stopped talking.

"You're going to have difficulty getting to that box," he warned. "Banks are famously protective of safe-deposit boxes, and merely having the key won't get you access. Did your sister leave a will?"

"No." What sort of healthy young woman with no responsibilities had a will?

"Then the contents of the box will go to Gwendolyn's nearest living relative. I believe it would be your parents."

"I don't want to involve them in this," she said quickly. "They can barely function, and I want to be sure I can find the box before I raise the possibility with them."

He nodded. "Most of the banks are in the financial district. I'd be happy to accompany you, as I'm dying to know what's in that box."

She smiled in reply. It would be good to have him as a guide, for she knew almost nothing of Boston outside of City Hall. Just the thought of spending more time with him made her heart speed up. The magnetism that hummed between them seemed to get stronger at each meeting.

Or was she as delusional as poor, pathetic Daisy, who'd fled the office in tears only a couple days ago? The last thing Stella wanted was to join the ranks of pitiful women trailing after Romulus with forlorn hope in their eyes.

But she wasn't a pitiful woman. She was a strong one who was willing to fight for what she wanted.

And she wanted Romulus White.

Romulus looked forward to squiring Stella through the financial district in search of the bank box that matched the key found in Gwendolyn's jewelry case. He would be patient, pleasant, and the soul of decorum as he helped her on the ludicrous quest to explain her sister's death.

The girl drowned. He was convinced of it. After all, he'd heard every word as Dr. Lentz tried to explain the situation to Stella, who clearly didn't want to hear it. Perhaps it was only natural. Who wanted to think that a healthy, vibrant young woman with her life stretching before her could be snuffed out so quickly due to an unlucky slip on a bridge? Dr. Lentz had excellent credentials and was a man of sterling reputation. Romulus wouldn't use him as a reviewing consultant for *Scientific World* if he didn't have personal faith in the doctor's abilities.

He spent the morning escorting Stella to three banks clustered along Milk Street and Water Street, asking the clerks if Stella's tiny bronze key opened their boxes. Three banks, three negative replies. Only four more banks to visit, but it was a small price to pay in exchange for luring Stella ever closer to employment at *Scientific World*. Neither money nor prestige seemed to matter to her, but help solving her family problems did. He wasn't above using gratitude as bait to get her onboard at the magazine.

Besides, it was no burden to escort a stunning woman down the fashionable streets near Post Office Square. He enjoyed watching Stella turn heads as they strolled down Water Street. She had class and style, but most important, she had the heart and soul of a lion.

He needed to be on guard with her. He'd always been an unrepentant flirt, and Stella seemed game, but he needed to pull back. If all went according to plan, Stella would soon be working for him, and that made her untouchable.

He held the door as she swept into the muted interior of a formal bank lined with ferns in brass planters, imported carpets that muffled footsteps, and the smell of old money.

He lingered in order to fully appreciate the way Stella's fishtail skirt was cut to a perfect flare at her ankles as she walked to the bank counter. It wasn't an easy style to wear, but Stella carried it off with aplomb. It also revealed that she had a superb figure beneath all that polished cotton twill. He tore his gaze away and dragged his thoughts back to respectable territory, then followed Stella to the front counter, where a balding man with horn-rimmed glasses sat behind the teller's window. Stella extended the key.

The clerk eyed the key and nodded. "You will be wanting access to your box, ma'am?"

Romulus bit back a smile. They were at the right place.

"Yes," Stella said a little breathlessly, but the clerk's next words wiped away her smile.

"I'll just need to see your paperwork for access to the box," he said.

"It's my sister's box, actually. She died last December, and I am her heir. I'd like access to her box, please."

The clerk's brows lowered. "Allow me to summon the bank manager," he said delicately.

The distinguished gentleman who emerged from the back office looked as rigid and starched as his high-stand collar. He expressed the proper condolences upon learning of Gwendolyn's passing but explained the bank would need to see either a will or a form transferring ownership and signed by a judge before he could permit access to Gwendolyn's box.

It was bad news. Romulus already knew there was no will,

and getting the attention of a judge to hear the case could take weeks or months. Given Stella's agitation, he doubted she'd have the patience to wait that long.

"My sister and I had no secrets. Might she have added my name to the list of people authorized to see the box?"

He could tell where Stella was heading with this. If Gwendolyn had made such a list, it was likely her parents or perhaps even the mysterious A.G. would be on that list. The bank manager excused himself to check the paperwork, and when he returned, he carried a notebook and a troubled look on his face.

"It seems your father has already claimed the contents of the box," the bank manager said.

"My *father*?" Stella asked. "But my father didn't know anything about this box. Surely you must be mistaken."

The bank manager consulted his notes again, now looking distinctly uncomfortable. "Our records indicate he was here on December 15th, five days after the unfortunate accident. He had a death certificate and a copy of your sister's will, granting him access. He emptied the box and turned ownership back to the bank."

Stella looked as if she'd been struck. She staggered a bit as she reached out for balance on the bank counter. Romulus put an arm around her.

"What did he look like?" Stella demanded. "My *father*—what did he look like?"

"I'm sure I don't remember, ma'am," the bank manager said, taking a step back and fiddling nervously with the paperwork.

"Try harder," Stella demanded.

"We deal with hundreds of customers each week—"

"There is only one customer I care about," Stella bit out. "Her name was Gwendolyn Eloise Westergaard, and she was a beautiful, courageous woman who trusted this bank." The agitation in Stella's voice increased, her temper unraveling. She stepped closer to the hapless bank manager, who drew back in the face of Stella's mounting temper. "My father didn't set foot in this bank on December 15th!" she cried out in a voice beginning to crack. "I know because I was with him all day at my mother's bedside in a mental asylum, where she had been committed because she couldn't even feed herself."

Romulus blanched at the image. Stella had alluded to her parents' difficulties, but he hadn't realized they were so severe. He didn't know her parents, but they shouldn't have the most private details of their life spilled out in a bank lobby. She was going to regret this. Her voice rose in an angry crescendo, causing people to turn and stare.

"My father never left her side! He was never in this bank because we were two hundred miles away, watching my mother starve herself—"

"Stella, come with me," Romulus said, trying to nudge her toward the door.

"I'm fighting for my sister's legacy!"

He lowered his voice. "And I'm fighting for your family's future. Come along. This isn't the place."

His words were like cold water thrown on a fire. She froze and swallowed back whatever she'd intended to say. After a moment, she nodded.

He guided her to a streetcar. It was the middle of the day, and the streetcar was half empty, so they found a bench to themselves near the back, where Stella's hard-fought stability slowly unraveled. Her face crumpled, her shoulders rolled forward.

She wept quietly the entire ride home, tears dropping onto her lap, each breath a shuddering moan. He'd never heard such bleak despair in a woman's voice. The profound love Stella had for her family was unknown to him. He'd grown up in a home with a chilly and disapproving father, and his parents' bitter marriage had poisoned anyone who got too close. Stella's family was different, and when the bedrock of that idyllic, storybook family had fractured, it had broken her, as well.

He skated through life on the surface, making friends with ease but never letting anyone get too close. And if there was an occasional void—an emptiness—well, that was all right. But Stella's shuddering sobs reminded him of a callow young man who had once thrown his entire being into the crucible of love and had come away scarred. He remembered. He understood. He put his arm around her and cradled her head against his shoulder.

"Shhh," he murmured, anything to soothe her pain. "You'll be okay."

"I'll never be okay," she said on a broken whisper. "Nothing will ever be the same again."

He believed her. It was why he held himself at arm's length from such turbulent, unrestrained passions. Casual friendships could never break you or plunge your world into despair.

"Nothing will ever be the same," he agreed softly. "But you are strong and resilient and still have a grand life ahead of you. I don't know why God called Gwendolyn so early. We'll probably never know, but you've still got a purpose."

"He should have taken me," Stella said. "Gwendolyn was the good sister, I was the bad one. If anyone deserved to die, it should have been me."

It stunned him that she should think of herself this way. He wasn't a theologian or a doctor of psychology, but the tortured guilt in Stella's voice was hard to hear. "You will be okay, Stella. I have a feeling God is still expecting great things from you, and so am I. You are going to survive this and flourish again."

Stella closed her eyes and sagged. "I wish I were a better

person. If I were, maybe I could find some meaning in Gwendolyn's death, but all it has done is broken my mother and made me angry and bitter. I don't like myself very much anymore. I don't like what I've become."

He didn't know how to help this suddenly weak, insecure version of Stella. He knew how to spar with the flamboyant woman who bragged about her art and hurled barbed jests for sport. He adored matching wits with *that* Stella, but this one somehow slipped beneath his defenses. She touched the weak, vulnerable part of himself he usually kept locked down and hidden, but he needed to draw upon that part to comfort her.

"Gwendolyn brought a wonderful gift into your family," he said. "She's gone now, but those memories will illuminate your world for the rest of your life."

That much he knew was true. His mind cast back more than a decade to Laura. It was hard to recall the beautiful memories without the bitterness that followed, but yes, he was glad Laura had been a part of his life. She had widened it, strengthened it, given him a little glimpse into a shining world where he wanted to live forever. His happiness had been fleeting, but he could not regret it.

Perhaps that was the nature of joy. There was a poignant sense of yearning that somehow pointed to a deeper spiritual world. It was impossible to appreciate the beauty of it without first knowing loss and yearning. Stella's grief was still too raw to have that perspective. She was like a bird thrashing in a net, angry and frustrated with the injustice.

He would help her find a way out.

S tella recovered quickly after her pathetic breakdown in the streetcar. It was embarrassing to have blubbered like that in front of Romulus, but the terrible weeks at the mental asylum were a memory she rarely touched. She and her father had stood by helplessly while Eloise stared, broken and vacant, unable to feed herself or even rise from bed. Her mother's complete mental breakdown had terrified Stella. Could it be possible to lose both Gwendolyn and her mother in the same month?

And yet her mother rallied. By January, Eloise was ready to return home, but to Stella's surprise, her father asked her not to accompany them.

"We need to heal, baby girl," he said, tears filling his eyes as he cupped her face between his hands. "Every time Eloise looks at you, she sees Gwendolyn. Go back to your life and create beautiful pictures. Fill the world with color and joy and splendor. Your mother and I need to be alone now. We need to make new memories together, instead of dwelling on the past."

It had hurt, but she had gone. The morning her parents es-

142

corted her to the train station, the three of them had clung to one another and wept anew. Sometimes dawn was a long way off, and there was nothing to be done to hasten its return. Her parents needed time, and Stella needed to uncover what had really happened to her sister.

Well, what she'd just learned at the bank was a giant leap toward helping her find A.G., and she needed Romulus's help even more now. They went to his office to discuss it. He sat behind his desk, rocking in his swivel chair as he watched her pace across the tight confines of his office.

"I think the man who passed himself off as my father was A.G. I've been trying to find him on my own, but what if I change tactics and get him to come find me? If he is the honorable man Gwendolyn believed him to be, he will seek me out once he knows I am here."

"*If* he is an honorable man?" Curiosity and caution were heavy in Romulus's voice.

"I don't know what to believe anymore. If A.G. was on the list of people with access to Gwendolyn's box, he had no reason to impersonate my father. Or maybe the man wasn't A.G. at all, and it was someone who knew what Gwendolyn was up to and played a part in her death." In which case, finding A.G. and recruiting him to her side was more important than ever.

"How do you propose we flush him out?"

"Gwendolyn would have told him about me. He would surely know my professional name, and even if he doesn't, I'll spell it out for him."

Over the next five minutes, she outlined her plan. A powerful man like A.G. would read at least one of Boston's three newspapers. She would agree to work for the magazine if Romulus would lean on his connections in the press to publicize that he had just hired renowned lithographer Stella West, also known as Stella Westergaard, to produce brilliant full-color lithographs for *Scientific World*.

"It would benefit both of us," she said. "You will be the first magazine to routinely publish full-color plates, and I get my name publicized throughout Boston. Either A.G. will come forward, or he won't. And if he doesn't . . ."

If he didn't, it became more likely that A.G. had played some nefarious role in Gwendolyn's demise.

Romulus was intrigued. That quiet flare had lit behind his eyes, and he was holding on to barely leashed excitement. "If I make that announcement, I expect you to honor it."

"Of course." Her job at City Hall was gone, and there was nothing to stop her from taking a new opportunity, especially if it might coax A.G. to reveal himself.

Romulus vaulted out of his chair, triumph in his gaze as he reached across the desk to shake her hand. "Then we have a deal, Miss West."

~·~

Romulus sat frozen in his desk chair for five minutes after Stella left. Had he just scored a brilliant coup or done the stupidest thing of his career? He'd been trying for years to get Stella onboard at *Scientific World*, but that was before she'd walked across his line of sight and sparked a flare of attraction unlike anything he'd ever known. Even from Laura. Stella could slip beneath his defenses, and he had no desire to plunge back into the turbulent whirlwind of his youthful mistakes.

A knock on the door dragged him back to the present. Roy Tanner met his eyes through the window and held up a flat wooden box. Roy was the magazine's chief typesetter, and despite the burns that limited his facial expressions, it was clear

Roy was delighted about something. Romulus nodded, and Roy opened the door.

"Just got the new boldfaced font for the linotype. Here's a sample."

Romulus grinned. The new font had cost almost six hundred dollars, but it would help them create better sidebars and enhance the readability of the magazine.

"Is it too late to use it in the next issue?" he asked.

"Jake is already learning how to set the new slugs. We should have enough time to get it done before we start printing."

"Excellent!" He'd stay up late tonight figuring out which snippets of text to highlight in each of the articles. The diversity of stories appearing in every issue made it unlikely that many people read *Scientific World* cover to cover, so the sidebars would help readers identify stories of interest. Or at least inform them of the salient points in the stories they chose not to read.

"There's talk on the third floor that you were ranting again about not getting married until forty," Roy said.

"Some principles need periodic reinforcement." Even if only to remind himself. Stella wasn't the sort of woman who would tolerate being strung along for the next eight years. Nor would she be a suitable wife for him, anyway. The irrational attraction he'd felt for her could get out of hand, and he didn't need or want it.

"You may want to rethink that," Roy said. "My wife and children are the center of my universe. I thank God for them every day. Nothing gives me greater pleasure than the sixty seconds after I step through my front door at the end of the day, when three little children come racing into my arms and I see my wife's smiling face across the room."

Romulus said nothing as he picked up a piece of 16-point font, inspecting it from all angles. He was glad Roy had found happiness in marriage. Roy Tanner was a black man trying to survive in a largely white city. Having been burned by a grease fire as a child, Roy's face was a mass of frightening scar tissue that made most people turn away, but he'd found a wonderful woman who saw beneath the scars to the kind, gentle man beneath.

A sudden commotion in the main office grabbed his attention. Evelyn was arguing with two men he'd never seen before. He could see Evelyn only from the back, but her stance was rigid as she shook her head. He rose, prepared to go out and see what was happening, and then Evelyn turned around, her face white and frightened.

He opened the door. "What's going on?"

The two men crossed to him, one of them handing him a document. "Sir, we have an injunction against the further distribution of *Scientific World*. All publication of your magazine must stop until a complete investigation can be conducted."

"On what charge?" he demanded, flabbergasted.

Evelyn answered. "They claim the articles we have been running about electricity are full of errors. That they are dangerous and inaccurate."

"Our articles are written by leading engineers and vetted by college professors," he protested. "I don't publish 'dangerous and inaccurate' information."

One of the men, wearing a badge from the Suffolk County Superior Court, had an oily, supercilious look on his face. "We hear your upcoming issue carries another article extolling the virtues of electricity as a heating element. Something women can use in their kitchens! We cannot permit its circulation until all doubts about your magazine have been put to rest. Until then, you are ordered by the court to cease distribution."

This was a nightmare. He'd never heard of a magazine being

ordered to stop publication, but the court document looked official. He blanched at the sight of his magazine's name, the only thing in the world of which he was truly proud, typed onto a form that smeared its credibility. The document was signed and notarized. He was going to need a lawyer. Fast.

"What about the First Amendment? It's called freedom of the press, perhaps you read about it in school."

The court clerk smirked. "We've also read about judges who arrest people who ignore court orders."

He watched in stunned disbelief as the two men left the office.

"What are we going to do?" Evelyn asked, her voice trembling. "The next issue is due to ship in ten days. If we can't ship it, we can't collect our advertising revenue." She swallowed hard. "And we'd have to issue refunds to all our subscribers. We can't afford . . ."

He knew they couldn't afford it. They made a fortune with each issue, but their expenses were high.

A white-hot anger began building inside him. Their articles were solid, vetted, and legitimate. Whoever was behind this was merely grasping at straws. Beside him, Roy Tanner clutched the box of new type in his hands. His eyes were panicked.

"Roy, send a message to our attorney. Get him here immediately. Tell him it is an emergency."

Roy handed him the box of type. "Yes, sir."

The door slammed behind Roy, and the office went eerily silent. Everyone had heard what had just happened. The worst thing was, he didn't know what to do. This magazine was his only success in the world, yet he hadn't a clue about how to save it. The only sound in the office was from the construction noise in the street below.

Clyde!

Clyde Brixton was one of the nation's leading experts on

electricity. It was his knowledge of electricity that had made him so valuable to the Transit Commission, for the subway was going to be powered by electricity.

Romulus turned to look at Evelyn, whose dark eyes were wide. "Evelyn, I'm going to send someone down to the street to ask Clyde to come up here. We need his help. If there is anything in the series of articles we've published that is wrong, he'll be able to spot it."

Mercifully, Evelyn nodded in agreement.

─◦◦◦◦◦◦─

Clyde arrived ten minutes later. He wore a laborer's coveralls, his face streaked with dirt and sweat, but concern was carved onto his features. He seemed bewildered as he scanned the legal document that had just brought Romulus's world crashing down.

Clyde and Evelyn joined Romulus in his office, but through his window, he could see the other employees clustered in groups, their heads leaning close together in hushed discussion. How was he going to pay them? There was some money in the reserves, but without incoming revenue, it would evaporate quickly.

"What do you need from me?" Clyde asked as soon as they all were seated.

"Our last three issues have featured articles on the various applications for electricity. I need you to read those articles and let me know if there is anything questionable in them."

"There isn't," Clyde said. "I've already read them."

"You did?" Evelyn asked, her voice astounded.

Clyde's face softened. "I've always read each issue. I wouldn't miss it for the world."

Evelyn glanced away. The last thing Romulus wanted to deal

with was the endless turmoil between Evelyn and Clyde, and he dragged the conversation back to the task at hand.

"Are you certain?" he pressed. "The injunction specifically noted the articles on electricity. If there is anything that is in the least bit questionable . . ."

"If there was, I would have notified you immediately." Clyde's voice was full of the confidence that came from a West Point education and work in some of the most prestigious research laboratories in the world.

That was the difference between Clyde and him. From the time Clyde was a boy, he knew exactly what he wanted and chased after it with single-minded zeal. Romulus was the opposite. He spent his years at Harvard dithering at one course of study after another, and he hadn't been able to find gainful employment until the magazine had come along. From the moment he and Clyde bought *Scientific World*, the magazine had been his whole universe. And it was about to come crashing down unless he could lift this injunction.

His lawyer arrived within the hour. Everett Wilcox worked only a few blocks away. He was a fine attorney who handled their basic legal matters, but Romulus had no idea if he was up for the pitched battle this injunction was going to cause.

Everett looked through the paperwork, still flushed and breathless from the run to this office. "It looks as if they've scheduled a hearing for three weeks from now," Everett said. "I expect we'll learn more about their concerns at that time."

Romulus nearly exploded. "I'm not waiting three weeks!" They were to start printing in two days, and the magazine was scheduled to ship in ten days. If news of this injunction got out, the prestige of their magazine would plummet. He needed this addressed now, not in three weeks.

"I suppose I could request an emergency hearing," Everett said.

Romulus was tempted to break something. He didn't want a timid attorney who would politely ask for expedited service. He wanted a gladiator to hurl fire at whomever was threatening his magazine. For the first time in days, he had sympathy for Stella West's sense of outrage at bureaucratic hurdles, but he still believed that holding on to the threads of self-control was the best way to cut through the red tape that threatened to strangle the life from his magazine. "Please do so."

And in the meantime, he'd work behind the scenes to speed up the process, for the court system was infamously slow. Romulus had spent years glad-handing and accumulating goodwill among men of power in Boston. It was time to start calling in some of those favors. Tomorrow morning, he had a standing boxing match at his club with Michael Townsend, the highest-ranking attorney in all of Massachusetts.

That boxing appointment was his best shot at cutting straight to the heart of this matter.

―◦✦◦―

Stella snapped awake in the darkness, rearing upright and clutching the sheets to her chest. It was pitch-black in her room, but someone banged on her door loud enough to rattle the furniture.

"Open up, lady! Boston Police Department."

She scrambled to pull on a robe. Could there be a fire in the boardinghouse? Or an intruder? The banging continued while she rushed to turn on the single electric lamp.

"Open up, lady, or we're kicking the door down!" The voice was impatient, and she didn't know what to do. At least her door had a chain. Her fingers trembled as she struggled to get it into place before she twisted the bolted lock and cracked the door open.

"What's wrong?"

Two men wearing police uniforms stood in the hallway, one of them thrusting his badge up to the crack in the door. "Open the door unless you want to be charged with interfering in a police investigation."

She was still groggy as she slid the chain free and opened the door, staring in confusion at the two officers. Her room seemed dwarfed as the two men pushed inside, filling the tiny space. She didn't even have anywhere for them to sit. Aside from her bed and a chest of drawers, the room contained only a modest desk and a single chair.

They didn't seem to care as they inched forward until her legs backed up against the mattress of her bed.

"We hear you're unhappy with the way the police handled your sister's drowning," an officer with a thick neck and heavy whiskers growled. "That you're threatening to register a complaint with the city. What's that all about?" he demanded.

"Our guys risked frostbite to pull her out of that river," the other said.

Stella was not a timid person, but she felt weak and disoriented as she blinked the sleep from her eyes. "I—I still have questions . . ." she stammered.

"And you've asked for your sister's body to be exhumed!" one of the officers roared.

It was true. After learning that Gwendolyn's safe-deposit box had been robbed, she was more convinced than ever that there was foul play involved. She didn't like the thought of having her sister's rest disturbed for yet another autopsy, but she didn't trust Dr. Lentz. It must have been her official request to have Gwendolyn exhumed that had set off this new flurry of resentment from the police.

"It is my right to request another postmortem," she insisted. "I still have questions."

"And we've answered them," the thick-necked man said. "Detective Tillis met with you in February and answered everything you asked him. Just because you don't like his answers . . ."

"Hey, Smith," the other said in an artificially bright voice. "Maybe we should reopen the case, after all. Detective Tillis said he did the girl a favor by declaring it an accident instead of a suicide. The little piece of fluff was running around in the middle of the night, probably meeting strange men. Girls like that usually come to a bad end."

The thick-necked officer leaned in closer. "Would that be a good idea? Spread the word around that your sister was walking the streets at night, meeting strange men, and probably jumped to her death? We'd be happy to do that for you."

"My sister did not commit suicide," she insisted. But if they thought she'd overlook foul play simply to avoid having Gwendolyn's reputation smeared, they were in for disappointment. She and Gwendolyn were both made of stronger stuff than that.

The officers growled and stamped and threatened, but she refused to back down. She would keep hounding the police with regular visits until she could talk to someone higher up than the original investigating detective.

The officers finally left after twenty minutes, letting her know they'd return with more *updates* in the future if she didn't stand down and let them do their job.

It was three o'clock in the morning, but her entire body was tense and shaking. It would be impossible to sleep again. Each time the old building creaked, she startled anew, and she resigned herself to waiting for dawn.

She paced the room, her mind awhirl. Her plan for finding A.G. through the newspapers would take a few days. In the meantime, she needed to move quickly on getting a second autopsy of Gwendolyn's body. The more time that passed . . .

and as the weather got warmer . . . she hated even thinking of it, but that autopsy needed to be done as soon as possible.

Dr. Lentz had promised to deliver a copy of the original autopsy report to Romulus by today. She would need that report if she was to hire another physician to perform a private autopsy. After what had happened at the bank, it seemed Romulus was coming to believe her about the suspicious circumstances of Gwendolyn's death, and she needed his help now more than ever.

The thought of seeing Romulus again brought vast relief. His easy manner and irreverent way of deflecting problems helped her put everything into perspective. He'd been like a mischievous angel of mercy, alternately making her laugh and saving her at the next turn.

As much as she liked to consider herself independent, sometimes she simply needed another person to lean on. And she needed Romulus now.

10

Romulus belonged to the Boston Athletic Club not only because of its location across the street from *Scientific World*, but because its membership included hundreds of men from the corporate, academic, and governing elite. Only the well-to-do could afford membership, but on any given day, the club offered a priceless opportunity to mingle with the influential men who made this city operate. Rooms were set aside for fencing, billiards, and bowling. A steam room, barber shop, and a smoking lounge were all heavily used, but Romulus always went straight for the boxing ring. Boxing was a sport he'd practiced ever since college. The competitive drive to match his strength, speed, and agility against another man's was an addiction he indulged to this day.

But today he wasn't here to box. Pacing on the tiled floor in the foyer, he waited for Michael Townsend, his regular Tuesday morning sparring partner, to arrive. A few men he knew wandered in and headed to the changing room. Romulus nodded grimly, wondering if rumor of what had happened to him was already beginning to circulate. It wouldn't take long for news of the injunction against *Scientific World* to spread like wildfire through parched savannah plains. Miraculously, it seemed no one knew anything yet, with men offering their normal greetings and nods as they entered.

Romulus swallowed hard. Unless he could get this injunction lifted, soon those pleasant greetings would be replaced by sidelong glances, suspicious looks, and pity. He kept his hands fisted in his pockets, probably ruining the line of his trousers, but hiding the white knuckles and tension in every line of his body.

At precisely nine o'clock, Michael strode through the door, a pair of boxing gloves dangling from his hands. "You haven't changed?"

"I'm not sparring today," he replied. "I wanted to speak with you about something privately."

Michael nodded. "I had a feeling you might," he said, a trace of unease on his distinguished face. "Let's head back to the restaurant. I doubt anyone will be there at this hour."

The club's restaurant was dark and empty, but the door was unlocked, so they headed toward the mahogany bar along the back wall of the room. Potted palm trees and hanging chandeliers loomed in the dim interior. It was a gray and drizzly day, but weak light filtered in through the window blinds.

"So you've heard about the injunction against my magazine?"

"I've heard," Michael confirmed.

"Who is behind it?"

"Someone filed at the Superior Court. I don't know who."

"But you know *why*. And don't tell me it has anything to do with electricity, because those articles were vetted, and they are all aboveboard." Romulus was fishing, but given the way Michael shifted his weight and kept glancing away, the attorney knew plenty.

"Yes, it is about electricity," Michael said. "Although that's not all. In the past year, the magazine has published other articles that may not be safe. You've written laudatory articles about x-ray technology, and it is known that x-rays can cause radiation poisoning. There are also concerns about articles on vaccination."

Anger began to simmer. Scientific innovation often came along with risk, but most people understood that the potential benefits usually outweighed the danger. "So if I discredit the concerns about electricity, I can expect more injunctions? Who is behind this?"

"I don't know," Michael said again. "I gather a hearing has been scheduled, and both sides will have a chance to air their concerns in due time."

"And how am I supposed to pay forty employees next week? Or collect revenue from my advertisers when I know I won't be circulating an issue this month?"

"Romulus, this is a matter of public safety."

"We've been publishing this magazine for almost ten years. We've built a reputation for quality scientific information that some anonymous troublemaker is trying to tear down. And you expect me to sit still for that?"

Michael turned away, bracing his hands on the back of a chair and staring out the window, his gaze troubled. "There's more to it than just the articles."

"I suspected as much."

"There is some gossip calling your judgment into question. Rumor has it you have been running around town with an unstable woman, causing a ruckus in the police department and the medical examiner's office."

Romulus felt the blood drain from his face. "This is unbelievable."

"Nevertheless. People have always been willing to grant you

leeway despite some of your eccentricities, but Stella West is rubbing people the wrong way. It calls your good sense into question. Apparently she just filed a report to have Dr. Lentz fired because she disagreed with one of his findings. She has also asked for her sister's body to be exhumed for another autopsy in hope of discrediting Dr. Lentz. It's all very unseemly."

Romulus rocked back on his heels. It was hard to believe that even Stella would ask for something so appalling, but hadn't she told him that it "wouldn't end here"? Now her wild-eyed accusations were reaching out to taint him, as well.

"I barely know Stella West," he growled.

"But you've been seen escorting her around town while she throws daggers at people. It hasn't shown you in a good light." The concern lifted from Michael's face as he clapped Romulus on the shoulder. "It's all merely a tempest in a teapot. Don't worry too much. This will all blow over soon. Just let the process work."

"And how am I to pay my bills in the meantime? My employees depend on me." Roy Tanner's scarred, gentle face rose in his mind. That man and his entire family depended on Romulus being able to pay him on Friday. They could make payroll this week, but what about next Friday? And what if their advertisers started pulling their business?

"How can I find out who is behind these accusations?" he ground out from behind clenched teeth. "I need your help."

"Show up at the Suffolk County Superior Court in three weeks," Michael said. "I don't have any influence to speed up the process, nor can I look into locked files to gather confidential information. Please don't ask again."

Romulus looked away. Michael Townsend's reputation for honesty was well known, and he wasn't going to risk it over a magazine.

"I hope you'll understand my need to cancel our sparring appointment this morning," Romulus said as he reached out to shake Michael's hand. "Next week, perhaps." He could only pray to have found a way out of this quagmire by then.

"I'll look forward to it." Michael's tone was understanding, which only made Romulus feel worse. The pity was beginning.

—᧐᳀᩠᳀᳀᳀᩠᳀᳀᳀᩠᳀᳀᳀᩠᳀᳀᳀᩠᳀᳀᳀᩠᳀—

Stella arrived at *Scientific World* early. She dreaded the prospect of arranging a second autopsy on Gwendolyn's body, but this was something that couldn't wait for more evidence or the chance that A.G. would miraculously appear and solve all the riddles. Every additional day that passed made a second autopsy more problematic, but it was her best chance to discover if Dr. Lentz had botched the original examination. Romulus ought to have a copy of the original postmortem by now, and he would help her get things rolling.

Never in her life had she felt so comforted as when he'd held her on the streetcar while she'd blubbered like an infant. He looked flashy and flamboyant on the outside, but in those few moments, she'd witnessed a tenderness that took her breath away. She needed a bit of that comfort now. She hadn't slept since the early-morning invasion by the police officers, and she was desperate for a chance to soak up Romulus's effortless humor.

He was not in the office, but Evelyn was at her desk. Which was disappointing. Evelyn seemed so frosty, with a reserved, almost queenly demeanor. To Stella's surprise, Evelyn invited her to take a seat beside her desk for a chat.

"I'm eager to know how a woman found a foothold in the London publishing industry," she said. And since there was nothing Stella liked better than talking art and publishing, the two of them had a fascinating hour trading information on women in business, high-speed printing machinery, and rates of compensation.

"Wasn't it scary?" Evelyn asked. "Moving to another country where you had no one to lean on?"

Her parents had accompanied her to London, but after a month, she was on her own. It hadn't been scary, it had been exhilarating. London was a city that found room amid its royal palaces and stiff reserve for flamboyant artists and poets. It was a city where, on any street corner, she could witness layers of British history from the Romans all the way up to Charles Dickens. No, she had never been frightened in London.

She winced at the memory of two Boston police officers invading her room.

Evelyn noticed. "What?" she prompted.

She tried a smile. All morning, Stella had been trying to recast the incident in a less ominous light, hoping it would lose its power to frighten her. And yet, when she told Evelyn what had happened, the effect was precisely the opposite.

"How did they get in?" Evelyn asked. "Isn't your boarding-house locked after hours?"

The front door was locked each night at ten o'clock, and Mr. Zhekova warned all his boarders that if they weren't home by that hour, they could expect to sleep on the front stoop. And yet that locked door hadn't provided any protection against the police.

"I guess my landlord must have let them in." It was an un-settling thought. Ever since the incident with the bees in her mailbox, Mr. Zhekova had grown increasingly suspicious of her.

"You are welcome to stay at my townhouse," Evelyn said. "I live on Hanover Street and have plenty of room. It's only me, my housekeeper, and her two children."

"I couldn't impose on you like that—"

"Nonsense," Evelyn said. "We professional ladies must band together, if only until you get to the bottom of what happened with the police. If women don't band together, we'll fall beneath the stampede of men."

Stella had never felt trampled on by men. In London, she laughingly mingled with dozens of male colleagues and never sensed hostility. But this wasn't London, and nothing had been easy since she'd come to Boston. The companionship Evelyn offered seemed like a safe harbor in a storm. "I'd be grateful for your hospitality," she said, and Evelyn beamed in reply.

"I hope you like little children. Miss Delaney has two, both under the age of three. They are delightful—but can sometimes be a trial."

"Miss Delaney? Is she your housekeeper?" Stella hoped she didn't sound critical, but wouldn't a woman with two children be a *missus* rather than a *miss*?

A bit of humor faded from Evelyn. "Miss Delaney falls into the category of women needing to stick together. Her fiancé was in the navy. She eventually learned he already had a wife in Richmond, but by then . . . well, by then she had a baby and another on the way. I hope that won't be a problem for you."

It seemed that Stella was unpeeling layers of kindness hidden beneath Evelyn's frosty demeanor. "No, it won't be a problem." She was in no position to throw the first stone. Ever since Gwendolyn's death, she'd been consumed with a driving anger that blotted out the finer aspects of Christian charity. Perhaps it was time she tried a little harder in that area.

As they waited for Romulus to return, Evelyn filled her in on her housekeeper and the two children. She'd found Bridget Delaney living in a poorhouse, seven months pregnant and on the verge of having her two-year-old son seized by authorities at a state-run orphanage.

"That little boy had these huge, liquid eyes that just broke my heart," Evelyn said. "The way he looked at his mother . . . well, I've never seen so much love distilled into a single look, and I couldn't bear the thought of having him torn from his mother to be raised by strangers. They moved into my home that very day and have been with me ever since."

Evelyn proudly showed her the photograph of two children she kept on her desk. The boy looked about three years old, and his arm was around a little girl barely old enough to stand.

"I have to confess to entirely selfish motives," Evelyn continued. "I don't have any children of my own, and the thought of being able to help Bridget with the newborn appealed to me. For the first few months, I was more Bridget's housekeeper than the other way around, but now things have settled into a nice arrangement. I think of Bridget and the babies as family."

And the photographs of the children on Evelyn's desk certainly attested to that. But what was taking Romulus so long? When she asked, Evelyn filled her in on the strange injunction that had been filed against the magazine.

"He's meeting with the state's attorney as we speak. I'm sure they will be able to sort everything out." But Evelyn didn't look certain as she drew a long sip of tea.

Stella shifted uneasily. This was probably the worst day she could have chosen to come looking for that autopsy report, but she needed it, and as Evelyn had said, surely Romulus would have been able to draw on his vaunted connections to solve this silly injunction by now.

─◦◦◦◦─

Romulus headed across the street, his anger simmering hotter with each step. Tremont was now completely excavated, and he had to cross on a rickety pine-board bridge erected for pedestrians. The purpose of the temporary overpass was to get people to cross the street, not loiter on the bridge to gawk at the activity below. Why were people so fascinated by a hole in the ground? The trench was now fifteen feet deep and teeming with workers rerouting the gas lines. The gawkers clogged traffic and annoyed respectable people who needed to get to work without having to push through the crush of sightseers on the bridge.

By the time Romulus made it to his building, he was too angry to even exchange a greeting with the elevator attendant. Normally he chatted with Caleb on his way to the fourth floor because the boy was bright and hoped to go to college someday, but he wasn't able to look Caleb in the face today. Caleb was the oldest of eight children, and his wages were important for keeping his family fed. Even accepting help from the elevator attendant ratcheted Romulus's anxiety tighter.

The last person he wanted to see as he stepped inside the managerial wing was Stella, but there she was, chatting away beside Evelyn. They both looked up as he slammed the door.

Stella rose. "Thank goodness you're here," she said. "I need your help."

"Help with what?" he snapped "Exhuming bodies? Trying to get good men fired? Trying to destroy my magazine? It seems you are making progress on all three fronts, so I am breathless to hear what you need next."

Evelyn had a placating look on her face. "Romulus, please. Stella has had a difficult night. A couple of Boston policemen broke into her apartment and—"

He looked at Stella, dressed in a spectacular green and gold ensemble offset by a black velvet choker around her neck. On the side of the choker, she'd pinned a showy silk blossom, the white petals of the oleander looking fresh and spectacular. His eyes narrowed. "You don't look any worse for wear."

"They didn't attack me," Stella said. "But they came to frighten and intimidate me. A few weeks ago, someone put bees in my mailbox. And they broke my window, too. I think it must have been the police all along."

He struggled to maintain a calm voice. "You are insane," he said tensely. "And in supporting your insanity, I have put my magazine at risk. Get out of here and go draw your pictures for someone else."

She blinked. "You don't really mean that, do you?"

Honestly, the arrogance! Stella West might be a fine artist, but he'd swallow a dose of arsenic before doing business with her again. Swiveling his attention to Evelyn, he forced a tight smile on his face.

"I just came from a meeting with the state's attorney to get to the bottom of this nonsense. Do you know what he relayed about my professional reputation in Boston? Apparently it is taking a beating by squiring Miss West about town in hopes of chasing her ghosts. Literal ghosts. She's asked for the exhumation of her sister's body in a macabre quest to cast aspersions on Dr. Lentz's abilities."

Evelyn blanched, but Stella only lifted her chin, confirming his suspicion that she really was prepared to head down this revolting path.

"I know he botched Gwendolyn's autopsy. He got the scar on her wrist wrong."

"Do you know how crazy you sound?" he roared. "I was a fool for letting an irrational woman with no scientific training beyond her own stupid impulses to lead—"

"That's enough," Evelyn said firmly. "If you want to cut ties with Stella, that's your prerogative, but it won't be because she is an 'irrational woman.' I know a thing or two about being pushed aside for that exact reason. I won't tolerate such backward thinking in a company for which I am fifty percent responsible."

A piece of his anger drained away. Stella had taken a battering ram to his reputation and still had the effrontery to look spectacular on a day his professional life was crumbling to pieces. And it infuriated him that he found her attractive despite the chaos sweeping into his life.

He glanced at the silk flower on her choker. "Oleander blossoms are highly toxic and can shut down a man's heart and central nervous system. The irony is blinding."

Before Stella could reply, the door opened and Roy Tanner entered, rubbing his hands on an oily rag and shifting from foot to foot. "I'm sorry, Miss Evelyn," he said. "I've been fooling with that linotype machine all morning, but there is no way I can retrofit it to print envelopes."

"Why would we want to reconfigure the linotype machine?" he asked.

"Because we've got 160,000 subscribers to notify. That's a lot of envelopes to address by hand if we can't get the machine to do it."

Romulus sighed. The costs of this injunction were increasing by the moment. At least they had plenty of employees in the building to do the addressing. If typesetting, printing, and mailing the next issue of *Scientific World* was forbidden, at least he could deploy his people in mitigating the damage.

Evelyn was calm as she spoke to Roy. "Will you check the storage room and see how many envelopes we need to purchase? And organize the typesetting crew. They will be addressing envelopes by hand instead of printing today."

Roy nodded and left. Romulus waited until the door closed before he turned to rip in to Stella again.

"Do you see the man who just left?" he asked Stella. "Roy

Tanner's wife and three children depend on the wages he earns at this job. If this magazine goes under, it doesn't matter what kind of stellar recommendation I write for him, a man with that face and skin color won't be able to find comparable work anywhere in this city."

He was gratified to see a bit of starch drain from Stella's spine, but Evelyn stepped between them. "Yelling at Stella won't solve things. Nor will airing your grievances before the entire managerial staff. May we step into your office while we outline the next few days?"

A glance around the office proved the truth of her words. Ten employees, all frozen at their desks, stared at him with worried, anxious gazes. He didn't really believe the magazine was going to go under, and venting his spleen at Stella was only causing further worry among his staff.

"You can all go back to work," he said. "Please proceed with the next issue. It will be released eventually."

He tried to make himself believe it as he retreated with Evelyn to his office and closed the door.

─◦◦◦─

Stella didn't know what to do once Evelyn and Romulus disappeared into the safety of his office. She was relieved to be spared his glowering disapproval, but she still hadn't gotten what she'd come for this morning.

She watched him through the window into his office. He paced the confined space and dragged his hand though his hair. It was impossible to hear what he said, but he gestured grandly with each sentence. Evelyn sat calmly in a chair, taking notes and looking like a long-stemmed rose amid the hurricane named Romulus. Honestly, she didn't know how Evelyn could tolerate the onslaught without returning fire.

They emerged from the office after only a few minutes. "I have an announcement to make," Romulus said, and all motion and sound in the front office area quickly tapered away.

She was surprised at how relaxed Romulus suddenly looked, with a thumb casually hooked in his trouser pocket.

"It seems we will all be taking a brief holiday from the routine work of the magazine. No need to panic. Everyone will receive their wages on Friday, and all subsequent Fridays. For the next week, we will be contacting our subscribers and advertisers to alert them of the delay in this month's issue. This is merely a temporary interruption. An infinitesimal hiccup in the grand scheme of our distinguished magazine. As soon as we clear up a few minor details with the court, we will be back in full operation. In the meantime, we will be addressing envelopes for 160,000 subscribers." He turned to Evelyn with a smile. "Evelyn will be awarding a prize to whoever stumbles across the strangest town name. A quick glance at our subscriber list showed a town called Lick Skillet, Alabama. It is the current frontrunner. Anyone who can beat that name shall be treated to a dinner at Vercelli's."

His teeth were so white they gleamed from across the room, but beneath the veneer of charm, Stella sensed tension. He masked it well, but the glint of determination in his eye hinted at the anger smoldering inside.

The veneer slipped as he saw her and crossed the office to stand before her. "Still here?"

"I'm wondering if you have a delivery for me?" When no understanding registered on his face, she clarified. "From the medical examiner's office? An autopsy report from Dr. Lentz?"

Autopsy was probably the one word guaranteed to stir his resentment anew. "No, Miss West, I have no autopsy report for you. And I'm finished with your quixotic quests to resurrect the dead, hunt down phantom enemies, or ruin my reputation."

"You don't *really* blame me for what's happening, do you?"

"Yes, Miss West, I really do." Icicles dripped from his words. He glanced at the door, then back at her. It was a wordless order to leave.

She left. There were times to stand her ground, and times to withdraw and regroup.

Back at the boardinghouse, she intended to retrieve her mail and pack her bags to move into Evelyn's townhouse for a few days.

Only a single letter awaited her today. There was no return address, but she recognized the British stamp on the envelope. It was probably from one of her former editors or artist friends from London. Curiosity prompted her to open the letter before heading upstairs.

Dear Miss West,

It has come to our attention that you are no longer living within the borders of the United Kingdom. As you are not a British citizen, copyright laws will no longer protect your works until you apply in person at the copyright office in Stationers Hall, London. Failure to personally appear and register your copyright privileges will result in a revocation of all your copyrighted artworks produced in the United Kingdom, and may not be retroactively activated.

Sincerely,
Director of Copyrights
& Registers
Stationers Hall

It was outrageous! A tingling began in her limbs, and she grew both hot and thirsty. She *needed* the revenue from those copyrights! The illustrations for a book of short stories by

Robert Louis Stevenson alone brought her a healthy income, one she depended upon.

She was going to need a lawyer for this. The letter said she needed to appear in London in person, but my goodness! How was she supposed to drop everything and rush across the Atlantic? And why should she have to? The wonders of modern telegraphy meant that she could communicate quite quickly and efficiently from overseas.

She sat down, her knees too weak to keep standing. The letter was so terse it was hard to even know who to contact. Flipping the envelope over, she studied the stamp and the postmark.

The postmark was too smudged to be legible. She had properly registered her copyrights, and that couldn't be taken away merely for traveling abroad. She knew dozens of writers and artists who made their home overseas, and they had no fear of losing their copyrights.

The letter was a fraud. A clever one that had succeeded in sending a temporary rush of panic through her, but it was a fraud.

And somehow, knowing there was someone so determined to frighten her away from Boston was even more worrisome than the threat of losing her copyrights. Whoever was behind this letter knew where she lived. He knew her history in London well enough to fabricate a believable threatening letter.

It made her more grateful than ever for the escape to Evelyn's house.

-ᘓᔆᘎᔆ-

It didn't take long to move into Evelyn's townhouse on Hanover Street. It was a narrow, three-story house that was two rooms wide on each floor. Bridget Delaney had her hands full with two little children who had just awakened from a nap, but

Stella didn't need much help as she carried her bags into the house. Bridget told her that Evelyn was at the office, but that Stella should make herself at home.

There wasn't much time for that. It was Tuesday afternoon, and her regular four o'clock telephone call to her parents was coming up. Would Ernest let her use the telephone in the archives now that she'd been terminated from City Hall?

There was only one way to find out. The archives telephone was so much quieter than using one in a noisy hotel lobby.

Ernest was surprised to see her as she entered the archives. Setting down a stack of cataloging records he was adding to a drawer, he looked up with concern in his face.

"I'm real sorry about what happened," he said. "I wish they hadn't let you go. You were the only nice lady in this whole building."

She doubted it, but given the snickering from her fellow stenographers whenever they spoke of Ernest, perhaps he had cause for his statement.

"I was wondering if I could still use the telephone," she asked. "My mother's condition is precarious, and I haven't been able to find a better spot to place a call. Please?"

To her relief, he nodded toward the telephone at the small desk near the map cases and went back to sorting records.

It took several minutes for the various switchboard operators to patch the call through to her father's house, but soon his warm voice greeted her. "How is my darling girl?" he asked in a hearty voice.

A little too hearty . . . as though he was going through the motions of happiness. "I'm fine. How is Mother?"

His pause was so long that she worried their connection had been severed, but finally he replied. "There are still bad days," he acknowledged. "This is one of them."

The hollow despair in his voice sliced through her. He went on to say that Eloise was going through a phase in which she obsessed over memories, dragging out Gwendolyn's old drawings, school essays, even the toys from their childhood saved in their attic.

"Gwendolyn wouldn't have wanted this," Stella said, leaning over to rub the pounding in her forehead. Gwendolyn had loved to dream about the day she would be married and have children. She already had baby names picked out and had even knitted two baby blankets, one in pink and one in blue. Just thinking about those things made Stella's heart ache over the dreams that would never come true for Gwendolyn.

"Papa, I'm worried," she said. "I know this scar will live with us all forever, but Mother's obsessing isn't natural."

"I know, baby girl," he said. "I'm hoping to coax her out on a trip, just the two of us. There's a resort hotel in Boulder Point I think she will enjoy."

"Boulder Point, Massachusetts? Why there?"

"Because it's where we went on our honeymoon, and she loved it. We need to rekindle what we've still got. I love her too much to watch her keep drifting away."

"I'll be praying for you both," she said before hanging up the telephone.

On the walk back to Evelyn's house, she stepped into a church with an unlocked door. She didn't attend here. The last time Stella had set foot in a church had been for Gwendolyn's funeral.

She'd always been a lackluster Christian. She didn't have time for mundane rituals like attending church services when the glittering temptations of London beckoned. The world was bright and dazzling, and withdrawing from it to pay homage to God seemed like an interruption. There would be time to settle down and become more devout when she was older. At least that was what she'd always believed. Who could anticipate how brutally short life could be?

At least Gwendolyn had been a good Christian . . . one of the many ways her baby sister was a better person than she. Gwendolyn had been the good sister, the modest one who obeyed rules and aspired to the simple joys of marriage and motherhood. It was Stella who lived recklessly, seizing each day with wide-open hands and squeezing every drop of joy from it. Why did God have the good sister perish and leave the wild sister unscathed?

Stella said a brief prayer for Gwendolyn, but mostly she prayed for her parents. The undertow of grief was dragging her mother farther away each day, and it seemed her brave, courageous father was floundering in his quest to help.

She squeezed her hands tighter, wondering if God would pay more attention to her appeals if she were a better person. It made her a little angry. Maybe she was a lousy Christian, but what had her parents ever done to deserve this misery?

It wasn't fair. Her parents were good people. Not perfect, but good. And Gwendolyn had been the best of them all. What kind of loving God—

She stopped the angry train of thought. She'd read the book of Job, she knew life wasn't fair, but it was one thing to read the words and another to take them into her heart and accept them.

—◦◦◦◦—

Stella hadn't realized quite how serious the injunction against *Scientific World* was until she noticed that Evelyn had not returned from the office until almost nine o'clock that night.

And in the middle of the crisis yesterday, she had waltzed in and pestered Romulus with pleas for more help. She had to make it right. So far, he and Evelyn were the only allies she'd made in Boston, and she couldn't afford to alienate half of that team.

Not that she regretted locking horns with him. Romulus was a force of nature whose personality would overwhelm any woman without a good, strong backbone, and Stella never shied away from a fight. Although she'd grown up in the loving household of Karl and Eloise Westergaard, their family was a boisterous, turbulent one. Her parents fought as fiercely as they loved.

The classic example came when Stella was twenty-two and had been invited to display her lithographs at the Royal Exhibition Hall in London. Her father refused to permit it, and since she didn't have the funds to buy ship's passage on her own, it looked as though the invitation would come to nothing.

But her mother was determined to see her daughter shine in London. Eloise called a family meeting at the modest kitchen table overlooking her rose garden, the place where disagreements were always thrashed out. Her father was intransigent. He refused to even sit at the table and kept pacing before the kitchen window, his hands clasped behind his back.

"Stella can display her pictures at the gallery in Cornell," he said. "No daughter of mine is traipsing off into a foreign den of iniquity."

"And no daughter of mine will be shackled in obscurity when she has the chance to fly with the eagles," her mother retorted.

Eloise set an amethyst bracelet on the table, the stones clicking in the suddenly silent room. It was the bracelet Karl had given Eloise on their tenth wedding anniversary. "I shall sell this bracelet and buy two tickets and accompany my daughter to London," Eloise said calmly.

"Don't you dare," Karl said, warning heavy in his tone.

They were fighting words, but Eloise did not rise to the bait. "What are you so afraid of?"

"What rational man wouldn't be terrified of sending his daughter alone to London?" Karl roared.

"We can find a solution without you shouting the house down and stomping on all of Stella's hopes and ambition." Her mother pushed the amethyst bracelet to the center of the table. "If it takes the sale of some purple rocks to make my daughter's dream come true, I'm willing to make the trade."

"Don't you dare," her father said again, but this time he whispered the words gently. His tone was laden with love, affection, and yes, a healthy dose of fear. He sank down into a chair, blotting his brow with a handkerchief. "Those amethysts are precious to me, as are Stella's dreams." He turned his attention to her. "I'm sorry, baby girl. I'm terrified of setting you loose into the world. Your mother and I will go with you to London. Perhaps we'll even wait for the spring so Gwendolyn can come with us."

Two months later, the four of them boarded a steamer to England, her mother proudly wearing her amethyst bracelet as she stood beside Stella on the deck of the ship as it pulled out of the port in New York. Her fear of water made it hard for Stella to endure the crossing, but if her father could be brave enough to send his daughter into the wider world, she could face her fear of water with no whining.

And the four of them had a magical time in London. Her parents stuck close to her side as the grand salons and museums were opened to her. She signed contracts with two famous publishing houses on Fleet Street, earning a healthy commission to illustrate a novel and three scientific textbooks. Her lithographs were sold for staggering sums. She moved through the art circles of London, dressed to the nines and laughing with an endless parade of suitors. Her popularity was due as much to her novelty and personality as her artwork, and she savored every moment of it.

At first, her parents worried about Stella's meteoric rise in the world of artistic acclaim. Karl accompanied her everywhere, hovering in the background like an archangel ready to descend at the least provocation. Some girls might have chafed at such vigilance, but not Stella. Every day of her life she was secure in the knowledge she was loved, protected, and supported to pursue whatever high-flying ambitions she could envision.

At the end of their one-month visit, her family returned home, while Stella chose to remain in England. None of it would have happened if her mother hadn't had the backbone to confront her husband, or if Karl didn't have the respect and patience to listen to an opinion he didn't want to hear.

Stella rolled from bed. This time it was she who was wrong, not Romulus, and she would make it right. Tackling him at his office probably wasn't the best strategy. Romulus was easily distractible, and he wouldn't welcome her intrusion when he was surrounded by his duties at the office.

Evelyn concurred when Stella brought up the subject. "He always takes breakfast in the dining room at his hotel," she said as she sipped coffee and fed bits of pastry to the housekeeper's two children while Miss Delaney scrambled eggs and bacon in the kitchen. It smelled wonderful, and a plate had been set for her, but Stella did not want to linger. She had no idea how long Romulus loitered at breakfast and wanted to intercept him before he left for the office.

The dining room at the hotel was almost full, but Romulus sat alone, reading a newspaper and sipping coffee. She had dressed to impress this morning and attracted her fair share of attention as she sauntered through the tables toward Romulus. "May I join you?"

His eyes widened in surprise as he set down the newspaper. He made a great show of surveying her emerald cutaway jacket, slim-fitting black skirt, and lingering on the Byzantine gold choker snug against her neck.

"Disappointing," he murmured. "I've always held to the belief in only one exclamation point per ensemble."

She raised a brow. "You are *not* going to give me fashion advice."

"A fancy choker *and* a cutaway jacket? Too much icing on the cake, dearest."

He turned his attention back to the newspaper. He had a point, but she'd swallow strychnine before admitting it. The tailoring of her jacket was a masterpiece of engineering, but she probably had overdone it with the choker.

"May I join you?" she asked again with forced brightness. She had an apology to deliver and could hardly do so standing up.

He gestured to the vacant seat opposite him.

"I'm sorry about the way I burst in on you yesterday. I was obsessed with my own needs and didn't realize the problems I had been causing you, so I'm truly sorry." She risked a wobbly smile and waited for his reply.

"Does this work for you a lot?"

"What?" She honestly didn't know what to make of his chilly tone. She'd just delivered a brilliant apology, and he was supposed to accept it.

"Batting your lashes. Gracing me with your presence. I just wondered if other men are so desperate for your company they roll over for it."

"They usually recognize a genuine apology when they hear one. I was wrong about asking for another autopsy. It was a stupid idea."

"What were you thinking?" he burst out, exasperation in his tone.

"I wasn't! I was letting my emotions run away with my judgment, and I was wrong. I wanted to find a villain in all this mess and was ready to skewer Dr. Lentz because he was convenient.

I truly am sorry. You've been nothing but helpful, and I've been an idiot."

The first hint of a smile curved his mouth. "Have you eaten? The eggs Benedict here are out of this world."

And that was that. A waiter delivered two platters of eggs Benedict and a bowl of freshly cut melon. They talked about everything from the horticultural properties of melons to the excavation of land beneath the Charles River for the subway. Stella had once illustrated a series of drawings about underground caves and karsts and had learned a great deal about how subterranean water could produce fissures and sinkholes beneath the surface of the land. Romulus took notes as she spoke, suggesting it might make an interesting article for the magazine someday.

This felt so comfortable. So domestic. She could imagine having breakfast with Romulus every morning. Which was a problem. Romulus was relentless in his determination to escape any woman who dared get too close.

And she was getting far too close. It seemed that when Romulus walked into a room, he sucked up half the oxygen. The clocks stopped, the world slowed its rotation. Honestly, if anyone could see the inner workings of her mind, she'd be locked up in a lunatic asylum. She'd never been clobbered with an adolescent infatuation, and her attraction to Romulus was equal parts thrilling and mortifying.

The instant Romulus suspected her level of attraction he'd start holding her at arm's length, but that didn't mean she intended to retreat. She would be smarter than the other women who'd tried to reel him in. She could repress the outward show of her growing infatuation, letting the natural affinity between them grow stronger and bloom while his guard was down.

"What are you smiling about in such glee?" Romulus asked.

"It isn't a smile of glee, but pity," she said. "I can't help but mourn the triumphs you might have accomplished had you gone to Cornell instead of the predictable choice of Harvard."

His laughter was so hearty it was impossible not to join in. "Such bitterness. I'm surprised it doesn't sour the fruit." That didn't stop him from wolfing down the last of the melon, but his mood soon sobered. "I wish I could make this breakfast stretch all morning, but a court case awaits my attention," he said as he pushed back from the table and stood.

As he left the restaurant, Stella noticed every female in the vicinity, young and old alike, following him out the door with their gaze.

Romulus didn't know who was behind the campaign to destroy *Scientific World*, but he suspected the battle was far from over, and he refused to supply his opponent with ammunition. The contract governing the distribution of subscription magazines required the publisher to notify subscribers of an interruption in their service within five days of learning of the delay. Typically it would be ridiculous to believe anyone would bring a lawsuit for such a minor violation, but these weren't normal times.

That meant he needed to get these letters in tomorrow's mail if he was to stay within the letter of the law. His staff had been addressing envelopes for the past three days. Overflowing bins of bundled envelopes crowded the office, ready to be stuffed as soon as the letters were printed. Roy Tanner had spent the entire morning reconfiguring the linotype machine to print a single-sided letter. Now stacks of letters were being carried up in batches of five thousand.

He couldn't ask his staff to stay late and stuff envelopes. He and Evelyn would do that on their own. It was going to be a long night, and Evelyn had gone downstairs to get them something for dinner. They might be here until the sun rose, but these letters would be ready for tomorrow's post.

He still needed to refute the charges against the magazine, and Clyde had been invaluable on that front. For the past three evenings, Clyde had come up to the office, tired and grubby after a long day of work on the subway. He took a seat at a vacated desk and wrote a point-by-point defense for each article they had published on electricity.

Evelyn had not complained. She didn't like Clyde's presence, but they needed him, so she swallowed back whatever remnants of bitterness still lingered in her mind. Evelyn's memory was a mixed blessing. It kept their office running like a well-oiled clock, but she was a master at storing and cataloging every slight Clyde had dealt her over the past ten years.

The door opened, and Evelyn shouldered her way in, followed by Stella, whose arms were weighed down with baskets of food.

"We have brought sustenance," Stella said gaily.

"What have you got?" he asked.

"Deep-fried clams, spiced lobster patties, corn bread, and of course, a nice big box of Belgian chocolates."

"She can stay," Clyde said, reaching out for the basket brimming with golden, crispy fried clams. Evelyn set out a plate with sliced corn bread and plenty of butter.

Romulus couldn't tear his eyes off Stella as she sashayed around the office, bearing her baskets of goodies like Lady Bountiful. It wasn't until she set everything down that he got a good look at her ensemble. Even for Stella, it was a bold choice.

"A Japanese kimono?" he asked in amazement.

Stella grinned. "It's going to be a late night, and it's the most comfortable thing I own. I overspent shamelessly on the chocolate, but I think we can all use a little something special tonight."

He resented the niggling sense of attraction that never left him in peace. He was grateful Stella had volunteered to help with stuffing envelopes, but that didn't mean he had to like it. He wasn't going to compliment her spectacular silk kimono. He wasn't going to ask if she'd made progress tracking down the mysterious A.G.—or anything else that might divert him from saving his magazine. All he wanted was to get these envelopes stuffed, sealed, and batched for tomorrow's mail.

Evelyn cleared space at a desk and passed out plates, and the four of them started tearing through the food. He was so hungry the first lobster cake was down his throat while he was still slathering butter across warm corn bread.

"This reminds me of old times," Evelyn said. "Except back in the early days when we addressed the magazines, the only thing we could afford was pretzels."

"I loved those pretzels," Clyde said.

Romulus held his breath. Dredging up old memories was always a risky sport for these two, but despite all the heartache, there had been good times, too. It seemed Evelyn was in a fond mood, smiling back at the memory of those pretzels.

They devoured the food quickly. Stella cleared the mess while he hefted the first bin of envelopes to the workspace. Each letter was folded into thirds, then inserted into an envelope. He'd paid extra for pre-gummed envelopes, and as he and Evelyn stuffed the envelopes, they passed them to Stella, who swiped a damp sponge over the flap to seal it closed. It took only a few minutes for them to sink into a routine, the work progressing quickly, but after an hour they'd stuffed only five thousand envelopes.

"I can help," Clyde offered, finally having completed the written defense for the last of their electricity articles. "Although a man of my brilliance being reduced to stuffing envelopes seems a painful waste."

"A man fired by Thomas Edison?" Romulus quipped, but Clyde was having none of it.

"So was Tesla! So was Westinghouse! All the great electrical engineers have run afoul of Edison. It's a badge of distinction."

Once Clyde joined Stella in sealing envelopes, their productivity picked up. The next hour saw almost ten thousand letters sealed, and at this rate, they ought to finish by morning.

"Do you remember the summer of the hummingbirds?" Evelyn asked.

How could any of them forget? It was the summer Clyde had come into their lives, showing up at Evelyn's house with the tools to electrify their greenhouse in order to create the right conditions to keep hummingbirds alive.

"The summer of the hummingbirds?" Stella asked. "It sounds like a play by Oscar Wilde."

Evelyn laughed. "It was about as improbable. His senior year of college, Romulus captured some hummingbirds just to prove he could do it. He set them free in our greenhouse, and we intended to enjoy them for only a few days . . . but by the time we got ready to release them, a pair had laid eggs, so we had to create a suitable environment in which they could hatch."

Stella seemed enraptured as Evelyn spoke. "You must tell me everything!"

"Only so long as you keep gluing those envelopes," Romulus said.

Stella nodded and went back to sweeping the sponge across the gummed flaps. "Continue," she prompted.

It was a little painful, listening to Evelyn resurrect that long-ago summer of dreams and halcyon days. They added a fountain to the greenhouse to ensure proper humidity for the hummingbirds. They stocked the greenhouse with flowering plants to provide an endless supply of nectar. Romulus, Evelyn, and Clyde then spent countless hours building a microcosm of paradise, ostensibly for the hummingbirds, but really just for the sheer love of the challenge.

"I would love a chance to study hummingbirds," Stella said, her voice saturated with the same kind of wistful longing he'd always felt when overcome by a surge of inspiration. "I've seen them a couple of times, but they always fly away before I can get a good look at them."

"Hummingbirds are the spoiled darlings of the avian kingdom," Romulus said dismissively. "When they grow bored of New England, they fly to the Caribbean in search of greener fields. Very fickle."

Evelyn apparently felt compelled to defend the hummingbirds' character, referencing the stamina contained in their tiny bodies. By the time darkness fell, they had forty thousand envelopes stuffed, and Clyde opened the window. Somewhere in the distance, the Boston Symphony was playing one of their outdoor promenade concerts. Whenever they performed outdoors, they played lighter, popular selections, and it was always a treat to open the window to listen.

"Brahms by moonlight," Clyde murmured. In the distance, the violins and cellos rolled through a concerto laden with longing and reverence. "When my last hour on earth arrives, I hope to be listening to Johannes Brahms," Clyde said softly.

"Not me," Stella said. "I'd want to be listening to Puccini. I think *La Bohème* is the most sublime piece of music ever written. I'll never tire of listening to it."

"It would be nice to see the concert in person," Evelyn said as she folded another letter. "I'd like to simply sit on the lawn, close my eyes, and let the music wash over me."

"Not me," Clyde said. "This room is exactly where I want to be. We are at the heart of scientific creation. We are a megaphone for launching news of discovery and innovation out to the world, distilling it into articles that inform and inspire. There is no place on earth I'd rather be."

Evelyn gave him a gentle nudge with her elbow. "You sound as flamboyant as Romulus."

Other people might take that as an insult, but Clyde and Evelyn both knew the magazine's success had been built on Romulus's grandiose celebration of scientific wonder. And Clyde was right: There was magic in this room tonight. They were trapped in the most mind-numbing task imaginable, and yet the evening was transcendent. It contained a perfect combination of energy, intellect, and comradery. Evelyn was the rock, the sensible foundation that kept them all grounded. Clyde was the academic and intellectual engine. And Stella? Annoyed as he was with her, she fit into this group perfectly. She brought the artistic flare to capture abstract ideas and translate them into images the rest of the world could understand.

Were he the type to analyze or dissect what made this evening so perfect, he would try to break it down to its component parts. He'd credit part of it to the captivating music of Brahms, part to his happiness at seeing Clyde and Evelyn behaving kindly to one another, and part to the smile he couldn't repress whenever he admired Stella's daring fuchsia kimono. But in large part, the magic of this evening came from a higher power that occasionally provided glimpses of pure, unrefined joy to those who were open to the message. Happiness was not an abundance of riches or amusements, it was evenings such as these, when people were engaged in a worthy pursuit and surrounded by kindred spirits.

It was four o'clock in the morning when the last envelope was sealed. His hands were so cracked and dry, it was a wonder he had even been able to keep folding the pages. He was bleary-eyed, hungry, and tired, but he had the satisfaction of a job well done.

"I'll walk you both home," Clyde said to Evelyn and Stella.

"We'll be okay," Evelyn replied.

Already, Romulus could sense Evelyn's invisible shields erecting as she retreated behind them. She was able to let down her guard here in the office, but stepping out into the real world alongside Clyde would be another matter.

"Don't be foolish," Clyde said. "It's on the way to my hotel, and Boston can be a dubious place at this hour."

"He's right," Stella said.

Romulus hoped Evelyn would concede; otherwise he would feel compelled to accompany them the three miles to her home, and his hotel was right next door to the office.

He breathed a sigh of relief when Evelyn nodded.

It was almost dawn, and Evelyn ought to be exhausted, but every nerve in her body was disturbingly alive because Clyde was so close on the narrow sidewalk that their hands were in continual danger of bumping against each other.

How unsettling to feel so stiff beside a man she was once married to. She battled the instinctive impulse to clasp hands with him, for although he knew her better than any man on the planet, it was essential that she keep her distance from him. In the eyes of the law, they were still married, but they had a formal separation agreement outlining the exact terms of their rights and obligations to each other.

Which was essentially nothing. They owed each other nothing anymore.

"Here we are," Evelyn said as she mounted the steps to the townhouse and fumbled with the key.

"I'll see you inside," Clyde said as he mounted the steps behind her.

"There's no need. Stella and I will be perfectly fine."

He didn't listen to her. Of course, he didn't listen. Why should she expect Clyde to change his stripes now?

Stella made her excuses and headed up the darkened staircase to the guest bedroom, leaving her alone with Clyde in the parlor. She didn't want to be brusque, but Clyde rarely responded to subtlety. It had taken her years to consign him to her past, and he'd broken his word by returning to Boston. She was under no obligation to extend hospitality or even be polite to him. "Thank you for walking us home. I'm sure you can find your own way back to your hotel."

"Evelyn."

"Don't." He was going to try to reopen old wounds and fight battles that were long over. Perhaps he had a hide thick enough to endure another beating, but she had no appetite for it.

"We said vows, Evelyn."

"Yes, and you broke them. Please, Clyde. I'm very tired, and there's no point in resurrecting this argument."

She turned to head toward the stairs, but his hand curled around her elbow. When she tugged, he tightened his grip.

"You said you can't have more children, but that doesn't mean we can't adopt. For pity's sake, I've seen the pictures of your housekeeper's children on your desk as though they are your own. If you want children, we can have them."

She wrenched her arm away. "And would these hypothetical children have a father? Or will you dash off to the Rockies or South America or to whatever engineering project grabs your fancy? You weren't even here when our son was born."

"If I'd known the baby would come early, I would have tried to get home," he said. "I came back as soon as I learned it had died."

"*He.* His name was Christopher, and he was a real baby, not an *it*. And if you can't—"

"I took that job in Wyoming because you wanted me to. Did you think it was fun for me, all those months in the middle of nowhere? The snow was blinding, and it was so cold the skin on my face blistered and peeled, but I didn't give up because the pay was good and you needed money to feel secure. I did it for *you*, Evelyn."

She retreated. He'd always accused her of being obsessed with money but she wasn't—she was obsessed with feeling *safe*. Clyde and his barrel of problems had no place in the strong, independent world she'd built for herself.

But a piece of her would always love him. She sighed. "Neither of our lives has turned out the way we hoped. Every time I see a hummingbird, it makes me sad. I survived our breaking apart once before. I don't think I could endure it again."

She didn't wait for him to reply as she headed up the stairs.

Romulus rose early to haul the bins of envelopes to the post office. Tremont Street was completely excavated for the subway construction, making it impossible to pull a carriage close to the building, so several trips lugging heavy bins the three blocks to the post office was his only option. To his surprise, Stella was at the building and offered to lend a hand. She wore one of her prison-garb dresses, smiling and ready to help haul bins alongside him.

They were tired and sweaty after the first trip, and it would take six more before all were delivered. While riding the elevator down the second time, he looked over to admire her. Her face was flushed with good health. With her sleeves rolled up, she looked strong and ready to tackle the world.

"You look like the peasant women from Millet's painting *The Gleaners*. Strong. Salt of the earth."

The Gleaners was an infamous painting in France because it glorified the nobility of women laboring in the fields, but Stella beamed. The elevator doors opened, and they both leaned over to heft up the next bins.

"I like a little manual labor," Stella said as she walked beside him. "I feel like one of those female penguins who spends months lugging stones across the ice to build a suitable nest. It's good to feel strong."

He smiled reluctantly. He loved that she could so effortlessly trot out animal science trivia, but it terrified him, too. Flirting with women was one of his favorite pastimes, but rarely was he moved by it.

Stella moved him, and it wasn't a good feeling. And yet he couldn't resist flirting with her the rest of the morning as they made trip after trip to the post office, loving every moment of it. When the last bin had been delivered, Stella sagged with tired, happy satisfaction.

"I'm going back to Evelyn's house for a long soak in her bathtub," she said with a weary smile, and he silently groaned. The last thing he needed distracting his mind was images of Stella in her bath. He kept his eyes trained on her as she sashayed down the street toward the streetcar stop. Even in that drab muslin outfit, she mesmerized him. He stood in the street and gawked like a schoolboy until she disappeared from view.

Which was insane. He had work piling up at the office and needed to get back to it.

"Is it done?" Evelyn asked the moment he walked through the door.

"Done," he confirmed. His back ached and hands hurt. His wallet was six hundred dollars lighter after paying the postage fees. The supply room needed restocking, but they'd squeaked in under the deadline to notify their subscribers of the halt in production.

"I'm not even sure I know what to do with my time," Evelyn said.

That was a first. Normally, Evelyn's day was consumed with

balancing accounts and getting the articles assigned, edited, and typeset.

"We probably need to make an appointment with the bank," he said. "We may need a short-term loan to cover operating expenses before we get back into production."

Evelyn nodded and made note of it in her journal. "And what about the series on electricity? Shall we find alternative stories in case—"

A tremendous *boom* sounded from the street below, so loud it hurt his ears. The windows rattled, and screams rose from the street. Everyone in the office leapt up, looking wildly about.

He dashed to the windows. A cloud of smoke and dust swirled in the street near the intersection of Tremont and Boylston. The pedestrian bridge had collapsed, storefront windows had shattered, and wagons were overturned. Electric wires and wooden planking from the overpass dangled over the gaping hole blown into the street.

Romulus tugged open the window to get a better view of the catastrophe. Before he could get a good look, Evelyn scooted in front of him, leaning out to see the full horror of what lay below.

"Oh no . . . Clyde," she whispered.

He swallowed hard. It was impossible to see into the trench; it was still obscured by a cloud of dust hanging in the air, but tongues of fire flickered in the dusty cloud of smoke.

"I'm going down," Evelyn said.

He grabbed her, hauling her back from the door. "It's a gas explosion. It's not safe down there."

"I don't care. If Clyde is in that trench, I need to get him out."

A black cloud billowed up from the trench, followed by a hiss of white steam. A horse lay thrashing on its side, its panicked screams audible even from up here.

As they watched, a second explosion blew a wagon into

the air. It was on fire before it landed, and the windows of the Boston Athletic Club shattered and came crashing to the ground. Evelyn sagged and would have fallen had Romulus not grabbed her.

The electric lights in the room flickered and went out.

"Stay here," he warned. "The gas lines may still be blowing."

"Clyde," Evelyn said faintly again. "Dear God, please keep him safe. Please don't let him burn."

He wished he could comfort her, but he didn't know any more than she. Even now, his best friend could be burning to death. He clenched the windowsill so hard his hands hurt. Last night Clyde had stood at this very window and listened to the music of Brahms, savoring every note. It was impossible to believe he could be dead today.

Men began staggering out of the pit, bystanders leaning over to haul them up and out. A bit of his strangling fear loosened. If survivors were coming out of the trench, there was no reason to believe Clyde couldn't be among them. He peered down at the men in an effort to spot Clyde, but they all had soot-blackened faces and were impossible to identify.

Roy Tanner burst into the office. "Is there anything I can do?" he asked.

"Just go down to the power room and make sure there is no danger of electrical fire." Romulus didn't expect it, but at this point, it was impossible to know what they were dealing with.

By the time he looked back at the window, Evelyn had fled the room.

He had better go down after her. If he couldn't save Clyde, at least he could help get the wreckage cleared away so the firemen could do their work.

—⟋⟍⟋⟍⟋—

The air was thick with dust and smoke, coating the back of Evelyn's throat and making it hard to breathe, but the stench of gas was worse. The sulfuric smell hung in the air as she plowed forward, her handkerchief clutched over her nose and mouth. Glass and gravel crunched beneath her feet, and the shouting of men added to her sense of panic. The clang of fire engines could be heard in the distance, and people began hauling away lumber from the collapsed overpass. The fire engines couldn't get through with the road this badly blocked.

A group of men hunkered down on the street, struggling to lift a man from the trench. His face was streaked with sweat, but he appeared uninjured as he got his feet beneath him.

"Clyde Brixton," she shouted at the man. "Have you seen Clyde Brixton?"

The man shook his head and gestured toward Boylston Street. "He usually works farther down near the electrical switches. I haven't seen him today."

She whirled and headed south toward Boylston, where the dust and confusion were even worse. Along the sidewalks, men held rags to bleeding wounds, and she paused only long enough to see if she recognized Clyde among them. Each time another man emerged from the trench, she asked the question. "I'm looking for my husband. Have you seen Clyde Brixton?"

Each time the men shook their heads. At last, she reached a grassy area near Avery Street where a dozen men were stretched out on their backs, passersby doing their best to render aid. She walked across the grass, looking each man in the face, growing more desperate by the minute.

Two men half guided, half dragged a third man whose face was streaked with blood and dirt. She studied him only long enough to know he wasn't Clyde, but then she saw the other man propping him up. "Clyde!" she burst out in relief. His face was darkened with soot, but those impossibly blue eyes were as clear as ever. He grimaced as he lowered the injured man to the bench, but he was alive and standing upright, and everything was going to be okay. Relief nearly sapped the strength from her legs as she staggered toward him, calling his name.

He must be in pain, for he cradled the side of his head with one hand as he lumbered toward a lamppost, bracing his hand against it.

"Clyde!" she shouted again, but the street was loud with the clanging of fire engines and the panicked yells of men. She reached out to touch his shoulder and nearly wept with relief when he recognized her and flashed a dazzling, heart-stopping grin, his teeth white against his sooty face.

"Are you all right?" she asked. "Do you need anything?"

He looked at her strangely, his eyes puzzled as he shook his head. He kept glancing between her mouth and her eyes, appearing more agitated and confused by the moment.

"Where are you hurt?" she asked.

He shook his head. "I can't hear you!" he yelled. "Say it again."

Oh dear God, have mercy. She swallowed hard, cleared her throat, and spoke as loudly and clearly as possible. "Where are you hurt?"

His confusion faded as fear tinged his face. She was frightened, too, for in all the terrible scenarios she'd obsessed over while wandering through the street, she had never imagined this.

Clyde was completely deaf.

─ ⚘ ─

Romulus stood in the corner of the examining room, keeping a close eye on his two best friends in the world as a doctor examined Clyde.

The hospital was crowded, noisy, and filled with panicked people. They had waited three hours on a hard bench in the hallway as the critically injured people were treated first, then finally they'd been shown into this small examination room. Clyde sat on the patient's cot, looking pale and stoic as the doctor examined his ears.

In order to get a proper view of the middle ear, the doctor wanted Clyde to go through a series of simple commands, such as swallowing and taking a deep breath. Clyde didn't understand their pantomiming, and Evelyn's hands shook too badly to write, so Romulus wrote the commands and Clyde followed the instructions as the doctor studied both ears. A rubber tube and balloon was used to blow a puff of air into the ear canal while the doctor studied the reaction.

The results were not promising.

"His right eardrum is shattered," the doctor said. "I can see some feeble movement in his left ear, but it is not enough for any hearing to register."

Evelyn's face crumpled at the news.

Clyde had been watching Evelyn, not the doctor. "What did he say?" Clyde asked.

Romulus scribbled the doctor's conclusion as quickly as he could. There was no point in trying to soften the blow. Clyde would want to know exactly what was going on, but it hurt to even write the words.

You are completely deaf in your right ear. Little hope for improvement there. Left ear is badly damaged. Might recover, might not.

Clyde was stoic as his eyes traveled across the page. His mouth turned down, but he gave a brusque nod of acknowledgment.

"Is there anything we can do to help the recovery?" Evelyn asked.

The doctor did not look optimistic. "I am not a specialist in auditory issues, but the inner ear is a delicate mechanism, and the sound waves from that explosion did serious damage. Mr. Brixton is in considerable pain with each additional vibration, and this can't be good for his recovery. There is a sanitarium west of the city where he can have complete bed rest and as much silence as possible. The less disturbance to his ear, the better. Only after the swelling goes down and his body has a chance to heal will we know if he will regain any hearing."

Evelyn nodded. "I will take him."

When Romulus wrote out the doctor's recommendation, Clyde shook his head. "I can't leave my men," he said, but winced before he even finished the sentence. How ironic that although he was stone deaf, the sound waves from his own voice were painful.

Romulus took the time to write out the doctor's advice. Avoid physical movement, avoid loud noises, avoid anything that jarred his badly damaged tissues. The doctor recommended that Clyde not even be moved for a few days. He left to make arrangements for a bed for Clyde, and from there Clyde would be transferred directly to the sanitarium.

Clyde grabbed the pencil. "What has happened in the subway? I need to examine the damage and get back to work. They need me."

This was going to be a battle. It was in Clyde's nature to plow through any difficulty. Romulus wrote a response.

I'll find out what happened. Wait until we know more. Then we can argue.

A fleeting smile crossed Clyde's face and he nodded, but given the way he winced, even that simple nod had caused Clyde pain.

Even from a mile away, Stella had heard the blast, and it was all anyone was talking about. A late edition of the *Boston Globe* reported the few known details about the explosion. One of the sandhogs excavating near the six-inch gas main on Boylston Street noticed a crack in the pipe and the smell of gas. He reported it to a policeman, who put in a telephone call to the Boston Gas Company requesting help. Business went about as usual on the street above. Witnesses reported that a trolley took the curve at Boylston and Tremont too quickly, causing sparks to fly from the metal rails and into the nearby pit. The explosion happened moments later.

At two o'clock in the afternoon, a messenger boy came banging on Evelyn's front door with a message for Stella. It said that Clyde had been injured in the blast and to prepare the downstairs bedroom immediately.

"What's wrong with him?" she asked, but the boy knew nothing. He was just carrying messages from people at the hospital.

"What about the scene of the explosion? Did you see any of it?"

"Yes, ma'am. It made a real mess of the subway tunnel. Who's to say if they'll even be able to fix the damage? My father is a sandhog on the job, and they told him not to come back to work tomorrow."

Stella was a doctor's daughter and had often helped at his practice. She snapped into gear, putting fresh sheets on the bed, laying out clean towels and a little bell for the patient to ring. Bridget and the children had left town for a few days, but she ran to the market to buy veal and beef marrow bones for a broth. Her father swore by the nutritional properties of hearty beef stock, and she'd start making it by the vat. She quartered carrots, onions, and plenty of flat-leaf parsley for added flavor and nutritional punch. She didn't know the nature of Clyde's injuries, but sitting here twiddling her thumbs would do no good, and a nourishing beef broth couldn't hurt.

It was dark before she heard a carriage roll to a stop in front of the townhouse. She sagged with relief when she saw Clyde propped between Evelyn and Romulus, slowly inching his way toward the steps up to the townhouse. He placed each foot cautiously and with great deliberation, but at least he was walking on his own two feet, so surely he couldn't be too badly hurt.

She was wrong. As Clyde entered the house, she could see he was pale and trembling, barely able to stand upright through the pain. She asked him how he felt, but he didn't meet her eyes and kept walking at that slow, measured pace.

"I need to get him settled quickly," Evelyn said. "Every step is excruciating for him."

Clyde looked like a stranger to Stella. The laughing, reckless grin was gone, replaced by haunted eyes and a mouth clenched with pain. She couldn't see any obvious injuries, but he moved at a snail's pace as Evelyn guided him to the back bedroom.

She swiveled to Romulus for an explanation and listened with a sinking heart as he recounted Clyde's probable deafness. They sat at the small dining room table, a kerosene lantern softly illuminating the room.

She'd never seen Romulus so pensive. "It's hard to believe it was only last night when we were all stuffing envelopes," he said. "It seems like a million years ago, but this time yesterday, Clyde was standing at the open window, listening to the Boston Symphony play Brahms. It's probably the last music he will ever hear."

She wasn't used to this level of sorrow from him. Romulus was supposed to be laughing, grappling with whirlwinds, flirting.

"I would trade places with him if I could," Romulus continued. "Everything I've accomplished I owe to Clyde. I owe him more than I can ever repay, but there's not a thing I can do for him, and it's killing me."

"I thought Clyde hadn't been involved with the magazine for years?"

"He hasn't. But there never would have been a magazine without Clyde. I would have flunked out of Harvard my senior year if Clyde hadn't been there to haul me across the finish line."

Her eyes widened in surprise. "Flunked? I thought you were brilliant at everything."

For the first time that evening, a bit of humor lightened his eyes. "I am. That doesn't mean I can't be a grand idiot on occasion. Two months before graduation, I set off on a course of destruction from which it was almost impossible to recover. Clyde and Evelyn came to my rescue."

Over the next few minutes, Romulus told her the entire story, sparing himself none of the embarrassing details. He'd struggled throughout his years at Harvard, continually changing programs of study and delving into academic obsessions for a brief time before getting distracted by something else. The only constant throughout his four years at Harvard had been a girl named Laura. Even the reverent way he spoke Laura's name made Stella sit up and take note. Laura was everything to him. She was laughter and beauty and inspiration, and he hoped to marry her immediately upon graduation. It didn't work out that way. In February of his final year, Laura had abruptly severed their relationship, sending him into a spiral of despondency.

"I quit going to classes," he said. "I stayed in my room, got drunk, and wasted two months of my life blubbering over Laura in an inebriated fog. Clyde was in his final year at West Point, but when he heard that I was on the verge of failing, he hightailed it to Harvard and spent the next week getting me sober, tutoring me in trigonometry, and pounding some sense into my head. I needed to score a ninety-seven on my final trigonometry exam in order to pass the class. I was always lousy at trig, but Clyde had a way of explaining it that made sense. I got a perfect score on the test and passed the class. I wouldn't have graduated were it not for Clyde."

Stella's smile was gentle, but Romulus hadn't finished speaking.

"What I didn't know . . . what I was too drunk and despondent to realize . . . was that during that week while he tutored me, Clyde was absent without leave from West Point. There are consequences for things like that. He ended up getting expelled from college. Instead of graduating and joining the Army Corps of Engineers as an officer, he was required to serve two years as an enlisted soldier. He never did earn a college degree."

"Oh," Stella said, overwhelmed by the sacrifice Clyde had made on Romulus's behalf. It was a heroic act of love, humbling in its magnitude. The quality of a friendship was not shown during the sunny days, but in dark times of trouble. In that act of sacrifice, Clyde had proven himself a true friend. Romulus was somber as he told her more.

"That's why he and Evelyn were so poor during their first years of marriage, but between the three of us, we were still able to buy that dying magazine and turn it into something great."

She nodded, feeling strangely proud of him. She had no part in the success of *Scientific World*, but she applauded the creative inspiration behind the endeavor and the three people whose harmonizing strengths combined to make it happen. She was honored to be associated, however obliquely, with such a publication. "Whatever happened to Laura?"

"She married a doctor a few years ago. I spent a humiliating few years trying to win her back, but nothing ever came of it."

"Is she the reason you've stayed a bachelor all these years?"

It was a terribly personal question, but from the moment she'd met Romulus, they had formed a bond, a sense that they had no secrets from each other. He did not seem to mind the question.

"No. I've simply come to accept that I would be a terrible husband. The problems between Laura and me were entirely my fault. Even though I was obsessed with her, it came in bursts. For a few days, she was all I could think about, and I showered her with devotion, gifts, and praise. But then something would snag my attention and I'd go off hiking in the Adirondacks to study conifer trees or become fixated on training to win a title in a boxing championship. That summer when we created the habitat for the hummingbirds in Evelyn's greenhouse was a perfect example. Laura invited me to the annual Harvard–Yale regatta with her parents, and I entirely forgot about it. It was the week we installed a fountain for the hummingbirds, and that took all my energy. Laura was incensed. She said I was unfaithful and incapable of commitment."

"Did you step out on her?"

"Constantly. With boxing competitions and experimenting in the laboratory. One summer I became infatuated with learning to play the cello and could concentrate on little else."

"Did you step out on her with another *woman*?" she asked pointedly.

He looked appalled. "Of course not! My father was never faithful, and I had a front-row seat to witness what that does to a woman. No, I never cheated on Laura, but she still thought I was disloyal. The final straw came in February of my senior year. We went to see the opera of *Tristan and Isolde*. She was dazzled by it and decided I'd never be able to love her the way Tristan worshipped Isolde. I couldn't give her the sort of constancy she needed, and she cut me free."

Stella thought that might indicate a problem with Laura

rather than a failing from Romulus, but she wasn't in a position to judge. "It seems rather drastic to condemn yourself to bachelorhood just because of an unhappy love affair."

A faint smile hovered on his face as he peered at her through curious eyes. "Have you ever been in love?"

The question took her aback, and she hoped he didn't notice the sudden blush heating her face. Her feelings for Romulus grew by the hour, and she didn't want to talk about it, but she could hardly clam up when he'd been so forthcoming.

"No, I've never been in love, but I hope to be someday. My parents have a remarkable marriage, one for the ages. They both come alive when the other walks into the room, and it's as if the air suddenly carries an electrical charge. Do you know how difficult it was to grow up in a house like that? There were times when my parents couldn't keep their hands off each another. My sister and I had to cover our eyes and run shrieking from the room." Her smile faded. "It was rather sweet, actually. They don't behave like that anymore."

Her throat closed up. Nothing remained the same after Gwendolyn died. Her father managed to find his footing and begin pulling the pieces of his life back together. Not so her mother, who still seemed to be drifting in the shadowlands.

She shook off the bleak memories. "Anyway, I want a marriage like my parents have. I want that kind of friendship and inspiration and challenge. I want a strong husband who can pick me up when I stumble, and I want to do the same for him when he falters."

She looked at Romulus, whose face had softened with tenderness while he listened to her ramble. He was such an affectionate man, with a big heart and boundless sense of energy. It seemed a shame that he would let a single tainted experience with love sever him from a normal family life.

Sensing her scrutiny, he hastily straightened in his chair. "Well, don't look at me," he said. "I would be a terrible husband. Everything Laura said about me was right. My lack of attention, my erratic character, my inability to focus. It wouldn't have been so hurtful if it hadn't been true. I'm getting better about things as I get older." He flashed one of those reckless smiles, but it didn't quite reach his eyes. "I figure when I'm forty, I will have settled down enough to be a tolerable husband."

He retreated behind a stiff formality as he shrugged into his jacket. He was once again a polite but distant man as he took his leave.

She would be a fool to ignore his warnings. Romulus had been fending off women for the past decade and showed no sign of a chink in his armor. She didn't want to be one of those pathetic women trailing after him and begging for a scrap of affection, but she couldn't ignore the truth, either.

She had fallen in love with Romulus White, and she did not know if he was capable of returning the sentiment.

—◦✦◦—

The next two days were the most stressful of Romulus's career. Avalanches of bills were coming due, and he had no way to pay them.

To make it worse, Evelyn needed money. He'd learned of the problem this morning when he'd visited her house to check on Clyde and ask if there was anything she needed. She had been mortified when she'd asked him for a loan.

"There is a clinic in the Adirondacks that will take Clyde," she said. "They have excellent doctors and can provide him with his best chance to heal. I'm afraid it's terribly expensive."

And the previous week Evelyn had used all her ready cash to help her housekeeper. Apparently, the housekeeper had been estranged from her parents for years, but they were beginning to soften. When the parents suggested they'd like to meet the children, Evelyn had gladly purchased three train tickets to Richmond and bought new clothing for the children. Who could have guessed that in a few days Evelyn's entire world would be upended?

"I'm so sorry, Romulus," she said, her eyes downcast and chin trembling. "I will pay you back as soon as I can liquidate some investments next month."

Of course Romulus gave her the money. He took an advance at the bank, which only loaned him the money on the condition that it be repaid within one week. And the only way he could do that was to start selling his shares in *Scientific World*.

It was like selling a piece of his soul, but he would sign the papers tonight. A New York investment firm had been trying to diversify into publishing for years and had jumped at the chance to buy a few of Romulus's shares. He'd felt honor-bound to tell them of the injunction, but they were willing to proceed with the sale at a slightly reduced price. Romulus had no option but to accept.

The evening was cool, and Romulus braced himself as he walked into the Parker House Hotel, where one of the finest restaurants in the city took up most of the ground floor. The moment he had always feared had arrived. He would rather cut off his right hand than lose control of the magazine, but Clyde and Evelyn needed money fast, and Romulus had only one way of getting it.

The three men representing the New York investors were jovial as they joined Romulus at a table near the back of the restaurant. Parker House only allowed men in the main dining room, and the atmosphere was relaxed as liquor flowed, cigars were lit, and hearty steak dinners were set before them. It tasted like sawdust in his mouth. As expected, the investors all made chitchat about politics and baseball as they dined. That was the way business was done, with glad-handing and small talk before the serious negotiating began.

Romulus played along, but beneath the table his hands clenched into fists. Every moment of this meal was excruciating. He just wanted to sign the paperwork, take his bank check, and bolt from the room, but that would reveal his desperation.

After consulting the account books this afternoon, he had decided exactly how much money he needed. Forty employees were to be paid on Friday, rent on the building was due, and he had less than a week to repay the bank. It was impossible to know how much he'd have to fork over in lawyer fees to battle the injunction, but it wasn't going to be cheap. Even so, he could pay it all if he sold ten percent of his stake in the magazine.

The New York investors weren't interested in ten percent. "Such a small investment isn't worth our attention," the lead banker said. "We are not interested in anything less than a thirty-percent stake."

Romulus owned half the magazine. If he gave the investors what they wanted, he would be down to twenty percent. Perspiration rolled down the side of his neck. He swallowed hard. Once he signed those papers, he would be only a minority shareholder in the magazine he'd founded. These New York investors would have more say in *Scientific World* than he. He could retain his title of publisher, but he would lose control of the magazine.

And Clyde had lost an engineering degree because of a sacrifice he'd made ten years ago to help Romulus out of a tight spot. He'd always said he owed Clyde more than he could ever repay. It was time to make good on that assertion.

His hand shook as he signed the papers.

~⌒∽⌒~

Evelyn asked Roy Tanner to find the softest, best-sprung carriage in all of Boston. She didn't care how much it cost, she couldn't stand the thought of Clyde being jostled about in a cheap rented hack, the damaged, delicate tissues deep in his ears being bumped and abused for the three-mile journey to the train station.

Clyde hadn't complained, but he'd been in agony during the carriage ride home from the hospital that first night. Every rut in the road caused him to break out in perspiration and his knuckles to go white as he squeezed his fists. Clyde was used to discomfort. He'd lived in a tent during Wyoming winters and did heavy labor while on construction sites.

No, Clyde never complained. She complained plenty. When he left her for months on end to live at faraway engineering sites, she complained of abandonment. When the baby came early, she complained that he hadn't been there to comfort her. When Romulus wanted to expand the page count of the magazine, she complained that they couldn't afford the risk because Clyde had lost his job again.

It was time for her to be a better wife. For the first time in their marriage, Clyde was floundering, and she needed to come alongside him on this difficult journey. And if getting a ridiculously plush landau with elliptical springs for the smoothest ride would make Clyde more comfortable, she'd turn the city upside-down until she found one.

It had taken the combined will of both her and Romulus to convince Clyde to go to the health clinic. It went against his nature to walk away from a job, and he didn't understand the need for it. Rest was rest. He insisted it would be cheaper and easier to simply stay in Boston.

Romulus had told him there was value in removing himself from the barrage of stresses and temptations Clyde would be exposed to in Boston. When he still wasn't convinced, Evelyn wrote her plea in plain, eloquent language. *We need time alone together. We both need time to heal.*

Clyde finally agreed.

Romulus carried their bags and secured them to the back of the carriage. Clyde needed help getting into the landau, and she knew he wouldn't want her to see his weakness. She dashed back to the house on the pretense of fetching something so Romulus could help him board in private.

When all was ready, she returned to the street and tried to summon a brave face to say goodbye to Romulus. "I'm sorry to be abandoning you while the magazine is in such a mess."

"Not to worry," he said with a wink. His face was typically carefree and confident. "It's high time I learned to manage my own calendar."

But she was walking out on so much more than managing his schedule. There was the injunction, the looming court hearing, and the problems with issuing refunds to the advertisers who had paid in advance. She excelled in managing daily operations, while Romulus struggled with such details. Even so, in her pocket she felt the weight of a roll of bills Romulus had loaned her to pay the fees at the clinic. Dearest, wonderful Romulus, always coming to her rescue, and now she was abandoning him in his hour of need. She scrambled to tell him everything he would need to know in the coming weeks.

"If you need to consult previous financial statements, I've stored them in the filing cabinets on the third floor. I usually work with Reginald Pitkin at the bank to issue payroll checks. He'll be the best person to consult if you need—"

"I don't need anything," he assured with tender compassion in his dark eyes. "Go take care of your husband. We'll be fine."

A sheen of tears blurred her vision, and it took a moment to blink them away. Romulus moved to open the carriage door for her, but she shook her head. "I'll be walking to the train station," she said. "The roads in this part of town are a disgrace, and the city won't repair them since everything will be ripped up for the subway. I'll walk ahead of the carriage and alert the driver of the spots to avoid."

Romulus nodded and pulled her into a hug. She squeezed him tightly, fighting to hold on to her unraveling strength. The weeks ahead would be filled with challenges she had no experience handling, and she was going to miss Romulus and his bottomless well of good cheer.

"Take care, Evelyn," he whispered. "Don't be too hard on yourself."

She extracted herself from his embrace. With a nod to the carriage driver, she and Clyde set off on their journey, moving at a snail's pace to keep the ride as smooth as possible.

Evelyn walked ahead of the carriage. She guided the horse around bumps in the road and every few yards stooped over to toss aside sticks and debris that might jostle the wheels. She wept the entire walk to the train station.

Romulus fired his lawyer and hired a new one first thing on Monday morning. Grover Linde specialized in the First Amendment and was the best lawyer in Boston for leading a battle over freedom of the press. Grover had won two earlier cases in which the government had tried and failed to stop the publication of controversial subjects. Unfortunately, Grover and his legal team were in court all week and would have limited time to devote to *Scientific World's* case.

His new lawyer was confident he could win the case. Grover said that six years ago the city had attempted to ban a labor union from publishing news about organizing a strike. The government had been soundly defeated, and the records of the case were stored in City Hall's archives.

Romulus intended to lean on Stella for help wading through old archival records, since it was likely the same arguments would be used in the case against *Scientific World*. She knew the filing system at City Hall as well as anyone, and she owed him a favor. It might be best to simply follow his new lawyer's advice and patiently wait for the lawyers to handle the work, but that was impossible. Romulus needed something to focus on to stop his thoughts from straying back to Clyde and Evelyn, who had been plunged into an ordeal neither of them were equipped to cope with. He longed to help, but this was a journey they would have to navigate on their own.

So the chance to bury his head in *Scientific World's* court case was a welcome diversion. Thus, he found himself strolling toward City Hall with Stella West on his arm.

He liked walking beside her. She turned the head of every warm-blooded male on the street, and he was narcissistic enough to enjoy soaking up the effect she had on people. Wearing a silk shantung walking gown of royal blue and black stripes, Stella might possibly be the most fashionable woman in the city, but it was the confident way she sauntered down the street that was the most attractive thing about her. Stella didn't walk. She glided, she sashayed, she strutted. Even the way she ascended the stairs to City Hall, confidently entering the building where she'd been fired a mere two weeks earlier, was attractive.

He could see why she'd been the toast of London. She had confidence and a wit that was diamond bright, and yet when she entered the archives, she headed straight for the awkward man hunched behind the counter and chatted with him like they were old friends.

"Ernest!" she said with a bright smile. "Did you go to the typeface auction in Philadelphia?"

The archivist straightened and adjusted the horn-rimmed spectacles on his face. "Indeed I did! I was able to buy the Caslon type. Can you believe it? There were only two other bidders, and I outlasted them both."

If Romulus were not so intent on making progress on his injunction case, the discussion of typeface would have been a temptation. A new set of typeface was always of interest, but today he couldn't let himself be distracted by the wonderful vagaries of production issues.

Within ten minutes, Stella had pulled two boxes of notes and court filings regarding the old labor union case. They sat at a large oak table, surrounded by acres of wooden filing cabinets that created a cocoon of privacy.

"Start reading through the notes and pay special attention to the names and titles of anyone eager to shut down the labor union newsletters," Romulus instructed. He still didn't know who had filed the injunction against *Scientific World*, and the more insight he could get into the people at City Hall, the better. Stella's slender fingers were capable and efficient as she riffled through a dozen files, extracting relevant meeting notes. Soon she had amassed a stack three inches thick for them to pillage.

The paperwork was lethally dull, but he did his best to skim each page for relevant details. The burden was going to be on the government to prove his magazine was a danger to the public, which gave him an advantage, but it was still aggravating. How was he supposed to pay his employees next week? Evelyn always handled such details, but it would be up to him now.

Evelyn's shattered face as the carriage had pulled away still tugged at him. She didn't deserve what had happened to her. And Clyde! How could Clyde function as an engineer if he couldn't communicate with a team of sweaty construction workers? Design work in a laboratory was a possibility, but Clyde belonged out in the field, battling the elements, building the infrastructure of the coming century . . .

"Concentrate," Stella murmured beside him.

He glanced at her. "How do you know I'm not concentrating?"

"You're staring straight ahead instead of at the papers in your hand."

"And you have perfect concentration?" he challenged. "Even

209

when your world is falling apart, your friends are howling in need, and everything you've worked for is teetering on the brink of disaster?"

"That's when my focus is strongest," she said simply.

Something uncomfortable stirred deep inside him. Stella tugged at emotions he'd long since buried and wanted to stay dead, but she made it hard. She did everything at full throttle, with fire and determination and strength.

"That's what I like about you," he said. "You never go half-way."

Her eyes sparkled as she met his gaze. "I think you've been doing the same thing from the time you bought a failing magazine ten years ago."

His shoulders sagged a little. Ever since he'd signed that deal with the New York investors, the proudest accomplishment of his life was no longer *his* anymore. He'd found the perfect outlet for his erratic interests by publishing *Scientific World*, but his zeal came at a cost. He wouldn't be an easy man to live with, but at least Stella understood the all-consuming appetite for creative expression and exploration. She was a good match for him that way.

She sat three feet away from him, and he had to clasp the arms of his chair to keep from moving toward her. "Time to get back to work, Miss West," he said, turning his attention to a stack of legal drudgery. This page seemed pointless, so he flipped it over, hoping the next would be more useful. He skimmed the document quickly and, failing to find anything pertinent, went on to the next.

Yes, he would be a terrible husband. In all likelihood, he would have the same trouble Clyde had with Evelyn. When a man was too obsessed with his career, women felt neglected. He should have warned Clyde about how needy Evelyn could be.

Not that he could blame her. Any girl who had been abandoned by her father the way she had was likely to need—

Stella grabbed the page from his hands and set it down. "You've lost focus again."

He glared at her but remained mute. He really hated it when she was right.

"Wait here," she said as she placed his document back on the stack of unread papers. "I have an idea."

She walked to the front of the room to speak quietly to the archivist. After a moment, she returned with a ring of keys in her hand. "I'm going back into the stacks. Come with me," she suggested. She explained that the stacks were where volumes of old books and boxes of records kept track of two centuries of Boston history.

He glanced at the work mounded around them. Her papers were sorted into tidy stacks, with a page of handwritten notes complete with pagination and court case citations. His was a sloppy mound of unsorted papers. His eyes had dutifully traveled across every line of text on those pages, but he couldn't remember anything of what he'd read.

If she had something in mind to help him make progress on the mess he'd made of the notes, he wanted to hear it.

～◦✦◦～

Stella's nose twitched at the musty scent of old paper and leather bindings as she traveled several aisles deep into the storage room. Romulus followed, and with every step, she felt her attraction burn brighter. She cared for him beyond reason or restraint. The more she tried to ignore the untimely attraction, the more it magnified.

Which meant she was losing sight of Gwendolyn. She didn't resent Romulus's request for help with his court case. After all, he'd done plenty to help her navigate the quagmire of Boston political circles, and she was happy to repay the debt—but not if he was going to dither and waste time.

She finally reached the back aisle, probably the most isolated, private spot in all of City Hall. She turned to face Romulus and fought to maintain a calm expression. "What do you need to do to quit obsessing over Evelyn and Clyde?" she asked.

"How do you know I've been doing that?"

"Because you've glanced at your pocket watch four times in the last fifteen minutes, and I have a strong suspicion it's because Clyde is meeting with a specialist today."

"If all went well, the meeting happened an hour ago. They ought to know something by now."

"Then put it from your mind and get down to work."

He slanted a frustrated glance at her. "I seem to be incapable of compartmentalizing pieces of my soul the way you can." Some people might have taken that as an insult, but not Stella. She was proud of her ability to plow toward a solution to her problems and not wait for rescue.

"All that means is that I am capable of focusing on the task at hand, something you've confessed you struggle with. I'm here to help. For the past five days, I've neglected my search for A.G. or anything else relating to my sister's death to help you with this legal injunction, and all you can do is stare into space and fiddle with your watch. So quit wasting my time, Mr. White. Spill out all your vexations so we can get back down to work."

An avalanche of frustration came tumbling out. "Clyde and Evelyn are great, shining, idiotic fools!" he said. "They always have been. They've squandered the best years of their lives being angry at each other, and now any hope of reconciliation is almost lost. So, yes, I've been distracted. I count it as a sign of human compassion and a beating heart."

"Aren't you also guilty of squandering the best years of your life? You had a failed love affair as a young man, and now you've avoided any romantic liaison that delves deeper than the admittedly fine tailoring of your silk vest."

Wading into these waters was risky, but Romulus didn't seem to mind as he drew an inch closer to her. His face had an alive, alert look that always took her breath away. His scattered concentration was gone. His lids lowered, his voice softened, and he appeared entirely captivated by this conversation. "And why should the manner in which I carry out my romantic liaisons, or lack of such, be of any concern to you, Miss West?"

Never had she heard a voice so laden with goading, and it spurred her onward. This might turn into the biggest mistake of her life, but she'd never wanted a man as desperately as she longed for Romulus White.

And when a person wanted something this badly, it was only natural to reach out for it with both hands. She risked terrific humiliation, but there were worse things than enduring a little embarrassment. Going through life only half living was one of them.

She stepped closer, resting her hands on the lapels of his suit jacket, a faint smile hovering on her mouth. "I disagree with your arbitrary declaration of forty as an end to your eternal bachelorhood."

"Too soon?"

"Too cowardly and timid. And you don't strike me as a timid man."

She stood on tiptoe and touched her mouth to his. For a moment, he didn't move, didn't even breathe. Then, to her immense relief, he leaned down and kissed her back. A moment later, his arms hugged her close, and the world tilted and swayed as he curled her tighter into his embrace.

She'd been kissed before, but not like this. There was a sense of urgency and need that was impossible not to respond to. And when she withdrew, the faint grin on his face made her heart turn over.

"Why did you do that?" he asked softly.

"Because I care for you. And life can be short. I don't want to waste a single hour daydreaming about what might have been. I'd rather work toward making it happen."

His fingers were light as he tucked a strand of hair behind her ear, all the while smiling down at her with fondness. With affection. And something else she couldn't quite name. Regret?

"You know this is a mistake," he said pointedly.

"I don't see why it has to be." It felt absolutely perfect, but even now Romulus was glancing over her shoulder, his eyes widening as he scrutinized something directly behind her. The faint smile on his lips grew wider.

"Miss West," he whispered in a voice full of wonderment, "do you know there is an original edition of Audubon's *Birds of America* on the shelf behind you?"

Impossible! But when she whirled around, there it was, laid flat on a shelf to prevent damage to its antique binding. For any scientific artist, *Birds of America* was the Holy Grail, the *Mona Lisa*, the alpha and the omega of excellence in illustration. A labor of love filled with 435 full-color illustrations of birds painted in exquisite detail. No other collection of paintings came close to the stature of *Birds of America*. Her fingers trembled as she touched the dry leather binding.

"Let's find a table and explore," Romulus urged.

"Okay," she said breathlessly. It was impossible to tell who was more excited. She'd seen unbound plates from Audubon before, but never an entire volume. She didn't trust her trembling hands to carry the oversized book, but she trailed after Romulus as he carried it to an oak work table set deep in the stacks. The volume was three and a half feet tall and barely fit on the table.

"I'll bet you shirked your duties to the Transit Commission to come down here and gawk," he said with a grin.

"If I'd known it was here, I surely would have."

She held her breath as Romulus carefully opened the volume, revealing the splendid plumage of a belted kingfisher, the cerulean feathers of the bird's outstretched wings beautifully offset by black bands of color.

"Your dress matches the bird," Romulus whispered, making a bubble of laughter escape with a snort. He continued to point out the similarities in shade, striping, and the ruffle of her collar to the kingfisher's feathers. Then he asked if she could emulate the squawking rattle of the kingfisher's ungainly call.

"Stop," she begged. "We are looking at John James Audubon, the man in whose shadow I am destined to live in perpetuity. You're not demonstrating the proper degree of reverence."

"Don't tell me you are intimidated by Audubon."

She let her gaze devour the next illustration of a wood stork's weirdly asymmetrical body leaning over to pluck a snail from a marshy swamp. Its brilliance was humbling, and her ego needed a little propping up. "I am a peasant compared to Audubon. I'll never be this good . . ."

"Darling, you're twenty-eight years old. You have plenty of time to improve."

It wasn't the answer she wanted to hear, and she grinned as she elbowed him in the ribs. He replied by pulling her into his arms for another round of kissing. It went on until she was breathless and had to pull herself away.

"Audubon's engravings were all colored by hand," she said. "Each one took weeks. I can produce forty impressions per minute on a high-speed lithographic press."

"Excuses, excuses," Romulus sighed, but he was smiling as he turned back to the volume. She loved the way he teased her. Most men were intimidated by her, but not Romulus. He knew precisely how to let the steam out of her ego without truly hurting her feelings, and she adored him for it.

The next hour was possibly the most magical of her life. They turned pages and admired the masterpieces of the greatest naturalist painter ever to have lived. Time and again, they stopped to laugh, kiss, and flirt outrageously. But it didn't take long to get pulled back into the book beside them and marvel at the perfect dovetail of art and science in the antique volume.

Then they went back to kissing. At one point, she ended up on Romulus's lap as he tried to properly assess her weight by jostling her on his knee. At any moment, someone could enter the stacks and she'd have to spring up and scurry to the other side of the table, but for now, this interlude was too idyllic to worry about such things.

"Will you go for a ride on the swan boats with me next week?" Romulus asked. "I think I've verified your weight will not sink the boat."

"What are the swan boats?" she asked, still perched on his knee. She'd heard of the swan boats but couldn't quite remember where.

"They are paddle-wheeled boats on the lagoon at the Public Garden. They've got oversized swans carved onto their figurehead. The tourists love them. I see them as a perfect excuse to sit too close to a fetching lady while someone else paddles us around the pond."

Now she remembered where she'd heard of the swan boats. It was one of the first times she'd visited Romulus at *Scientific World*, and a woman had run sobbing from his office. Daisy— that was her name. Romulus had said she'd made far too much of their jaunt on the swan boats and now she wouldn't stop pestering him.

She rose from his lap and went to turn another page of *Birds of America*. "Is that where you take all your casual dalliances?"

"It's where a nice afternoon can be had," he said, a hint of tightness in his voice. "A simple day in the sunshine, entirely free of hysterics."

Hysterics. The word set her teeth on edge. "Don't think I'm ignorant of the origin of that word," she said. "It's from the Greek word for womb and is used by male physicians who wish to dismiss or belittle female emotions."

"I asked you for a boat ride," he said tensely as he replaced the oversized Audubon book in its place on the shelf. "That's all, just a boat ride. I've been very frank about my disinterest in a lasting romantic relationship because it's best to avoid setting up false expectations. The world is filled with attractive women, and I have no desire to be shackled to just one. Not yet."

And she had no desire to prolong this conversation.

"Fine," she said tightly. She brushed past him to head into the main room of the archives, where their stacks of paperwork were still scattered across the table.

Romulus adjusted his cuff links and refused to meet her eyes. "I trust we will be able to return to our respective roles and put this incident behind us?"

"Incident?" An incident was a mishap, like a glass of spilled milk. It wasn't a glorious hour of perfect delight with the other half of your soul.

"Now don't look at me like that," Romulus said. "You've always known how I felt about delving into any serious romantic rapport with any woman. Not before I'm forty—"

"If I hear the word *forty* one more time, I'll strangle you with your own cravat."

He rolled his eyes. "You remind me of our accountant, Millicent O'Grady. How often did I warn her? And still she's set her sights on me. It is embarrassing and awkward for us both."

"Is that what I am to you? Embarrassing and awkward?" She didn't bother to lower her voice, and Ernest sent a disapproving look at her from behind the front counter.

"Not unless you continue pestering me over things I've been very clear about. And forget about that boat ride. It was clearly a catastrophically bad suggestion."

Heat smoldered inside her, but the worst thing was, everything he said was right. From the day they'd met, he had laughingly asserted his desire to live as a carefree bachelor, and she'd ignored it. Somehow she'd thought the rules didn't apply to her because of this overwhelming, unwieldy, and glorious attraction. And he felt it too, she knew he did, but for some reason he shied away from it like a bat afraid of the sunlight.

"You're inherently shallow," she accused. It was childish, but she didn't care.

"I'm honest." He started gathering up the notes they had taken. Notes that *she* had taken. He'd done nothing but stare into space while she toiled away on his behalf. Even now, he was aimlessly paging through the stacks of notes and making a mess of things. He didn't know which papers belonged in which file.

She sighed in exasperation and pushed him away. "I'll do it," she muttered. She had too much respect for Ernest Palmer to return a pile of disorganized files to him.

"I'm not a complete idiot," Romulus said, and she handed him her page of handwritten notes.

"Here," she said. "This is a list of the case law the labor unions used to overturn the city's ruling six years ago. You can give it to your lawyer."

Romulus said nothing as he tucked her notes into the pocket

in his suit jacket. She didn't know if any of the work she'd done would yield results, but she needed to get out of here. She wasn't going to become a pest like Millicent O'Grady, and she'd neglected her own affairs too long on his behalf.

Silence raged as she completed sorting the rest of the documents into their proper files. She carried them to Ernest, who regarded her with serious eyes. For once, he didn't want to jabber about typeface or printing techniques, for which she was grateful. He had probably overheard every word of her embarrassing exchange with Romulus, but at least she wouldn't go to her grave wondering if Romulus might have proven to be the love of her life. She'd taken a peek beneath his glamorous exterior and found only an immature man incapable of growing up.

The carriage ride home was long and uncomfortable. She remained as far to one side of the padded seat as possible, her body snug against the carriage wall. He stared ahead, his expression like stone. Each time the carriage bumped or jostled, she clung to the armrest to avoid any possible contact.

It was a relief when the carriage drew to a halt before Evelyn's townhouse.

Before she could tell him not to bother, Romulus sprang down and offered her a hand. "Take care, Miss West," he said formally.

He'd probably used a similar phrase dozens of times over the years to extract himself from difficult situations.

"Thank you, Romulus. You are surely the glibbest man in all of Boston." Why was she acting like this? She hadn't behaved this childishly since, well . . . since she'd been a child. She just didn't know what to do with these bewildering emotions swirling inside. She couldn't be the only one feeling them, could she?

Romulus walked her to the front door. She needed to make it clear she'd have nothing more to do with *Scientific World*, to tell him she'd neglected her own responsibilities for too long.

Did he even care that she'd ignored her hunt for A.G. because of him?

"I'm going home to my parents," she said. "They may have insight into Gwendolyn's final months and should be healed enough to speak about it by now. I've neglected that shamefully in the past week."

"Give your parents my regards," he said politely.

She fumbled in her reticule for the door key. "After that, perhaps I'll go back to London. A new publishing house is set to open on Fleet Street." *Please ask me to stay. Please don't be so indifferent that you won't care if I get on a ship and sail three thousand miles away.*

But he said nothing, just dipped his head in a little bow and returned to the carriage.

She ought to go to London just to prove how little he meant to her. But why stop at London? She could go on to Rome. Or to Moscow. She'd heard Japan was becoming interested in lithography.

But in her heart, all she wanted to do was race home to the tiny village of Hudson, New York, with its village green and Sunday picnics and her mother's legendary lamb stew. She wanted to sit at her father's rolltop desk with all its hidey-holes and tiny drawers where he used to stash candy for her and Gwendolyn to find. She wanted to curl up in the turret bedroom she had once shared with Gwendolyn and dreamed of knights in shining armor and faraway lands. Her life had been perfect in Hudson, and she couldn't wait to get back to it.

Romulus White was nothing in comparison. He was fickle. Erratic. He was exactly what his long-ago love had accused him of being. An impossible man who couldn't commit to anything.

And yet Stella loved him anyway.

14

Stella had grown up in a rambling Queen Anne home with a wide front porch, spindle columns, and a turret that rose two stories tall. She and Gwendolyn had shared a bedroom in the upstairs turret. From one window, they could see all the way to Hudson's quaint main street, and to the right was her mother's two-acre rose and herb garden. On summer nights, they watched fireflies glimmer in the garden, and in the autumn they could open the window and smell apples brewing in the cider mill down the road.

Her father used the front two rooms of the house for his medical practice, but there were no patients here today. "I've sent everyone to Dr. Willis during your visit," her father said warmly as he pulled the carriage to a halt. "My beautiful daughter is home, and the proverbial fatted calf shall be slain. We shall have a feast, and her path shall be sprinkled with rose petals."

"Rose petals in April?" She laughed.

The front door opened, and her mother came bounding out the door, her smile blinding as she shrieked and tugged Stella into her warm, vanilla-scented embrace. Tears pricked the corners of Stella's eyes as she hugged her mother, for it had been years since she'd seen Eloise look so vibrant.

The instant she stepped inside her childhood home, the scent of lamb stew and peach cobbler enveloped her. The first few minutes back home were filled with laughter and good cheer, and Stella kept glancing over at her mother. Eloise looked healthy, with a bit of color in her cheeks and no longer so gaunt. She'd taken time to carefully style her fading blond hair into a neat coil on the back of her head, a welcome change from the scraggly braid her mother was too dispirited to comb while at the asylum.

A seed of hope took root. If her parents had managed to pull themselves out of the fog of despondency, perhaps she could begin asking the kinds of questions that had been impossible in the devastating weeks following Gwendolyn's death.

They moved through the front rooms toward the family's parlor, dining room, and kitchen. She let her eyes drink in the cherished, familiar sights. The grand old rolltop desk where she and Gwendolyn used to play, her father's collection of antique clocks lined up on the mantelpiece, her mother's potted herbs growing on the windowsill, and the steady pulse of the grandfather clock ticking in the corner. All of it brought a rush of comforting memories.

But something was wrong. Beside the grandfather clock was a stack of boxes that didn't belong.

"What are those?" she asked as her mother pressed a glass of sweet tea into her hands.

Some of the pleasure faded from her father's face at the question, but Eloise seemed unusually bright. "Oh, that's my little project," she said. "No need to worry about it today. I'll show it to you tomorrow."

Her gaze drifted back to the boxes. One of Gwendolyn's old dolls was propped up against the boxes, and it was an odd sight. That doll had been consigned to the attic twenty years ago—what did her mother want with it now?

"Your mother has been sorting through Gwendolyn's old things again," her father said. "It's harmless."

But he didn't sound very convinced.

Eloise went to the kitchen to spoon the stew into bowls. It had been a four-hour train ride from Boston, and Stella had craved her mother's slow-simmered lamb stew the entire time. Eloise always simmered it so long the carrots and potatoes almost blended in with the gravy, which used to be the only way she could coax Stella to eat her vegetables. To this day, it was the perfect meal to Stella. These overcooked vegetables and savory lamb stew signified home and comfort and every warm childhood memory.

They made small talk while Stella ate. Eloise chatted about their upcoming trip to Boulder Point, where they'd spent their honeymoon and would now spend four days at the finest suite in the resort hotel. Stella asked her father for his insight into sudden hearing loss. He couldn't give her much more information than Clyde's doctor at the hospital, but he promised to send an inquiry to a hearing specialist in New York. The inner ear was a mystery that was hard to study, and science had made very little progress in treating hearing loss.

At last the meal was finished, the plates cleared away, and her gaze strayed back to the tower of boxes. Her mother brightened when she saw Stella's curiosity.

"I've been organizing Gwendolyn's old things," she said as she lifted the lid from the top box. Inside were stacks of old childhood drawings and schoolwork in childish printing. Her mother had always saved anything her precious daughters produced, and now Stella suspected she tortured herself by endlessly sorting through them and reliving the memories in each faded piece of paper.

Eloise lifted out the top drawing, a wild splash of pastel colors on an oversized piece of paper. Stella remembered that painting, done during a summer they'd spent at her grandparents' farm in upstate New York because her father wanted to teach them about the natural world. On days when rain kept them trapped inside, she and Gwendolyn had opened a huge box of pastels to draw with.

Even as children, their distinct personalities were apparent in their artwork. While Stella captured the exact details of things like the fine threads of a bird's feather, Gwendolyn drew idealized images of castles and knights. Even as a child, Gwendolyn had dreamed of a perfect world.

Stella set down Gwendolyn's exuberant drawing of a castle. She pawed through the other papers in the box, finding only more artwork. "Are there letters from Gwendolyn in any of these boxes? From after she moved to Boston?"

"Oh my, no," her mother said. "Gwendolyn called us on the telephone once a week, but she never wrote."

Her spirit sagged, but only for a moment. "During those telephone calls, did she ever mention meeting with someone outside of work?"

"Like a beau?" her mother asked.

"Maybe. Or someone she was working with on a project. A mission." She hesitated to say Gwendolyn had been engaged in some sort of clandestine intrigue. It would only upset her parents, and they would hound her for more information. She didn't even know how to characterize the nature of Gwendolyn's relationship with the mysterious A.G. It seemed to have been a combination of hero-worship, romantic longing, and a crusading partnership all wrapped up into one puzzling liaison.

"The only thing your sister seemed to be obsessed with in

those final months was some high-flying ambition to attend law school," her father said.

Gwendolyn wanted to go to law school? It was the first Stella had ever heard of such a thing. As far as she knew, Gwendolyn's sole ambition in life was to find a good man to settle down with and have a passel of healthy, happy babies.

"It was pure nonsense," Eloise said dismissively. "She met some fellow who was encouraging her to reach higher than a secretarial position in City Hall. The law school at Buffalo had begun accepting women into their program, and this Michael fellow convinced Gwendolyn she ought to attend."

"Michael?" All of this was new information—and so out of character for her sister. "Who are you talking about?"

Her father's face darkened. "He was an attorney Gwendolyn met in Boston. He was far too old for her, but he was the one nudging her toward law school. I'm not sure why she was so keen to go—"

"It was to impress Michael," her mother interrupted. "And why shouldn't she? I didn't want my daughter to be a spinster, and just because he was a few years older—"

"He was forty-nine!" her father burst out. "No man that age ought to be prowling around my twenty-six-year-old daughter."

Stella's mind whirled. Gwendolyn hadn't told her a single thing about law school or this Michael fellow, and it was worrisome. She and Gwendolyn told each other everything, but now it seemed there were layers of secrecy Gwendolyn had built around herself, and Stella needed to know why. "Who is this Michael person?" she demanded.

"He was an attorney," Eloise said.

"*Is* an attorney," her father corrected. "Michael Townsend. He's very high up in the government and works at the State

House. He's a widower but still has no business hankering after a girl Gwendolyn's age."

Stella closed her eyes. She knew that name . . . she'd met him outside the Boston Athletic Club. The handsome man with prematurely gray hair. He and Romulus were sparring partners.

Romulus had introduced him as *the top attorney* in Massachusetts. At the time, she'd thought it was just an overblown compliment, but if Michael Townsend worked at the State House and was the *top attorney* in the state, it meant that Michael Townsend was the attorney general of Massachusetts. A.G.

It made perfect sense. In her letters, Gwendolyn had written that A.G. was a powerful and well-connected man. He had the authority to bring men to justice. He was a principled man who longed to remake Boston along the idealistic lines of their Puritan forefathers.

He also used a naïve and unprotected woman to spy on a network of corruption at City Hall. A.G. had a lot to answer for.

"I have to get back to Boston," she said.

"So soon?" her mother said.

She rushed over to place a kiss on her mother's check. "I'll try to come back next weekend," she said breathlessly, her mind flooding with the rush of new information. Was Michael Townsend a friend or an enemy? The only way she'd find out was by confronting him.

─◦⟨๑⟩◦─

Only in a state like Massachusetts would they call a State House built in 1798 the "new State House," but since the previous one had been built in 1713 when colonists were still paying homage to Queen Anne, perhaps the name was appropriate. Sitting on a prime lot at the top of Beacon Hill and featuring a classical redbrick façade, white columns, and golden dome, the State House was designed to look imposing.

Stella climbed the elegant staircases to the third floor, where the executive offices dominated most of the space. The office of the attorney general was in the rear wing, fronted by a reception room lined with hand-carved mahogany paneling, oriental carpets, and soft illumination from green-shaded lamps. A number of gentlemen waited in the fancy leather chairs lining the room. Oil paintings of white-wigged men from the eighteenth century stared down at her as she made her way to an official's desk in the front of the reception area.

"I'd like to see the attorney general, please."

The young man with thinning hair and an unfortunate herringbone tweed suitcoat looked up at her in disapproval. "Do you have an appointment, miss?" The man spoke in a low voice, made even softer by the muffling from the carpet and swags of draperies surrounding the windows.

"No. I'd like to make one for today. Now, if he's available." She spoke in a voice brimming with confidence, for timidity was not likely to get her a meeting with the state's highest attorney.

The young man coughed delicately. "I'm afraid the attorney general is an important man who is unable to meet with every person who wanders in from the street. The usual manner of contacting him is to send a letter to his office, where it will be addressed in due course."

In other words, where a clerk would process the letter with as little fuss as possible. She glanced down at the papers spread across the clerk's desk. Most appeared to be official correspondence, but the open appointment book was likely to contain Mr. Townsend's schedule for the day. She turned the book to face her, ignoring the sputtering outrage from the clerk.

"I see Mr. Townsend has an opening at one o'clock. Shall I

write my name in, or would you care to do that? Please mark down Stella Westergaard."

The only time she'd met Michael Townsend was on the steps of Boston Athletic Club, and Romulus had introduced her by her professional name, Stella West. Ever since she'd arrived in Boston, she'd deliberately kept her real last name private from everyone except people connected with the investigation, for she wanted no one making an association between her and Gwendolyn. That time was over.

"You have no authority to write anything in Mr. Townsend's schedule. I suggest you leave immediately, or I will be forced to summon a member of the security staff."

Some of the gentlemen in the room lowered their newspapers to peer at her, but she didn't care. Last night she had passed up an evening with her parents to race back to Boston, and Gwendolyn lay dead in a grave because of her association with Michael Townsend.

She leaned forward and lowered her voice. "Get up out of your seat and tell Mr. Townsend that Gwendolyn Westergaard's sister is here to see him. Tell him that I've been at City Hall and I know what the two of them were doing."

Something in the intensity of her voice must have cracked the young clerk's sense of decorum, for he nodded to a chair in the reception area as he stood. "Please have a seat. I will return momentarily."

She sat. She didn't know if the clerk was carrying her message to the attorney general or was in the process of summoning security, but she'd find out soon. If they threw her out of the State House, she'd be at the boxing club first thing on Tuesday morning to intercept the attorney general before his weekly appointment to spar with Romulus.

It turned out not to be necessary. A moment later, the door

to the administrative wing opened and Michael Townsend emerged. He was a tall but slender man, with silver hair neatly groomed and combed back from his face. With his blue eyes and patrician features, he was exactly the sort of cultured gentleman who would have appealed to her sister.

She stood as Mr. Townsend approached, guarded curiosity on his face. "We met outside the Athletic Club," she said bluntly. "Gwendolyn was my sister."

He nodded and gestured down the hall. "I remember. Please follow me, Miss Westergaard."

He led her into an office at the end of the hall. In contrast to the luxuriant furnishings in the reception area, Michael Townsend's office was spartan, with minimal furnishings and only a few framed diplomas on the wall. He offered her a seat in the leather chair facing his desk.

She got straight to the point. "I returned to Boston when I learned of Gwendolyn's death. I've been looking for you." She let the sentence hang in the air like a challenge.

He refused to take it. "First, let me extend my condolences about Gwendolyn's death. She was a wonderful young woman, and her death was a tragedy."

Despite his smooth words, there was a hint of sincerity in his eyes. She wasn't used to talking to strangers about Gwendolyn, and it hurt. Rather than looking at the compassion in Mr. Townsend's troubled eyes, she let her gaze roam around the office. Usually it was possible to glean insight into a person by looking at how they furnished the space where they spent most of their time, but there was little of a personal nature here. His desk was a glossy surface of polished walnut, with only two framed pictures in the corner, facing toward him. He noticed her gaze.

"My children," he said briefly and turned the frames to face

her. The first photograph showed a young man in college graduation robes, standing beside a girl a few years younger. The other
photograph was much older. It was a family portrait with Mr.
Townsend when his hair was still dark, seated stiffly beside a
handsome woman who held a baby girl on her lap, with the
boy standing beside them.

Stella's father had said Michael Townsend was forty-nine
years old and had no business consorting with Gwendolyn in
a romantic capacity. Despite the adoration in Gwendolyn's letters, possibly their association had been entirely platonic, but
his next words dispelled that notion.

"My wife died shortly after that portrait was taken," he said
as he returned the photographs to their proper places. "I've
been a widower for almost twenty years. I had hoped that was
coming to an end. It turned out not to be the case."

Stella said nothing, too intent on the pictures he had set back
on the desk. The surface of his desk was wide and spacious,
but in the far corners there was an almost imperceptible sheen
of dust. She noticed it only when he lifted the frames to reveal
narrow rectangles of clean space beneath.

There were three rectangles in the dust. A third photograph
must have been removed right before she came into the room.
She wanted to know whose photograph he felt compelled to
hide from her, but she had too many questions to squander on
idle curiosity.

"Why did you empty Gwendolyn's safe-deposit box?" She
was fishing, but given the way he shifted and looked away, she'd
hit the truth.

He recovered quickly. "Miss Westergaard, I gather you are
aware of my relationship with your sister. Gwendolyn was doing
heroic work in helping me root out corruption in the city. In
so doing, she had gathered important and sensitive informa-

tion. I needed to retrieve it quickly before it could fall into the wrong hands."

"So you admit she was spying at City Hall on your request?"

He held her stare, his face so still it might have been carved from stone. She grew uncomfortable beneath his unwavering scrutiny, but at last he answered.

"Of course. And I know from the letters the two of you exchanged between Boston and London that you were well aware of Gwendolyn's activities."

"I want those letters back," she snapped. She was certain Gwendolyn would not have thrown them away. Michael Townsend had stolen them from the safe-deposit box along with everything else that was in there.

"I will have them delivered to you immediately," he said smoothly.

"What else was in that box?"

He took a moment before answering. "Gwendolyn was well positioned within City Hall to keep an eye on things. She took copious notes documenting suspicious activities. Her notes were stored in the box."

"I want them, too."

"No."

His answer was firm and unequivocal, enough to heat her temper to a low simmer. She didn't know if Michael Townsend could be trusted or not. All she knew for certain was that if Gwendolyn had never met him, she would be alive today. She would be savoring dreams of a future husband, of decorating the house she would someday turn into a home for laughing children. She wouldn't have been pulled cold and lifeless out of a dirty river.

"You have no right to the contents of that box," she said. "My parents are Gwendolyn's heirs, and those notes belong to them."

"They were addressed to me. And Stella, you really *don't* want to get into a legal argument with me." The framed diplomas on the wall behind him gave proof of his credentials. He also occupied the most powerful legal office in the state, with armies of attorneys and law enforcement officials at his beck and call.

"You wanted Gwendolyn to go to law school," she said.

He nodded.

"Why?"

"She had the intelligence, but more important, she had a heart for it. She believed in standing up for people who had no voice. I've never met a woman with a greater sense of idealism just waiting to break free. She could have funneled that passion into a brilliant career in the law. With my backing, no one would have dared to slight her."

Stella didn't believe him. More than anything else in the world, Gwendolyn had dreamed of marriage and motherhood. While Stella reached out with both hands for a professional career, Gwendolyn was happy to take a secretarial position until she found the right man to marry.

"Who killed her?" she asked.

For the first time, he seemed taken aback. "What makes you think someone killed her?"

"Gwendolyn was a strong swimmer. She would not have drowned in five feet of water."

Mr. Townsend's reply was dismissive. "I saw the results of the police investigation myself. It was an accident. She drowned."

"What was she doing on that bridge in the middle of the night? Was she there to meet you?"

He shook his head. "We limited our meetings to no more than once per week, and always near her boardinghouse where the streets were well lit and safe. I have no explanation for why she was in south Boston, but Gwendolyn suffered from insomnia. It is possible she went walking when she was unable to sleep."

It was true that Gwendolyn often had trouble sleeping, but Stella doubted she would have been so foolish as to go walking after dark in a dangerous part of town. "Gwendolyn was involved in dangerous work," she insisted. "It's possible someone tried to silence—"

"You're exaggerating," he interrupted. "She noticed men skimming from the public coffers and called it to my attention. She was also keeping an eye on how contracts were being awarded, because I suspected some men of graft and bribery. We're talking about a few hundred or perhaps a few thousand dollars at most. This isn't the sort of thing men would kill over. I would never have asked that of Gwendolyn had there been any indication . . ."

His voice trailed off. Mr. Townsend looked rattled, his voice uncertain. Perhaps he wasn't so sure about the circumstances of Gwendolyn's death, after all. If he suspected foul play, had he done anything about it? Or was he protecting his reputation by letting this inconvenient death be quietly swept under the carpet? For all his fine talk about justice and valor, if word got out he was meeting a woman half his age under cover of darkness, ultimately leading her to a violent death, it would forever mar his sterling reputation.

She looked him in the eye and asked the question she needed to know. "Did you love her?"

Annoyance flashed across his face. "Yes, I loved her." His voice was harsh and defensive, but as his gaze strayed out the window, a shadow of pain darkened his eyes. "I loved her," he said again, softer this time. He turned farther away from her and swallowed hard. It might have been her imagination, but it seemed his entire body sagged beneath a terrible weight. "I loved her," he whispered. "I loved her very much."

He sounded shattered. It was impossible to doubt him. She'd seen too much of that haunted, lost look not to recognize it.

If Michael Townsend had truly loved Gwendolyn, then he would be the best person to help solve her death. Gwendolyn had trusted him implicitly. She'd called him a modern-day King Arthur, a man willing to battle dragons no matter how desperate the odds.

But Stella didn't trust him. Not yet. She glanced at the photographs clustered at the corner of his desk. "Who is in the third picture?" she asked and glanced pointedly at the third mark in the dust.

"Gwendolyn."

She drew a quick breath. "May I see it?"

He opened his top desk drawer with a whisper-smooth glide, removed a large silver frame, and handed it to her. The beauty of the photograph drove the breath from her lungs.

It was Gwendolyn, more radiant and beautiful than Stella had ever seen before. It must have been taken in a studio, for the soft illumination of light streaming from a window high overhead could have been created only by a master photographer. Gwendolyn's face was in three-quarter profile, her eyes tilted to look upward toward the light. Her skin was luminous, the glints in the coils of her pale hair adding subtle depth. Only the barest hint of a smile graced her face, but she looked glorious and lovely. Happy.

"It was taken at a studio on Tarnower Street," Mr. Townsend said. "The photographer keeps plates of his work, and I can have copies of this photograph made for both you and your parents."

The lump in her throat made it impossible to respond. Gwendolyn had always been pretty, but this photograph captured a depth of beauty Stella had never seen before. She instinctively knew it was because Gwendolyn was in love, flush with radiance and joy so powerful they made her glow.

"Thank you," she managed to say. "I would like that very much."

She handed the picture back to him, and he set it beside the other two photographs on the desk. "I will also make arrangements to have the letters you wrote to Gwendolyn returned to you. Please understand, I cannot return the other notes she compiled. Your sister's greatest accomplishment was the information she gathered in those months before her accident. I cannot turn them over to you while the investigation into corruption at City Hall is still pending." He paused and swallowed, his gaze straying to Gwendolyn's photograph. "She had the heart of a warrior. I won't abandon her mission."

He told Stella to make an appointment with the clerk at the front desk for next week, when he would have her letters and two copies of the photograph ready for her.

It was a dismissal. A gentle one, but not something she could ignore.

As she left the office, she knew only one thing for certain. Michael Townsend was lying to her. Gwendolyn's photograph was much larger than the modest outline in the dust from the third photograph.

There was someone else he did not want her to know about.

Romulus dragged out the bottom drawer from Evelyn's desk and set it alongside the others on the table. He was making a mess of her carefully organized drawers, but he couldn't find the accounts-receivable ledger and was tired of bending over to peer into the back of the oversized drawers.

He'd come to the office an hour early today to search for the ledger before his staff began to arrive. It was embarrassing to be this incompetent in managing the weekly operations of the magazine, and he didn't want an audience as he stumbled through managing his first payroll. His employees were already skittish about the stability of the magazine, and with Evelyn gone, that concern was compounded. Everyone depended on Evelyn, and although Romulus could be counted on to swan about town solidifying their reputation as the premier science journal in the nation, they didn't know if he could run it.

His staff expected to be paid today. The infusion of cash from the New York investors was being paid in installments. He wasn't certain there was enough cash in their account to cover all the pending expenses, so yesterday he'd gone to a pawn shop to earn a quick five hundred dollars for his diamond cuff links.

He'd stayed up past midnight writing out bank checks, but he couldn't make sense of the double-entry bookkeeping method Evelyn used. She'd tried to explain it to him once, but it was so convoluted he'd quickly lost interest and swore she could have his firstborn child if she promised never to burden him with an accounting ledger again.

It was going to be a while before Evelyn returned to rescue him from his incompetence. He'd had a telegram from Evelyn saying there had been no improvement in Clyde's hearing, so they would be staying at the health resort until the swelling in his ears had diminished entirely.

It meant Romulus was going to have to handle all the financial aspects of the magazine, and frankly, that terrified him. What was the difference between the bank-payments ledger and the magazine-invoice ledger? They seemed to keep track of the same payments, and he didn't want to be dinged twice for the same bills. Should he ignore one of them?

The office door opened with a gentle *snick* and Millicent O'Grady entered, gaping at the catastrophic mess on Evelyn's desk. The redheaded accountant had been with them for two years, and she'd been making calf eyes at him for most of it. She was the last person he wanted to ask for help. It might stoke the romantic fantasies she harbored toward him, but he couldn't have his incompetence exposed to the rest of his employees. He had the best staff in all of Boston, and they might start jumping ship if they sensed the magazine was in danger.

"Miss O'Grady," he said pleasantly as he slid Evelyn's drawers back into their slots. "I'd like a word with you about the accounting ledgers." With luck, he'd be able to dump them all on her desk so he could return to battling the injunction against the magazine. The first court date was next week, but he'd made little progress in mounting a defense while also trying to manage Evelyn's responsibilities.

Millicent removed her hat, smoothing strands of hair back into her coif. "Yes, sir," she said a little breathlessly and approached the desk.

The door opened again, and three members of the editorial staff wandered in. A copyeditor and his lead chemistry writer followed. He exchanged nods with the men as they removed their coats and drifted toward their desks.

"Let's speak in my office, please." He didn't like encouraging her and had a firm rule about never meeting with any female employee aside from Evelyn behind a closed door, but this couldn't be helped. He scooped up the sales-invoice ledger and all the bank registers.

He dumped the ledgers on his desk and waited until Millicent was inside before closing the door. He adjusted the blinds on his office window to be sure they were as open as possible. "Evelyn always handles payroll and the financial ledgers," he said. "I know you handle our basic accounting, but can you shed any light on Evelyn's double-entry bookkeeping? It would be best to hand that task to someone with experience."

Millicent blanched. "Oh my, I've never even tried it. Miss Evelyn is very particular about the way she handles the books. I just keep track of accounts receivable."

He tried to block frustration from leaking into his voice. "Is there anyone else in the office who would know how she did it?"

"No, sir. I handle the arithmetic aspects, but she handles the complicated things."

"I see," he said, trying to force back the rising tide of panic. He could hire a professional accountant, but after completing payroll last night, there wasn't a lot of leeway in the budget for new staff. Two of their advertisers were demanding refunds rather than accepting an extension of their advertising contract, but he didn't want to pay. If word of that got out, others would want refunds, as well.

"Thank you, Miss O'Grady. That will be all."

Millicent left, and he stared at one of Evelyn's accounting ledgers, wondering what to do next. He picked up a pen and tried to make a list, but it seemed overwhelming.

The office door opened with a bang, startling him and causing a glob of ink to spill across Evelyn's tidy accounting ledger.

He looked up to see Stella tearing through the main office door. She careened through the desks in the front office and yanked open his door without knocking. It was impossible to tell if she was terrified or delighted.

"I need your help!" she gasped out. "Michael Townsend is A.G. He admitted it."

Romulus stood. "What are you talking about?"

"The man Gwendolyn was meeting. A.G. I assumed A.G. was someone's initials, but it's the *attorney general*."

That was a surprise. He'd always known Michael Townsend to be a straight-laced, bookish type of man, not the sort to run around under cover of darkness.

He sat down, using his handkerchief to blot the ink stain on the ledger before it soaked through to damage other pages. "What do you want me to do about it?"

"I need your help! He's brushing me off and refuses to turn over Gwendolyn's papers, even though he admits he took them."

He balled up the handkerchief and tossed it into the trash. It was a fine silk handkerchief, ruined because Stella West couldn't walk through a door without terrorizing the office. "Does Michael Townsend think your sister was murdered?"

"No."

"Excellent. You can stop gallivanting around town and pestering law-abiding citizens."

"But I think he's lying! Or at the very least, he isn't telling me everything. I can't just walk away. He knows more than he's telling. I'll bet you can get through to him."

His hands clenched into fists. Stella's sister had died five months ago, and there was no need for urgency in reopening the case of a woman who probably died due to an unfortunate accident. "My magazine is hanging on by a thread," he said tightly. "Payroll is due today, and the books are a mess. Advertisers are starting to line up for refunds, and if I can't keep this ship afloat, members of my staff will start leaving. My association with you has called my professional judgment into question and may well have contributed to the injunction against the magazine. And you want me to drop everything so I can go pester the state's top attorney?"

She winced a little but did not back down. "Would you?"

"Look around you!" he hollered as he shot to his feet. "On the other side of my office window are men and women who depend on this magazine for their livelihoods. And downstairs are another thirty people who are expecting to be paid. Forgive me for not having you at the top of my priority list today."

"You don't need to talk down to me." She said it as though he were the irrational one in this conversation. Didn't she understand what was happening?

"I had to sell a pair of diamond cuff links to ensure the payroll checks won't bounce!"

"Horrors. However shall you hold your head up when so shabbily dressed?"

His eyes narrowed. This wasn't about the attorney general; she was angry he wasn't ready to fall on his knees and lavish her with rose petals and love poems. He drew a steadying breath. "Look, I'm sorry if I disappointed you—"

"Sorrow pours from you like a tidal wave. It's a miracle I'm able to remain standing in the path of it." Her voice was hard, and her eyes glittered.

"I don't want to get married," he snapped. "I have no room in my life for any kind of romantic commitment, and since that seems to be the direction you are pushing us, it's best to be frank. I have no time today to go chase down your ghosts."

Stella sucked in a quick breath. "Gwendolyn isn't a ghost. She was *real*. She was beautiful and courageous and one of the finest—"

"And she's dead." He pointed to the people on the other side of his office window. "They are alive. They depend on me, and I owe them my loyalty. Now, get out of my office so I can work. Find someone else to be your knight in shining armor. I'm done. Finished. I truly have no desire to see you again or pursue our association any further."

"You don't mean that."

He paused, closed his eyes, and counted to ten. She was right. If he never saw Stella again, it would be a loss he'd never forget. She'd become a good friend. Even during the difficulty of the past few weeks as they'd navigated through this unwieldy and unwelcome attraction, Stella would forever hold a place of fondness in his heart. He couldn't even look at her as he blotted the remainder of the spilled ink on his desk.

"Stella, I'm sorry. You're right, I don't mean it, but I'm terrified of my business going under, and I don't have time to indulge your need to hunt down mysteries that will probably never be solved." He stacked the accounting ledgers in the center of his desk. "And I'm not ready for the kind of relationship you seem to be hoping for. I'm sorry."

A braver man would have looked her in the face as he spoke, but he wasn't feeling particularly brave or proud of himself right now. Stella was a once-in-a-lifetime woman, and he didn't have the backbone to reach out toward what she offered him. "It would be best if you left now," he said as kindly as he could while his world crumbled around him.

"I'm sorry for disturbing your day," she said through gritted teeth, then marched out of his office with the pride of a queen.

~*~

After leaving *Scientific World*, Stella stood on the bottom step of the building, staring stupidly at the wide trench of the subway. She'd managed to hold on to the unraveling threads of her dignity before leaving Romulus's office, but it had been hard.

What was she supposed to do now? Romulus had rejected her again. It hurt even worse than before.

Hurt was such a mild word for this aching, confused sense of disappointment. No matter how long she lived, she couldn't imagine meeting anyone quite so perfect for her as Romulus White. He was a bold, flamboyant force of laughter and inspiration who seemed to be her perfect match. He would be the measuring stick against which she judged all future men, and no matter how much she wished it otherwise, she doubted anyone could ever surpass him.

She didn't know what to do. She stood on the street and watched the dozen carpenters working in the subway trench before her. The rubble and debris from the explosion had been cleared away, the gas lines repaired, and the men had returned to work. The trench had been completed, and cranes lowered pre-assembled wooden braces into the tunnel. Carpenters nailed them into place, filling the air with the steady clatter of hammers. Progress on the monumental infrastructure of this amazing city continued at full steam.

It was as if the explosion had never happened. Her heart

was broken, Clyde might never hear again, and Gwendolyn was dead, but work on the subway plowed ahead. Someday soon, thousands of people would ride on this new and miraculous underground train, and no one would remember the people who had labored and sometimes died during its construction.

It was time to put her broken heart into perspective. Romulus had been honest since the very beginning, but in her arrogance, she'd refused to believe such rules applied to her. She probably deserved a humiliating set down like this. And she shouldn't have pestered him on a day like today. All her life, she'd hoped to be the type of supportive woman who would prop up her man when he needed strength. Instead, she'd let her emotions overrule her better judgment.

Well, enough moping. It was time to renew her commitment to finding out what had happened to Gwendolyn, and that couldn't happen if she kept becoming distracted by Romulus.

She wanted a copy of that photograph of Gwendolyn. She'd keep it on her nightstand and use it as a talisman to remind her why she'd come to Boston in the first place. It wasn't to flirt with Romulus or draw pictures for the magazine.

Without further dawdling, she turned and headed toward Tarnower Street and the photographer's studio. Michael Townsend had said he would have a copy made for her, but she wanted one now.

Tarnower Street was far from the commotion of subway construction, and for a moment, Stella was able to walk down the cobblestone, tree-lined avenue and see what Boston ought to look like. Shops of tidy red bricks, glossy iron railings, and bow-fronted windows. The photographer's studio was nestled between a stationer's shop and a lawyer's office. A little bell rang when she stepped through the front door.

There was nobody here. The room was small and barren, with

only a few waiting chairs and a counter at the front, bearing a sign. *At work in the dark room. Please do not disturb.*

"I'll be with you in three minutes!" a voice hollered from behind a closed door.

"Thank you," Stella called back. In the meantime, she admired the photographs hanging on the walls. Gwendolyn was not among the portraits on display, but the photographer's artistry was astounding. He didn't merely sit a person in a chair and record the image. He seemed to capture something of each subject's spirit. One picture showed a withered old woman holding a photograph of a soldier in a Civil War uniform. Had the soldier been her husband? Son? Whatever the story, the old woman's face contained a blend of pride and grief as she looked directly at the camera with a glint of challenge in her eyes.

Other photographs contained no people but captured a ray of sunshine as it broke over a rusted wagon wheel in a field of rye. Photography was evolving into an entirely new form of artistic expression, but she was surprised to see it on display here at a photographer's studio. There was no money in such photographs—only portraiture could pay a photographer's bills.

The door to the dark room opened, and the acrid scent of developing chemicals wafted from the open door. A man with shaggy gray hair emerged, wiping his hands on a cloth. "Peter Mc-Kendry," he introduced himself. "What can I do for you, ma'am?"

"I am hoping to commission two copies of a photograph you took last year. Gwendolyn Westergaard," she said.

"Certainly, ma'am! What a lovely young lady. She is doing well, I take it?"

Why should she expect this man to know of Gwendolyn's passing? It had barely warranted a brief paragraph buried deep in the Boston newspapers.

"No. My sister passed away in December."

After his initial shock, the photographer expressed all the proper condolences, then proceeded to open his ordering book and write up her request. While he completed the paperwork, Stella continued to admire the photographs on display.

She nodded toward the portrait of the steely-eyed old woman holding the picture of the soldier. "There *must* be a story behind that portrait."

"Indeed, ma'am. The woman is Mrs. Henry Grosjean. She and her husband had plans for missionary service abroad, but the war interrupted their dream. Her husband was killed at Chancellorsville, but after the war, she sold everything and headed out on her own. That photograph was taken when she returned to Boston after thirty-two years of service in India."

Stella gazed at the woman with new respect. Her husband's death must have been devastating, but Mrs. Grosjean hadn't let it derail her dream. Such fortitude was humbling, for Stella had done little but indulge in anger and bitterness since Gwendolyn's death. That bitterness had blotted out the finer aspects of her character, spurring anger at God for the injustice dealt to her family.

It seemed Mrs. Grosjean peered out of the photograph, straight into the moral failings of Stella's soul. *Do you love God only when he is good to you?*

Stella flinched. It was as if the old woman had spoken the words, but they came from inside Stella. It made her uncomfortable, and she stepped away to examine a photograph of dew drops glistening on a cobweb.

"You have a very unique style," she commented. "I love the artistry in your work."

He straightened in pride. "Thank you, ma'am. I've had the studio for two years now, and it has truly been an honor to be able to do this sort of work."

"I am surprised at how many landscapes you have on display. I thought portraiture was the only way to make photography profitable."

"It's the fastest, but there are plenty of other ways photographers are using their skills these days. Newspapers are using photographs for big events. Then there is more mundane work like pictures for product catalogs or architectural work. I got my start photographing for the police department." He shuddered a bit. "I'm glad I'm not there anymore."

"What did you do for the police department?"

"Mostly booking photographs for criminals. Sometimes I went to photograph a crime scene. The worst was the murder victims. Like I said, I'm glad I'm not there anymore."

Stella's mouth went dry. The medical examiner claimed to have taken no photographs during Gwendolyn's autopsy because he did not consider it a suspicious death, but might the police have taken one after they pulled Gwendolyn from the river? At that point, they would not have known if it was a case of foul play or not.

She forced her tone to remain calm, even though every nerve ending in her body seized with tension. "Do the photographers work for the police, or are they commissioned case by case?" She'd already been frozen out by the police department, but if their photographers were booked for special jobs . . .

"They are commissioned by the job. The police don't have a dark room or space for equipment, so a bunch of photographers lease space at a shared studio near the wharves. The police always know where to find a photographer when they need one."

She swallowed hard, her mind whirling. It was a long shot, but one she needed to pursue. If there was a photograph of Gwendolyn taken on that morning anywhere in the city, she was going to find it.

16

The White Oak Health Resort was nestled in the middle of the Adirondack Mountains in upstate New York. The sprawling lodge looked like a place where rugged outdoorsmen and hunters might come spilling out the door, shotguns in hand as they trekked into the wilderness. That illusion was destroyed when nurses wearing white uniforms and little folded caps on their heads pushed patients in wheelchairs outside, walking them to the wide slate terrace that had an excellent view of the mountains. Some of the patients came for the thin air to recover after pneumonia, but most suffered from an assortment of broken bones, nerve complaints, or other disorders that required long-term care.

Evelyn furrowed her brow as she headed to the small room that served as a library for the resort's patients. None of the books she'd brought to Clyde so far had been of interest, but perhaps today she could stumble upon the perfect novel or history book that would cut through the veil of his melancholy and spark his curiosity back to life.

Had she done the right thing by bringing him here? It didn't feel like it. The doctors in Boston had advised complete rest and immobility, and in those first terrible days after the explosion, he had been in such excruciating pain from every jolt or vibration that she'd assumed the health resort was Clyde's best chance of letting his shattered eardrums recover.

They hadn't. Each day, he let her push him in a wheelchair onto the terrace, where he stared in stony silence at the mountainside. It was chilly, and she always draped a blanket over his lap, making him look even more like an invalid. His ears no longer hurt, so the wheelchair was no longer necessary, but the majority of his day was still spent in a chair, staring into the distance. When she brought him books, he managed a polite smile in acknowledgment, but it vanished quickly. Within a few minutes, the book would lay open on his lap as he went back to staring at the mountainside. There had been no improvement in his hearing.

She squatted down to get a better view of the British literature collection. Might Shakespeare interest him? She'd just opened a copy of *A Midsummer Night's Dream* when a nurse entered the library.

"Mrs. Brixton?" she asked.

Evelyn stood. She'd resumed using her married name at the clinic. It avoided the strange looks and made tending Clyde easier, even though they still did not share the same room. "Yes?"

"A telegram has arrived for your husband, but he's sleeping. Shall I leave it with you?"

Evelyn took the telegram and thanked the nurse. Should she open it? It might be urgent, but Clyde got so little sleep, and she didn't want to awaken him unnecessarily. Opening the note, she quickly read the demoralizing news.

The Boston Transit Commission had fired him. They didn't use that term, of course. They used pretty language thanking him for his service and wishing him a speedy recovery, then suggested he need not feel compelled to return to Boston. They had hired another engineer to oversee the Tremont segment of the subway, and his services were no longer needed. She sagged as she read the note.

This telegram was going to be a kick in the teeth. Maybe she shouldn't even give it to him, for he didn't need this kind of stress.

She went for a walk among the pine-scented trails that meandered around the resort. The peaceful calls of mourning doves and the gentle rustle of pine needles were in stark contrast to the turmoil in her mind. This latest news was going to devastate Clyde, and she'd give anything if she could shield him from the blow.

She hadn't been a very good wife to him. He hadn't been a very good husband, either, but the qualities about Clyde that frustrated her had all been in full view while they were courting. At the time, she'd thought his reckless spirit and his high-flying dreams had been thrilling. Why had she assumed he would suddenly be tamed after walking down the aisle?

A man could not be expected to turn those qualities off and on as her whims dictated. He hadn't been the best of husbands, but there had been stretches of real happiness, and she missed them. By the time Clyde had tried to become a better husband, she had given up, and that was her fault, not his. It wasn't his fault she'd lost the baby, even though for years it had felt good to nurture that bitter seed of anger against him. It was easier to be angry than to keep hurting.

She wanted a man in her life again. A real man, not one from a girlhood fantasy. She didn't need a man to bring her chocolate or flowers. She needed the kind of man who saddled up and got the job done, whether it was picking up a shovel to work on

a subway or rushing across the state to help a friend in need.
A man who could fix the leaky roof or provide electricity to
a greenhouse to ensure the hummingbird eggs would hatch.

Men like Clyde Brixton were the heart, soul, and muscle that
made the world go around. Clyde could be clumsy, brash, and
thoughtless, but she was no princess, either. They were both
flawed, broken people, but she loved him. She'd spoken holy
vows with him that could never be set aside, even though she'd
done her best to ignore them for the past six years.

She wished with all her heart she didn't need to deliver this
terrible telegram to him, but it was time. When she returned
to the lodge, he was out on the terrace, a book lying open and
unread on his lap as he stared into the distance. He hadn't yet
noticed her approaching.

She bowed her head and said a short prayer. It was impossible
to know why God had sent this calamity into their lives, but
there was a reason and they needed to accept and deal with it.

She walked to Clyde and set the telegram on his lap.

He smiled a bit in greeting, his eyes impossibly blue. She
tried to memorize his face, his expression, the faint hope in
his eyes. This was the last moment before the final foundations
crumbled beneath him.

He turned his attention to the telegram, staring at it for a full
minute. A meadowlark chattered in a nearby bush, and a squirrel
gnawed on a piece of bark in the garden. Clyde was motionless save for the muscle in his jaw that repeatedly clenched and
released. Finally, he handed the note back to her. There was no
change in his expression. She grabbed the small notepad and stub
of a pencil she carried in her skirt pocket and scribbled a message.

Clyde? Talk to me. Tell me what you're feeling.

She tried to give him the notepad, but he pushed it aside and
looked the other way.

She changed sides to hunker down next to him, but he shifted again and looked in the opposite direction.

A man had to have some dignity. In his own way, he had just asked for privacy, and it was not an unreasonable request. She complied, but left instructions to the nurse to keep an eye on him. She didn't think Clyde would do anything foolish, but it seemed he was being systematically stripped of everything that mattered to him.

She retreated to the lodge's library to sulk for only a moment before regrouping to start a battle plan. Clyde Brixton was not going to become a useless cripple. She didn't know precisely what fate had in store for them, but it wasn't going to be staring mutely into space while the seasons passed. The library had medical texts, history books, and inspiration. As long as she and Clyde both had a brain, they would not give up. It wasn't in their nature—not since the day they'd met more than a decade ago and had the impossible task of figuring out how to keep hummingbirds alive in captivity.

Clyde was falling deeper into a hole. He was the only one who could pull himself out, but she could throw him a lifeline. The seed of an idea took root and grew. She dragged out dozens of books, flipping through them quickly and assessing various angles. She scribbled notes and made plans, not even breaking for dinner. She'd had no coffee all day, but excitement thrummed through her veins, and it was going to be impossible to sleep with all the hopes and possibilities swirling in her mind.

She sat at the table long into the night, dialing up the flame in the kerosene lantern as she plowed through book after book. Her plan would only work if Clyde cooperated, and he was notorious for kicking up a fuss.

After breakfast the next morning, she went in search of him. As expected, he was sitting on the terrace, a blanket over his lap, staring at the mountains. Already he was starting to look more like an aging, depressed invalid. Dark circles shadowed his eyes, and she suspected he must not have slept much last night, either.

She'd spent an hour this morning drafting a carefully worded note to him. She knelt on the chilly slate stone beside him and set the note on his lap. It didn't take him long to read it. He rolled his eyes, snorted, and threw it on the ground. She picked it up.

"Beethoven was stone deaf when he wrote the Ninth Symphony," she said, angling to stand in front of him so he could see her. "If he can write a symphony, don't tell me you can't design an electrical grid or write a book about it."

She repeated the words and pointed to her note, which said the same. It was unlikely Clyde could work out in the field again. Communication was too important on a large-scale engineering site to have a deaf man at the helm, but that didn't mean he had to abandon his calling. Half of Clyde's professional troubles stemmed from his inability to get along with Thomas Edison, a man who had starkly different views about how the cities should be electrified. It was an important technological issue that so far had remained confined to engineers, city planners, and corporate financiers. As city after city began to build electrical grids, not many ordinary citizens understood the controversy about alternating currents versus direct currents, and yet it was those ordinary people who would be most affected by the outcome of the controversy.

Evelyn knew how to communicate to laypeople. Clyde did too if he would take the time to do so. Together they could write a book about the history and turbulent development of how electricity was planned, financed, and being unrolled across the nation. Was there anything more significant to the lives of everyday Americans than getting electricity into their homes?

She and Clyde could write about everything from the plans to use Niagara Falls to deliver hydroelectric power for the entire eastern seaboard to the bold plans to light up the nation house by house.

Clyde's mouth tightened. "I am an engineer," he said loudly. "It's the only thing I know how to be. The only thing I want to be. I'm not a writer." Already his speech was starting to regress. His words were a little slurred, almost as if he were drunk.

She reached for the piece of paper and scribbled quickly. *We can do it together. I'll help you.*

He grabbed the paper and crumpled it up, tossing it aside. "I don't want your pity."

"Then think of something else to do. Teach. Learn how to design houses. Just do something besides sitting in that chair and staring at the mountains."

He looked at her blankly, for she had been babbling too quickly again. She reached for the notepad and wrote out her thoughts. There were plenty of things Clyde could do if he would pull himself out of this despondency. She wanted to come alongside him and be a team again, and it had nothing to do with pity.

Last night when she'd been cocooned in the library and had tentatively outlined the possible chapters for a book about electricity, she hadn't been feeling pity, she'd been excited. She could be more than Romulus's managing editor. She could create something on her own and learn how to be a better wife to Clyde.

She scribbled another note. *It will be fun. It will be something new for us.*

Clyde frowned. "It won't be fun. I've never been able to make you happy."

Her heart squeezed. Nobody could make another person happy, but she had certainly been masterful at blaming Clyde for everything that went wrong in their marriage. She hunkered down before his chair so she could be on the same level as he.

"I love you." The words were simple enough she knew he'd be able to read her lips, and he did.

"Shut up."

"I love you," she repeated. When he turned his face away, she framed his head with her hands and turned it so he couldn't look away. "I love you. *I love you.*"

He jerked away. "Don't lie to me. I swear that will push me right over the edge." He stood and stalked toward the path skirting the meadow. It was hard to keep up with his long-legged stride.

"Don't walk away while I'm talking to you!" she yelled after him, but he didn't break stride. It was idiotic to shout at a deaf man's back, and they were going to have to figure out some way to communicate with each other. She didn't know if his deafness would last another week, another year, or forever, but she loved him and couldn't stand aside while he withered beneath despair.

The path took them past the outdoor patio, where a number of patients still lingered at the outdoor breakfast table. People gawked at them, but she didn't care. Neither did Clyde as he shook off the hand she clapped on his shoulder in a vain attempt to slow him down.

She hiked up her skirts and sprinted ahead of him, stepping into his way and blocking the path. "Don't run away from me!" she hollered. Which was stupid, but it made her feel better to yell.

"Go home, Evelyn. Let it go." He averted his face again, and it was maddening. They couldn't go through the rest of their lives if all he had to do was turn his face away like a child refusing to eat whenever he wanted to shut her out.

"I won't ever let you go," she said, and two fat tears plopped down her cheeks.

He looked back at her, the first hint of curiosity in his expression. She smiled, and it was a genuine smile mixed with a little laughter as more tears spilled down her cheeks. He was definitely intrigued now, and he waited as she scribbled more words on the notepad.

I was a lousy wife. If you can forgive me, I want to do better.

Now he looked confused. "You're always angry," he said. "I don't know how to make you happy. Now I can't even earn an income. I'm useless to you."

She blanched. This was the second time he'd accused her of caring only for the money he earned. It was unfair, and she drew a breath to defend herself, but then paused.

His concern was valid. She'd been furious when he'd lost one job after another because he couldn't get along with the financiers who controlled the projects.

"I don't need you for an income," she said, but he shook his head in frustration. He couldn't understand her, so he pointed to the notepad. It was progress. At least he was listening to her. She wrote as quickly as possible.

I don't need you for an income. I can work until you are on your feet again. We are partners. We should never have lost sight of that.

This time when he read the note, his face softened. He swallowed hard, his Adam's apple bobbing. She stepped in front of him, a thousand watts of love and affection blooming inside.

"I love you," she said. "I love you, and I don't pity you. You're too pig-headed for that." She used grand gestures to illustrate her point, and he must have understood most of it because he looked partly amused, partly indignant. But for the first time since the accident, the lopsided grin she'd always loved tilted across his face.

He tugged her into his arms and held her tightly, rocking

them both from side to side. How many years had it been since she'd let him hold her? It felt like coming home.

At last, Clyde pulled back, holding her shoulders and smiling down into her face. "I think everyone is watching us," he said loudly. He glanced at the dozen patients and nurses on the breakfast patio, staring at them in amusement.

"They are, beloved." Evelyn laughed.

Let them watch. She had found the man she loved. Beneath the careless insults, the forgotten anniversaries, and socks thrown on her clean floor, she had found a man. And she loved him desperately.

This was love. This was a marriage, in all its shining, imperfect glory.

It didn't take long for Stella to locate the shared photographers' studio down near the wharves. It was in a dilapidated section of town, the streets crowded with fishmongers carting in their haul. The repetitive slosh and slapping of the waves against the seawall was worrisome, a constant reminder of the cold, briny seawater just yards away.

It was a good thing she hadn't had breakfast this morning or that sloshing water would have made her feel even more ill. Besides, how could she have an appetite when she was pursuing the slim chance that the police had a photograph of Gwendolyn's dead body? Such a photograph seemed like a gross intrusion on her sister's dignity, but Stella prayed it existed.

The studio was in a windowless brick building amid the fish stalls and meat markets. The rent must have been inexpensive, for there was nothing pleasant about the space. She banged on the door, but there was no answer. A passing fishmonger told her the police had been by earlier to drag one of the photographers to a textile mill where an overnight fire had caused two deaths. The others were at lunch. Stella had no choice but to wait on the cracked and rickety bench outside the studio for the photographers to return.

A pair of herring gulls bobbed in the harbor, making her seasick just looking at them. It would be easier to cross the street and avoid the sight, but was she really going to go through the rest of her life at the mercy of this pathetic fear of water? She lowered her chin and glowered at the water, determined to overcome this ridiculous fear. As soon as she solved the mystery of Gwendolyn's death, she was going to learn how to swim.

An hour later, one of the photographers returned. He looked tired and bedraggled, but he gestured her inside. The interior smelled of sawdust and ammonium chemicals, but she was lucky he was the photographer who regularly manned the morning shift, for he had been the man on duty when Gwendolyn's body had been discovered.

"I remember the lady," he confirmed. "Someone came down early, before the sun was even full up. I went straight over to Cooperman's Bridge and took a few pictures. I developed them that day."

Stella's hands clenched, and she could barely breathe. "Do you remember anything about her? Anything that might suggest foul play?"

He thought for a moment but shook his head. "I take a lot of pictures, ma'am. Hundreds every year. After I develop the photographs, I turn it all over to the police. It isn't my job to think too much about what I see. To tell the truth, I don't want to think too much about it. Those things haunt a man, you know?"

"Do you still have the plates? Can I get a copy?"

He shook his head. "It's too expensive to keep the negatives.

After I develop the photographs, I scrape off the emulsion and reuse the glass plates."

"So it's gone?"

"Afraid so, ma'am. I turned the photographs over to the police, but most things usually end up getting filed in the city archives. Maybe they've still got them?"

Her heart thudded so loudly it could probably be heard in this barren room. She'd had no idea the archives contained old photographs, for it was a cavernous space she'd never fully explored. She'd already seen Gwendolyn's file at the police department, but what if the photographs had been sent elsewhere for storage? It was a long shot, but if pictures still existed, the only surviving copy of what Gwendolyn looked like immediately after being pulled from the river was in the archives at City Hall.

The streetcar ride to City Hall was maddeningly slow. It was nearing the end of the day, and Ernest Palmer locked the archives promptly at five o'clock. She wouldn't be able to sleep if she had to wait until tomorrow to get her hands on those photographs—if they even still existed. Looking at Gwendolyn's dead body was the last thing she wanted polluting her mind, but it had to be done.

It was four o'clock by the time she raced up the staircase to City Hall. She couldn't tell Ernest what she'd come for. If Gwendolyn's troubles stemmed from her work at City Hall, it was important to keep a tight lid on what she was seeking. Stella didn't like lying to Ernest, but she needed to get back into the stacks, where boxes of documents from the police department were filed.

As usual, Ernest was hunched over a vintage letterpress tray at the front counter, using a pair of tweezers to poke amid the hundreds of tiny compartments that held individual slugs of type. Normally she'd spend a few minutes chatting about whatever typeface or memorabilia had caught his fancy, but she had only an hour before closing and no idea how many boxes she'd need to plow through.

"Can I borrow the key to the stacks?" she asked. "Romulus White is still looking at that old lawsuit about the labor union. I'd like to poke around some more."

It wasn't technically a lie. They'd made very little progress last week because Romulus had distracted her with that volume of Audubon prints. Ernest said nothing as he reached for the key. His attention had already returned to the letterpress tray as he extended the key toward her.

The key made a scraping sound as she twisted it in the heavy metal door. It clanged shut behind her. How cold and ominous this space seemed compared with the last time she was here. She walked down the center aisle, scanning the books and boxes towering to the ceiling in imposing walls of information. She had an hour to find those police photographs.

At least she knew where to begin. The old police reports were kept in two aisles near the back of the stacks. She jerked out the boxes and quickly poked into them to see if they contained photographs. It didn't take long for her fingers to become dry and coated with dust, but she kept moving through dozens of boxes. Dust swirled in the air as she lifted the lids. Her nose twitched and she could taste the air, but time was growing short and she couldn't wait for the dust to settle.

The first box of photographs was on the bottom shelf. Crouching down on the cold concrete floor, she jerked out the first file. They were booking photographs, for the first one she grabbed featured the ugly mug of a tough-looking man staring angrily at the camera. It didn't take long to flip through the remaining files in the first box.

She moved on to the next box. More booking photographs,

but when she flipped open the third box, she blanched at the sight of three bodies sprawled in the street. The title printed on the tab of the file was *Irish Street Riot, May 21, 1896*. All the photographs in the file seemed to be from the same incident. One of them showed a close-up shot of a dead boy who couldn't have been more than fifteen years old, his face contorted in a grimace.

She'd never seen a dead body, either in person or a photograph, and it was chilling. She swallowed hard. This had to be done, no matter how distasteful.

Fortunately, each file had an identifying tag, and she made quick progress as she ignored the files marked *Milk Street Bank Robbery*, *Fourth Street Arson*, and *Samuelson Murder*. Most of the files had names on them and most were murder victims, but she didn't see Gwendolyn's name anywhere.

She moved on to the next box.

Well, this was strange. Most of the files were labeled *John Doe*, and a dozen others *Jane Doe*. It was a common term dating back centuries for unidentified people. She was about to return the box and move on to the next, for the police had identified Gwendolyn fairly quickly, but something made her grab the first *Jane Doe* file.

A middle-aged woman sprawled in a filthy alley with a liquor bottle by her side. Stella was able to dismiss the next three just as easily.

But the fourth file contained a photograph of Gwendolyn.

She dropped the file, doubled over, and looked away. Had Stella not already been crouched on the floor, she would have fallen down. Nothing could have prepared her for this. She didn't want to look, but this was what she'd come for.

She waited for her stomach to settle, took a deep breath, and picked up the file. There was only a single photograph inside. Gwendolyn lay on the grass, her eyes wide open and staring vacantly into space. Her hair was wet, plastered to her skull, and a few reeds were tangled in her clothing.

The worst thing was her throat. Her milky white skin still glistened with dampness, and the dark bruises tracking across her neck were stark and obvious.

Gwendolyn had been strangled.

─ ᎶᎥ Ꮿ Ꭷ ─

Stella curled over the file, her breath coming so hard and fast she was dizzy, but for the life of her she couldn't stop her lungs from this helpless gasping for air. In her hands, she held proof that Gwendolyn had been murdered.

And it was the only remaining photograph to prove it. The negative plates had been destroyed. She couldn't ask Ernest's permission to take it out of the archives, nor did she trust it with the police or any attorney affiliated with City Hall. Dr. Lentz had falsified his report when he'd claimed Gwendolyn had no injuries. He had looked Stella in the face and lied. And she had no explanation for why Gwendolyn's case was filed as a *Jane Doe*, but that wasn't what mattered.

What mattered was protecting this photograph. She couldn't leave it here. It would have to be smuggled out, and she had no satchel or books in which to hide it.

She tried not to look at the photograph as she closed the file. Hiding it in her jacket would have to do. She'd worn the worst possible jacket for the task: her absurdly stylish black cutaway tailcoat. She'd have to hope the tightly cinched tailoring of her jacket would hold the file secure, although the satin lining was going to be a problem. As she stood and buttoned her coat, she felt the file slide with each step.

She was going to have to do this. Ernest Palmer was harmless, but even he would not be able to overlook the outright theft of a document if it slipped free of her coat as she left the archives. She made sure all the police boxes were replaced, then darted to the aisle containing the labor union cases where she and Romulus had been working last week. She jostled the boxes from their positions, just in case Ernest might check where she had been working.

Before leaving the room, she adjusted the file inside her jacket one final time. She jammed it as high as possible until it was snug beneath her underarm, but if it sank even an inch, the white file would be visible beneath the black velvet hem of her coat.

"Okay, Gwendolyn, let's go," she whispered. She opened the door and headed into the reading room. From behind the service counter, Ernest watched her with unusual attention as she strode toward the front of the room. Those oversized eyes made her want to fidget, but she held her head high as she drew closer. She dared not release her breath for fear the file might begin to slip.

As she passed the front counter, she nodded to Ernest and flashed him a cordial smile, every muscle in her body tense as she glided toward the door. The file was starting to travel, snaking across the satin lining and moving toward her front. She reached for the door, the knob cold in her sweating palm.

"Miss West," Ernest's voice called out as she twisted the knob. She froze, barely turning her head. "Yes?"

When he didn't respond, she turned a bit more to see him walking from around the counter toward her.

"The key," he said simply, and she almost fainted in relief. The key to the stacks was still in her front jacket pocket. Clamping one arm against her side to secure the file, she plucked the key from her pocket with her other hand and turned it over.

"Good day, Miss West," Ernest said as he returned to the counter.

She had made her way down the hallway, up the stairs, and onto the public street before her heart resumed its normal rhythm.

262

17

Ernest Palmer watched Stella as she left the archives. She was so obvious. Even with those flashy clothes, he could see that every nerve ending in her body was as uptight as a newly strung piano. She was on to something.

The urge to go back into the stacks and see what she'd been up to was tempting, but there were still two visitors in the reading room and the rules prohibited him from leaving the room unattended. *Lawyers*, he thought with a roll of his eyes. While he might be willing to bend the rules if the visitors were low-level civil servants, it was best to obey protocol when lawyers were in the room.

Besides, he wanted to finish loading up this compositor's stick with the new typeface he'd bought in Philadelphia last month. He hadn't had much time to experiment with the Caslon typeface, which was a shame. He plucked a capital M from the tray and slid it into place. Modern-day typesetters did this sort of work by machine, but Ernest did it by hand as a labor of love. Nothing was quite as satisfying as sliding the type and slugs into place, inking the final product, and then experiencing the thrill of producing hand-set documents. His ability to forge stationery, legal documents, and official-looking telegrams had proven quite lucrative over the years. What a unique dovetail of craft and financial gain.

He wished the lawyers would leave. It was after five o'clock, and he'd told them the archives was closing, but apparently rules didn't apply to people like them. City Hall was filled with people he didn't particularly like, but lawyers were at the top of his list. Women weren't much better. They laughed at him because of his thick glasses and the fact that most of them were taller than he. He liked Stella West, though. She was friendly and respected the diligence it took to master the challenging trade of typesetting. She always had interesting questions to ask, and he liked hearing her talk about the publishing industry in London. That was before he'd learned she was Gwendolyn's sister.

He never would have realized they were sisters but for eavesdropping on the weekly telephone calls Stella placed to her parents from the archives. The two women looked a little bit alike, but Stella and Gwendolyn were as different as chalk and cheese. Gwendolyn had been a nuisance since the day she'd arrived, sniffing about and poking her nose into other people's business. A real goody-goody. And now it seemed Stella was getting too curious about what had happened to Gwendolyn.

Which was a shame. He liked Stella, but business came first.

It was fifteen minutes after closing time before the lawyers put away their paperwork, stood, and left the room. They didn't even thank him for staying late.

When the door closed behind the lawyers, Ernest walked the entire length of the room, scanning to be certain no one else lingered. When he was convinced he was alone, he picked up the telephone and asked the operator to connect his call. It was answered promptly on the second ring.

"She was over here again today," Ernest reported.

"What did she want?"

"I have no idea, but she was alone. No sign of Romulus."

"Good." The satisfaction bleeding through the telephone line was annoying.

"No, it's not good," he snapped. "She's still poking around where she has no business. You need to get her out of Boston. If you can't do it, I'll take care of her myself."

The voice on the other end of the telephone uncoiled like a snake. "If you touch one hair on her head, I will turn you in. I swear it, Ernest. You are to leave her alone."

"If I go down, you go down. That's the way it's always been." He disconnected the line without waiting for a reply.

—◦◦◦—

Dusk had fallen by the time Stella reached the street where Evelyn lived. Gas-lit lamps created pools of light in the darkness, but there were few people on the street and she quickened her steps, anxious to get home.

Gwendolyn's photograph still chafed against her side, but she dared not take it out until she was safe behind the solid walls of Evelyn's townhouse. Maybe she was being paranoid, but it felt like someone was watching her. A glance over her shoulder showed two men in dark wool business suits following her. They'd been on the trolley with her. It didn't matter that one of them was old enough to be her grandfather and the other carried a parakeet in a birdcage, they worried her.

Evelyn's house loomed like a safe haven at the end of the block. She was only a few yards from safety, and she clenched the cold iron key in her fist. The first thing she would do once inside would be to turn on every electric bulb and light every kerosene lantern until the place was illuminated like a Christmas tree. Terrible things lurked in the darkness. She wished Romulus was here. She wanted someone to lean on, and beneath Romulus's irreverent sense of humor was a man whose strength she desperately needed.

No, she didn't. No matter how badly she longed for him, she didn't need Romulus, and it was time to quit imagining that she did. But wasn't it strange they were both going through such terrible calamities at the same time?

She paused. Or was it?

Michael Townsend had disavowed any knowledge of who had initiated the injunction against *Scientific World*, but how likely was that? As the attorney general, he probably had the power to find out anything he wanted. Romulus had been the first real ally she'd had in Boston, but the moment the injunction had been filed, his attention had been fractured and his help began unraveling.

Then there was the bizarre letter purportedly from London that had threatened the revocation of her copyrights. She'd recognized it as a counterfeit, but the legalistic tone was something a good lawyer could cobble together.

It was frightening. Someone had been trying to scare her for months, and she couldn't put it down to simple paranoia anymore. It was real. The men following behind her made her nervous, and she hurried to Evelyn's door. She vaulted up the short flight of steps with her key in hand.

Something wasn't right. When she'd left the house this morning, the lace shade over the front-door window had been securely closed. Now there was a sliver at the bottom. Someone had been inside.

The housekeeper and her children had gone to visit family, so the house should have been empty all day. Could the gauzy lace covering have been disturbed by air currents in the house? It had never seemed drafty inside the house before.

The two men following her were drawing closer. She inserted her key into the lock and twisted the knob. She stood in the partially opened doorway and listened.

The front of the house was dark, but a light glowed in the kitchen. The scraping of a chair being moved and the swish of fabric were unmistakable.

"Hello?" a voice called from the back of the house. "Stella?"

She almost doubled over with relief. It was Evelyn, silhouetted in the light coming from the hallway. A larger figure moved behind her.

"Clyde?" Stella asked.

"Yes, we're home," Evelyn said. "We're having dinner in the back. Will you join us?"

"I'll be there in a moment."

Thank heavens she wouldn't need to be alone tonight. Normally she didn't fear anything, but that was before she saw the dark, mottled bruises on his sister's throat. She scurried to her bedroom to slip Gwendolyn's photograph beneath her mattress. It wasn't the sort of image anyone should see without warning.

Evelyn was already preparing a plate by the time Stella arrived in the kitchen. It was a simple meal of sliced bread, cheese, and salami. Evelyn's smile was radiant as she handed over the plate.

"Is Clyde better?" It was the only thing she could think of that would cause such exuberance, but a glance at Clyde showed him to be standing politely and looking to Evelyn for interpretation.

"There has been no change in his hearing," Evelyn said. "But things are going well. No matter what happens, we are going to be all right."

And with that, Evelyn crossed the floor to where Clyde stood and slipped her hand in his. The way he smiled down at her, only the tiniest curving of his mouth but tenderness blazing in his eyes . . . well, this was unexpected. The warmth between these two could heat the entire house. It was almost embarrassing to be standing here and intruding, but Evelyn straightened and smiled at Stella.

"Please, you must be hungry. We've already eaten six links of salami." Evelyn scribbled something on a pad of paper and handed it to Clyde, who read it quickly.

"Evelyn scarfed down five links all on her own," Clyde said. "I barely had one."

Evelyn burst out laughing. "What a liar." But her eyes sparkled, and given Evelyn's trim waistline, Stella had no doubt it was Clyde who had put the largest dent in the salami.

Over the next twenty minutes, Stella made her own dent in the bread and cheese as she listened to Evelyn recount their time at the White Oak Health Resort. Every few moments, she stopped to scribble a note to Clyde, who read them and usually responded with a couple of words, but mostly what he did was watch Evelyn. With his fingers gently tracing Evelyn's wrist, he gazed at her with a fondness that took Stella's breath away. If a man ever looked at her like that, it would be hard not to melt on the spot.

She'd always heard that tragedy could tear people apart or draw them closer together. It seemed that Clyde and Evelyn had decided to be the type who emerged from the firestorm stronger and more resilient than before. She envied them, and could only pray that her parents would find a similar path out of the darkness.

After the last of the cheese and salami had been finished and the plates scraped clean, Evelyn asked Stella how things had been going.

Should she tell them? This evening had been lovely, an unexpected island of joy amid the days of stress. She hesitated to spoil it with what she'd learned today, but she needed their advice. It was a certainty that Gwendolyn had been murdered, but Stella couldn't trust the police, the medical examiner, or even the district attorney. Boston was a tight-knit community, and most of these men socialized together, ate meals together, and sparred at the same athletic club.

But she could trust Evelyn and Clyde. Since Romulus was no longer interested in helping her, they might be the only two people in Boston she could trust.

"I found a photograph," she said. "It is proof my sister was murdered." She retrieved Gwendolyn's picture and relayed how she'd found it buried deep in a file labeled *Jane Doe*.

"The medical examiner lied to me," she said. "Rupert Lentz is a friend of Romulus's, and he looked us both in the face and lied."

"He is a friend to *Scientific World*, as well," Evelyn said, her brow furrowed as she scribbled out her words for Clyde. "He reviews our articles relating to medicine and anatomy. I've always found him to be a fine man."

"I gather he never performed an autopsy on one of your family members? And botched the job horribly?" She felt bad about the scorn in her voice, but how many months had been wasted because of a shoddy postmortem report?

And *shoddy* was the best possible term for what he'd done. It was far more likely to be a case of fraud or outright collusion in a murder.

"I think I should bring an official complaint against him, but I don't know how to do that. To whom does he report? It seems the government leaders of Boston are such an insular group of people, I don't know how to move forward without stumbling into someone related to Gwendolyn's case."

Evelyn looked troubled. "I'm afraid it's even worse than you realize. Did you know that Rupert Lentz is the attorney general's son?"

Stella gasped. "No!" She'd seen a picture of his son on his desk that day, and there had been no resemblance to the medical examiner at all.

"Well, his foster son," Evelyn clarified. "Rupert was orphaned at a young age and was sent to be raised by his grandmother. He is from a humble background. I believe his grandmother was a housekeeper to a wealthy family up in Marblehead, the same village where Michael Townsend came of age. In any event, the housekeeper died when the boy was only eight or nine, and he had nowhere to go. Michael Townsend got word of it and took him in. He raised the boy as his own, and even paid for Rupert's college. I gather the two of them are still quite close."

Perhaps this was the explanation for the missing photograph on Michael Townsend's desk. She'd bet her bottom dollar the attorney general had a picture of Rupert Lentz on his desk, and for some reason he didn't want her to know of his connection to the man who had performed Gwendolyn's postmortem.

It made her even less eager to trust the legal system to handle Gwendolyn's case. She had only a single photograph to prove Dr. Lentz had falsified the report, and all it would take was a lit match to burn this inconvenient photograph to ash.

"What about the press?" she asked. "If I took all this information to a reporter and made it public, wouldn't that force the government to address the issue?"

Evelyn shrugged but wrote down the question and handed it over to Clyde, who shook his head vehemently the moment he read it.

"If a journalist gets wind of this, you will lose control," he warned. "They will take your information and run with it in whatever direction they want. Wait. Hire a private detective, someone who works for *you*, not a newspaper."

His suggestion had merit. Frankly, she was at the end of her rope and was ready to hire a professional who could devote his full attention to the case. Just as Romulus had no more time for her, Clyde and Evelyn were at a delicate stage of their marriage. They didn't need her as a third wheel while they took their first tentative steps toward building a new life together. It was time to turn to a professional for help.

"Do you know of a private detective you would recommend?"

Evelyn looked a little amused. "It depends on the strength of your intestinal fortitude."

"It's rock-solid," she replied. "I want the best."

Evelyn stated that Riley McGraff was the best investigator in the city. He used to work for the Boston Police Department, but they'd fired him for being "intolerable." Stella had already met a few Boston police officers, none of whom seemed to have attended charm school, so Mr. McGraff must really make an impression.

"I'll call on him tomorrow," Stella said, already feeling a renewed rush of energy from having a plan in place.

—◦⁀◦⁀◦—

Riley McGraff was as unpleasant as Evelyn had led her to expect.

He lived on the top floor of a five-story building, and the private detective's apartment doubled as his office. The front room smelled of cigar smoke, fried oysters, and a sour mood. Riley McGraff sat behind a cluttered table in a room crowded with cabinets too overstuffed with paperwork to close properly. He was unshaven and had black eyes that matched his shaggy hair. Spread out on the table before him was an exotic game of solitaire that must have used at least three decks of cards. A pair of cats constantly meandered around his legs.

But the instant she started talking, he set aside his hand of cards and listened intently to everything she said, scribbling notes on a pad of paper. When she told him of hunting through police archives and finding Gwendolyn's photograph misfiled under the *Jane Doe* records, he seemed both impressed and surprised.

"The folks in the Homicide Department are good. That isn't the kind of mistake that happens by accident."

She caught her breath. "Then who is responsible?"

"Couldn't tell you," he said. "Keep talking. What else have you got?"

"Shortly after I arrived, someone threw a baseball through my window. They planted a nest of bees in my mailbox, too."

Riley snorted. "That sounds like Izzy Smith at the first precinct. His father used to be a beekeeper, and he's never been afraid of them. He uses bees to annoy people who have been giving the police a hassle. It doesn't mean anything. Same with the baseball. They just wanted to intimidate you into dropping the case. What else have you got?"

She spoke of her suspicion of the connection between the attorney general and Dr. Lentz, especially the fact that the attorney general did not mention it during their meeting, but Mr. McGraff was dismissive.

"Everyone knows Dr. Lentz was raised by Michael Townsend. When the governor nominated Dr. Lentz for the position, Townsend made a great show of disclosing their relationship and even asked for an independent panel to review Dr. Lentz's credentials to avoid any hint of favoritism. Everything Townsend does is by the book. He probably figured you knew about it."

But she didn't know anything, and that omission set off resounding warning bells in her mind.

"I think the key lies somewhere in their relationship," she said. "Are they somehow covering for one another? Or maybe it is the opposite. What if Dr. Lentz is blackmailing the attorney general? All I know for sure is that someone hid that photograph and mislabeled it as a *Jane Doe* for a reason. I want to know who and why."

"I agree. My retainer fee is three hundred dollars."

"That's outrageous!" It was more than most people earned in a month, and there was no guarantee this man was going to find anything.

"That's the going rate for someone who gets results. Look, lady, I'm perfectly happy to sit at home playing card games all day. I don't *need* to work. But it looks like you need to find out who killed your sister, and I'm your best bet for that."

She narrowed her eyes. Everything he said was true. There were three tables in this room covered with various card games in mid-play, making it easy to see how he typically spent his day, but she'd heard of the renowned Riley McGraff when she'd worked at City Hall. A man didn't get a reputation like that without a solid foundation. She needed the best, and such men didn't come cheap.

"If I pay your shameful extortion, I want you to begin work immediately. Today. And I want to be your exclusive client. I'll tolerate no distractions until my case is resolved or we agree to sever our relationship."

"Lady, I only take cases I'm interested in, and not many people can afford me. I'll start today."

She didn't need to like Riley McGraff or approve of his obsession with card games. All she needed was a competent man exclusively devoted to Gwendolyn's case. No middle-of-the-afternoon flirtations. No payroll distractions or romantic squabbles. She never should have gotten so deeply entangled with Romulus in the first place. "Very well," she said. "I'll visit my bank and have payment by the end of the day."

Before she even stopped talking, he swiveled his chair and turned his attention back to the card game. "You know where to find me," he said as he expertly shuffled a deck of cards in one hand.

Arranging for the withdrawal of cash took a frustratingly long time. First there was a delay because the manager with the vault key was out at lunch, and after that she had problems verifying her identity. The man actually had the gall to ask if she had a husband or father who could vouch for her.

Would a man have had this much difficulty withdrawing his own money from a bank? It didn't really matter. She managed to withdraw the money and marched up the steps to Mr. Mc-Graff's apartment with determination, liking the sound of her tightly-pleated twill skirt swishing behind her. She was on the warpath now. She had the city's best private detective and had pointed him squarely in the right direction. All she had to do was unleash him, and soon she'd be tearing away the smoke-screens thrown up by most of the departments in the city. She knocked on Riley's door.

"Come in!" he hollered.

Couldn't he even be bothered to get up and answer the door? But she wouldn't let his rude behavior unsettle her. She was the embodiment of poised efficiency and would allow no inconvenient emotions to distract her from the mission.

He was sitting at another table, hunched over an entirely different game of solitaire. She set the stack of bills on the corner of the table.

"Well?" she asked. "Have you learned anything more about why my sister's photograph was misfiled as a *Jane Doe*?"

He didn't move, but those black eyes swiveled to glare up at her. "I don't start work until I've been paid." His hand shot out and scooped up the money, counting it quickly, as though she couldn't be trusted to count accurately.

"I thought we agreed you would begin today. Immediately."

He rolled his eyes as he tucked the bills into his pants pocket. "You waste three months before hiring a competent investigator, then complain when your case isn't solved by five o'clock. Some people are too stupid to be worthy of air and water."

Okay, she probably deserved that one. Besides, she rarely began work on a commission until she'd received a down payment, so she couldn't be too annoyed. She pasted a smile on her face. "Then when may I expect you to begin work on the case?"

"Now. Come on, I need to see that photograph of your sister."

He shrugged into his coat and started heading toward the door. The cats crowded his legs as though trying to stop him from leaving, but he moved them aside. He made no small talk as he descended the stairs with brisk energy, and she had to struggle to keep up with him, but she didn't mind. Riley Mc-Graff was a ham-fisted and obnoxious steam engine plowing straight into the case.

Maybe she was going to get along just fine with Mr. Mc-Graff, after all.

─◦⟨๑⟩◦─

It was six o'clock, and there was still plenty of light when she arrived back at Evelyn's townhouse. A note on the kitchen table informed her that Evelyn and Clyde were enjoying the day exploring the Boston Athenaeum but should return by nightfall. Stella invited Riley inside and back toward the dining room. She set Gwendolyn's photograph on the table before Riley and moved to the window to watch a squirrel scrabbling through the mulch in the garden outside. The sight of Gwendolyn's bruised throat was already burned into her memory; she didn't need to see it again.

"This picture was taken at dawn," Riley said. "I'll lean on someone at the police department to tell me who was on duty that day. I'll have a chat and find out what they know."

A loud pounding at the front door made them both jump. Riley met her eyes. "You expecting anybody?"

She shook her head, and Riley withdrew a pistol as he headed to the front door. It seemed a little paranoid, but she was grateful for his vigilance and the fact that he was willing to open the front door while she hugged the back wall.

"Is Stella West living here?" She recognized her landlord's thick accent.

"Mr. Zhekova?" The wide-shouldered man entirely filled the front stoop. "What are you doing here?"

"You're three days overdue on your rent. Just because you're staying here now doesn't mean you can skip out on your rent."

She'd given Mr. Zhekova her forwarding address when she'd left to stay with Evelyn, but most of her belongings were still at the boardinghouse. Now that she was no longer working at City Hall, she would find a nicer place to live.

"I'll be moving out soon," she said. "And I've already paid rent through the end of the month, so I don't owe you anything."

"You've still got my room and haven't given notice that you're leaving," he said. "You owe me for next month's rent."

"I told you, I'll be out before the end of the month," she said tightly.

He held up a small card. "This telegram came for you a few hours ago. I'll take it back to the boardinghouse, and you can have it when you pay next month's rent."

Her eyes slid to the telegram. The last time she'd received a telegram was on that terrible morning in London when she'd learned of Gwendolyn's death. It was impossible to know who had sent this new telegram or why, but a growing sense of urgency clawed at her. She reached out to grab it, but Mr. Zhekova jerked it back.

"Not until you pay your rent."

"You can't do that! It's addressed to me!"

Mr. Zhekova made a great show of scrutinizing the words printed on the front of the cardstock. "Looks like it was addressed to my boardinghouse," he concluded. "Either you live there and are entitled to this telegram, or you don't. Which is it?"

"What you are doing is illegal and you know it," she snapped. "Hand that telegram over or I'll sue you into the next century."

Mr. Zhekova pretended to fan himself with the telegram. "Oh, so we should wait until the next century to see what the telegram says? That's fine with me, Miss West. Just keep paying the rent on that room, and we'll let the lawyers figure it out."

Riley stepped in front of her. "I got an idea," he said as he hefted his pistol before him. "That telegram looks like it would be good for target practice." He twisted the cylinder a few times, the metallic clicking sounding ominous in the night. Riley wasn't a large man, but the reckless gleam in his eyes was plenty threatening. "Or you can keep fanning your face with it and I'll shoot it now. What's your pleasure?"

Mr. Zhekova dropped the card and ran. Riley smirked as he picked it up and handed it over.

"You wouldn't really have shot at him, would you?" she asked.

"Would you have sued him?"

"I most certainly would have!"

Riley rolled his eyes. "Lady, you seem smart, but sometimes I swear you have the intellectual capacity of a pine cone."

She took the telegram back to the kitchen, where the light was better, and tore open the flap, holding it to the light of the window to read.

Miss West,

With regrets, your mother has attempted suicide. Condition critical. Come immediately to the Boulder Point Hospital.

It was signed by the director of the hospital.

"Oh no," she whispered. The fact that the message was signed by a member of the hospital staff meant her father was either too busy or too distraught to send the message himself. Her mother could be dead even now. From the corner of her eye, she saw Riley reading the telegram, but she didn't care.

How could her mother have done this? It seemed she had been getting better, finally starting to rally. Perhaps the visit to the resort hotel in Boulder Point where she and her father had spent their honeymoon thirty years ago had overwhelmed Eloise's fragile stability.

But suicide? *Suicide?* Stella curled over and collapsed onto a chair, clasping a hand over her mouth. She felt hot and sick, too shocked to think clearly.

A blue and white washbasin plopped into her lap. "If you're going to throw up, use that," Riley said.

This was going to destroy her father. He doted on Eloise and was going to blame himself for not figuring out how to rescue her. Fear mingled with anger and despair. And panic. She tossed aside the washbasin. "I've got to get out of here." She ran to her room, dragged her traveling bag from under the bed, and yanked it open. The last trains stopped running in a few hours, and she needed to be on one of them. Boulder Point was only sixty miles to the north, and if she hurried, she could get there tonight.

Her father was going to need her. Losing Gwendolyn had been bad, but to have his wife, his anchor, the woman he'd built his whole world around, torn away from him like this? And by her own hand?

She balled up a dress and shoved it inside her bag, then glanced at Riley, who leaned against the doorframe of her room. "I need you to write a note to Evelyn for me. Tell her what's happened and where I'm going."

ELIZABETH CAMDEN

"What am I, an errand boy?"

"You're the man I just paid three hundred dollars to make my life easier," she snapped.

Mercifully, he did not argue with her and wrote out the note while she finished stuffing her bag. He even accompanied her to the train station, where fortune must have been smiling, for she was able to secure a ticket on a train heading for Boulder Point. It would make half a dozen stops before it got there, but by eight o'clock tonight, she would be in Boulder Point.

She sent her father a telegram, in care of the Boulder Point Hospital, alerting him of her arrival. Perhaps knowing that she was on her way would provide a sliver of comfort.

She sat on the hard bench in the railway station, the clatter and chugging of engines a constant rumble in the air. The station reeked of coal-fired steam and creosote, but she was oblivious to it. She tried to pray, but she was too angry. Was it a sin to be furious with her mother? It felt wrong, but it was easier to be angry than quaking in terror. That telegram must have been sent several hours ago, and her mother might be dead before she stepped off the train in Boulder Point.

Her anger subsided, replaced by fear and despair. Again she began to pray.

—⁘⁘⁘—

It was dark by the time the train arrived in Boulder Point. A few circles of gaslight illuminated the train depot, but all Stella could see of the surrounding area was the dark silhouettes of trees looming in the distance.

There weren't many people on the platform, and she scanned them frantically, searching for her father. He wasn't here. Was that a good thing or not? If her mother was still alive, surely he'd be at her bedside.

She waited for the porter to unload her traveling case from the baggage compartment, scanning the station for a hack she could hire to take her to the hospital. Boulder Point wasn't exactly a bustling city, and at this time of night, the train station was almost deserted. There seemed to be only one carriage at the far end of the platform, and she prayed it was for hire. She grasped the leather handles of her bag and headed toward it.

"Miss West!" a familiar voice called behind her.

She was surprised to see Ernest Palmer from the city's archives heading toward her. He had a flushed, eager look on his face. The last thing she needed right now was to get entangled in a conversation with him.

"Hello, Ernest," she said. "You'll have to excuse me. I'm here on urgent family business and need to move along quickly."

"I have a carriage for hire. I believe it is the only one at the station. I'd be happy to share it with you." He gestured to the single carriage at the far end of the platform. The horse was already harnessed, and a cabbie waited on the driver's bench.

"Let's go," she said, heading off at a brisk pace, her heels thudding on the wooden planking of the station platform.

Thank heavens there was a carriage available. It was a miracle that Ernest was here and willing to—

She froze. "What are you doing in Boulder Point?"

The pleasant expression on his face never wavered. "I've come to meet Horatio Kettering, a fellow typography enthusiast. He has a fine collection of eighteenth-century Garamond type. I can never visit without . . ."

He continued rambling about the unique qualities of Garamond type as they walked toward the carriage. It was darker over here, with no other passengers or station employees. She glanced nervously at Ernest, who continued to speak, but she could no longer focus on his words. All she noticed was his tight, smiling expression. Ernest never smiled. Usually when he discussed typeface he was solemn and intense. Collecting was serious business to him.

And it was altogether too much of a coincidence for him to be at this train station at the same time she'd arrived. A part of her was tempted to hop back on the train and continue heading toward the next stop at Ipswich. She could return tomorrow, when it was daylight and more people were about.

But was she merely being paranoid again? Her mother was in a hospital bed at this very moment, clinging to life by a thread.

Or was she?

On the far side of the platform, the stationmaster strode down the length of the train, shutting the doors. The noise from the engine rose as steam pressure escalated. It was too late to get back onboard.

"I'll hire my own carriage," she said as she headed back toward the brightly lit ticket counter.

Ernest sprang in front of her, and she almost bumped into him. "But there are no other carriages to hire," he said. "I told you I have the last carriage."

Yet another coincidence? With trembling steps, she moved backward, almost stumbling over a loose plank. Ernest reached out, his hand clamping around her arm, tugging her forward.

"What are you doing?" she shrieked. A foul rag clamped over her nose. She tried not to breathe, but the chemical stench was already in her nose, her mouth. Everything went black.

Romulus was thrilled to see Evelyn waltzing into the managerial wing of *Scientific World* just before lunch. Even better, she'd brought a skilled accountant from their bank who was prepared to take over the accounting books until she could return to work. She would be staying at home with Clyde for at least another week, so the accountant was a blessing. As soon as they had him set up at a desk, Romulus rushed Evelyn inside his office for a complete update on Clyde.

"There's been no change in his hearing, but everything is going beautifully," she said, looking happier than he'd seen her in years. She filled him in on their arrival home and their plans for a book. Depending on Clyde's recovery, she warned Romulus that she might be frequently absent in the coming months.

"Are you really going to write a book together?" It seemed impossible that these two, who hadn't cooperated with each other in years, were suddenly undertaking such an ambitious project together.

"Who knows?" Evelyn said with a shrug. "If his hearing returns, he'll go back to work in the field. If not, he will find some other use for his talents, but I couldn't bear seeing him stuck in that chair, staring off into space. In the meantime, we have a project. A mission. And it is making us very, very happy."

Considering the gorgeous blush staining her cheeks, he suspected there was something else making her happy, and he was glad for them.

But he was also desperately eager to return to the injunction against *Scientific World*. During the most hectic professional crisis of his life, his time had been completely fractured, first by Stella, then Clyde's accident, and then Evelyn's absence and the accounting mess. At last he could shift his attention back where it belonged. His new lawyer had just delivered a lengthy brief he needed to read and answer. The hearing for the injunction was coming up soon, and he could afford no more delays.

He crossed the floor of his office and held the door open for her, but Evelyn lingered at the desk, watching him apprehensively. He forced a pleasant expression on his face. "Anything else?" he asked. *Please say no.*

"It's about Stella," she said.

"What about Stella?" He deserved a medal for how cordial he pretended to be. He wasn't going to let Stella interfere with saving the magazine, not again.

"Close the door and have a seat," Evelyn said.

It was hopeless. It seemed he was biologically incapable of resisting news of Stella. Frustration had built to a low simmer by the time he sat down behind his desk, but it evaporated the moment Evelyn told him about the photograph Stella had found misfiled in the city archives. A photograph showing her sister's bruised throat and staring, vacant eyes. It was the only remaining photograph of Gwendolyn's body after it had been pulled from the river. She'd left it at her home for safekeeping, but Romulus did not need to see it. He believed her.

"We can't trust Dr. Lentz," Evelyn said. "He flat-out lied when he said there was no sign of foul play."

His gaze drifted out the window, trying to take it all in. *Rupert Lentz?* What possible motive could Rupert have for lying about Gwendolyn? For the first time in his life, Romulus was completely speechless.

"Stella has hired an excellent private investigator," Evelyn said. "I'm not sure how this is going to play out, but I think she's in good hands now. She had to leave town on family matters, as I gather her mother has taken a turn for the worse. When you see Stella again, you might be a little kinder than usual. She may look like solid steel on the outside, but like any metal, she will eventually crack when under enough pressure."

Evelyn quietly closed the door as she left.

He sat in dumbfounded silence, barely able to accept all the news he'd just heard. Stella had been right all along.

Romulus was fairly certain that, as long as he lived, the biggest regret of his life would be Stella West. The timing of their relationship had been catastrophically bad. Why did she have to drop into his life during his worst professional crisis? Why did she have to be so angry and distracted by her sister's death? Nothing had gone right for them.

Most of all, he regretted he hadn't had the common sense to recognize that Stella was perfect for him. He'd been an idiot time and again.

When had he started thinking of his future with her beside him? Probably the night they were stuffing envelopes. She'd embraced the mundane chore with the same bright vitality she did everything. A woman like that was to be cherished, not casually tossed aside because she had the gumption to arrive in his life before the expiration of his self-imposed bachelorhood.

He bowed his head as the magnitude of the realization sank

in. Stella was the one. He'd felt a connection with her even before they'd met. He could travel the seven continents and never find someone whose spirit flew alongside his in such harmony. And yet the last time he'd seen her he could not have been ruder.

He covered his face with his hands, trying to beat back the smile that threatened. She was going to make him grovel in epic fashion before she'd take him back, but he was good at fighting for what he wanted. At the very least, he would take more care in unraveling the mystery surrounding her sister's death. Stella didn't need him to grovel so much as she needed his help—

A crash startled him as his office door burst open, banging against the back wall.

"We've got trouble," Michael Townsend said. The normally straightlaced attorney looked frazzled, his tie askew and a frantic look in his eye. Overwhelmed with the backlog of work, Romulus had cancelled their regular boxing match at the club this morning, which should have sent a signal he didn't need any more interruptions in his day. And frankly, Michael Townsend wasn't on his list of favorite people after his refusal to lift a finger on behalf of *Scientific World* and this ridiculous injunction.

"Trouble like the imminent collapse of a business you've spent more than a decade building and nurturing? That kind of trouble?" He didn't even try to mask the sarcasm in his voice.

"Trouble like Stella West disappearing from town under suspicious circumstances."

The note of panic in Michael's voice was worrisome. "What are you talking about?"

Without a word, Michael tossed a telegram on his desk. Romulus read it quickly.

Miss West,

With regrets, your mother has attempted suicide. Con-dition critical. Come immediately to the Boulder Point Hospital.

The breath left him in a rush. Evelyn had warned him that Stella's mother had suffered a setback, but this was a blow Stella didn't deserve. She idolized her parents.

"Where is she?" he asked.

"I don't know. All I know for sure is that telegram is a fake. I found half a dozen practice copies of that same telegram in the trashcan at the City Hall archives. The archivist is a master forger. He collects typeface for just this sort of purpose. He can imitate the stationery of the police department, a court of law, and certainly the Western Union Telegraph Company. She is being lured to Boulder Point, and I see only trouble for her there."

Romulus stood, trying to grasp the fast-moving implications. "But why? What would the archivist have against Stella? I thought they were friends."

"We don't have time for this," Michael said. "I know that a woman matching Stella's description boarded a train last evening for Boulder Point. We need to get there quickly, and I could use some help. I can explain on the journey."

Alarm bells started ringing. Stella had tried to tell him there was something dubious about Michael Townsend, but he had refused to hear it. She was a newcomer to Boston and prone to putting the worst possible spin on things, but perhaps she had been correct. She'd certainly been right about Dr. Lentz.

Romulus reached for his jacket, fastening the buttons with great care as his mind raced. He couldn't afford to be stupid about this. Stella had been spooked by a frightening telegram and possibly lured into danger. Could Michael have played a part in it and was even now ensnaring Romulus into the same trap?

He would keep an alert mind as they headed to the train station, and if Michael tried anything shady, he'd pounce. They had been sparring together for six years, and Romulus knew who was stronger, quicker, and more nimble. Michael wouldn't stand a chance against him.

"I'll summon a carriage," he said. "I use a livery service one block down."

Michael waved an impatient hand. "I've already got a carriage waiting in the alley behind us. It will be faster than navigating around the subway construction."

Romulus ignored him as he strode into the editorial room and picked up the telephone receiver, the polished wood piece cool in his hands. "Please connect me to the Tremont Street Livery," he instructed the operator.

Michael's mouth tightened in annoyance, but Romulus didn't trust anyone right now. It might take an extra twenty minutes to navigate around the mess on Tremont, but he intended to be firmly in control all the way to Boulder Point.

―◦◦◦◦―

"Tell me what's going on," Romulus said once they were both in the enclosed carriage and on their way to the train station.

The carriage moved at a snail's pace, rocking over the temporary path bisecting the park during subway construction. The interior was so cramped their knees bumped with each jolt of the carriage. It was vexing to be trapped in a confined space with a man he distrusted. Tension coiled in his muscles, and he longed to spring out and run the entire three miles to the railway station, but he needed information.

A muscle bunched and twitched in Michael's jaw, and he stared out the window. A combination of panic and despair warred on his face—so odd for a man who'd always seemed cool and refined in all the years Romulus had known him.

"Well?" he pressed again.

Michael continued staring out the window. "Some sins you never stop paying for," he whispered.

Romulus said nothing. Now that the door had been cracked, the rest was likely to come out soon. Michael drew a heavy breath and finally turned to look at him.

"I grew up with Ernest Palmer in a little village at Marblehead. We had nothing in common, but there were no other boys our age, so we played together, studied together. Got into trouble together."

Michael swallowed hard and went back to staring out the window. "The richest family in town was the Aldens. Joseph Alden had a big house out on the point and owned a fleet of merchant ships. There was land, too. Mostly they used it to graze cattle, but the real money came from shipping. They had a grand house, but their barn was in bad shape because Joseph Alden was a miser and wouldn't pay for repairs.

"I was thirteen the summer Ernest and I started getting into trouble. Marblehead is isolated, with little to keep adolescent boys occupied, and playing pranks on old Joseph Alden seemed like an amusing way to pass the time. One night we thought it would be funny if we could lure him out to the barn and dump a bucket of water on him. After sunset, we snuck into the barn and filled a three-gallon bucket with water. We propped it up on the top of a door left partially open, then hid in the barn. I had a brand-new turkey call that could send up quite a racket. I blew into that call so loud it could probably be heard all the way to Lighthouse Point. The cows didn't like it. They were outside in the field but woke up and started complaining. We figured it wouldn't be long before Old Man Alden came out to find out what was amiss in the barn."

Michael's eyes closed, and he scrubbed a hand over his face. It was shaking. Romulus said nothing but could barely draw a breath. Adolescent mischief was nothing new, but from a man as composed and refined as Michael Townsend, it came as a surprise.

"I kept blowing into that turkey call like I was an angry tom trapped in the barn. Mr. Alden jerked the door open, and the bucket came down on his head. I still remember the sound it made. He fell to his knees, then pitched over flat on his face. We thought it was hysterical until he didn't move. He didn't ever move again."

Michael expelled a ragged sigh. "We ran out of there as if our lives depended on it. By late the next day, word started circulating that Mr. Alden was dead, and the constable suspected murder. Samuel Alden, the old man's only son, had been in the house that night. Samuel lived in New Bedford and rarely visited. Everyone knew the two men weren't on good terms, and suspicion immediately turned to the son. Samuel stood to inherit the shipping fortune, and he was the only logical suspect."

Romulus waited. This was so much worse than he'd suspected.

Michael turned to him with the grief of over thirty years in his eyes. "I think you can guess where this is going," he said. "Ernest and I were both terrified but thought if we came forward, we would be put on trial for murder instead of the son. For months, I couldn't sleep or eat or think of anything but Samuel Alden sitting in a jail cell for something I did. The trial came, and he was found guilty. He was sentenced to life in prison, and then my guilt intensified. Every morning when

289

I woke up in a room filled with sunlight, I thought of Samuel in a windowless cell. When my mother served hotcakes with maple syrup and crispy bacon, I wondered what he was served for breakfast. I knew if I came forward and confessed to what I did, they would let him go, but then I assumed I would have to take his place. Ernest warned me not to tell. If I went down, he would go down, too. So I stayed silent."

Michael clenched and unclenched his fists. Outside the confines of the carriage, the normal noise of the city continued. A vendor hawked pickles, and hammering came from the construction site. The world around them was lively, but Michael was trapped in a thirty-year-old nightmare.

"Ernest and I are the only two people in the world who know what really happened," he continued. "In those years, we did everything together, and this sort of prank isn't something a boy does on his own. One of us couldn't come forward without exposing the other. So we agreed to stay silent."

"What happened to the son?" Romulus asked.

"He died in prison two years later. He contracted a lung infection in jail, and you don't last long after that happens." A bitter smile crossed his face. "After that, there seemed no point in coming forward. Samuel Alden paid the ultimate price for a stupid prank I committed and was too cowardly to own up to, but there was no going back and repairing the damage. The only thing I could do was look to the future. I cut all ties with Ernest Palmer and committed my life to making the world a better place. I earned a fortune but tithed half of everything I made to charity and the church. The Alden fortune went to distant relatives in New Hampshire, and the people who had supported Samuel over the years were left destitute. There weren't many. He never married, and as far as I could tell, the only friend he had in the world was his housekeeper.

She was the only person to visit him in prison, and when she died twenty years later, she left an orphaned grandson behind. That was Rupert Lentz. He was seven years old, and I couldn't bear the thought of seeing him go to an orphanage. Were it not for me, Samuel Alden would have been alive and able to pay his housekeeper a decent wage, but her association and loyalty to a murderer tainted her reputation. I adopted the boy and gave him everything. I treated him like my own son because I knew Samuel cared about his loyal housekeeper and wouldn't want her grandson to end up on the streets. It was the only thing I could do for the ghost of Samuel Alden.

"Beyond that, I fought to clean up corruption wherever I saw it. I wanted to create a city on a hill, modeled on the ideals of our pilgrim forefathers. I dedicated my life to it. I thought that if I worked hard enough, kept to the straight and narrow, I could atone for my sin.

"And then I met Gwendolyn," he said. His voice softened, and for the first time, a hint of a smile appeared on his face, but it vanished quickly. "I first saw her at a meeting where she was the stenographer. I spoke about my concerns that graft was creeping into the subway contracts. Costs were skyrocketing, and contracts were going through convoluted channels, opening the door to corruption. She sat at the secretarial table in the corner, faithfully recording every word I spoke. And after the meeting, she ran after me on the street as I prepared to board a trolley. She said that she'd spotted signs of corruption and didn't know where to turn. I asked her to turn to me."

His voice dwindled. "She was as rare as pure platinum . . . shining and strong and wholesome. She was too young for me, but she didn't care—and I didn't, either. The problem was that the more she looked for corruption at City Hall, the more she found. She turned over a rock and found Ernest Palmer beneath it. When she brought me evidence of kickbacks in the tax assessor's office, Ernest was the ringleader. I arrested everyone but him. He was the one man I didn't care to take on. Gwendolyn continued bringing me incriminating evidence, and I stopped it where I could, but I stalled when it came to Ernest. Gwendolyn couldn't understand why I hadn't arrested him, and I told her I needed to wait until the time was right. I tried to divert her attention. I encouraged her to quit her work and attend law school, anything to get her out of City Hall. I saw her heading toward trouble and didn't want the stink of Ernest Palmer to taint her. She died before anything came of it."

"Who killed her?"

"No one killed her," Michael said, annoyance creeping into his voice. "Gwendolyn slipped on the ice and fell from a bridge, but Stella's crusade to prove otherwise has set Ernest off. Over the years, Ernest has been able to fund a very comfortable lifestyle by being the spider at the center of a web of corruption. He's not going to let Stella endanger that, and now she's gotten herself into trouble. I've overlooked a lot from Ernest, but I'm drawing the line here. I have no idea what he's got planned for her in Boulder Point, but it's not good."

"He plans on killing her," Romulus said softly, his voice vibrating with tension. Stella was alone, isolated, and may not even realize she was in danger yet. He pictured her as she'd been the last time he'd seen her—her chin tilted high in self-confidence, wearing an emerald-green suit, with a spectacular scarf tied to one side. Her audacity and sense of style weren't going to get her out of this one.

"I think he's just trying to scare her," Michael said. "Both of us know what it is to have a murder on our conscience. He won't do it again."

"He killed Gwendolyn."

Michael's voice lashed out. "Why do you keep insisting on that? Gwendolyn's death was an accident. Rupert did the autopsy. He saw no signs of foul play."

"Stella found a photograph of Gwendolyn's body. She had bruises on her throat."

"Nonsense. Rupert told me it was a clear-cut case of accidental drowning," Michael insisted. "I saw the postmortem report filed in the police department. There is no mention of bruising and Rupert didn't take any photographs, so I don't know what Stella thinks she saw, but it's wrong."

"The photo was taken by a police photographer right after Gwendolyn was pulled from the river. It was filed in the city archives under *Jane Doe*."

The color drained from Michael's face. He looked as if he'd been shot. "No," he whispered.

At least Romulus could be assured that Gwendolyn hadn't died by Michael's hand. His skin was chalk white. No man could feign that reaction.

Michael turned his face to the carriage wall. He did not speak again.

19

The rocking of the boat slowly roused her. The boat pitched and swayed, adding to the nausea in her stomach and the pounding in her head, but Stella remained motionless and kept her eyes closed. Too many times over the past few hours, she'd started to stir, only to have that sickeningly sweet rag pressed over her face again, fogging her mind until she slipped back into oblivion. So she remained motionless and strained to hear the voices in the boat through the sloshing of the waves.

Were they on the ocean? The air smelled salty, but with the foul taste in her mouth and the lingering stink of chloroform in her nose, it was hard to tell.

"What a wreck," a voice mumbled.

"What would you expect? The place has been abandoned for thirty years. Ever since the sea cut the promontory off from the mainland." The voice sounded like Ernest Palmer's, and Stella stifled a groan. Ernest knew all her business. How often had she used the telephone in the archives? She'd thought he was being kind by letting her call her parents, but all the while he must have been eavesdropping. It explained how he knew her parents had been planning a trip to Boulder Point. He certainly would have known all about her mother's fragile mental state.

"It still seems like a waste to me," another voice said. "I'll bet that cannery employed at least fifty people. They probably made millions."

"It will be a fine place to wait until . . . well, for as long as we need."

The steady sloshing of oars dipping into the water and the corresponding tug of the boat made Stella suspect they were rowing out to an island. Just knowing she was surrounded by water caused a sweat to break out over her skin. Cold, slimy boards mashed against the side of her cheek, and she fought the urge to panic.

The boat tilted, and a slurry of cold water hit her face. Not much, but she instinctively recoiled as salty water ran into her nose.

"Hey, I think she's awake again."

She wasn't going to let them stuff that rag over her face anymore. She pushed upright, sputtering from the water in her nose. Every muscle in her back and neck ached, but this was no time to baby her abused muscles.

It was hard to see through the glare of sunlight, but her eyes soon adjusted. Four men sat in the boat, but Ernest was the only one she recognized. Two men rowed, and one held a rifle pointed straight at her. Instinct urged her to flee, but she was surrounded by water on all sides.

"Now, don't panic," Ernest said, holding up a hand as though to quiet a barking dog. "We aren't going to hurt you."

They'd already hurt her. That drug had fogged her brain, and water was everywhere . . .

"I've always liked you," Ernest continued, "but we needed to get you out of City Hall for a spell, see?"

"Why are you doing this?" It was hard to speak through the cottony feel in her mouth.

Ernest winced in pretend sympathy. "Well, you've been a little on the nosey side, ma'am. Asking a lot of questions and poking into files where you had no business. And that's a problem. So we'll keep you out here for a short spell, then we can all go home, right?"

His tone was placating, but the others in the boat looked tough. On second thought, her gaze trailed back to one of the men rowing. She recognized him from City Hall, and he had an odd name. It rhymed. She struggled to recall it . . . Mason . . . yes, Jason Mason. He was a clerk in the Harbor Department.

None of the men had made any effort to disguise his face from her, which meant they didn't fear she would report them to the authorities, and that wasn't good. In all likelihood, she was going to end up at the bottom of the ocean. Her parents would never know what had happened to her.

The boat was getting close to land. To her left was a rocky shoreline. There wasn't much of a beach. Most of it was jutting gray boulders.

Looking farther ahead, she saw that they were nearing an island that couldn't have been even a half mile in diameter. It was covered with decaying buildings, probably the abandoned fish cannery Ernest had mentioned. The outbuildings looked ready to topple over. Some of the roofs had collapsed, exposing heating tanks, pulleys, and a water turbine. Were they headed to the shore or the fish cannery? Neither looked safe.

A man with a thin mustache jiggled the rudder of the dinghy, while the man with the rifle still had it trained on her.

"Where are we going?" she asked.

"We're going to land on the beach," Ernest said. "There is a cave tucked into the cliff where you'll be safe and won't be able to get into any trouble. All you need to do is cooperate and everything will be fine."

She wondered if Gwendolyn had cooperated. Assault, kidnapping, and drugging people were not the crimes of a novice criminal, and in all likelihood one of the men in this boat was responsible for strangling the life out of her sister.

"Hey, do you remember that Caslon type I bought in Philadelphia?" Ernest asked. "It turns out another set just got listed for auction in London. The lowest bidding price is twice what I paid for mine last month." He looked pleased, as though he expected her to be impressed.

"Congratulations," she managed to say in a pleasant enough voice. "It seems you found quite the bargain." Find common ground with him. Perhaps that would help him see her as a human and not some inconvenient insect that needed squashing.

"It's a rare set, and one of great beauty," he said. "I think all the modern printing methods have really lost something. The artistry of the typographer is gone. It's all just machine printing now."

She scrambled for something, anything, to say that might placate Ernest. "You're right," she said. "The soul of a craftsman can be seen in all kinds of type. Even bookbinding has a certain beauty to it, don't you think?"

It seemed to be the right thing to say. Ernest's smile was broad as he nodded his head. "Wonderful artistry! Of course, leather bindings are far more fragile than good metal type. That's why I never bothered collecting books. The leather ages and decays, and the lifespan of a book is so short. Not like good steel type that can last for millennia."

Stella felt a little sick inside. She was like the fragile, mortal leather book, except instead of being able to age and decay with time, she suspected she was about to come to a swift end.

They were almost ashore, and Jason Mason of the Harbor Department hopped into the surf, the water rising only to his hips. Grabbing the front of the boat, he dragged it toward the boulder-strewn beach. A bump and a rasp below her indicated the boat had run aground. The fourth man still kept the rifle trained on her.

"Time to go ashore," Ernest said brightly. "Here's the part where it is important to keep your wits, Miss West. Raymond is going to keep that rifle trained on you the whole time, so don't try to get stupid or heroic. All you have to do is follow instructions, and everything will be fine. Hop on out now. Don't worry, the water is shallow. You might want to hike your skirts up, because the surf is cold and you don't have a change of clothes on shore."

A sheen of frothy bubbles swirled atop of the gray surf. Her knees wobbled and her head pounded, but she could do this. They didn't know she couldn't swim, and she had no intention of telling them. Jason stood beside the boat and reached up to guide her out.

The last thing on earth she wanted was to touch that man's flesh, but she needed his help.

The water was so cold! She yelped, and almost lost her balance, but Jason grabbed her elbow and righted her before she fell.

"Come on, move along," Jason grumbled.

She focused on the shore ahead of her—anything but the water swirling around her knees. Dry land was only a few more yards away. It was a good thing she'd worn tightly laced boots. Otherwise the sucking pressure from the surf would have pulled them off.

Relief trickled through her as she reached the shore. The man let go of her arm, and she stepped carefully amid the wide, flat-topped rocks littering the shore. She kept moving toward a sandy area ahead, water squishing out of her sodden boots with each footfall.

"We made it," Ernest crowed when they were all ashore. While one of the men hauled the dinghy higher onto the beach, the other two each raised their rifles. Ernest had a pistol strapped to his belt, as did the man dragging the boat ashore. Four men, four guns. What did they need so many for? If they were going to kill her, one would do the job just fine. Although didn't firing squads usually use a team of men?

"What now?" she asked.

"Now we head toward that cave on the north end of the cliffs. I've brought a canteen of water, and we can all have a bit of a rest." Two men set off toward an outcropping of rocks, but one of the men with a rifle stood behind her.

It wasn't until Ernest mentioned the canteen that Stella realized her thirst. Her mouth was cottony, and her raging headache was probably from dehydration. The canteen dangled from Ernest's hand as he set off toward the cave, and she followed as quickly as possible. Her limbs trembled and her entire head ached, but the canteen of water motivated her steps.

The cliffside ahead was made of pitted black rock, flecked with bits of mica and carved away by thousands of years of surf. A deep indentation in the rock lay straight ahead, and the three men headed inside. Stella hurried to follow. The canteen was small, and she didn't want the others drinking all the water before she had a chance at it.

It was dim inside the cave. The bottom of the cave was mostly sand, with a few jutting boulders and some shallow tidal pools with water puddled inside. It was tall enough to stand in, but not by much. She instinctively ducked and covered her head as she moved farther into the dank cave.

Ernest extended the canteen. "Ladies first," he said with a smile.

She took the canteen, a metal canister about the size of a small loaf of bread. The nozzle was open, and she sniffed. No matter how thirsty she was, she didn't fully trust anything out of Ernest Palmer's hand.

"I'd prefer if you drank first," she said, handing him back the canteen.

He understood, and with a grim smile, he took a hearty sip.

"More," Stella said, and he drew more, his throat bobbing. When he handed the canteen back to her, it was lighter. A glance inside showed the water level had gone down significantly.

She put the cold metal opening to her lips and drank. She didn't care that Ernest had just been drinking from it, she was dying of thirst and couldn't swallow quickly enough. A few trickles dribbled down her chin, and she stopped for a moment to breathe, then went back to drinking. Good manners dictated that she offer the canteen to the others, but manners didn't come into play when dealing with kidnappers.

At last she'd had enough. She carefully twisted the lid back in place while surveying the four men standing in a semi-circle around her. Now that her immediate thirst had been quenched, the fear returned.

"We are going to leave you here for a spell," Ernest said. "You are welcome to keep the canteen, but we need to be on our way now. It is important to stay in the cave until we return for you, hmm?"

"And when will that be?"

"When our business is done," Ernest said. "Don't be difficult about this, Miss West. I'm sorry things have gotten so unpleasant. As I said, I always liked you. I find you so much more interesting than the other women who work at City Hall, most of whom are nothing more than cackling harpies worried only about clothing and suitors. You had real worth."

She swallowed hard, wishing he hadn't referred to her in the past tense, but the men were already turning around and heading out of the cave. Was she really supposed to stay here? But she didn't mind putting a little distance between herself and those guns. It was hard to hear over the pounding of the waves, but their voices did indeed seem to be fading into the distance. Stepping a few feet closer to the mouth of the cave, she saw all four men walking back to the dinghy, and a surge of hope took root inside. They were clearly up to no good, but if they really intended to leave her here while they set off on some nefarious task, perhaps she had a good shot at escaping.

As the men drew closer to the dinghy, they occasionally looked back over their shoulders to be sure she remained at the cave. One of them even pointed his rifle at her casually, and she immediately jumped back behind the sheltering wall of rough basalt rock. A few minutes later, she saw the dinghy back at sea, all four men inside.

Where were they going? Before she had long to ponder, a rush of chilly water raced toward the cave in a gentle hiss. It swirled around her ankles and replenished the water in the tidal pools, then raced back out, but the damage had been done. Her skirts were soaked to her knees. Leaning over, she grabbed hunks of fabric and wrung out the water. She liked this skirt, too! It was hand-dyed twill and shouldn't be abused like this, but it wouldn't do to stand about in wet clothes. Heavens only knew how long they intended to make her wait here.

Another rush of water came only moments later, undoing her work. She squeezed out the skirt again, then scooted to a natural rock ledge in the wall. She had to hop up to sit on it. It was horribly uncomfortable, but at least her feet were above the surf.

She clenched the canteen in her lap, tempted to drink again, but this might prove to be a long wait and she should probably ration it.

It stank like wet stone in here. The cave only went back about fifteen feet and had rough, uneven walls and ceiling. The back of the cave was completely submerged in water.

How long had she been here? It felt like hours but was probably no more than fifteen or twenty minutes.

A surge of water brushed her boots and she lifted them higher, grabbing at the canteen to prevent it from falling into the water, which rose higher than ever before. Even though she lifted her feet as high as possible, they still got wet.

This was ridiculous. She waited until the surf rushed out of the cave, then pushed off the ledge to see where the dinghy was. She had no intention of staying in here and getting soaked once those men were out of sight. The palms of her hands scraped against the grainy rocks, but she'd worry about them later. Almost a foot of water remained inside the cave even after the waves retreated.

She slogged to the front and peeked out of the cave, scanning the water for the dinghy, but she couldn't see it. How could it have disappeared from sight so quickly?

A movement on the island a quarter-mile away caught her attention. That's where they were! Sitting amid the abandoned fish cannery, all four men casually lounged on the pier, two of them leaning back against a corrugated tin shed. The dinghy was tied to the pier.

One of the men spotted her and scrambled to his feet. The other three men stood, and within moments, all four guns were pointed straight at her. She froze.

Another wave came rushing toward the cave, hitting her at the knees. She grabbed the side of the cave for balance as the waters churned around her. The grainy rock hurt, but the undertow was strong as water rushed back to the sea. One of the men fired a warning shot in the air, then aimed the rifle back at her.

Now she understood their plan. The tide was coming in, and there was no escape from this cave. They wanted her drowning to look natural, for they had messed up Gwendolyn's murder by leaving bruises on her throat. They'd learned. Her drowning was going to be genuine, not staged. Once she was dead, they could take her body back to Boston and do whatever they wanted with it. She had a morbid suspicion they'd dump her precisely where Gwendolyn had been found, for it would surely appear to be a suicide.

The four men still stood on the pier, guns trained on her. They would only shoot as a last resort, she realized. She closed her eyes as despair knifed through her. It looked like she'd never get a chance to marry, which was a shame. It would have been nice to have had a chance to mend fences with Romulus. They would have been great together.

The wind made her sopping clothes seem even colder, and another wave was on its way. The sight of the guns was nerve-racking, and she retreated back into the cave, wading through the calf-high surf toward the ledge. There was still water in the canteen, and she drank. It hadn't been an act of kindness on Ernest's part to offer her the canteen. It had been a way to lure her into the cave without a fuss, and she had stupidly walked into his trap. All for a drink of water.

She pulled up her feet and huddled on the ledge, clutching the canteen to keep her hands from trembling.

—ᕫᣟᕬ—

Two hours later, the water was at her waist. The men were still outside, still scrambling to their feet each time she poked her head outside the cave. She was getting shaky, whether from hunger, the cold, or fear was anyone's guess. Probably all three.

But the peculiar thing was that a faint glow came from beneath the water at the back of the cave. It wasn't until it got darker in the cave that she noticed the strange source of light. It was barely visible, but it wasn't going away. What was it?

The cave was completely flooded. It hurt her palms to cling to the rough crevice above the ledge, and as the water rose higher, the tug of the waves was harder to resist. The water was so high she could smell it—salty, dank, and horrible—but when she tried to scoot higher on the ledge her head bumped against the ceiling of the cave. There probably wasn't more than an hour left before the tide would be too high to keep her head above water.

Would it be better to wander outside the cave and let them shoot her? It would be a quick death and easier than drowning. And if her body had bullet holes, there would be no question that it was a murder.

Salty water rushed against her chest, the spray hitting her face and going up her nose. She sputtered, trying to clear her nose without loosening her death-grip on the crevice that kept her anchored on this narrow ledge.

She didn't want to die. This was going to destroy her parents. Her parents deserved to have grandchildren they could spoil and open presents with on Christmas mornings. She wanted to watch her father take her children out into the meadow and teach them how tadpoles developed or why the sky was blue. She had really looked forward to that someday. They didn't deserve to lose both their daughters.

She had to stop thinking this way. Getting weepy wasn't going to help, and she really didn't want to knowingly walk before a firing squad.

The cave dimmed as the tide obscured the opening, making the light at the back of the cave more noticeable. She didn't know what it was, but it might be her only chance out of here, and there wasn't much time to think about it. Scooting off the ledge, she waded through shoulder-high water toward the weird source of light coming from low in the cave.

She explored with the toe of her boot and found an opening. A tunnel? A karst? She struggled to remember the research she'd done for the series on subterranean caves she'd illustrated years ago. Most of them had been carved out by water. This could be one of them. It might be the only explanation for the light. And the tunnel couldn't be that long or the light wouldn't be able to penetrate.

What did it matter? She wished she had learned how to swim, but she hadn't, and there was nothing she could do about that now.

Another wave hit her in the face. This wasn't going to get any better. She either had to stay here and drown, or go out and face the firing squad.

Or she could force herself to sink down into the water and find out what was causing that strange source of light. If it was a tunnel and there was daylight on the other side . . .

She closed her eyes for a quick prayer.

Dear Jesus, I need help. I've been a lousy Christian up until now, and I'm sorry for that. Another wave slapped her in the face, and she sputtered again. *I'm doing this for my parents as much as me, so if you can lend a hand . . .*

And if it didn't work out, she prayed her parents would live through this, that they would make it despite the death of another daughter. Karl and Eloise Westergaard were a love story for the ages, and Stella had to believe they could weather another storm. She would be rooting for them from the other side.

But she wasn't dead yet, and her parents hadn't raised sissies. She was going to do this.

She took a deep breath and dove under the water.

It was freezing! Cold water penetrated her hair and scalp. She couldn't see, but she thrashed toward the tunnel opening, struggling to get low enough in the water, arms flailing madly. Pain scraped across her knuckles as she found the underside of the tunnel and pulled herself lower. She tried to force herself into the tunnel, but it was impossible to get that low. Pain exploded as she banged her head against the top of the tunnel. Her breath expelled, and she sucked in water.

She had to get out. Panic ruled as she thrashed back out of the tunnel, jagged rocks ripping at her palms and arms. The instant she was free of the tunnel, she braced her feet and shot back to the surface, sobbing as she flailed her way back to the ledge. She sucked in air and didn't have the strength to haul herself back up onto the ledge.

"I'm sorry, Mama," she sobbed. "Oh Mama, I'm so sorry."

It turned out she was a coward, after all.

If she could live her life again, she would do things differently. She would be a better Christian every single day, not just on the occasional Sunday. She wouldn't have waited so long to get married and have children. She would have done so many things differently . . .

No. No, she wasn't going to spend her last moments on earth counting her regrets, for all in all, she'd had a good life. No, scratch that . . . she'd had a *fantastic* life. She'd been blessed with the best parents imaginable, and she'd gotten to pursue a career most people could only dream about. Just remembering it all made her start to laugh through chattering teeth. No one could say that Stella West didn't wring out the best each day had to offer, and she had loved every moment of it.

Thank you, God! Things didn't end so well . . . but I had a wonderful life. It was the best. Thank you, thank you . . .

She should have been thankful for it every day, not just here at the end.

A trickle of blood slipped down from her scalp, and her hands were scraped and bloody, but her panting began to ease. The air flowed in and out of her lungs at a normal rate as her panic subsided.

It was that air in her lungs that had been the problem, preventing her from sinking low enough to get through the tunnel. She had taken a huge breath of air just before attempting to swim the tunnel, and that had been a mistake.

A hint of a smile came back. She wasn't ready to give up. She had enough strength for a second run at that tunnel, and she would be smarter this time. It seemed illogical and frightening, but this time she would go under with empty lungs.

Please, she whispered in the fading light. She closed her eyes, summoning up the image of her parents, then blew out all her air and dove under. Sinking was easier this time. And she kept her eyes open, ignoring the painful sting as she headed straight for that blur of light ahead, grabbing the side of the tunnel wall to pull herself forward, then forward again.

The light intensified as the darkness overhead lifted. She rose, sputtering and pushing the hair from her eyes, trying to get her bearings in this new, strange cavern. It was flooded with light and air. It was like a tunnel going straight up. Was she in an old fishing hole? Or a sinkhole? It was hard to tell, but directly above her was a channel of volcanic rock, and at the top of it she could see a smattering of late-afternoon clouds in a blue sky.

She dragged herself to the edge of the water. There was enough of a slope that she could at least get out of the water. Her muscles trembled as she crawled out. She was sopping wet, freezing, and trembling from thirst and exhaustion, but she had made it.

The opening was at least twenty feet up. She would never be able to crawl out of this cavern, but it would keep her safe until dawn.

The patch of blue sky overhead was the most beautiful sight she'd ever seen, and she couldn't stop laughing. Perhaps it was her imagination, but she sensed warmth and love in the patch of sunlight streaming down. There was a radiance here, brilliant and blinding in its intensity. It felt like warmth and compassion and forgiveness.

Tears slipped from the corners of her eyes and leaked into her hair. The awesome power in the sunlight above was deeper and more intense than the human mind could grasp. It had been strong enough to power her journey through the tunnel to get here.

She was thirsty, her hands were scraped and bleeding, and her head throbbed, but she felt God's love surrounding her. Even in this most desperate of hours, she was not alone. She might die tomorrow morning, but she had six hours until the next low tide. Six hours was a blessing, and she'd savor every moment of it. What was six hours or six years or six decades in the grand scheme of things? God had saved her, and every second from this moment forward was a gift for which she was infinitely grateful.

Laughter bubbled up once again. She was alive to fight another day, and it was a gift she intended to seize.

20

By the time Romulus and Michael reached the railway station, the last train heading north had already departed, and another would not leave until tomorrow morning. A long carriage ride through the night had been their only option to get to Boulder Point.

As attorney general, Michael was able to pull some strings to smooth their path. Before leaving the station, he'd wired the police in Boulder Point to be on the lookout for Ernest Palmer, described as a short, stocky man with thick glasses who was probably traveling with a young woman. The woman was to be warned and taken into safe custody.

Romulus could only imagine Stella's reaction to being detained, but it was better than heading off into the wilderness with a criminal like Ernest Palmer.

The rented hack was poorly sprung and the padding on the benches had been matted down long ago, but Romulus welcomed the jarring ride. Anything to get his mind off Stella. All he could do was pray the telegram reached the police department in time to waylay Ernest Palmer. If it didn't, or if Stella was not with Ernest when Romulus finally arrived in Boulder Point . . . well, it didn't bear thinking of. Maybe someday he would look back on this miserable evening and laugh about the needless panic that had sent him hurtling off into the darkness, but for now, he was sick with anxiety. He'd never been the sort to suffer from ulcerative complaints, but it seemed his stomach was awash with acid. He couldn't sit still, couldn't focus. The combination of guilt and fear was a powerful motivator, keeping him awake through the long night.

They arrived in Boulder Point just as the sun was rising. The wheels of the carriage hadn't even come to a complete stop when Romulus unlatched the door and sprang to the ground, Michael not far behind. They raced into the police station, a modest building at the end of the town's main street. If Ernest or Stella had been detained last night, someone here would know about it.

Unlike the bustling police stations in Boston, here the front room looked more like a doctor's office, with a grouping of empty chairs, a service counter, and a bleary-eyed night attendant still on duty.

"The wire didn't arrive until late last evening," the young sergeant said. "The captain sent a pair of officers to the train depot, but we think it was too late. A man matching your description was loitering around the depot most of the afternoon. A young lady arrived in the early evening. The clerk thinks they left together."

Romulus felt as though he'd been punched in the gut. They were too late.

~ ᴏⳡᴏ ~

It was a difficult night. After the rush of exhilaration from surviving the underwater journey to get here, Stella stared up at the blue patch of sky until it darkened into gray, then black, then speckled with tiny stars.

She was freezing and thirsty. The canteen was long gone, and the darkness was unnerving. All she could hear was the slap of waves, oddly comforting in that it reminded her she was still alive. A few times, she slipped into a hazy kind of sleep, but the lapping of the waves caused her to jerk awake every few minutes.

There was no getting out of this tunnel, and that meant that tomorrow at low tide she was going to have to slip beneath the water and make that journey through the underwater tunnel again. She ought to be terrified at the prospect, but she was too exhausted to worry anymore. And sometime in the middle of the night, it rained. She opened her mouth, frustrated by the meager drops of fresh water that had landed on her tongue, but she'd take what blessings came her way.

Low tide came at sunrise. The fumbling swim through the tunnel wasn't nearly so difficult to accomplish the second time, and she emerged in the awful cave she had come to despise. Were Ernest and his minions still about? Or had they assumed the tide had done its work and headed back to Boston?

There was only a few feet of water in the cave, and she cautiously approached the opening, clinging tightly to the wet, grainy wall. Holding her breath, she peeked outside the cave opening and scanned the old fish cannery. The men and dinghy were gone.

Her relief was so great she went dizzy.

"Thank you, Lord," she murmured. "Thank you, thank you." She would thank him every day for the rest of her life. She leaned against the cave wall long enough for the trembling to subside, then headed outside in search of civilization.

Romulus was glad Michael was willing to pull rank at the Boulder Point Police Department to get men posted at the train station, the two local stables where horses could be leased, and at the only ferry on the peninsula. Unless Ernest intended to walk home to Boston, they would catch him at one of these spots.

Romulus put his money on the train station. It was how the archivist had arrived in town, and it would be the quickest, most anonymous means of getting back to Boston. Two members of the local police were at the station, one a sergeant and the other a young officer who looked barely old enough to shave.

Romulus took a seat on one end of the station platform, while Michael monitored the other. They both wore caps pulled low over their foreheads. The worst thing would be if Ernest recognized them and fled before they could catch him.

Hours crawled past as Romulus scrutinized dozens of strangers who passed through the station. Against all hope, he kept looking for Stella. It was hard to imagine her dashing figure sauntering up to this rural train depot, but he couldn't stop hoping and praying for her safety.

He refused to believe she was dead. Not Stella.

A commotion at the far end of the platform caught his attention. The two police officers emerged from behind the coal shed, guns drawn. Michael had given the signal, pointing out Ernest Palmer, who was approaching the ticket window. He was with two others, and all three men looked baffled as the police sergeant ordered them to stay put. There was no sign of Stella.

Romulus raced down the platform as the officers drew their pistols on the three men.

"What's going on?" Ernest asked, his voice bewildered and hands raised high. The other two men joined in the universal sign of surrender. With his short stature and mild-mannered bearing, Ernest was playing the confused victim to the hilt, but the other two men looked like they'd had toughness bred into them from birth. One was a brawny redhead, and the other had an ugly mustache and a bolt-action rifle in a sling across his back. He didn't look frightened. He looked angry.

Michael strode forward. "Where's Stella?" he demanded.

"Stella who?" Ernest replied with admirable calm.

"You know who I'm talking about," Michael said. "Where is she?"

Perspiration dotted Ernest's forehead, and he gave a weak little smile. "Why are you playing games? I don't know what you're talking about."

Romulus scanned the situation. Three criminals, one with a powerful rifle on his back. Two police officers with pistols, but Michael and Romulus were unarmed. With lightning speed, the redhead standing beside Ernest drew a pistol from his coat and shot the young police officer. The officer recoiled and collapsed.

Without hesitation, the sergeant shot the redheaded man between his eyes. Bystanders panicked and raced for cover, but there was almost no place to hide on the boardwalk platform. The clerk behind the ticket window rolled down the wooden cover with a loud thump. A woman and her child huddled behind a metal bench, terrified. The man with the mustache got his rifle off his back and aimed it at the sergeant, who was fighting to overcome a misfire while the wounded young officer struggled to rise. The fallen policeman had blood running down his arm, but he managed to lift his gun, his hand wobbling badly.

"Enough!" Michael shouted. "It's over. Enough!"

"It won't be over until that copper drops his gun!" Ernest shrieked.

"And what will you do then? Shoot both officers dead? That's a hanging offense. Shoot me? Shoot at them?" Michael asked, gesturing to the bystanders huddled behind benches and lamp-posts. "It's over! We killed a man thirty-five years ago and have been hiding it ever since. Samuel Alden went to prison for it, and it was all our fault."

Michael shouted the words loud enough for everyone at the train station to hear. There was no going back now.

Ernest still held his hands in the air, but they shook wildly, making the sergeant nervous.

"Quit moving!" the sergeant bellowed, his weapon trained on Ernest.

A click sounded somewhere behind a cluster of trees near the hitching post. Romulus caught the glint of a rifle barrel in the shrubbery. "Behind you!" he shouted.

The crack of the rifle cut him off, and the sergeant pitched forward, his gun spinning out into the dirt. The man who had had the rifle on his back fired at the wounded officer still on his knees. The young officer rolled aside just in time. The henchman jerked back the bolt to eject the cartridge and reload another round.

Romulus wasn't going to let him take another shot without a fight. Leaping across the platform, he kicked the rifle, sending it twirling onto the train tracks, then hauled back and landed a right hook on the henchman's face.

He was vaguely aware of the hidden sniper emerging from the bushes and joining the fray, but Michael was already on him, dealing a swift series of combination punches.

He and Michael fought back to back. It was two against three, but raw speed, strength, and agility won out over men who couldn't raise their weapons amid the onslaught of flying fists. When Ernest managed to get his pistol drawn, Romulus kicked it so hard it went flying and smacked against the wall of the train depot.

But another gunshot rang out, and Michael fell to his knees. The man from the bushes even now struggled to chamber a new round. Romulus bounded toward him and grabbed the barrel of the rifle before the sniper could reload. He tore the weapon away and swung it like a bat against the side of his attacker's head. The man fell and did not move again.

There were more gunshots behind him, and Romulus hit the ground, uncertain where the shots were coming from. The young police officer who'd been grazed had risen to his knees and fired off a steady series of shots, taking down Ernest and the remaining henchman.

It was over.

For a few moments, it was as if time had stopped, the sound of gunshots still echoing in his ears. Romulus glanced frantically around the station, searching for any other henchmen who might still be in hiding.

No one emerged. It seemed that it was all well and truly over.

The sniper Romulus had clobbered had a sizeable wound on the side of his head but was still breathing. A newspaper boy who'd taken cover behind a bench came forward and landed a heavy boot on the wounded man's back. "I'll keep him locked down if you want to see to your friend."

Romulus nodded in gratitude and darted to Michael, who lay curled on the bare platform. His face was pale, and the wheeze as he gasped for breath didn't sound good. It gurgled, and blood trickled from his mouth. He'd been shot in the lung.

Romulus knelt beside him. "Can you hear me?" he asked.

Michael managed a single nod. "Sorry," he whispered.

"I know you are. You did a brave thing." Michael probably wouldn't live to face the legal ramifications of his adolescent prank, but he'd confessed it openly and without reservation. That counted for a lot.

"Tried to be a good man," Michael wheezed.

Romulus grabbed his hand. "You were."

Whatever his old friend's sins, Romulus could not doubt his remorse. He held Michael's hand as the life faded from his eyes and the tension eased from his body. He could only pray that, in death, Michael would find the peace and forgiveness that had eluded him in life.

The sergeant was badly wounded but would probably live. The young police officer had only a flesh wound to his arm and helped sort out the mess. Of the four men involved in Stella's disappearance, only the sniper in the bushes survived. By the time he roused from the clobbering Romulus had delivered, he had been handcuffed to a bench and had three police officers training their guns on him.

"You've killed the attorney general of Massachusetts," Romulus said. "Your only prayer for mercy is if you tell us what you did with Stella West."

Romulus held his breath, praying that, against all odds, Stella was still safe, but the guilt flushing the man's face filled Romulus with dread.

"It was that slimy archivist's idea," the sniper said. "We didn't want anything to do with it. We told him not to do it."

Romulus couldn't breathe, couldn't move. All he could do was brace himself for what was coming, but nothing could have prepared him for what he heard next.

"We cornered her in the cave down by the old Wallingford Fish Cannery. You can't get out of there once the tide comes in. She drowned last night."

He recoiled. Of all the ways for Stella to die, that had to be the worst.

It was possible this man was lying. Or that she had somehow escaped. He knew he was grasping at straws, but it was easier than facing the reality of her death. He would never have a chance to say that he'd been wrong about the two of them, that he was sorry.

But if there was a prayer that she still lived, or if her body hadn't been dragged out to sea and could be recovered, he would find her. Her parents deserved the finality of a decent burial.

The tiny police force of Boulder Point was overwhelmed by the deaths of four men and two injured officers. They weren't going to send anyone to help him, and frankly, he didn't want their help. He needed to be alone right now.

He was warned the dirt road leading to the abandoned cannery was neglected and too bumpy for carriage traffic, so he rented a horse and set off.

※

It was late in the afternoon before Romulus could smell the salt from the sea as the horse carried him closer to the cannery. Thick pine forests framed both sides of the dusty rural lane.

He must be getting close, for the forest had thinned, giving way to reeds and sand dunes. The scent of pine was overwhelmed by the briny tang of salt. As he rounded a bend, pale blue water finally came into view. He kicked the horse into a trot, anxious to find the cannery and the dangerous cave where he might find Stella. He would need as much daylight as possible to begin the search. A glance to the right showed the ramshackle old cannery, cut off from the peninsula by about fifty yards of water. He looked in both directions for the cave, but the cliffs on both sides looked equally rocky and forbidding.

Wind buffeted him, and once again he cursed this bleak, depressing sight. It was an abandoned stretch of beach, where everything was shades of gray, blue, and black. It wasn't the kind of place someone as brilliantly colored as Stella West should have met her end.

It was impossible to know which direction would lead him to the cave, but to the south, a lone beachcomber picked his way along the shoreline. The beachcomber was almost a mile off, but perhaps he would be able to direct Romulus to the cave.

He guided the horse into the shallow surf, where the footing was pure sand and clear of the treacherous rocks. Water splashed onto his legs as he spurred the horse forward to catch up with the beachcomber. As he drew closer, it became clear the beachcomber was a woman, stopping every few yards to pick at something in the sand. He winced. She was eating the whelks that had washed ashore. Whelks were nasty little mollusks that were rubbery even when cooked and purely revolting when eaten raw.

A scraggly blond braid hung down her back, and the filthy dress looked as if she'd been rolling in the surf. She tossed another whelk shell behind her as she continued heading up the beach. He shuddered, glad he'd never been so hungry as to eat raw whelks.

The way she walked . . . he swallowed hard and refused to hope. Stella had an unmistakable saunter, full of grace and confidence. The beachcomber seemed close in size and shape to Stella, but in his wildest dreams he could not bear to hope . . .

"Excuse me, ma'am," he called out. His voice was carried away on the wind, and he cleared his throat to shout louder. This time she heard him and turned around. His heart nearly stopped beating.

She gasped. "Romulus?"

He sprang down from the horse, staggering through the surf toward her. She was laughing as she ran toward him, flinging her arms around his shoulders as he hoisted her in the air, twirling her in circles above the surf. Her skin was grubby and speckled with sand and salt, but her wind-chapped complexion had never looked prettier.

This felt like a dream, but it was too real, with the sun glaring in his eyes and the chilly rush of the water at his knees. One shoe had gotten pulled off as he'd twirled her in the air.

"I was afraid you were dead," he whispered against her neck. His voice wasn't too steady, and he was grateful he got the words out without choking up. He set her down to get a better look at her. Leonardo himself couldn't paint anything more radiant than the happiness in Stella's face.

"I was afraid of that for a while, too," she said. "It's been a rough couple of days."

He nodded. "I know . . . and I've lost my shoe. Help me look for it?"

Her jaw dropped. It looked as if she didn't know whether to laugh or choke him. "I nearly drown, get shot, die of thirst, and get scraped to pieces on volcanic rocks . . . but hold on, everyone! Romulus has lost his shoe!"

She doubled over with peals of laughter, and he was helpless against joining her in a full-bellied laugh that echoed down the beach. This might be the funniest, happiest moment of his life. Fits of laughter seized so hard he doubled over and had to brace his hands on his thighs to stop from falling into the surf.

"That shoe was handmade in New York," he managed to gasp out before another round of laughter overtook him, and she laughed just as hard. She was almost hysterical, with big gulping sobs of laughter.

"Are you laughing or crying?" he asked.

"I don't know!"

"Well, come here and let me hold you until you decide."

She slogged through the water toward him, and he held her tight as the waves churned around them. This moment was perfection, and he leaned down to kiss her. They fit perfectly together, and he held her tightly, savoring the solid sense of relief and joy and happiness at being alive. The sky was cloudless, and they had both survived the worst trial of their lives.

But he still wanted that shoe back, and it was rolling in the surf a few yards away. He grabbed her hand and tugged her along as he slogged toward it. After snatching the shoe from the water, he trudged up higher on the beach and sat on a boulder to wiggle his sandy foot back into the waterlogged shoe. It was probably ruined.

"What are you doing here?" Stella asked as she sat down on the boulder beside him.

"I came looking for you." He tugged on the sodden laces, suddenly unbearably fatigued. The exhilaration of the moment began to fade as memory of dark tragedy intruded. "Rumor had it you were destined for a bad end in a cave."

Her smile was sad and exhausted. "That was the plan."

Over the next half hour, she told him everything that had happened to her. He held her hands on his lap. Her palms and knuckles were covered with bloody scrapes, but she was alive and breathing and would make a full recovery. Her body would, at any rate. No woman could live through the night she'd just endured without carrying those scars for the rest of her life.

He traced the outline of her hand, avoiding the swollen scrape marks but knowing it was impossible to avoid the pain of this conversation. "Michael Townsend is dead," he said, filling her in on how the man had made a full confession of his role in the death of a man decades earlier, and the string of cover-ups stemming from it.

During the overnight carriage ride, Michael had admitted he

and Ernest created the trumped-up injunction against *Scientific World*. It was an attempt to drive a wedge between Stella and Romulus so she would lose her best shot at getting close to the people who could help her discover the extent of Gwendolyn's activities at City Hall. Michael and Ernest had also drafted a fraudulent letter from London, implying she needed to return as soon as possible to reassert her copyright privileges.

"I don't know if it's any comfort," he said, "but I truly believe he loved Gwendolyn. He didn't know Ernest ordered her death. The surviving henchman admitted that Ernest bribed a City Hall employee named Jason Mason to lure Gwendolyn to that bridge by implying he wanted to join her crusade. He killed her instead."

Stella nodded, but her face was unbearably sad. Wind tugged at locks of her hair that had broken free of her braid, and he gently smoothed them behind her ear. She turned her face into his hand, pressing a kiss to his palm. He would give his right arm if he could pick up and carry some of this grief for her. In a bittersweet way, he envied her. Aside from Evelyn, he'd never had the sort of tightly knit family that was such a central part of Stella's life. He leaned forward and kissed her forehead.

The wind, the salt spray, the roar of the surf . . . it stripped away the bright artifice he and Stella usually wore, and they were just a man and a woman, open and without armor to protect against these raw, nascent emotions.

"When I thought I was going to die, I realized that I wanted so much better for myself."

He nearly choked. "You've had your work displayed at the British Museum!"

"I meant I want to be a *better person*," she hastily amended. "Not so self-absorbed. Someone like Gwendolyn, who cared about more than her career or her wardrobe. I want to be the sort of person who ends each day by saying a prayer of thanks to God for everything I've been given. My parents did a good job of teaching me about faith. The fact that I drifted was my fault, not theirs. I'm ready to do better."

He touched his forehead to hers, clasping her hands. From the moment he'd met Stella, she'd presented herself as an overly confident, somewhat imposing personality. Now she had stripped away that façade and was willing to share her insecurities on this most perfect of days.

"I love you," he said. "When I feared you were dead, I wished I'd told you. I should have told you every day." It looked as if she was going to cry again, and that was the last thing he wanted.

"I love you, too," she said, hugging him tightly and pressing her salty cheek against his.

This was all going very fast. The distant prospect of marriage was suddenly looming very close, and it was terrifying.

"I don't know if I can be a good husband," he confessed. "I've never been around a marriage that worked. My parents were always at each other's throats."

"Don't worry, my parents have a great marriage, and I know enough for the both of us," she said, the old confidence creeping back into her voice. "We'll be positively brilliant. *I* will be, anyway. You'll just have to watch and learn."

He grinned. "I want you to know how much I deeply admire your spectacular ego. Sometimes it's large enough to blot out the heat of the sun."

Her laughter was like music. With her face tilted to the sky, golden hair flying in the breeze, she was as brilliant as she'd claimed. And he loved her, high-flying ego and all.

They walked along the beach hand in hand, eating ghastly whelks because it was the only thing available and neither one of them wanted to return to civilization quite yet. It was as if, when they returned to the real world, this luminous, other-worldly happiness might vanish.

"It will be getting dark soon," he whispered.

Both of them were damp, and it would get chilly the moment the sun began setting. The horse could only carry one of them, and Romulus helped Stella into the saddle. He arranged her skirts to cover her legs. "Forgive me for being an idiot about the whole waiting-until-forty thing?"

"It depends on what kind of engagement ring you buy me."

A shudder raced through him. "You do know how to send a bolt of sheer terror straight into a man's soul."

He had always jested about his fear of marriage, but it was real. It was one thing to fail privately, but a failed marriage swept innocent casualties into the firestorm. He didn't know how to tame the wild streak inside and conform his life to another person's expectations, and he was not confident of his ability to do so.

He loved Stella, but the thought of letting her down petrified him. The only other woman he'd ever loved had been brutally frank about his shortcomings, and Laura was entirely correct in her assessment. He was distractible. Scattered. Disorganized. Could a man like him be a proper husband to a woman like Stella? He toyed with her ankle as he struggled to form these rambling, unwieldy thoughts into words. "I want to be your husband, but marriage is too important to rush into. I need a little more time, all right?"

He was glad she didn't sling a witty retort back at him. Sometimes he needed to lower the shields and simply be honest. This soft, vulnerable piece of him wasn't used to the bright light of day, and it needed to be handled carefully.

Stella's face was gentle as she smiled down at him. "I understand," she said softly.

He gathered the horse's reins and set off toward town, Stella riding the horse behind him. They were silent for the walk back to town, but it was a companionable silence. He breathed deeply of the pine-scented air, the trees looming tall around them in the gathering darkness. These few days had been marked with tragedy and joy, and the whirlwind of emotions was something he would never forget. He'd found the woman he loved, and by God's grace, she had survived an almost certain death sentence.

Both he and Stella had huge, howling inadequacies as people, but these past few weeks had taught them humility. They'd both let themselves be manipulated by anger and professional crisis. When his magazine had begun failing, he'd put his work before Stella. When Stella was consumed with bitterness over what had happened to Gwendolyn, she had trampled on everyone in her quest for justice.

They would learn from their mistakes. Had they relied on the timeless principles of faith in God's enduring promise, they would have supported each other better through this time of trial.

A soft breeze caressed his face, and he smiled into the wind, grateful for the chance to begin again.

─ ⟋⟍⟋⟍ ─

Evelyn lay in bed, staring at the ceiling as the early-morning light illuminated the muted tones of her bedroom. It was a plain room, with simple but well-made furniture, almost puritanical in its sparse design. The only real decoration was an oil painting on the wall across from the bed. It was of a hummingbird suspended before a honeysuckle vine, delicately sipping from a bloom. That painting had been relegated to the attic for years, but she'd asked Clyde to help her hang it again after they'd returned from the health resort.

Clyde slumbered beside her, his breathing deep and even. She dared not move, lest she awaken him. He'd been sleeping so little in the past few weeks, and she wanted him to have as much rest as possible. Clyde had been dealt a terrible blow and had needed to hibernate in the mountains for a while, but they were both glad to be home. They hadn't been this happy since their honeymoon. Neither expected perfection of the other, and that was making all the difference in the world.

The swelling was finally subsiding in Clyde's ears, letting the doctor get a better view of what was going on deep within his ear canal. The doctor said Clyde's right eardrum was shattered and would never recover, but there was still hope for his left ear.

Her suggestion that they write a book together had been an attempt to get Clyde to focus on something meaningful rather than counting his losses. If his hearing recovered, would they still write it? In the past few weeks, they'd had fun outlining the contents, arguing over which details were significant and which were merely Clyde's chance to grind an axe against his rivals. When she pointed that out, he had grinned and told her he *liked* grinding an axe!

Beside her, Clyde sighed and snuggled closer. She smiled. Life hadn't turned out as they had planned, but it was an extraordinary life nevertheless. A heavy arm flopped over her waist and pulled her closer. She reached over to stroke his hair. There was no point in trying to avoid waking him, for he was now propped up on his elbow and smiling softly in the early light.

"Good morning," she said, brushing a lock of hair from his forehead. "How is my handsome husband today?"

"Feeling very handsome," he replied.

She hadn't expected an answer, and she shot upright in bed. "Did you hear what I said? Or were you reading my lips?"

He tapped his left ear. "When you say nice things, this ear picks it up. Just a little, but I can hear it."

Her smile was so wide it hurt. "And when I *don't* say nice things?"

"Then I'm stone deaf again."

She flopped back onto the mattress, her mind awhirl. "Thank God," she whispered. "Thank you, God."

Over the next few minutes, Clyde told her he had begun hearing the first traces of sound a few days earlier. It was so faint that he feared he was imagining it, but gradually he was hearing a little more each day. He hadn't told her because he thought it might fail again, and he couldn't bear to see the disappointment in her eyes.

She hugged him tightly. "We are going to survive this, no matter what happens."

Somehow the accident had brought them closer instead of driving them farther apart. Clyde was her husband. She'd chosen him first among all others. Their vows were sacred, and she would never again lose sight of that. From this day forward, they would weather whatever storms or joys came their way—together.

It was a new beginning.

21

Stella's parents arrived in Boston within a few hours of her return. One of the policemen in Boulder Point had telephoned them as soon as Stella and Romulus had staggered back into town. Upon hearing of this latest calamity, her parents rushed for the train station.

"How could you think I would do something so foolish?" her mother shrieked, her voice loud enough to be heard throughout the entire first floor of Evelyn's townhouse.

This wasn't the right time to point out her mother's obsessive sorting and organizing of every piece of paper Gwendolyn had ever touched. Besides, it felt nice to sit on the sofa and let her mother fuss over her, cuddling, hugging, and smelling of lavender and vanilla. Her father was more circumspect, asking Stella to recount everything that had happened in the cave and the events leading up to it.

To her vast relief, a Boulder Point police officer also had notified her parents about what actually happened to cause Gwendolyn's death, so Stella hadn't needed to break the news to them. It was a shock to her mother, but less so for her father.

He'd known the circumstances of Gwendolyn's death were odd but was busy trying to save his wife.

"I simply couldn't fight on all fronts," he said. "I wish I'd known that was the reason you were in Boston. I would have helped you, had I known."

"It's over, Father," she said. "These last few months were terrible, and I didn't always handle it well, but it's over now."

And she would do better in the future. She had been granted a reprieve, and she would learn to count her blessings every day, rather than enumerate the offenses.

"Come, let's go shopping!" Eloise said. "I think this calls for a new dress or two, hmm?"

How good it felt to step out into the utter normalcy of shopping for clothes. She and her mother tried on a dozen blouses, skirts, and scarves while her father looked on in gentle amusement, giving his opinion when asked, which she and her mother blithely ignored. Few men, Romulus being the notable exception, were qualified to pass judgment on women's apparel.

Where was Romulus, anyway? After those few hours on the beach, it seemed as if they were destined to become inseparable for the rest of their lives, and yet she'd barely seen him since returning to Boston. Still, she'd bragged about him incessantly to her parents.

"He's charming," she had said. "Watch out for that because he uses it to get away with a lot, but I do love him, and I can't wait for you to meet him."

Her parents were staying at the same hotel where Romulus lived, and they finally saw him in passing one morning while they were at breakfast. It seemed he intended to head straight to the office, for he passed the dining room without sparing them a glance. Stella had to chase him down in the lobby and prod him into the dining room to meet her parents. Even then, he seemed anxious and distracted as they approached her parents' table.

"Mother, Father, this is Romulus White, the man I've been telling you about."

Her parents both rose, and Romulus shook her father's hand and dutifully leaned over to kiss her mother's hand.

"Now I know where Stella got her looks," he said. "Mother and daughter both look lovely enough to have just stepped out of a Botticelli portrait."

Her mother flushed with pleasure. Stella thought he was laying it on a little thick, but she was relieved he had finally made an appearance after three days of being mysteriously absent.

"Will you join us for breakfast?" her father asked.

"My apologies," Romulus said. "I have a full schedule today and am already running late." He was heading out of the restaurant before any of them could utter another word.

Well! After she'd so enthusiastically praised Romulus to her parents, his distraction was a little embarrassing. Her parents smoothed over the awkward moment by suggesting a visit to the Public Garden, where they could walk along the paths meandering through the tulip beds.

Stella agreed. What else could she do, since the man she was practically engaged to did not even have time for a cup of coffee with her? Romulus had asked for *a little time*, and she was going to supply it whether she wanted to or not.

─◦⟨⟩◦⟩◦─

Romulus could practically see the steam coming from Stella's ears, but he could not spare the time for her this morning. An urgent note from Evelyn had been delivered only moments ago, and he needed to meet with her as quickly as possible. Frankly, he'd prefer a leisurely breakfast alongside Stella and her parents, instead of the tongue-lashing he was about to get from Evelyn and Clyde.

Breaking the news to Evelyn about selling his magazine shares needed to be handled gently, but the investors from New York had beaten him to the punch. They were legally obligated to inform existing shareholders regarding any change in ownership of the magazine, and apparently that document had arrived on Evelyn's doorstep this morning.

He straightened his collar and smoothed back his hair before entering the managerial office. The last thing he wanted to discuss was why he'd been so desperate for money when he sold those shares. Clyde and Evelyn ought to be celebrating the rekindling of their marriage and the return of Clyde's hearing. He didn't want to make Clyde feel guilty for seeking much-needed treatment at that ridiculously expensive health resort.

Romulus plastered a relaxed expression on his face as he strode onto the fourth floor. Clyde sat on the corner of Evelyn's desk, playing with the miniature gyroscope she used as a paperweight, but their smiles fled the instant they saw him.

"Hello, dearest," he said cheerfully.

Evelyn shot to her feet. "We need to talk," she snapped.

"I expected as much," he said as he gestured to his private office. They both followed close behind, the air crackling with tension. Everyone in the office had stopped work to stare at them. The typewriters slowed, Millicent's adding machine ceased, and every eye was on him.

"There's no cause for alarm," he said loudly enough for everyone to hear. "We've got a magazine to publish by the end of the week. Please get to it."

The noise in the office resumed, for it was going to take a sprint to get the magazine released on schedule. By the time Romulus had returned from Boulder Point, his new lawyer had finally gotten around to fighting the injunction, only to learn it had never been officially filed at the Sussex County Court. The paperwork was all a forgery from Ernest Palmer's clever typesetting operation, just a ploy to throw Romulus off track and away from Stella. The interruption in the magazine's production had been a costly setback, but they were back in full operation, and he expected subscription rates to soar now that they had the ability to produce full-color images.

He held the door for Clyde and Evelyn. Clyde took a seat, but Evelyn began pacing. "What in pity's sake were you thinking?" she harangued the moment the door was closed. Clyde merely glowered from the chair.

There was no getting around this, no way to soften the blow. The three of them had been through so much since they'd bought the magazine, but the circle of owners was about to get a lot larger, and there was nothing they could do about it.

"I needed some quick money," he said quietly. "You know Bertie Watson and his New York investors have been eager for a piece of the magazine for years."

"Yes, and we always agreed not to sell," Evelyn retorted. "*Thirty percent?* Are you insane?"

There was no way to make this easier. He drew a deep breath and looked her in the eyes. He really did not want to go into the details. "We've had a lot of expenses in the past month," he said simply.

"What, did you buy a new watch?" she demanded "Perhaps a new stickpin?"

He didn't answer, and the silence stretched between them. Understanding hit Clyde first. He winced and curled over, cupping his bent head in his hands. Evelyn still didn't understand.

"It was the clinic, wasn't it?" Clyde's voice was sick with regret, and the color dropped from Evelyn's complexion. Her face transformed, and she looked ready to cry as she gaped at him as though begging him to deny that was why he needed the money. He rushed to assure her.

"It was also postage for 160,000 letters," he said. "And a lot of fancy new typeface and lithography equipment, all of which sapped our reserves. And frankly, a ridiculously over-priced parquet floor that I simply had to have. That one is entirely my fault but, yes, I also needed money to pay for a health resort."

Clyde pushed to his feet. "I've got some money saved. Maybe we can buy the shares back."

It'd be nice if that were an option, but the New York investors would have no interest in it. The deal was a sale, not a loan. Romulus's limbs felt heavy as he pulled out his chair and sat, running his hands along the smoothly polished walnut surface of his desk. This magazine and all its trappings had always been his greatest pride. It still was, but changes were coming, and there was nothing he could do to stop them. "There's no going back, Clyde. It's water under the bridge."

"But we owe you," Evelyn said. "We've got a fifty-percent stake, and it's not fair you are down to twenty percent because of us. At the very least, we need to repay you for what you gave me for the resort."

He swiveled his chair around so he wouldn't have to look at them. They *did* owe him, and if nothing changed, his minority ownership would eventually sting and chafe as the years rolled by. This was going to have to be handled delicately, because their expenses were about to go up again, and it would be a while before they could earn a profit from the increased subscriptions Stella's color illustrations would bring. He turned the chair to face them. "Stella will be joining the staff as a full-time illustrator," he said. "We don't have any reserves to pay her a salary.

If you sign over ten percent of your shares to Stella, I think she will work for free."

It ought to have been an easy solution, but Clyde's face darkened. His fists clenched, and he looked away as he spoke.

"That's not a good idea," he said. "I know we need to sign over some of our ownership, but not to Stella. It would be a volatile situation. She's not family. The New York investors aren't either, but they live two hundred miles away, and we won't be dealing with them on a daily basis. And as businessmen, they are going to defer to us about the direction of the magazine. That won't be the case with someone who works on the third floor. And if things go south between you and Stella, we'll be stuck with her."

A reluctant grin twisted Romulus's mouth. He was *already* stuck with Stella, and he didn't particularly mind. "Um . . . about Stella not being family," he said. "I have a strong feeling that is about to change."

The beginning of a smile lit Evelyn's face, but she still looked guarded. "If I remember correctly, you are still eight years away from turning forty."

She let the sentence dangle, and heat flushed his face. Clyde and Evelyn both looked ready to leap up to congratulate him, but his palms were sweaty and his heart rate was picking up. Before him sat two people whose marriage had been pockmarked with calamity, yet still they seemed to think he ought to take the irreversible plunge. This was the biggest commitment of his life, and he wasn't going to bungle it.

He tugged at his collar. "Yes, well . . . the number forty was somewhat arbitrarily selected." Mostly it was simply a barrier he used to insulate himself from the prospect of something that had always mildly terrified him. Part of his reluctance was due to Laura, a wonderful person but not the right woman for him.

With the wisdom that came along with the distance of years, he could see that he couldn't offer the sort of undivided devotion Laura needed to be happy. Stella was far more self-sufficient, and they would get along smashingly well. "Nothing is official yet, but Stella isn't the sort who'd tolerate being strung along for eight years, so I will need to step things up."

Clyde and Evelyn put their heads together, whispering behind cupped hands. He'd known from the instant he'd signed the contract selling his shares that it would result in some exquisitely awkward conversations, and this was only the first of many. What did he need a fancy parquet floor for, anyway? He could probably benefit from a dose of Evelyn's practicality, even though he did love admiring this floor every day as he walked into the office.

After a few minutes, Clyde and Evelyn separated and looked up at him. "We owe you five percent of the shares to pay you back for what you advanced us for the resort," Evelyn said. "And an additional ten percent to Stella would make a wonderful wedding present, don't you think?"

It meant that each couple would have a thirty-five percent stake in the magazine. Mathematics had never been his strong suit, so he couldn't compute the precise value of what they were offering versus what Stella would be paid if she were an employee rather than a shareholder, but he trusted Clyde and Evelyn. Over the years, they had all sacrificed for one another, and they each gratefully accepted help when needed. Counting pennies and keeping score had never come into play between people who loved and trusted each other.

"It's a deal."

As Evelyn and Clyde left his office, Riley McGraff walked in the front door. The private detective had warned Romulus that he didn't like working early-morning hours, and he looked bedraggled and surly, but there was a lot of work to accomplish and not much time in which to do it. Stella's parents were going to be in town only for another week, and it was going to be hard to get everything organized in time.

But Stella was going to really love what he had planned, and that knowledge gave him the surge of energy necessary to keep working.

─ ⌒ ᘐ ⌒ ─

Stella was tired but happy after a day of sightseeing with her parents. After hearing about the swan boats for months, she finally had a chance to ride one. Her parents enjoyed it, but she did not. She'd probably never get over her dislike of water, but at least she managed to conquer her fear long enough to step into the roomy boat with elevated sides and let a boat-man paddle them about the large pond. Fountains, statues, and blooming flower beds abounded, giving her plenty to focus on during the boat ride.

Now came the most difficult part of the day . . . buying a copy of all three of Boston's newspapers and retreating up to her parents' hotel room to read. Each day they did their best to avoid looking at the newspapers until evening, when they could quietly read through them and absorb the latest revelations about the scandal that had killed both Gwendolyn and the attorney general. News of Michael Townsend's ignominious fall was reported in great detail, going all the way back to Samuel Alden's wrongful conviction in his father's death.

Acting on a tip from Romulus, the police searched the attorney general's home and retrieved the notes taken from Gwendolyn's safe-deposit box. The notes proved to be a blueprint for corruption at City Hall. Although Ernest Palmer was already dead, some of the men who'd been on the receiving end of kickbacks were alive and well. They were systematically rounded up and charged with a litany of crimes.

Dr. Lentz made a full confession about falsifying Gwendolyn's postmortem report. As an orphaned boy taken in by Michael Townsend, his loyalty to his adoptive father was profound. Ernest Palmer convinced Dr. Lentz that his father had caused Gwendolyn's death in a momentary fit of anger during a lover's quarrel that he immediately regretted. Knowing of his father's clandestine meetings with Gwendolyn, Dr. Lentz agreed to falsify the report. He'd been riddled with guilt over the deception, prompting him to preserve a single copy of the police photograph of Gwendolyn by misfiling it as a *Jane Doe* in the city archives.

Upon his confession, Dr. Lentz was stripped of his office. He was another case of a good man who bent the rules to protect a friend. He'd been lucky to keep his medical license, and rumor had it he intended to move out West to practice medicine in the territories.

Stella received a letter from the police department, thanking her for helping expose the corruption at City Hall. She also heard that Izzy Smith, the police sergeant whose father had once been a beekeeper, had admitted to planting the bees' nest in her mailbox to teach her a lesson for being so obnoxious. He'd been assigned to a month of walking the night beat as punishment for leading the charge to systematically bully Stella. It wasn't much of a punishment, but she didn't care. The police were now acting swiftly on the evidence Gwendolyn had gathered, and that was all that mattered

After a week, the scandal began to fade away. The scrapes on Stella's hands healed, the newspapers reported fewer stories about the scandal, and life was settling into a normal pattern. Romulus had neglected her shamelessly all week. At first she'd thought it had been considerate of him to let her have some time alone with her parents, but after a few days, his disregard had become quite embarrassing.

She was *not* going to become like Laura and demand his daily attention. He'd warned her about this, hadn't he? But deep in her heart, she hadn't really thought he'd actually be so neglectful. It was humbling. And annoying! Her parents would need to return home soon, and she wished Romulus would find a little more time for them.

Her father rarely liked to be gone this long from his medical practice, but he'd decided to stay in Boston for Gwendolyn's birthday, for it was going to be a difficult day for them all. She feared that if they returned home, Eloise would spend the day dragging out Gwendolyn's old mementoes, obsessing over every detail, and slipping back into depression.

On the morning of Gwendolyn's birthday, Stella met her parents early for breakfast in the lobby of their hotel. Her fears were confirmed when her mother announced her plans for the day.

"We would like to see City Hall," Eloise said, and Stella blanched. That building held no fond memories, and it was Gwendolyn's work there that had led to her death. Stella tried to dissuade them. There wasn't much to see, and it would only summon painful memories for them all.

She cast a worried glance at her father. "Are you sure this is a good idea?"

Her father's smile was gentle. "Yes, we'd like to see City Hall."

It was hopeless, for her mother was determined to go. They were crossing the lobby toward the front door when the most heavenly fragrance surrounded them.

She paused. "Do I smell orange blossoms?"

The scent was unmistakable, for it had always been her

favorite. She glanced around the lobby and spotted an immense bouquet of splendid white blossoms in the arms of a hotel porter as he carried them down the hall.

"Come!" Stella said. "We must go see if we can purchase some for your room."

Her mother tugged her arm. "Nonsense. Let's be on our way."

But Stella had already flagged down the hotel porter, who told her the orange blossoms were a special delivery from Florida and were not for sale. Stella leaned forward to inhale the heady fragrance, flooded with a sense of wellbeing. How odd that a lovely scent could have that effect, but the scent of orange blossoms had always been soothing for her.

"What a shame," she murmured as she watched the porter carry the armful of flowers away.

"Come, let's hurry," her mother said.

Stella followed her parents toward the front door, but from the corner of her eye, she caught a glimpse of Romulus shuffling toward the elevators with a short, stocky man in tow. "Romulus!" she burst out, heedless of the dozens of people in the lobby who swiveled a disapproving stare her way. Why should she care? It had been a full week since that glorious afternoon on the beach, and so far Romulus was doing a miserable job of courting her.

After she'd bragged about his flawless sense of style, why did he look so disheveled before her parents? His shirt was rumpled, and it looked as if he hadn't shaved in days, and was that *cat hair* on his trousers?

"Where have you been?" She wanted to be angry, but his slovenly state was alarming.

He passed her a sheepish smile. "I got caught up playing cards. Baccarat is a fascinating game; it is completely addictive. I've become obsessed."

Romulus angled his body away from her, his hand wrapped around a slim box as though he was trying to hide it from her, but it was awfully large to hide. He slipped it to the man beside him.

To her annoyance, she recognized Romulus's companion as the most unpleasant man in the entire city. Riley McGraff looked just as slovenly as Romulus. "Hello, Riley," she said testily. "Is it too much to hope you are here to return the three-hundred-dollar retainer you gouged from me?"

"Lady, I earned that retainer."

The surliness in his tone was appalling, and she looked to Romulus. "Are you going to let him talk to me like that?"

"Maybe he's right," Romulus said with a shrug.

"Three hundred dollars and all he did was threaten my land-lord with a pistol? I can—"

"Now, now," Romulus intervened. "Don't be nasty. Mr. Mc-Graff has done heroic work training me in the intricacies of baccarat, and I will be forever grateful."

She stepped back to get the full view of Romulus. He was tall and disturbingly elegant despite the rolled-up sleeves and open collar of his shirt. But honestly, cat hair! The pieces were beginning to fall into place. Romulus had warned her about his periodic obsessions that sometimes descended, and it looked like he and Riley McGraff had just spent a six-day bender play-ing cards.

She cleared her throat and strove for a calm voice. "Father, Mother, I hope you remember Romulus White?"

"We're thrilled to see you again!" her father boomed, and Eloise looked just as delighted, especially when Romulus ex-ecuted a courtly bow and leaned over to kiss the back of her mother's hand.

"I apologize," Romulus said. "My hands are cold."

"Like your heart?" Stella couldn't resist adding.

"Stella!" her mother scolded. "We think it's perfectly splendid that Mr. White is learning to play baccarat. Perhaps he can teach us all to play?"

Romulus turned to Riley. "Mr. McGraff? Can I trust you to show Dr. Westergaard and his wife some of the basic rules of baccarat? Perhaps in the tea room? I'd like a quick word with Stella."

The last thing she wanted was to subject her loving, decent parents to that beady-eyed private detective who'd already swindled her out of three hundred dollars. "No need, we are on our way to see City Hall."

Once again, her mother interceded. "We'd be delighted to learn a new card game, wouldn't we, Karl?"

"Mother!"

Eloise leaned forward to whisper urgently. "Just behave. I'm sure Romulus knows what he's doing."

Stella glared at the man in question, who looked annoyingly handsome despite his week-long binge of card games. Even now, half the women in the lobby couldn't resist ogling him, for he did have a pirate-like appeal with that open shirt and tousled hair. That didn't mean she was going to fall into his arms after a week of neglect, nor was she going to subject her parents to Riley McGraff's atrocious manners. "I think I'd rather spend the day with my parents. Alone."

"Stella . . ." her father said in his warning voice.

Something wasn't right here. Her parents were a little too bright, especially toward the man who'd been ignoring them for the past week. And the way Romulus had just flashed her mother a wink was a dead giveaway. The three of them had been up to something behind her back.

Her mother caught her eye. "Just speak to him!" Eloise implored.

"Mr. McGraff," her father said in a hearty tone, "let's repair to the tea room to discuss this card game. Baccarat?"

The three of them were already turning away, Riley still carrying the gold-foil box Romulus had passed to him.

Stella swiveled her attention to Romulus. "Have you been meeting my parents behind my back?"

"What makes you think that?"

She narrowed her gaze. "Because my father is usually worse than the Spanish Inquisition toward any man who shows interest in me, and my mother is fawning over you like the first rose of spring."

"My charm is legendary. You can hardly hold it against them."

"What are you up to?" she asked, completely bewildered.

"Maybe your parents and I have shared a drink or two in the evenings," he admitted. "I bumped into them in the lobby their first night here, and after that we usually had a nightcap in the evenings. Come on, let's go over by the piano. I'm not in the mood to be raked over the coals in front of half of Boston."

No one was playing the piano nestled in the corner of the grand lobby, and it offered as much privacy as they could get. A cluster of potted palms provided an additional screen, and Romulus drew her behind them, standing deliciously close and holding one of her hands. He leaned over to whisper in her ear.

"When we were on the beach, I confessed to living in terror of marriage. When I asked for a little time to become accustomed to the idea, did you think six days was too much to ask?" Instead of velvety words of praise, his voice was riddled with frustration. "Because it's been only six days," he continued.

"You could have told me where you were."

"I just did. Playing baccarat. I warned you these obsessions sometimes get the better of me." Gentle fingers stroked her hair back from her forehead. "I know I should have contacted you, but I've been scheming with Riley to do something nice for you. Oh, and he really *did* earn every dollar of that retainer. Your parents and I paid him another two hundred just to keep him working. The man is a miracle worker."

Her parents had already met Riley McGraff, as well? This entire conversation was so baffling she sunk down onto the piano bench, her knees no longer capable of supporting her weight. "Tell me," she managed to stammer.

"There's something at City Hall we want to show you. It's taken Riley and me some time to get the necessary approvals, which is what we've been up to most of the past week. So I've actually only spent the past two days playing cards as the final details got worked out." He gave her a reluctant smile. "And I knew I couldn't see you without spilling the secret."

"Spill it. Please." She loved surprises and had a feeling Romulus could deliver a good one. Jewelry? Maybe something to make lithographs with? Maybe even . . . She swallowed hard as the image of Audubon's *Birds of America* popped into her mind. Acquiring one of those volumes would take time, and he knew how much she admired it. They'd had their first kiss while standing over *Birds of America*.

"There's something I want to ask you first, but I'm afraid the surprise I planned is falling apart. You've already spotted the orange blossoms, and I suspect your parents and Riley are already tearing into that box of the Belgian chocolate you like so much. To top it off, I just got word that the orchestra won't be at dinner tonight."

"An *orchestra*?"

"Just a quintet and an opera singer. Apparently the singer has laryngitis and has lost her voice, so all my grand plans are falling apart."

"Oh dear," she said, her heart squeezing at the wry amusement on his face. She had no idea how he'd managed to get orange blossoms here, but it wasn't an easy task to accomplish and she was sorry to have spoiled his surprise by chasing after that hotel porter.

"They were going to play *La Bohème* at dinner. You said it was your favorite."

"It is."

"Your mother told me you have a fiendish love for orange blossoms, and I already know about your weakness for Belgian chocolates. I wanted everything to be perfect for a first-class marriage proposal. I'm only planning on doing this once, you know."

Her heart split wide open, for now she understood where this had all been leading. Dearest, sweetest Romulus. She didn't need orange blossoms or fancy music, she just wanted the man standing before her, imperfections and all.

"I was going to propose at dinner tonight, but since everything has fallen apart, and I . . ." He swallowed hard. "Well, I suppose I should still try to do this properly."

He sank down onto one knee and took her hand. His was trembling, hers was rock solid. He looked terrified. "Miss West," he said on a ragged breath. He cleared his throat and looked like he was about to pass out.

"Please don't have a heart attack," she said. "Stand up before you fall over. Come, there is room here on the bench."

She scooted over to make room for him, and they were both laughing by the time he joined her. It was a tight fit, and he clasped both her hands in his. The laughter broke his tension, and he suddenly seemed more relaxed. His smile was genuine and tender, his expression soft.

"Miss West," he said in a much calmer voice, "I love you desperately and would be honored if you would marry me."

"Thank you, Romulus. I would like that very much."

For a few moments, all she could do was gaze at his face, so dear, so kind. From the moment she'd read his first wildly enthusiastic letter to her over three years ago, she had been attracted to him. "Half the women working at the magazine will go into mourning when they hear you are off the market," she said. "Of course, they don't know what they'd be getting."

She'd meant it as a joke, but his eyes grew somber. "I know," he said seriously. "I won't be an easy man to be married to. You just saw it with the baccarat. Most of the time I really was working with Riley on the surprise for you, but once that was done, I got distracted by that blasted card game. It's just the way my mind works. I latch on to something and can't let it go—"

She pressed a finger to his lips. "I know. And I love you anyway."

He pulled her finger away. "Do you? Because I'm pretty good at creating an impressive smokescreen, but behind it there is a whole world of scatterbrained thinking and maladjusted behaviors."

She didn't care. She loved him, flaws and all. "Romulus, you make me smile all the time. I'm moved beyond words that you tried to get an orchestra for me, but you didn't need to do all this. All I want is you. I love the man who would drop everything to watch monarch butterflies as they migrate south. Who would hold his mother's hand when she was in despair. Who would send me letters for three solid years because he admired my artwork. I want *you*. You're vain, you've got cat hair on your trousers, and you've just wasted forty-eight hours of your life you can never get back playing cards with Riley McGraff, but I love you desperately."

Her comment seemed to humble him. His eyes softened, and he touched the side of her face. "Give me a quick kiss. Then I'll get your parents and we will go to City Hall. There is something else we want to show you."

She shot to her feet and obliged. What was supposed to be a quick kiss grew. And got deeper. And more magnificent.

Finally, she pulled back. "Show me!"

He led her toward the front of the lobby, where her parents waited for them. There was no sign of Riley McGraff, for which she was grateful. Her parents beamed in expectation.

"What's this all about?" she asked. It was baffling that her parents could have been planning some sort of clandestine surprise with Romulus, but they refused to divulge any details on the walk to City Hall.

When they entered the building, Romulus walked straight past the elevators and headed toward the east wing and the Hall of Heroes. The marble hallway was lined with busts of famous Bostonians, and the walls held portraits of notable people, documents, and the architectural wonders of the city.

Romulus led the way, and she followed with her parents on either side of her. The gallery was nearly empty, and their footsteps echoed in the corridor. They walked past the busts of long-dead people and headed toward the section documenting more recent history.

Romulus slowed before a portrait hanging on the wall. "Here it is," he said gently.

It was a portrait of Gwendolyn, the beautiful photograph made at the studio on Tarnower Street. Stella whirled to her parents, who gazed at the portrait with tears pooling in their eyes.

"Gwendolyn deserves to be remembered by more than just your family," Romulus said. "Riley McGraff has been pulling strings at the State House to make the case that your sister belongs in this hall alongside the other notable Bostonians. A plaque will be added with Gwendolyn's name and a line of text outlining her contribution to the city."

Stella's finger trembled as she touched the cold silver frame, staring at the perfection of Gwendolyn's idealistic, hopeful profile, looking upward at soft light shining on her face. "She will be forever young," she said in a choked voice. "Why did you do this?"

Romulus said, "Sometimes art captures the human spirit in a way no words can ever hope to do."

She rushed into his arms, hugging him tightly. Romulus knew, he understood. She buried her face in his neck, knowing she'd embarrass herself with noisy weeping the instant she pulled away. Gwendolyn was no longer here, but this lovely portrait would inspire people for generations to come.

Her parents did not want to mark Gwendolyn's birthday by mourning. Rather, her mother had planned a celebration with a picnic on Boston Common.

Romulus joined them in the park, and they found a spot beneath a huge oak tree where men once gathered to agitate for freedom, willing to risk their lives for a cause. It was a fitting place to toast Gwendolyn, for she, too, had been a fighter, worthy of her revolutionary forefathers.

It was spring. Crocuses bloomed, and children played while parents looked on. The park represented a timeless haven that memorialized the city's long and magnificent past. Gwendolyn herself was now a part of that storied history, having given her life for the city she loved so well. The actions of a brave, modest stenographer were already echoing through City Hall and creating change for the better.

Her father spread the blanket while Eloise laid out sliced fruit, cheese, and jam tarts packed for them by the hotel's restaurant. Romulus popped a cork on a bottle of champagne in order to have a proper toast to Gwendolyn.

A rush of sentimentality came over Stella. How close she had come to dying only a few days earlier, but now she had been granted the gift of a cloudless afternoon like today. "At times like these, I feel like Gwendolyn is right here with us," she said.

Her mother's eyes had a sheen of tears, but her smile was genuine. "She is, dearest."

And Stella knew it was true. Gwendolyn had not vanished into nothingness. She had merely gone to a different place. They toasted Gwendolyn, said a prayer in her honor, and then tore into the delicious meal Eloise had brought for them all. The memory of Gwendolyn would live with them forever, but it was time to move on, for they were alive to love and cherish every hour of the gift of life.

God still had a purpose for her. Stella wasn't yet certain what he intended, but wasn't that the beauty of it? She was alive. Her parents were happy. She and Romulus had been blessed with the talent and skill for meaningful work that inspired others. It was going to be a challenge to live up to Gwendolyn's legacy, but by the grace of God, she was still here to try.

A Note From the Author

Boston was the first city in America to build a subway. At the time, the only cities in the world with a subway were London, Glasgow, and Budapest, all of which were powered by steam and met with deep suspicion by the public. By the 1890s, developments in electrical power made the construction of safe, clean, and well-lit subways a possibility.

Boston and New York City began designing their subways at the same time, and both cities struggled with political wrangling, public skepticism, financial setbacks, and safety concerns. Construction on New York's subway was repeatedly delayed due to financing troubles and the challenges of tunneling through the hard bedrock that underlay much of Manhattan.

Construction on the Boston subway was halted after the gas explosion at the intersection of Tremont and Boylston. In all, six people were killed and sixty others seriously injured. Despite the explosion, the Boston subway opened on time and under budget on September 1, 1897. The subway in New York City opened seven years later.

QUESTIONS FOR CONVERSATION

1. At the beginning of the novel, Romulus's self-worth is defined entirely by his career as a successful publisher. What are the things that define your own view of yourself? Do these things ever throw other areas of your life out of balance?

2. Clyde's crisis after the explosion draws him and Evelyn closer together. It has often been said that tragedy will either pull couples apart or render them stronger. What qualities do people need to become closer rather than drift apart?

3. Michael Townsend tried to atone for his adolescent mistake by being "a good man." Is it possible for a sin to be atoned this way?

4. Stella believes the model of her parents' marriage will aid her in creating a happy marriage of her own. Is this a

valid belief? How can people raised without such a model build a successful marriage?

5. During her years building her career in London, Stella assumed there would be time "later" to become a devout woman. Do you ever see this quality in your own life?

6. Both Stella and Evelyn go through phases where they believe it is easier to be angry rather than hurt. Can anger ever be a useful emotion?

7. Romulus projects a bold, overly confident persona to mask deep-seated insecurities. Do you know anyone in your life who does the same thing?

8. Evelyn was well aware of Clyde's reckless streak when they were courting, but she assumed it would diminish after marriage. Can a woman make such an assumption about a man she hopes to marry? What should she do if she finds herself chafing against qualities she once accepted but now finds difficult?

9. Romulus was once wildly in love with a woman who ended their relationship. Is there value in having a first great love, even if it ends badly?

10. Do you predict Romulus and Stella will have a strong marriage? What about Clyde and Evelyn?

Elizabeth Camden is the author of eight historical novels and two historical novellas and has been honored with both the RITA Award and the Christy Award. With a master's in history and a master's in library science, she is a research librarian by day and scribbles away on her next novel by night. She lives with her husband in Florida. Learn more at www.elizabethcamden.com.

More From
Elizabeth Camden

Visit elizabethcamden.com for a full list of her books.

National Weather Bureau volunteer Sophie van Riijn has used the abandoned mansion Dierenpark as a resource and a refuge for years. But now the Vandermark heir has returned to put an end to the shadowy rumors about the place. When old secrets come to light, will tragedy triumph or can hope and love prevail?

Until the Dawn

When a map librarian and a young congressman join forces to solve a mystery, they become entangled in secrets more perilous than they could have imagined.

Beyond All Dreams

United in a quest to cure tuberculosis, physician Trevor McDonough and statistician Kate Livingston must overcome past secrets and current threats to find hope for their cause—and their futures.

With Every Breath